I0668198

TRUTH REVEALED

TRUTH REVEALED

BOOK 3 OF THE MANTLE OF THE GODS

TRICIA SPARKS

TRINITY GATEWAYS LLC

TRUTH REVEALED, Book 3 of the A *MANTLE OF THE GODS*

This is a work of fiction. All characters and events portrayed are fictional, and any resemblance to real people or incidents is purely coincidental.

Cover Design by Doris Ross

A Trinity Gateways LLC Publication
www.TrinityGateways.net

ISBN: 0988195178
ISBN-13: 978-0-9881951-7-2

DEDICATIONS

To my parents, you've been my life's compass, showing me my true north.

To Mrs. Dent, my high school English teacher, who took an interest in my writing and put the wind in my sails to pursue my dreams.

To Doris Ross, the captain of my ship. You've been behind me every step pushing me to go further and never give up.

To Lisa Gastineau, my creative partner and crew. You're the one that works behind the scenes and keeps my voyage smooth.

To Dustin, my life's partner on this grand adventure, you make each day brighter because you're in it.

Thank you all for helping me to reach this stop in my journey and I hope that you'll sail with me into the future as well.

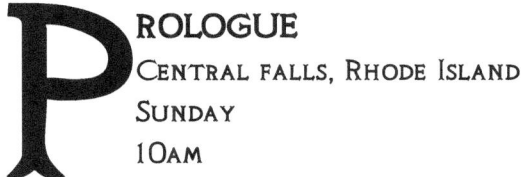

PROLOGUE
CENTRAL FALLS, RHODE ISLAND
SUNDAY
10AM

Sam sped down the busy streets of Central Falls, Rhode Island headed back to the hotel they'd acquired hours ago, despite his opinion that Catharine needed a hospital. As he raced on he found he was unable to get the images of what had transpired only moments before out of his head. He was once more in the winding passages under the Victorian three story house that had once been Catharine's home.

When they'd located Ares layer they'd found the room was lit within by hundreds of candles. He'd been forced to shield his eyes against the harsh light after wandering the dim corridors of the basement.

It struck him now that the room resembled more of a catacomb or mausoleum prepared for the dead than a basement. He and Lance had blinked trying to adjust their sight. When his eyes had adapted Sam had seen angels and demons alike. They ran throughout the décor their gaze fixed on the center of the room.

Thin wisps of translucent silken fabric had hung from the ceiling in hues of reds, oranges and yellows where the graven images looked on. The blending of which looked like a circle of flame.

Sam watched as the detective slipped past the filmy veil that surrounded a huge ornately carved bed. Laying upon it naked and bleeding was Catharine. Her arms bound to the head board her legs spread eagle feet bound to the foot board. The killer they'd hunted stood over her his eyes lit with madness as his fingers skimmed over her naked body and he gloated over her defenseless state. She struggled to escape him pulling at her restraints.

"YOU'RE SO WILLFUL, SERENITY, YOU MAKE IT HARD FOR ME TO NOT TREAT MYSELF TO A REAL TASTE OF YOU. I'VE NOT HAD A BRIDE THAT PLEASED ME SO COMPLETELY IN OVER TWO THOUSAND YEARS AND I WANT TO TAKE MY TIME WITH YOU," the spirit of the fallen within the man said amused.

He'd moved closer as if he intended to do just that then cursed. "HOWEVER, THE MORTAL WHOM I'M SHARING THIS BODY WITH WANTS ALL OF YOU NOW AND IN THE WORST SORT OF WAYS IMAGINABLE," Ares whispered with disgust. His host's fingers slid down into the valley between her breasts.

"Don't touch me," Catharine roared with disgust as she pulled harder at her bonds.

"Get your hands off her," Lance hissed as he moved out of the shadows.

Sam had been relieved when Lance had made his move, he hadn't wanted to let things get any further. He'd figured there was a trap waiting for them but he'd not fully understood it until he moved to aid his friend. Without warning the filmy veil that surrounded the bed became a blazing ring of flames that barred his passage.

Sam had cursed as he shielded himself against the heat of the flames that blazed between him and Lance. The trap itself had been far worse than he'd imagined. The game, being played there, for keeps. If Lance had given into the anger driving him and killed Catharine's tormentor then he would have become the War God. Worse still, Catharine would have fallen with him as the influence of Dionysus over her would have had her surrendering to Lance's desires and Ares would indeed have had a willing bride.

Sam groaned at the memory, it seemed each step they took on this twisted quest he was powerless to stop the hand of the god that moved. In the end he'd asked for help and gotten the strangest answer he'd ever anticipated.

Sam heard Hecate's final remark in his mind, the one he knew if their roles were reversed, and it had been Anna there defenseless, would have pushed him to the breaking point.

"SHE WANTS HIM DEAD."

Before another thing could happen, an angry voice had spoken from behind him.

"NOT AS MUCH AS I WANT ARES DEAD," Artemis had roared as she raced into the room like an avenging angel. She'd taken one look at the flames and her eyes had glowed with her power as she summoned a storm. Rain had poured within the basement putting out the flames as strong winds tore the curtains down.

Sam hadn't blinked. He hadn't hesitated. He moved across the line that had barred his passage and grabbed the killer by the arm twisting it behind his back separating him from Catharine, before putting his weapon on the man.

He'd watched as Lance freed Catharine, covered her with his shirt and carried her out of there.

"RELEASE THE WAR GOD'S PUPPET, MORTAL, OR FACE MY WRATH," Artemis hissed as she advanced.

Sam had let go of the other man he wasn't about to get in the middle of a battle between a pair of Fallen besides Hecate was getting away and he needed to try and catch her before the knife slipped beyond his reach.

He'd raced from the house but found no signs of Hecate's passage where ever the goddess, demon, witch, ah good grief he didn't know what to call her was she'd vanished. As he'd moved toward the car where Lance was loading Catharine in the backseat, Artemis had emerged from the house. A bolt of lightning was summoned setting the house ablaze.

Sam had turned to face the goddess, his gun at the ready not that it was much defense against her but he wasn't about to let her near Anna as she was under order to return her to Hermes.

"STAY YOUR HAND, MORTAL. OUR BATTLE WILL WAIT. MY BUSINESS FOR NOW, IS WITH HECATE," Artemis said before she walked off.

Sam had blinked, confused but grateful turning, he'd moved to the car joining the others. Lance was less than pleased with him.

"What took you so long?" Lance asked as he settled into the passenger side-seat, beside Catharine. He brushed his fingers through her hair needing to touch her just to assure himself she was real.

"Damn curtains became flames, they slowed me down.

Artemis showed up just at the right moment to help me."

"Man did she seem mad," Lance muttered as Sam pulled away from the curb and started toward the motel.

"Yeah, I'm pretty sure she killed him. Told me as she was leaving she's not after us for now, more interested in Hecate.

"Glad she's not after me," Lance said. Catharine's eyes opened, she looked at him and she visibly relaxed. "You okay?" he asked her.

"Yeah, he, didn't…" Catharine began, unable to finish the sentence.

"Good."

Catharine's assurance that they'd reached her in time had gone a considerable length to cooling Sam's fury at what he'd been witness to. As he drove back towards Anna he wondered if it had been her there if he'd have been able to resist the need to kill to protect her. Or if the fury that had risen in him would have been too much. He didn't know and it plagued his mind as he drove on.

"What's our next move?" Lance questioned.

"Get back to the motel, rest up and then move on. If you're still insistent she doesn't need a hospital."

"I'm not visiting an emergency room here." Catharine persisted.

"You heard her, if she needs help we'll get it when we land elsewhere."

"Fine. Artemis may not be on us but she works for Hermes and he'll know soon enough where we are. The sooner we get out of here the better." Sam answered.

1

Anna groaned as she rose from her work space yet again. She had been unable to concentrate since Sam left. Her mind was troubled. She was worried for him and Lance and feared for Catharine's safety. As she walked past the end of the bed, her gaze shifted to the night table where the gun Sam had given her earlier lay concealed. She felt a shiver run down her spine as she remembered the feel of the cool metal in her hands and the weight of it.

Ann blinked how had she gotten here? She wasn't a fighter. She was a scientist. Until a few weeks ago the most dangerous thing she'd ever faced was her parents' disappointment in a choice she made. Since her discovery at the dig site in Israel she'd been followed, had her home broken into and even been shot. The injury was healed but she'd bear the scar as a reminder.

She swallowed, aware she was in well over her head. Anna sat down on the end of her bed as reality began to sink in. Catharine was the prisoner of a serial killer; a man who would systematically torture and destroy her. Lance and Sam were on the move to save her. But the man they faced was no ordinary man. He like James Hardagen and Ian Broody were each possessed by the spirit of a fallen one.

She was being hunted by figures that had once been worshiped as gods. The thought of it left her exhausted. Anna lay her head down on the bed.

"I just need a few minutes," she told herself as she closed her eyes.

2

Anna's mind slipped into the dream world, the moment her eyes fell shut. As the dream began she saw Sam and Lance moving down an old stair case by flash light. Once on flat ground again, they switched off the dim light as they moved through a dark corridor.

"Maybe he's got her in the attic," Sam muttered as they moved on. The dark passage seemed to go on forever.

"He's down here; I can feel him," Lance whispered as they rounded another corner.

The darkness came to an abrupt end as the room that opened up before them was lit by hundreds of candles.

Anna's heart pounded with terror at the sight before her and unable to face it she turned and ran. Whatever they were facing now she didn't want to see it. She couldn't.

Anna slammed the door separating dark corridor form candle filled chamber and locked it. She leaned against the hard oak and trembled. Her breathing heavy and labored as she fought to keep the door shut.

Dionysus who lurked in the shadows smiled. He'd known if he waited that Anna would reveal herself. He moved from the edge of the dream realm where he'd lurked in wait for her return. With a precision that came from centuries of practice, he slipped into her nightmare without touching her mind and alerting her to his presence.

He watched from the shadows in the dark hall as Anna pressed a hand against the door she'd created to close out what lay on the other side. She drew it back as if burned and for a moment the door and the passageway were replaced by the candlelit room. A bed sat in the center of the room, on it lay a naked, bound and bloodied Catharine. Her kidnapper stood over her watching her. A hand brushed over her bare flesh. Lance stood gun at the ready poised to shoot and Sam's path barred by a ring of burning fire.

Anna turned from the image once more and the dark corridor with the door returned. Dionysus noted that oak had become like a vault door, his prey he noted was fighting hard to keep the image of that room and what was happening there from her thoughts. She was agitated and eager for anything else to latch onto. It would make influencing her that much easier.

Dionysus crept closer to his target.

"WHAT ARE YOU AFRAID OF ANNA?" he whispered gently, probing her mind for the source of her distress.

He watched as the image of the room resurfaced once more. Now only Sam and the killer remained in the room. The two men stood locked in battle, the struggle ending with Ares blade piercing the man Sam's flesh. Once more the image faded and the door reappeared.

Dionysus closed the distance between them with excitement. He was just a few steps away from his goal. Anna's mind was not yet aware of him, if he could just keep her busy he'd be able to pinpoint her location. Okay so the pretty doctor was worried about her Sam. He could work with that. Fear could be a great lever for pushing a mind to surrender to their lusts, he just needed the right hook to draw her in.

As the god of wine and excess dug deeper into the woman Anna's mind, searching for the right button to press, the man he possessed James Hardagen sat aboard a plane bound for the east coast and his prize.

3

Sam cursed as he was forced to stop at yet another light. He'd caught every one wrong since they left the house. He could feel time slipping away from him and it made him angry. His instincts were screaming for him to get back to Anna. He was aware that none of their enemies were there in the city but still he couldn't shake the sense she was in danger.

With each minute that passed the worse it grew. As he made his way toward the hotel the last words the angel had spoken circled round in his mind.

"I'm here to warn you the road ahead will be hard and fraught with danger. Do not give up hope or give into the influence of the fallen."

As he made his way to Anna, Sam wondered what the angel had meant when he said the road ahead would be hard. Hard for who? Was the message for him or for her?

Sam snarled as he was forced to stop for yet another light.

"You okay man?" Lance questioned from the back seat.

"No, this is taking too long."

"We're almost there."

"I know but I can't shake this feeling that Anna's in trouble."

"Artemis said she's not after her at the moment. No one else knows we're here, what danger could she possibly be in?" Lance asked.

"I get that but I'm telling you she's not as safe as we think."

Dionysus gave Anna's mind a nudge back toward the nightmare she was reluctant to face. He watched as the pretty doctor moved deeper into the room where Sam and the killer had been fighting. The man Sam lay on the cool stone floor in a pool of his own blood, his life slipping away. Anna ran to him falling to her knees beside him. With care she lifted his head into her lap.

"Sam, no. don't leave me," she whispered tears fell from her eyes as she kissed his forehead.

"Anna?" he asked his voice weak.

"Yes, it's me," she assured him. She watched as he opened his eyes and let out a breath she'd been holding. "You're going to be okay," she whispered trying to convince herself of it.

"HE'S DYING, ANNA, AND IT'S YOUR FAULT," Dionysus whispered to her troubled mind. He watched with delight as the lie was accepted.

"I'm sorry," she whispered before she kissed the dying man's lips. As her lips met his a flash of a memory flitted into Dionysus awareness.

The moment before Sam had left to go face the monster Anna now feared would kill him. Once more the room faded and the door separating it from the hall she hid in returned.

"FORGET THIS DARKNESS ANNA, AND SHOW ME WHAT HAPPENED. REMEMBER WHAT CAME BEFORE," Dionysus murmured.

He watched with pleasure as Anna turned away from the door to her nightmare to face what lay back down the dark corridor. The hall twisted and turned like a maze and Dionysus followed her every step with care not to get too close. When they came to the end of the winding stairs he found he was no longer in the house but a hotel room.

Dionysus lurked in the dark corridor careful to remain unseen he watched her memory play out like a scene in a movie with fascination. As it neared the end he moved in closer to hear what was being said.

"After I go don't let anyone in but me, not even Lance," the man Sam instructed. Dionysus watched as Sam drew Anna into his arms for a second time.

"I won't," she told him.

"Good, I'll be back as soon as I can," he promised.

"I know you will," she assured him before she kissed him. It was a short and quick meeting of their lips, but Dionysus felt the desire there for more and smiled.

"Yes that's it enjoy the memory," he whispered as he pressed his power against her mind a little, not wanting to startle her from the memory but wanting her to focus on it completely; needing her to build, dream upon it so that he could enter without her sensing it. If he could get inside her mind then he could locate her.

The nightmare began to recede as her mind slipped back into the memory.

"Be careful out there," she requested.

"I will," Sam assured her and unable to resist he kissed her again his hands sinking into her hair pulling lightly to get a better angle. She gasped startled by the silent demand. He took full advantage of her lips parting; drinking deeply.

Anna moaned as the taste of him hit her like a drug and made her flesh clamor with a need that left her weak in the knees and frightened her. How did he get to her so fast? She'd never had another man's kiss affect her so.

She burned for him and if she didn't have him soon she felt she'd die of it. Her arms wrapped around his neck holding him close not wanting him to let go. Sam eased back and his eyes locked with hers. "I love you," he murmured tenderly. She felt his hold on her ease and knew he meant to go.

Dionysus cursed. "NOT AS MUCH OF A MEMORY AS I'D HOPED FOR." he muttered to himself. "OH, WELL, SO MUCH FOR SUBTLE," the wine god groused. Desperate to keep Anna there in that moment he pushed at her with a tidal wave of his power.

As it swept over her and sank into her, Dionysus crossed from the dream world into her mind. He laughed as he felt his power crash through her, making a pleasant feeling of desire become a fierce painful hunger, whose teeth had her body aching for her Sam.

"Don't leave me like this Sam, I need you," she pleaded as she pressed herself against him, bringing memory and dream together, blurring the lines between truth and fantasy. Dionysus latched hold of the dream thread and built the lie about her wrapping her further in it.

"Anna," the dream Sam groaned her name at the feel of her pressed against him. His mouth crashed against hers in a bruising kiss that stole her breath away.

Dionysus thrilled in the feel of her lust stirring but knew not to linger in it, she was on guard against his influence and he'd risked as much as he dare. He needed to finish the job here before he played with her. Dionysus looked about the room created from memory and smiled as he noted the hotel name on the phone by the bed as well as the room number. "GOT YOU," he whispered with excitement. The fallen let part of his own mind return to his servant, it whispered the location of the hotel to the man whom for now, he shared a body with. Having gotten what he came for the wine god turned back to the woman's fantasy.

He noted with satisfaction her mind was running riot with the memory he'd pushed her to indulge in. Fear drove her now, to take, when before she'd hesitated. "THAT'S RIGHT PRETTY ANNA, GIVE YOURSELF OVER TO THE HUNGER. TAKE GREEDILY WHAT YOU LONG FOR NOW, LET ME IN DEEPER," he crooned tempting her to give into her desire.

Dionysus approached the sleeper boldly now and with the barest of touch he ran his index finger down her cheek.

Goose flesh rose under his caress and she tore Sam's clothes with frustration, she wanted his skin against hers. She wanted to touch him, to feel him.

As Dionysus finger skimmed lower tracing the line of her neck he reveled in the ease with which her mind was responding to his power. He fed her images of things she could do here with her Sam and her mind latched onto them like a starving beast. He cupped her chin much the way Sam had, blending his touch with the fantasy.

"YES, THAT'S THE WAY, ANNA, LOSE YOURSELF IN THE DREAM. IT'LL MAKE IT THAT MUCH EASIER TO GET

TO YOU WHEN I REACH YOU," Dionysus's mind whispered. The pretty doctor moaned as she found her dream lover's flesh.

5

Anna shivered as Sam brushed the thin silk straps of her gown from her shoulders and the blue green fell off her leaving her in nothing but her stockings and underwear. His hands were everywhere at once, it seemed and it was destroying her mind. She felt the pad of his finger brush against her kiss swollen lips and she imagined drawing it in her mouth biting lightly teasing making him groan, the finger became something more and she blinked startled.

What was wrong with her? She'd never thought of such things before. She'd never had any interest in such acts. She'd always been unsure, when it came to this sort of thing.

So why would she think it now? Opening her eyes she found Sam's blue ones staring back at her with question, pain, and need were written on his face, but acceptance. She knew that if she decided to bring an end to it now he'd respect her wish.

He panted, his breathing heavy as he waited for her to decide. She moaned as she felt his fingers play over her throat though he wasn't touching her. The phantom caress moved lower tormenting her breasts through the thin wisp of cloth that passed for her bra. She pictured his mouth latching there through the lace driving her wild and she felt the jolt of pleasure the image brought her, shoot right to the center of her need.

"Sam," she breathed his name trying to find her control as that phantom caress moved lower playing over her belly. She pictured his mouth there tasting, tongue pressing into her navel teasing her with the promise of what he would do if she allowed him to put his mouth lower. She licked her lips her mouth having gone dry.

"What do you want from me Anna?" He whispered as he brushed a strand of her golden hair out of her face. She felt the fingers playing over her body, slide over her hips to squeeze her backside and she jumped startled by the roughness of the touch here. She pictured Sam pressing his need against her here, bending her over teasing her…

God what was wrong with her? Where were these images coming from? This was not like her. All her dreams of this nature before had been tame; they stripped; he held her and she told him they couldn't. Where had this nearly pornographic imagery come from?

"Do you want me to let you go Anna, or do you want me to finish this?" Sam asked as those damn fingers took hold of her butt once more and pressed her more firmly against his aroused flesh.

Anna bit her lip to fight back a cry of delight, as more images flooded her mind ,she could see them together in the bed, Sam kneeling over her buried inside her his balls slapping against her ass as he took her hard from behind like a mindless beast.

She blinked. "I don't want that," she whispered with certainty. "Let me go Sam, this isn't going to happen," she said with a strength she didn't feel.

"Are you sure that's what you want?" Sam asked as he eased back a little. She felt those hands move elsewhere to cup her breasts. Sending another flicker of need through her but she ignored it and the image that followed it.

"Yes Sam, I'm sure I don't want a dream gone bad because Dionysus is playing with me, when we do touch this way I want it to be real. I want it to be the way God meant it to be a union of two people on every level seeking to become one flesh. Not a mindless empty fuck," she said with a smile before she brushed a kiss on his cheek and turned away from him.

6

Anna's eyes shot open as she came out of the dream. She lifted her head from the bed where she'd dosed off and wiped the sleep from her eyes. She gasped startled to find her body was running riot, screaming for relief from the lingering effects of the dream.

She ached for a man's touch in a way that she'd never known to be possible. Her own mind had been used against her and she didn't like it one bit. Aware of the cause of this desperate hunger she felt tearing through her, Anna prayed for strength. As the fire burning within her began to ease, she asked for forgiveness for letting herself get so lost in the dream Dionysus had lead her into.

Getting up from the bed she turned her attention back to the book she'd been reading before she gave into her fear. She still had work to do. There were three more mantles to find and if she was going to beat Hermes to them she had to stay one step ahead of him.

7

Dionysus raged as Anna shoved him out of her mind.

He'd underestimated her ability to draw back from his hold. Any other would be lost in the dream he'd created for her, powerless against its spell. A slave to their bodies need for ease. He should have been filling the role of her dream lover and cementing his hold of her mind, instead he was back inside the man James Hardagen's mind sitting on a private jet already winging it's way east.

The plane had taken off shortly after he'd realized his guests had slipped out of his home. He'd not known yet where he was heading, only that Ares power signature lay in the center of all this. It hadn't taken him long to figure out that the war god's power base was settled somewhere on the east coast. He'd been tracking it until it went out. He cursed now figuring that Artemis was the cause.

It seemed the huntress had caught up to her prey and slain him. It was of little concern, thanks to Anna's memory he knew exactly where they were going. It wouldn't be long before they reached their final destination. Turning his focus from the troublesome doctor, Dionysus let his mind press against that of Catharine's and he was delighted to find that the barrier the war god had constructed to keep him out was gone.

The lovely writer's mind was a mess of pain and turmoil created by Ares handy work. Fear and despair ran through her like a raging river that threatened to drown her. He reached out to touch her and she gave no response, unaware of him. He snarled. She was beyond his reach for now. No matter, with time the influence of his wine upon her would become the dominant force in her mind once more.

"James where are we going?" Emily questioned.

"To go help CJ my dear, I got a call from the detective they found her," the man James Hardagen replied.

"Is she okay?"

James smiled as the voice in his head assured him that she was. "Yes my pet, don't worry, Serenity's creator is just fine," he assured his pretty fiancé.

"Oh I'm so relieved, I like CJ and not just because she created Serenity."

"I know love, I'm fond of her too. We should be with her and the others soon." James assured her as the plane began its final decent.

Dionysus laughed to himself as his host disembarked from the plane in Central Falls Rhode Island. He was in a rental car within moments and speeding towards Anna's hotel.

8

Anna cursed as her eyes strayed from her book to the bedside clock noting the time. It had been six hours since Sam left and she was starting to worry.

She set down her book and looked over at her cell phone, she noted with disgust that since she last checked, no call had come through.

"Stop it Anna, you're just going to make yourself crazy," she muttered with irritation. She just needed to focus her mind on something else and work wasn't helping.

When she closed her eyes and drew a calming breath to clear her head and steady her nerves, unbidden the image of Sam's mouth crushing hers; his hand fisted in her hair pulling it back as he demanded more, filled her mind.

"Damn it, Anna, stop it," she snapped annoyed as her eyes flew open running from the image. She blew out a breath and flipped on the TV. Maybe the background noise would help.

She flipped the channel over to the Discovery channel and began to listen to some program about women who kill and she felt her mind recede. She figured that before the episode ended that Sam and the others would turn up.

9

James Hardagen made his way up the stairs of the small hotel and down the hall to room 207. He'd left Emily on the plane sleeping, with a little luck he'd have Anna on board and be well on his way to claim his reward from Hermes before Emily woke.

When he reached the door he tapped into the power he'd been given and watched as the door swung open. Anna's eyes shot away from the TV she'd been watching to the open door fear was etched on her lovely face as she crossed to the night table and pulled out the gun the man Sam had given her before he left.

"You don't need that doctor," James assured her as he moved closer.

"You're not welcome here," Anna snapped as she pointed the weapon at him and removed the safety.

"I BEG TO DIFFER, DOC. AFTER YOUR LAST LITTLE FANTASY YOU BASICALLY ROLLED OUT THE RED CARPET FOR ME," Dionysus teased from within his host. He moved closer to her, watching with amusement as she blushed.

"Take one more step and I will shoot," she warned.

"I DON'T THINK YOU WILL ,ANNA, I DON'T THINK YOU CAN," he whispered as he drew upon his power and pressed it against her mind, reminding her of the dream earlier, as he stalked towards her.

Anna's finger wrapped around the trigger as James came to stand before her. She felt lust coil in her belly and cloud her mind with the drugging promise of pleasure. She pulled the trigger twice but the act was far too late as James hand was already wrapped about her wrist turning the barrel so that the bullets missed lodging in the wall instead.

The wine god's fingers stroked down her arm teasing her with the promise of touch as his power pressed more forcefully against her mind.

Anna groaned under the onslaught, her fevered mind running wild with images from her fantasy earlier which she'd turned from.

"SHH, YES, MY DEAR, I KNOW," Dionysus murmured with excitement. His fingers moved from her arm to her face and down her neck. He turned her head exposing the vein there and he felt the need to bite her, there, burning in his blood. He wanted to mark her as his. To rub in Hermes face, his success, where the other had failed but he knew time was short.

The others would be returning soon and if he was going to seal his deal with his brother, he had to get Anna out of there. So he resisted the impulse and instead ran his fingers lower, stopping just above the swell of her breasts. Goose flesh rose in his wake and he watched as her hunger grew with a wicked glee.

"I PROMISE, I'LL TAKE CARE OF IT SOON," he teased as he drew back, "BUT FIRST THERE'S SOMEONE WHO WANTS A WORD WITH YOU," he quipped.

Anna blinked as his words moved past her lust fogged brain and sank in taking root. Hermes! He'd made a deal with the other fallen for his freedom and she was payment. She had to get out of there.

Fear driving her Anna pulled the trigger again the sound startling them both. As the TV droned on about some woman who'd killed others due to a need for blood, red exploded on the wall behind her as the wine god roared in rage as his host cried out in pain.

The gun fell from numb fingers the sound of metal clattering on tile struck her ears as she turned and fled from Dionysus' puppet.

10

Sam pulled into the parking spot he'd left earlier that morning and got out of the car. A sense of urgency driving him, he moved up the steps taking them two at a time. As he rounded the corner leading to room 207 his worst fears were confirmed. The door was flung wide open the frame busted but not by any natural force. Moving inside he found clear signs of a struggle.

The gun he'd given her lay on the floor, the smell of freshly discharged powder in the air. Two bullets were lodged into the wall, a third lower, along with blood splatter. Good, she'd managed to hit him. Maybe bought herself enough time to get away.

Sam drew his gun as he stepped out of the room looking for more signs of her passage. The blood was relatively fresh meaning she might still be out there. Sam followed the trail, marking her attacker's signs of passage. He swore as the trail came to an end at the top of the other set of stairs, there were signs here of a second struggle and to his regret, they all pointed to one conclusion Anna had been taken.

Rage coiled inside him as fear flooded his mind. Who? Why? The questions rose up like monsters to torment him but he brushed them aside. It didn't matter, he knew where she was headed and he had to get to her before she got there.

Sam ran down the stairs and back to the car. He was behind the wheel and on the move tires squealing as he pulled out.

Lance's eyes opened. "Where's Anna?"

"She's gone."

"How? Who? Do you think it was Hecate?"

"I don't know and it doesn't matter. Whether it's her or James cutting his losses, she'll be headed to the same place."

"Hermes."

Sam nodded his face grim.

"We'll get her back," Lance assured him.

"Damn it. I failed her, same as I failed Pamela. I was so caught up in doing my job I lost track of what really mattered.

All my instincts told me not to leave her."

"You haven't failed yet, Sam, we just have to find her," Catharine offered.

"No. You and Lance can't go where I'm headed. I need you to focus on finding that damn crown. I'll find her."

"Any idea where to start?" Lance asked.

"Just the airport. After that, no."

"Watch your speed, we don't need a ticket," Lance muttered.

Sam eased back from the accelerator. "Sorry."

"If we don't catch them at the airport--" Catharine asked.

"We split up, you find a quiet place to work off the radar and I continue the hunt. While I don't know where to go, I know someone who does."

"Pamela."

"Be careful, man, she's different now," Lance stated.

"I appreciate the warning. Watch out for Hecate. She's far more dangerous than the others."

"How do you know that?" Lance asked curious.

"I have a source."

"What else does your source know about all of this?"

"I don' know, but we should find out."

.

11

Zaharrah made her way to the break room on the dig site. She pulled out her drink and moved to the bulletin board. She pulled out of her back pocket a flyer she'd fashioned on her laptop on the boat back to the isle. Pulling down a pin she put it up on the board before turning to head for her work room. As she walked, she watched as Darrian rose from his seat at the table to check out the board.

He pulled the advertisement from the board and Zaharrah smiled. Her message was received. She'd been careful since her arrival at the dig not to draw attention to the young man with dark hair and dark eyes going by the name of Darian Hunter. They'd worked out a system of communication that kept them from meeting directly and so far no one had noticed but it was getting harder to maintain. Since the event in the throne room security was watching closer.

Broody was being even more secretive. There was tension at the site between him and his backer Russell York. All signs pointed to it being time to get clear of the place but she had to convince her brother of the fact.

As Zaharrah entered her office, the cell phone in her pocket began to vibrate. She drew the offending object out and seeing the number cursed. She'd have to keep this quick as she wasn't sure the room was secure.

"Hello."

"Zaharrah. How did you know about Hecate?" Sam Abrams voice asked.

"This isn't a good time to talk about Dad's health, Mom. I'm at work and they tend to monitor our calls for non-related work usage.

I don't want to get in trouble so I'll call you back," Zaharrah muttered before she hung up.

Sitting down behind her desk, she returned to the work she was responsible for, hunting for any leads on the locations of the remaining mantels.

12 CENTRAL FALLS, RHODE ISLAND

Sam cursed as the phone went dead. He understood the reason for it but at the moment he had little patience left for delays. As he pulled into the private hanger for Catharine's plane, he scribbled down the number for Zaharrah and handed it to Lance.

"She couldn't talk safely. Call her back later tonight, tell her who you are and how we know each other, then find out what you can about Hecate. I've got to get the rental back and hopefully find out if Anna's plane is still here."

"If it isn't?" Lance asked.

"Then I'll be looking for Pamela. I suggest you both get in the air before you start working. The last thing you need right now is Dionysus coming back for Catharine."

Lance nodded. "Be careful, man."

"You, too." Sam answered. He watched as Lance and Catharine climbed out of the car to board the plane before he sped off for the car rental terminal.

Once the car was back in the rental lot, he bailed out and ran in the direction of the control tower. He had to get those answers and at the moment, he didn't have the authority to demand them. Dragging out his phone he punched in the number of his contact at the agency and prayed for help.

"Mr. Abrams, there are a lot of people here waiting to talk to you about the information you sent us the other day. I hope you're calling to say you're coming in."

"I can't yet, I'm still working and I need a favor."

"You drop Kadar in our lap gift wrapped, then a mountain of intel on Russell York and his team without explanation, after being inactive for three years and start demanding favors, sorry, I can't help you, man, unless you come in."

Sam snarled, knowing he'd never get past airport security into the tower. Protocol was tight since 9-11. "Fine, get me on the first flight to you and we'll meet but I need that intel now."

"What are you looking for?"

"Flight plans for James Hardagen."

"The actor."

"Yeah, he kidnapped a friend of mine."

"I'm on it. You're on the first flight out to DC. It leaves in two hours--"

"Skip the flight, I've got my own ride. I'll be there within the hour, and you better have my answers." Sam snapped before he hung up.

Without skipping a beat, he punched in Lance's number as he ran back in the direction of the jet hanger.

13

Lance settled Catharine into her seat and moved to the storage area in search of the first aid kit. He was in the process of digging out the needed tools to tend to her injuries when his phone rang.

"Hello, Sam."

"I'm headed your way. I need you to drop me in DC. The agency is refusing to help me unless I come in."

"Got it, I'll let the pilot know where we're headed. We'll be in the air as soon as you get here." Lance assured him before he hung up. He grabbed the first aid kit and set it on the seat beside Catharine, before moving to the cockpit to inform the pilot of their destination.

"What did Sam want?" Catharine questioned as he reemerged from the front of the jet.

"A ride to DC." Lance answered as he knelt at her side to begin the task of tending to her injuries. He pulled open his shirt which he'd wrapped about her in his haste to protect her from the killer and hide her from Sam. He closed his eyes as he worked, reflecting on the irony of the moment, he'd been dreaming about taking her clothes off and little else since his encounter with Dionysus and now that he was, he couldn't bear to look. As he opened his eyes to look at the extent of the damage he hissed.

Sam was right, she should have been taken to a hospital. If it had been anyone else, he'd have insisted upon it but because she'd refused to go while in town, he'd reasoned he could take care of her, now he wasn't so sure. Opening the first aid kit he began to pull out the materials.

"Oh, that's perfect. We can work from there. I can do my observation if that's okay and--" Catharine began with excitement.

Lance smiled at her enthusiasm, the writer in her at work again. Unable to help himself, he leaned in and kissed her, both to quiet her, aware he shouldn't let her think too far ahead and to ease his own mind with the reality she was there. He'd nearly lost her and it had shaken him to the core.

Dana had left him. She'd chosen death over him, he saw that now and it disappointed him. Catharine on the other hand had been taken by the monster he'd once hunted. The Fury Killer as he'd been misnamed, had already begun his ritual to kill her.

Lance drew back from the thought, he didn't want his mind wandering back to the sight of her in that candle lit basement. She was there with him now and she was safe. The man who'd taken her was dead; slain by an angry goddess. His fingers brushed her face to sink into her hair and his hand brushed something moist and sticky.

Opening his eyes he found blood on his thumb from under her eye where her abductor had carved two of ten cuts. Lance drew back from the kiss, he needed to take care of her not indulge his own needs.

"That's fine, but before you start anything you're going to rest," Lance stated his voice gentle but firm broaching no argument.

Catharine nodded as she stared back at him, her blue eyes narrow slits, her lids heavy with fatigue from all she'd endured. Lance began the task of cleaning cuts and covering them. Little nicks covered her pale skin, bloody fingerprints marked her neck and arms. HIS bloody fingers marking her. They were the first thing to go. Nothing of the killer's touch would remain upon her when Lance was done.

As he began to bandage her wounds Lance spoke again.

"What did he do?"

"Not now, detective, please. I don't want to think about him for a while," she murmured her voice groggy and headed for sleep.

"All right, we'll leave it alone for now. Stay with me, Serenity, I still need to get you dressed," he whispered as he covered the last of the cuts along her body.

"I'm tired, Lance," she breathed.

"I know, princess, just hang in there a few more minutes," he requested as he got to his feet. Lance pulled out of the over head compartment her things which they'd brought from James home. He opened the lid to her case and dug through looking for something loose fitting.

A pair of sleep pants was what he settled on. Lance pulled the soft cotton over abused legs and to her hips. "Stand up for a minute," he requested and he watched as she rose slowly on shaky limbs. Lance draped one of her arms around his neck to steady her as he pulled the pants over her hips.

Lance settled her back in the chair and wrapped his own shirt around her once more taking the time to button it up. With the bulk of the work done, he turned his focus to her face. The two angry lines under her right eye were going to be far less easy to deal with. He wiped the skin clean and pulled out the bottle of liquid skin. It would do until he could get her in for stitches.

His work done, he gave her some meds for the pain and fastened her seatbelt preparing her for their departure. Once she was settled he closed up the first aid kit and returned it to its storage bin. He was closing up her bag when Sam boarded the plane and closed the door tight. Lance stowed her suitcase away before taking his seat beside her.

"How is she?" Sam asked, still concerned they were making a mistake by not taking her to a hospital.

"She's tired and sore, I imagine, but I've cleaned her as best I can for now. You're right, though, she should have gone to a hospital. She needs stitches."

"Did you want--?"

"No, I'll see her there when we land, the sooner you get to DC and get that meeting over with the better. You need to get to Anna before Hermes gets his hands on her. Given what Dionysus has done to her, I wouldn't want her alone with either of them for very long."

Sam nodded he took a seat next to the door. As Lance fastened his own safety belt, the plane taxied down the runway before taking to the sky.

14 UNKNOWN

Hecate moved down the corridor of Magnus Halden's private facility with a boldness few displayed. She walked past the guard and into his office without a word. None moved to stop her.

"Hades. You're late in your arrival to this realm. Hermes has already begun to build his power and soon even you will be no match for him. You must cement your return by presenting your mantle to the statue which holds your spirit captive."

"Hecate," the god of death breathed the name with a bit of surprise but he welcomed her with a kiss on the brow. "I'm working on the location of the image. Hermes has moved it. Is there anything we can do to slow his ascent to power?"

"Two things can be done. First, Artemis, his huntress, can be turned against him."

"How?"

"Reveal to her the truth of what happened to her mighty father." Hecate answered.

"And the second thing?" Hades prompted.

"Obtain Zeus's crown before him."

"I'll handle the huntress, as to the crown I know exactly where it is, as soon as I am restored to my full power I will get it."

"Excellent," Hecate purred with approval.

"What of the others?" Hades questioned as he took her hand in his own. Any information he could glean from her would be useful.

"Dionysus stands as Hermes' ally. Hephaestus, Eros and Helios are all fallen and Ares puppet is slain."

Hades smiled at the news as he lifted her hand to his lips and kissed it. "Ares sword?" he questioned, his hosts gray eyes gleaming with green sparks denoting his power.

"I have it," she whispered.

Hades gave her arm a tug and drew her closer to him. Aware that with Hecate, he couldn't rush her. She was not a hand to be forced. "May I have it?" he asked with patience.

Hecate reached out running a hand along Hades cheek to brush her fingers through his host's black hair "You can, though I'd not wield it if I were you," she murmured.

Hades smiled as he wrapped an arm around her waist so that they were face to face. "Why not, my lady?' he questioned.

"In order for you to match Hermes in his claim for the throne you'll need a second, an Ally to stand with you. Who better than the war god?" Hecate explained before she turned in his embrace presenting her back to him. Refusing his advance.

Hades didn't let it deter him, he simply brushed the kiss meant for her lip on the side of her neck. "So be it. Find me a suitable host for Ares and as soon as I get the location of the statues, we'll make our move." he stated before he released her.

Hecate turned to face him once more and bowed in a show of respect before departing.

Hades sighed at her departure, the witch was ever guarded. He cursed his fallen brother's foolishness for forcing himself upon her all those years ago. It made her slow to yield to a lover and a dangerous ally. Her motives were never fully clear. But he'd heed her words.

"Russell," Magnus bellowed.

"Yes, sir," his second answered, his voice shaky he'd been more frightened around Magnus since the candle arrived, Hades noted. Though he didn't understand what was happening he was aware of the change in his leader.

"Get Miss Walsh on the phone, it's time we paid her and Mr. Broody a visit."

"Yes, sir," Russell York answered with relief before retreating from the room.

Hades laughed it was good to be back. The emotions of these mortals fed him and he'd been starving inside that damn statue for too long. There were things he'd not indulged in for centuries and it was time to bring that to an end. With this in mind, his thoughts turned toward his chosen bride, he was looking forward to meeting her both in the dream realm and in the flesh. He'd marked her years ago and none had touched her since that time. When he finally did, she'd forget that anyone ever had.

15

Pamela was pulled from sleep by the chirp of her cell phone. Whiskey colored eyes looked about surprised to find Hermes gone. Reaching to the night table she picked up the offending object and through sleep blurred vision stared at the number and read it.

She cursed at the name on the screen. "Russell York." Pamela had hoped she'd have more time to prepare before she had to deal with the matter. Deciding that it was better to get it over with than string it out, she wrapped the sheet about her as she put up her mental wall before connecting the call.

"Miss Walsh. I trust you had a safe flight."

"I'm fine," she assured him.

"Good," Russell York said pleased.

"Can we skip the small talk and get to the point. I'd like to get back to sleep."

"Not even a hello for an old friend?"

"We aren't friends."

"We used to be. You were one of my better assets."

"'Was' is the operative word. I've moved on to bigger and better things since then."

"Yes, I know. I forgot you're all ambition, always looking to the next big step ahead. Fame, power, and greed are your great motivators. I can get you all of those if you do me a little favor."

"What do you want, Russell?"

"Just tell me where you are, Miss Walsh."

"That's not going to happen, Russell. My services are no longer free to your disposal or your employers. I'm not your errand girl anymore," Pamela hissed, making it clear she would not betray her husband.

"This is not the answer I wanted to hear from you, Miss Walsh. I thought you were smarter than this."

"I'm not afraid of you, Russell. You, or Magnus."

"You should be," Russell York warned. "He will find you, Pamela, and he will strip you of everything you've earned without him. When he's done with you, you'll beg him for his forgiveness." Mr. York muttered before he disconnected the call.

Pamela tightened her grip on the bed sheet about her involuntarily as old fears took hold of her. Magnus Halden was not a man to cross. She smiled at the thought and laughed. He was only a Man and she was married to a God.

16 Unknown

Russell York smiled as he set down his phone, the screen in front of him informed him that his efforts to track the call had been successful. Rising from his work station, he walked over to the heavy oak double doors that led into his employer's domain.

"Miss Walsh was less than helpful but I got the location. She's in Athens somewhere." Russell announced.

"Excellent work, Mr. York. Prepare the chopper. It's time we paid a visit to Ian and his new bride," Magnus stated.

Russell nodded before he made his way out of the office and headed back to his work space. He was relieved that things had run smoothly because he shuttered to think what sort of punishment the other man might have doled out if he'd failed.

Not for the first time he contemplated getting out. His employer had become more volatile since he got his hands on the candle. As Russell picked up the phone to call for the chopper he shook off the notion with regret. The only way he was getting free of Magnus Halden was in a body bag and he sincerely hoped that there wasn't a hell. Otherwise he'd never be free of the mad man.

17

Magnus Halden pulled out his portable communicator and pressed the button to connect him with his crew. "Team leader, report," he commanded.

"Troops are on standby awaiting orders, sir," his commander answered.

"Prepare for departure; your target is located in Athens, Greece. I expect to have complete intel on the site the moment I get on the ground." Magnus paused to consider where Ian would be and the voice in his mind reminded him he was not dealing with Dr. Ian Broody but Hermes.

"The team will be in place awaiting your command," the man answered.

Magnus ignored the response as he asked the voice in his mind where Hermes would have set up shop.

"My pompous and arrogant brother, who thinks he is omniscient, would be set up near the temple of sacrifice. He needs it to complete the ritual to make your Miss Walsh his true bride. By now, he's already wed her but it is of little concern to us. There are ways to undo what he has done."

"Perfect. The target will figure to be near the Parthenon," Magnus informed his team lead.

"Understood, sir," he answered before Magnus tuned him out once more. His focus shifting once more to the voice in the back of his head, "Hades," he breathed the name with both respect and amusement. As he drew the strange dark candle with its green gems out of the desk drawer to study it.

He'd heard the god of the underworld's voice ever since he encountered the text about the mantels in the council's library. A faint whisper in his mind nudging him forward promising him everything he'd ever desired so long as he obtained the candle and returned it to his hands.

Hades had warned him along the way to be ready for a battle. So as he'd worked in the shadows behind York's name he'd built himself a network of agents. Pamela, Ian, York and the others were but pawns he'd moved about to his own ends. The explosion that revealed the lost city was no accident. It had all been arranged. While Broody played at being god, he'd built himself an army to take what was his.

"WHAT IS OURS," Hade's voice corrected.

"You promised me her," Magnus breathed his voice hinted at impatience.

"SOON," Hades answered him.

"Sir, your chopper is ready," Russell York muttered nervously through the door having heard him speaking to himself again.

Magnus cursed he'd been careful to keep his conversations with Hades private. Only York had been privy to them. He wondered if it was time that Russell York vanished but Hades warned against it. He should not end his puppet until the job was done.

"Thank you, Mr. York, I'll be along in a moment," Magnus said. He put the candle in a steel case to keep it hidden before rising from his seat. He carried the case with him as he made his way to the helipad. Once on board the chopper, he strapped himself in. As the chopper took to the skies Hades bid him rest and as he fell into sleep the god of the underworld entered the dream realm in search of his bride.

18 Miami, Florida

Zaharrah made her way towards the Mexican cantina, mindful of her surroundings though she never looked behind her directly, she checked for a tail, aware that if she were caught meeting with Darrian they could both get in a lot of trouble.

She crossed the street casually as if she were just dropping in for a drink. Her brown eyes combed over the place looking for un-friendlies before she approached the bar where he sat. She took up the stool beside him and ordered a mojito. Once the drink was in her hand she crossed the floor to take a seat at an empty table in the back corner.

While it was not completely private it would serve for their meet. As she sipped at her drink a familiar voice spoke in a slightly slurred greeting.

"'ello, beautiful, mind if I sit?"

She shrugged with indifference. "It's a free country,' she muttered. Zaharrah watched as her brother sank down into the seat across from her and smiled at the sight of him, it seemed Darrian had learned how to play the drunk well.

"What's up sis it's not like you to break cover?

"It couldn't be helped. Look it's time for both of us to get off that dig sight…"

"I'm not done with my assignment yet," Darrian hissed.

"I know that but the stakes have changed. Broody is getting dangerous and I'm not convinced he's the one in charge anymore. Security has tightened up. Soon, not even I'll be able to get anything past them. I'm telling you it's time to go."

"I can't yet. I've got something I've got to finish first."

"Damn it, Darrian, you're playing with your life. If I have to I'll drag you out. I'm not about to sit by and watch the order get you killed."

"The hell you will this isn't about them."

"If not them then what?"

"I promised a friend."

"Okay if it's not family business then let me help you."

"I'm sorry, Zaharrah, but I can't…"

"Fine be that way stubborn fool, but be careful."

"I will," he assured her.

"When it's done get clear of this place."

"I will," he assured her in a low whisper with a cocky grin that had always made her laugh. She didn't feel much like laughing at the moment, in fact the look only seemed to heighten the fear growing in her gut. "I mean it, Darrian, I don't want…"

"Relax, sis, I'll be fine," he assured her before he turned and walked away from the table. Zaharrah finished her mojito before she turned and left. She hoped he was right.

19 WASHINGTON DC, VIRGINIA
SUNDAY
6PM

Sam was out of his seat and moving for the planes exit before the engine had even been cut off. He was aware of Lance and Catharine moving behind him, but didn't wait. He needed to get to the agency headquarters as fast as possible. Each second that slipped away, was precious time Anna didn't have.

Sam was down the steps and in the hanger the second it was safe to be outside. He was in the process of arranging for a rental car when the quiet hanger became alive with activity. Two dozen men came out of the shadows, guns raised ready to fire.

"Stand down, Mr. Abrams."

Sam cursed, even as he did as he was told, putting his hands in the air in a show of surrender. He figured the ambush was to be expected. He'd broken his agreement with the agency; been active for over a week. His silence hadn't helped his case any. For all they knew he'd gone rogue. "I came here to speak with you in good faith," Sam reminded.

"Yes, we are aware but until we get some answers I've been ordered to bring you in or take you out."

Sam nodded. If it was answers they wanted he'd give them but he wasn't about to wait for them to get around to him. "You'll get them but understand I can't wait long, there are lives at stake here," Sam stated, his blue eyes calm. If he let on this was personal they'd only slow this thing down more.

"I'll be sure they're made aware," the other man answered as his team moved into secure Sam. His hands were twisted behind his back like a common criminal and a plastic zip tie used to secure them. A black hood lowered over his head to blind him before he was loaded into a company vehicle and driven off.

20

Lance blew out a breath as the black SUV sped away. He heard the commotion in the hanger as Catharine had moved to exit the plane. He'd held her back raising a finger to his lips indicating she stay quiet as he'd watched his friend be taken away.

"What happened? Where's Sam?"

"They took him?"

"Who?"

"His former employers," Lance muttered.

"I thought Sam was a reporter?"

"He was a spy," Lance hissed before he looked back out into the hanger, checking to be sure they were really alone.

"A spy? Why didn't you help him?"

"Did you want to be held for questioning on matters we know nothing about until they came to the conclusion we were innocent by-standers in this mess," Lance questioned.

Catharine shook her head. The idea of an interrogation was not pleasant after what she'd endured in the last 48 hours.

"I didn't think so. Sam will be fine and with a little luck he'll get help in locating Anna," Lance assured her.

"And if he's not lucky?" Catharine questioned.

"They'll hold him indefinitely."

"But Anna…"

"Sam won't let it come to that," Lance stated. "Come on you still need stitches. The faster that is taken care of, the sooner we get back to my place and you can get some rest." Lance took Catharine by the hand and led her out of the plane into the hanger.

"A spy," Catharine said amused before shaking her head and grinning weakly.

"Yeah," Lance said uneasy, he hoped she didn't decide to pick Sam's brain; he wasn't fond of questions.

"That explains a lot," she said, amused before she brushed a kiss on Lance's cheek and pulled out her phone to call for a car.

"No questions?" He asked surprised.

"I told you before who he is doesn't matter to me where my book is concerned."

"Speaking of books, I saw you typing away today by the pool I thought you were stuck."

"I was but I had a breakthrough, I know how to fix *Dark Heart* and save Serenity," Catharine said with excitement.

"Will you tell me?" he asked.

"No but if you're a good host I may let you read," she teased before turning her attention to the phone and the task at hand. He shouldered his bag and grabbed hers before the pair began to walk down the tarmac in the direction of the car rental lot.

21

Sam stood for the second time in his life inside a 10 x 10 concrete room with a standard issue prison cot as its only focal point. He'd refused to sit, recalling that the damn thing was unbearably uncomfortable. He laughed at the irony of it all, the last time he'd been there had been over a woman as well. At least this time around there was no waking up dazed and confused, no trying to sort out where he was and who had him. He was just beginning to wonder how long they intended to make him wait when the cell door swung open and his contact stepped inside the room.

"Sam, Sam, you've been a bad boy, of late. DC, Israel, Jordan, Miami, LA. Road Island I thought when we relocated you we made it clear that you were not to leave Vegas without notifying us."

"I know but something came up I couldn't let wait."

"What?"

"Lance Roman sent me a civilian who was being tailed by Kedar."

"I see and who was this civilian?"

"A doctor, Anna-Lynn Gallagher. She's an arch…" Sam stopped in his explanation as his contact paled visibly at the name.

"What did you just say?"

"Her name is Anna-Lynn Gallagher, she's an archeologist for the Smithsonian. She gave me the intel on Magnus…" Sam began again but the other man wasn't listening instead he pulled out his phone and punched in a series of numbers. Sam wondered at the strange behavior even as he watched the other man.

"Get me *Rogue*," his contact demanded before mashing the

button to break the call.

"What's going on? Who's *Rogue*?" Sam demanded but the other man said nothing more. He simply sank down onto the uncomfortable cot as if he were expecting trouble. Sam paced realizing the interview was over. Whoever this *Rogue* was, something about hearing Anna's name had spooked the man. But what?

22

Lance unlocked his front door and switched on the light before stepping inside with his and Catharine's luggage in tow. She walked in behind him a bit groggy from the pain meds she'd been given at the hospital for her stitches.

"Have a seat, Catharine, I'm just going to take your things to the guest room and dump my own," he informed her before heading down the hall towards the back half of his apartment.

After dropping off their stuff, he moved back into the living room where she sat on his couch waiting. Lance studied her from a distance. She looked weak and weary, fragile even. He wanted to talk to her, ask her what she'd been forced to endure while she'd been held captive by the madman, but he couldn't find the words. They just wouldn't come together. Instead Lance moved through the living room into the kitchen and got her something to drink. He set it on the coffee table before moving back down the hall into the guest room.

Lance grabbed part of the bedding from the room. He carried them out to her placing the pillow under her head and covering her with the blanket in an effort to make her more comfortable.

"Thanks."

"Did you need anything else?" He questioned.

"No. I'm fine," she assured him, "sit down and relax," she entreated.

Lance nodded taking a seat in the chair at her side. He was careful to keep his distance, not wanting to inadvertently upset her. He flipped on the TV and crossed the room to his movie collection. "What do you want to watch?" he asked her needing a distraction.

Every time he looked at her his mind flashed back to the image of her in that basement, naked, bleeding, tied to a bed, and surrounded by candles. Kurt standing over her his eyes lit with madness and an unholy power as he touched her.

"Something funny," she requested.

Lance nodded and turned to pick a film, but his eyes didn't see the DVD's. "I'm sorry, Serenity, he never should have gotten to you," Lance blurted out giving voice to the regret he felt. He'd failed her.

"Stop it. This is not your fault, detective. I was the one who wanted to set a trap for him. You warned me against it...none of us expected an accomplice," Catharine snapped irritated by his need to take responsibility for what had happened. "Hell, you saw him for the monster he was...I really thought he was harmless."

"Yeah, I saw him but I turned a blind eye; let myself reason it was just the jealousy I felt...I nearly got you killed because I..."

"Don't, it's over. I'm safe now and he's not coming back. You got there before he could..." she began.

"I know, but he made you watch while he did those things to Gail first. He gave your mind enough time to run wild with what would happen to you when he finished. No one should ever have had to see that--"

"You looked at it for years," Catharine reminded.

"It was my job and I never saw it firsthand like you did. Beyond that you're an innocent..." Lance argued.

"Look at me, detective," she commanded. He turned reluctantly to face her his icy blue eyes met her gaze but moved to the stitches under her eye a testament to what she'd endured. "I'm fine," she assured him.

Lance nodded, not really believing her but aware she wished to end the discussion. Telling himself she'd dealt with enough for one day, he let the matter go turning back to the movies to select one for them. "If you want to talk about it..." '

"I know where to find you," she assured him.

Having said all there was to say on the matter for now, he pulled a movie and slid it in the DVD player before moving back into the kitchen to pop some popcorn. He used the task as a means to pull himself together before joining her once more. As the film started, he prayed they'd be able to forget, if only for a little, the nightmare they'd just survived .

23

James Hardagen moved out of the main cabin of his private jet from where Emily sat asleep in her chair to the sleeping quarters. Opening the door, he moved through the darkness to the bed where his pretty prisoner lay unconscious in a drug induced sleep. He reached out with eager fingers to touch the long golden tresses that surrounded her.

The soft silky strands were a temptation he found himself unable to resist. Anna was not anyone he'd normally give a second glance but she was the most like Serenity in appearance he'd ever encountered and he found he longed for a taste of her.

His blue eyes glowed with power as he sat down beside the sleeper. In the darkness, they were nearly violet as the fallen spirit within him moved to the foreground of his mind. Dionysus smiled as he studied his captive, he could see why his brother was so eager to get her back. It amused him that here in the darkness he had her where Hermes had failed to hold on to her.

In his mind's eye, he pictured waking her and bedding her, marking her bronze throat with his bite taking Hermes prize for himself but as much as he desired to finish the game with her he'd begun, he knew it was folly. Hermes power was growing and he dared not risk the other god's wrath. Instead, he drew out his host's phone. He punched in the woman Pamela's number and listened to it ring.

"Hello," the sirens voice purred over the other side of the wire.

Dionysus's mind reflected the image of her sprawled out in a bed of blue silk her body wound around her husband, skin still damp with sweat from their exertions and he smiled before he brushed her mind with his power, announcing his presence.

"Dionysus," she called his name her voice breathy with rising desire and he laughed.

"MY LADY, INFORM YOUR LORD THAT I HAVE HIS PRIZE PER OUR ARRANGEMENT AND I ONLY AWAIT THE KNOWLEDGE OF WHERE YOU ARE IN ORDER TO DELIVER HER."

"That is great news. Lord Hermes will be immensely pleased. We're in Athens near the Parthenon," she murmured.

"WE'RE OVER THE ATLANTIC NOW NEARING THE ENGLISH COAST. INFORM MY BROTHER WE'LL ARRIVE THERE SOON," Dionysus requested as he gave her body yet another playful nudge.

"We'll be expecting you," she stated her voice now thick and smoky with desire. He pictured her hands sliding over Hermes body before she ended the call.

Dionysus put away his phone and turned his focus once more to the woman sleeping in the bed. He let go of her golden locks and skimmed his finger down her neck to where her pulse lay below. The wine god pictured sinking his teeth in her there tasting the crimson liquid that lay within and wondered what it would hold in its taste for him.

Now was not the time to find out. He told himself. But he would know in time, Dionysus vowed. He contemplated the matter and smiled. Anna and the others had underestimated him and Hermes was no different. To him he was but a lesser fallen, no threat. If he played his cards right then he might just be able to maneuver Hermes into a position in which he'd be able to take that which he desired without reprisal.

Yes, he'd play Hermes right hand for now, as his brother desired. Let him think he'd won. Use his influences to build his own power in secret, and then when the opportunity rose he'd make his move and steal the throne right out from under him.

Dionysus licked his lips with excitement at the notion. Picturing his moment of triumph, he took a drink from his cup. His host had been the perfect choice, a figure already worshiped by others, the actor would help him to build his power and *Dark Heart* was the key. The wine god ran his tongue over his teeth that had already begun to change. His incisors were sharper it wouldn't be long now until he was restored to his full power. When that happened, he would be Baucus once more.

He smiled as he looked once more to the beauty beside him.

Once he'd cemented his foothold in this world the sleeper before him would succumb to his power as would any other he desired to have.

24

Hermes slipped from his bed and dressed. He looked to his now slumbering wife and smiled. She was an eager and even demanding lover. After informing him of Dionysus's coming she'd thrown herself into his arms and all but begged for him to take her. He'd been more than happy to oblige. Now it was time to get up and get to business. With Dionysus on the way it meant that Miss Gallagher would soon be there as well and the answers he sought.

While the child growing in his wife's body did much to prove his entitlement to the throne of Zeus it wasn't a strong enough claim to ensure his place as the new king of the gods. He needed the crown and the key. The sooner he located them the better. Within the pretty doctor's mind dwelled the knowledge to lead him to both. She'd been able to locate several of the other mantles; knew something he didn't yet. It wouldn't be long now until that changed.

With this thought in mind, Hermes threw open the ornately carved oak double doors that led from his personal chambers and moved down the short but wide corridor into his office. As he stepped into the room and headed for his desk, the spirits of his brethren still trapped within the stone figures that encircled the space hissed — all but the wine god, who laughed for he knew the key to his freedom would soon be there.

Hermes moved through the room to the parlor where his own image stood watch, like a sentinel over the home. "Anna's coming," he whispered to the man Broody's spirit living within it. The mortal laughed at the news and begged for the right to be witness to her fall. Hermes assured him he would and thrilled in the flood of power that washed through him as the mortal fantasized about what would happen to the troublesome woman who had spurned him.

Hermes studied the soul trapped within and smiled to find only a small speck of light remained. He'd make sure Ian was witness to Anna's fall, it would wipe out the last bit of light within him and then his soul would be ready to devour. "SOON," he assured the man before returning to his office and taking his seat behind the white marble desk. He turned his focus to Anna's notes and the stone tablets they'd unearthed in Sodom, hoping to find a clue of his own.

Hermes had just begun his work when he was alerted to the presence of another. Lifting his head he watched as his prized huntress walked into the room her blue eyes gleaming with pleasure.

"ARTEMIS, MY SWEET LADY, I TAKE IT YOU HAVE NEWS," he said pleased.

He watched with amusement as the demi-goddess bowed before him in a show of respect.

"THE WAR GOD'S PUPPET IS NO MORE; I HAVE EXTRACTED MY REVENGE. I LOST THE TRAIL OF THE MORTAL ANNA BUT WHILE I PURSUED HER, OBTAINED THIS," Artemis revealed as she presented the bow of Eros to him. Hermes rose from his seat and crossed the floor to her side lifting her head so that their eyes met. He brushed a kiss on her brow to show his delight.

"RISE, MY HUNTRESS," he bade her and watched as she got to her feet. He'd done well in utilizing her skills over the years. She was his best tool in his efforts to take the seat of her dead father. Her loyalty was total and, with time, he'd cultivate her other assets to his use as well. Her unspoiled body would be the perfect lure to ensnare his rivals' puppets. "WELL DONE, MY DEAR. DO NOT FRET OVER THE LOSS OF THE WOMAN; MY BROTHER THE WINE GOD HAS HER AND IS BRINGING HER NOW TO TRADE FOR HIS FREEDOM," Hermes assured her as he took the bow from her hands.

He looked to the graven image of his brother and moved to claim the power for his own but paused looking back to his servant and smiled, here was an opportunity to strengthen his hold upon her. To weaken the human blood that flowed within her veins. "THIS POWER, MY DEAR, IS ONE WORTHY ONLY OF A HUNTRESS AND A WEAPON MADE FOR YOU. FOR YOUR

LOYAL SERVICE TAKE THIS GIFT AND MAKE IT YOURS," he murmured as he set the bow back in her hands.

"MY LORD," she questioned unsure.

"COME, TAKE MY HAND. I'LL SHOW YOU," he whispered as he offered her his right hand. She took it and he led her over to the image of Eros. Within the statue, the god of love roared in outrage that Hermes meant to give his power to the demi goddess. "Place the bow in his hands," Hermes instructed. He watched with enjoyment as she did as he bade.

Artemis screamed as Eros' powers washed through her, her own devouring it and remolding it to her will. Outside, lightening crashed splitting a tree, setting it ablaze as thunder snapped shaking the house. Hermes watched as the image of Eros' face crumbled and caught Artemis as she fell back the jolt of power nearly knocking her off her feet.

"EASY, MY DEAR, I'VE GOT YOU," he assured her as he cradled her body close to his, thrilling in the feel of her so near lingering only for a moment before he helped her to stand. Not wishing to draw attention to the fact his interest in her was changing into something more than that of a guardian to a child. Knowing she wasn't ready yet to see him as a man. He had to lead her with caution or everything he'd worked for could be undone.

When she opened her eyes flecks of red danced within the blue pools.

"THANK YOU MY LORD, I AM HONORED," she said humbled now by the gift he'd bestowed upon her.

"YOU'VE EARNED IT, MY LADY. NOW I SENSE THERE IS SOMETHING YOU WISH TO ASK OF ME," He whispered as he led her back to the center of the room.

"THERE IS. I WISH TO RETRIEVE THE SWORD OF ARES FROM HECATE BEFORE SHE CAN FIND A NEW WIELDER FOR IT. I WANT TO ENSURE THE NAME ARES IS NEVER BORN BY ANOTHER MAN."

"HECATE?"

"YES, MY LORD. SHE IS LOOSE BUT HER POWER IS YET LIMITED."

"VERY WELL, THEN. GO MY HUNTRESS, TRACK DOWN THIS TROUBLESOME WITCH AND FIND YOUR ENEMY'S POWER. WHEN YOU HAVE IT, BRING IT AND HER TO ME," he commanded.

"AS YOU WILL, MY LORD, WHEN IT IS FINISHED WILL

YOU THEN HELP ME TO FIND MY TWIN AS YOU VOWED?" Artemis questioned.

"ONCE ALL THE MANTELS ARE FOUND, MY DEAR, I SHALL AID YOU IN YOUR SEARCH FOR APOLLO AS I SWORE," he assured her with a smile.

"THEN I WILL LEAVE YOU, MY LORD, AND SEE TO HECATE," she answered before she bowed and departed his presence once more.

Hermes smiled, his work with the huntress was nearly complete. Soon she would be ready to take her place in his new court.

25

Sam groaned with frustration at the continued delay in the interview. What was taking so damn long? He'd been there for hours now and there was still no sign of this Rogue person. Every minute that ticked by was another Anna was getting closer to reaching her destination. He didn't have time for this.

He watched with relief as the cell door finally opened and his contact stepped outside. He heard hushed voices beyond, whispers back and forth but couldn't make any of it out. A moment later, his contact issued him out of the concrete prison in the direction of an interview room.

When he stepped inside he expected to see the director but that wasn't who waited. No sitting on the opposite side of the metal table was a young woman with dark hair and sharp green eyes that measured him for a coffin.

"Mr. Abrams, have a seat," she commanded. Her voice was cold and harsh and held no patience. Whoever she was, she was clearly upset. Sam crossed the floor to sit down opposite her as his contact took the seat next to her.

"Now I want you to explain to me what the hell it is you think you're doing?" The woman shouted in fury.

"I've been trying to protect a civilian from a shit storm,"

Sam snapped back at the end of his tolerance for this delay. "You were given explicit direction not to leave Vegas under any circumstances." His contact reminded him.

"I know that but this woman, Anna, was being tailed by Kedar. What did you expect me to do? Ignore the matter and watch her die?" Sam muttered.

"No, we expected you to contact us with the intel. You're not a spy anymore." The other man stated.

"There wasn't time. Just like there isn't now."

"Damn it, Sam, don't you get the mess you're in right now. You were dismissed as an agent because you were burned as unsafe."

"By who for what?" Sam questioned

"By me." The woman hissed. "I had ya given your papers because ya were shacked up with that blonde bitch, Pamela Walsh."

"Pamela. Why? Because she was a reporter or my wife? Did you think I couldn't keep a secret? She knew nothing."

"No, because she was workin' for York," the woman spat with disgust.

Sam blinked at the revelation and then cursed.. That was how York had gotten to her so easily, why she'd left. The whole mess finally made sense. It hadn't been about her career; he was no longer of any use to her employer. "Not York, Magnus Halden," Sam corrected.

"What's he talkin' about?" the woman demanded looking to Sam's contact.

"New intel he just sent in. Russell York isn't our guy; some guy named Halden is."

"Why haven't I seen this yet? I told ya I was ta receive any movement on this matter."

"We've just begun sorting through it for validity, there was a lot of it and he was the source."

"Not me — Anna Gallagher. The woman you've left swinging in the wind for the last five hours."

"What the hell does that mean?"

"I don't know, **Rogue**, we didn't get…"

"How do you know Anna?" Sam asked curious.

"That's not your concern. I want ta know how ya know her and where she is right now!"

"Lance sent her to me. She'd had her place broken into after leaving a dig she was working. Kedar was following her. I offered my protection. Things got complicated with the dig, then worse when Lance's killer resurfaced. I left Anna at the hotel but when I got back I found she'd been taken."

"Taken where? By who?"

"I'm not sure who, there are too many players involved at the moment. As to where, I'm not positive on that either."

"What the hell do ya know, Mr. Abrams?"

"That Pamela can lead me back to her and she's in a lot of danger."

"If my sister dies because ya got her mixed up in this…"

"I didn't get her mixed up in this. You want to point a finger you point it at Ian Broody," Sam snapped.

"Ian?"

"You know him?" Sam asked amused.

"Yeah, he was her fiancé, mi parents loved him. What's this got ta do with Ian?"

"He works for York. Guess you missed that," Sam said.

"Son of a bitch. Okay, I'm sorry. I want everythin' on the case now," *Rogue* barked at Sam's contact. Sam watched as the other man turned and left. Anna's sister got to her feet and cut the zip tie restraining Sam. "Okay, Mr. Abrams ,you're with mi, we'll go get mi backup and then we're goin' ta find mi sister," Rogue stated before she turned and walked out of the interrogation room, Sam hot on her heels.

26

Lance rose from the couch to stop the movie as the credits began to roll. He put the DVD back in the case and returned it to the wall shelf with the collection. "What do you want to watch next?" he asked looking at the options.

Catharine blinked as she considered the matter. The comedy had done just what she wanted eased her mood and made her smile but now she wasn't sure what she was in the mood for. As she contemplated the matter Lance's cell phone rang. She watched as he drew the thing from his pocket and pressed the talk button.

"Hello."

"Lance, I heard you were back in town," a familiar voice stated.

"Yeah, chief, just got back earlier both cases closed officially."

"That's great news."

"What's up ,chief?"

"I've got a case I could use your help with."

"B&E?"

"No, a homicide. I know--"

"I'll give it a look." Lance assured him.

"You will?"

"Yeah, I've been bored in B&E, I needed the time away but my instincts are for homicide. When do you want to meet?"

"If you can tonight, I'd prefer it."

"Yeah, I can but I'll have a civilian with me," Lance warned.

"That's fine. Meet me in thirty minutes at the Brickskeller?"

"You got it, chief," Lance answered before he pressed the button to end the call. His blue eyes moved to his guest. "Want to go for a ride?"

"Where are we headed?"

"Famous cop bar. You'll get to see me work first hand."

"I'm in," she said with a smile. Lance watched as she pulled on her shoes and grabbed her purse. He grabbed his keys after switching off the TV and the pair left his apartment.

27

Zaharrah sat at the table in her hotel room, she'd converted into her work space. Her dark eyes skimmed over the information on the mantels she'd managed to gather. She wondered how Anna had managed to locate the ones she had so far, what was the key she was missing, and sighed.

Whatever it was it wasn't in her notes and the elusive detail continued to escape her. She smiled, glad of it. The idea of tipping Broody on anything pertaining to the hunt made her skin crawl. Her employer was no longer human. He was Hermes, the god of knowledge.

Zaharrah's thoughts drifted to the archives back in the Black Hand's headquarters. She found herself wishing she'd taken more than just the couple records from their files. Secrets to a great many things lay within those ancient walls and the texts they held. Answers to what was happening around her and how to stop it.

No one at the dig was safe now. She felt the need to flee but refused to go until she was sure Darrian was safely away from there. Zaharrah wondered what her brother was up to. She'd never known him to be secretive yet he'd been unwilling to explain this mysterious errand he had to complete. Zaharrah hoped wherever he was, her brother was okay.

She looked at her phone, sitting beside her work and contemplated calling Sam back. He had questions that needed answers. There were things she needed to explain and time was running out. Death's candle was gone. She had no illusions about what that meant.

Hades had picked a host. Soon he'd be coming for her.

28

Sam stepped inside the Brickskeller a few strides behind Anna's sister. She moved past the barkeep sending him a nod of greeting before taking a seat in a booth in a back corner.

"All right, Mr. Abrams, now ya goin' tell me 'what ya left out back in the interrogation room." *Rogue* demanded.

"Keep an open mind for me *Rogue,* as part of this will be hard to believe," Sam requested as he took a seat opposite her.

"I'll try," she muttered.

Sam nodded his thanks before he opened his mouth to tell her what he knew. "Your sister was called into a dig near the Dead Sea by Dr. Ian Broody to authenticate the validity of an artifact found there. She soon discovered the remains of Sodom."

"Bloody hell," *Rogue* hissed understanding the implications. "Why hasn't anyone heard about this?"

"Within those walls they found statues of their gods, a map of the kingdom and half a riddle. After unearthing Gomorrah, they uncovered the other half of it. Your sister played a key role in the discovery of Atlantis."

"Saints preserve us, she's not spoke a word of it."

"She couldn't. Broody's backer was this Magnus guy. He arranged for the city to be unearthed."

"Why?"

"The people of the lost cities worshiped ten gods. You know them as Zeus, Hades, Poseidon, Hermes, Dionysus, Hephaestus, Ares, Helios, Eros and Chaos."

"Those are Greek gods; they don't come into history until centuries later," *Rogue* stated.

"Right, but they were there at the dig sites, no different than the images of the Greeks. Each god possessed a mantle of power, which they bestowed as a gift to the kings of men. Our man Magnus was after them. I think he has one now and is looking to claim its power."

"Its power — have ya lost your mind, Mr. Abrams? Magic is a myth," *Rogue* snapped.

"Yeah, I thought the same but I've seen things of late that have turned me into a believer. They made your sister one as well."

"Okay, let's say for a moment I believe ya. What is it
Anna's done that's landed her in danger?"

"She took something from the dig and hid it from Broody. As a result she has been given the responsibility to protect these mantles."

"By whom?"

"An angel."

"Damn it, Abrams, that's crazy."

"Crazy or not, Anna's still caught in the middle of it and the men who are around her believe it's true."

"Shite. Damn ya, Mr. Abrams, if anythin' happens to Anna I'll kill ya." *Rogue* snapped.

"You won't have to because that alone will do the job for you," Sam muttered.

"What's that mean?" *Rogue* asked incredulous.

"I'm in love with your sister."

"Oh hell. Mr. Fenton, bring mi a bottle of whiskey."

"Coming right up. Something wrong, Terra?"

"This fool got mi sister in a world of trouble and now it seems he's set on keepin' her there," Rogue griped.

"No, I don't," Sam corrected.

"Being with ya puts her at risk, ya know that."

"And you know I'll do anything it takes to keep her safe," Sam countered.

"Shite. I don't suppose I can talk ya in ta walkin' away--"

"Not a chance," Sam stated.

"You want me to kill him for ya, Terra-Anne?" The barkeep asked as he set a glass in front of her. He poured her three fingers from the bottle of whiskey she requested and set down the bottle beside it. Blue eyes watched as she threw back the drink swallowing it in one gulp.

"No, luv, I'm afraid I need 'im alive yet ta find mi sis but ya get ready ta leave, Mr. Fenton, as we're going with this yank ta find her."

"As you wish, Mrs. Fenton. As soon as the bar closes, I'll be ready to go. Do us both a favor and don't drink too much of that Irish poison." He requested with a wink.

"I'll go easy. Bring a glass for, Mr. Abrams, I won't be drinkin' this shite alone," she muttered before pouring herself another glass.

"We're taking a barkeep?" Sam asked with doubt.

"No. Mi husband, Vince, is a lot more than a barkeep just as you were once more than a reporter," Terra muttered before she threw back another drink.

"Take my advice, Mr. Abrams, if you're plannin' ta get mixed up with one of the Gallagher ladies ya best learn ta enjoy the taste of a good whiskey," Vince stated as he set a shot glass on the table in front of the other man.

Sam nodded as Terra filled the cup. He picked it up and threw back the drink. He struggled with not coughing as it burned all the way down. Terra laughed.

"Damn! I like ya, Mr. Abrams. You're a hell of an improvement to that British prick Broody she'd been set on. Maybe Anna's finally learnin' ta live free of Ma and Da's shadow," Terra said as she filled their cups again.

29

As Lance made his way across the street toward the wooden doors of the Brickskeller Catharine smiled. "I remember this place. We met Miss Walsh here right?"

"Yes."

"Is this a favorite haunt for you, detective?"

"It is, I come here often during the after shift hours to discuss cases and think."

"Nice place to think," Catharine complemented as she stepped inside. "Hey, isn't that Sam in the back corner?"

"Yeah."

"Who's he with?" Catharine asked not able to make out the other figure.

"I don't know but we're going to find out," Lance muttered before he made his way to the booth, Catharine at his heels. "Sam, didn't think we'd run into you here," Lance said eyeing the other man with suspicion.

"Lance. *Rogue*, this is detective Lance Roman. He's a friend of your sisters. Lance, this is *Rogue*." Sam began.

"Terra, I'll be joinin' Mr. Abrams in his efforts ta rescue mi sister."

"Why haven't you left yet? I figured you'd have been gone by now?" Lance stated with concern.

"We're waiting on him," Sam muttered as he pointed his finger to the bartender.

"And he is?"

"Mi husband Vince."

"I see. Then we'll try not to keep him too long," Lance assured them.

"What brings you out here, Lance? I figured you and Miss

Nichols would be resting or in research up to your eyeballs," Sam muttered.

"Got a call from the chief about a new case."

"I see."

"Don't worry, we'll stay on top of the research for you," Catharine assured him.

"Thanks. We need the location of that crown."

"You'll get it," Lance vowed before he turned and led Catharine over to another booth.

They'd just sat down when the bell over the front door rang announcing the arrival of a new comer. Lance watched as his supervisor made his way from the door to the booth where he sat.

"Thank you for agreeing to meet with me detective."

"No problem. Chief, this is Catharine. Catharine, this is my boss."

"Hello," Catharine greeted.

"A pleasure to make your acquaintance, ma'am. I'll try to keep this brief."

"No rush," she assured him as she made mental notes on the older man.

"I felt that you should look at this case since you were the last one to see our victim alive."

Lance blinked. "What? Who?"

"A Dr. Phillip King."

"Shit, Anna's boss. What happened?"

"We're not entirely sure. We got a call on Friday from a concerned employee who said he hadn't shown up for work that day." The chief began.

"Less than twenty-four hours...who got the call?" Lance questioned.

"Detective Powel."

"He brushed her off then."

"Afraid so. He viewed her as overly concerned. Miss Wells went on to say her boss would never just, not show up without calling in. He advised her to come in and file a missing persons report if she hadn't heard from him by today."

"I take it she came in?"

"Yes, and when she did she mentioned you spoke to him Thursday about a stolen artifact from the museum."

"That's correct. A cup was swapped with a forgery. No one had noticed. She also mentioned that Dr. King had an altercation with

Dr. Gallagher."

"Yes. Dr. Gallagher tried to tell Dr. King about some less than reputable dealings going on at the dig she was working at. A colleague of hers who wished to discredit her claimed she'd gone mad. They had since worked out their differences."

"Right. So we sent a black and white by the doctor's residence and he found the door slightly ajar. Called for a crime scene unit. Philip King was dead. By the look of it, he'd been so since Saturday night. Whoever killed him tortured him first."

"Shit."

"There's more. When I heard about the theft I started looking into recent antiquities reported stolen."

"And?"

"I hit one in New York. That guy we brought in to ID — your thief — he claims someone stole a set of antique gauntlets out of his shop right under his nose while he was sleeping."

"Damn."

"They are connected then?"

"I'm afraid so, chief. Is anyone else aware of this theft?"

"Not local."

"Good. My advice: get this artist into protective custody because whoever killed Philip King may come looking for him next."

"Why?"

"The two objects in question are part of a collection. One that someone is willing to kill to get their hands on," Lance muttered.

"What kind of collection?"

"Myth based."

"Ah, hell."

"Philip King died because of what he knew about those pieces and no doubt Annalynn Gallagher. I'm sure if it hasn't been investigated yet, you'll find that his office was tossed and Dr. Gallagher's personnel file is gone."

"Why?"

"Because she holds the answers this guy is looking for."

"I take it you're in on this thing then?"

"Yeah. I need everything you have to this point on the case. I'll want to speak with the officer in charge--"

"I hadn't appointed one. I want you to run point on this."

"Chief, Powel will protest."

"Let him. You've got better instinct for this sort of thing than him. If you're ready I want to move you back to homicide."

Lance nodded.

"Good. I'll expect you at the station Monday night. In the meantime look this over and prep for the case. I'll see to it Dr. King's office gets looked at quietly this evening."

"Good."

"I'll see you tomorrow, detective," the older man stated before he rose from the booth.

"I think you had better give this news to Sam," Catharine stated speaking for the first time since greeting his superior.

"Yeah. Someone other than Ian is looking for Anna." Lance muttered.

He slid out of the booth and got to his feet. Turning he headed in the direction where he'd left his friend.

"Back again so soon, detective?" Terra teased with a laugh. He winced noting the other woman was by now a bit drunk.

"Sam, I hate to add more bad news to this mess but someone tortured and killed Philip King for Intel this weekend. I'll bet my badge, they were looking for information on the mantels and Anna."

"And I'll bet my fighting career it was someone working for Magnus Halden," Sam said with disgust. "Time we got moving, *Rogue*, before things go from bad to worse," Sam muttered.

"We're just headed out, I suggest you have your husband close up shop," Lance stated before he turned and headed for the door, Catharine right behind him.

"Why didn't you tell him about the other mantle being stolen?" Catharine asked once they were outside.

"Because I'm guessing that was Pamela's doing and he doesn't need to hear we've lost another one. Sam takes his job seriously, hearing another has slipped through his fingers will only mess him up more than he already is. He doesn't need any more guilt piled on him," Lance stated as he opened the passenger door for her.

He waited until she was inside before closing it and rounding the hood to get in himself. "Come on let's get home, " he stated before starting the car and pulling into the street to drive away from the famous bar. As he went, he hoped Sam would be able to find Anna before anything else happened.

30

Darrian crept down the dark corridors of the lost city with a care born from years of practice. Though there was no light to speak of, he knew the passage ways by heart. He'd memorized every hall, corner, nook, and cranny down to the last stone. He needed no aid to see, as the path he now tread was burned in his brain.

After watching the place the past several nights, he even knew where security would be making their sweeps and when. Zaharrah would be proud of him, he reasoned as he came to the Northern palace beyond the wall where the other project was going on. He slipped past the guard and into the lab careful to avoid the roaming eye of the cameras.

With care, he crossed to the computers and accessed the data he'd been sent to retrieve. Slipping a USB drive in the machine, he made a copy of the file. He then ducked into the shadows and waited as the camera panned over the machine.

When it had moved on again, he drew the device from the tower and repeated the process. He'd been asked to get a copy but Darrian had learned from experience that it was always best to have a backup plan. When the second copy was complete, he closed out the records and exited the system careful to cover his tracks so no one looking into the machine would be able to trace his entry back to the one who hired him.

The task done Darrian crept out of the lab and made his way through the dig site in the direction of the main temple.

He was aware that his sister had been stationed in the old library. As he slipped inside the main entrance from the north, the ominous stone table within the chamber made his skin crawl. He'd heard many a person speculate what its purpose was.

Darrian had a few theories of his own, based on what little he knew about the old gods, and none of them were particularly pleasant. He moved through the chamber in haste wanting only to get clear of it. As he stepped into the feasting hall the sound of footsteps alerted him to the fact that someone was making an undesignated sweep of the area.

The thief cursed as he ducked into the library a moment before the flashlight beam of security cut through the chamber. Darrian took cover behind the row of shelves and waited for the other man to leave.

"I'm telling you I heard footsteps in here," a woman's voice purred from the other room.

"You're paranoid there's nobody here," a man's voice answered.

"Yeah, well, if anything goes missing from this place we're as good as dead." a second man muttered.

"I think that's a bit of an exaggeration, don't you?" the woman teased.

"No, not after Dr. Gallagher went missing, I don't. Something weird is going on around here. The boss has been acting freaky. No tolerance for anything missed."

"Right, well, how do you think he'll react to you raising a false alarm." the first man snapped.

"I'd rather call in that than miss a thief," the other man answered.

Darrian blew out a breath. It seemed he was going to have to do something to stop the guards from rallying the troops. He stashed the drive in a place only his sister would find it, before scribbling a note for her. With his ass effectively covered, Darrian crept back in the direction of the feasting hall. He'd have to get a jump on the guards before they could call for help.

Carefully, he moved in behind them wrapping an arm around the closest ones neck, he covered his mouth to muffle his alarmed sounds as he squeezed putting him to sleep. Darrian was just laying the body down when the flashlight beam wheeled to where he stood. He cursed as the other guard sounded the alarm drawing his gun, the woman watched him with an intense interest that made his skin crawl.

Turning, he ran out of the feasting hall and through the southern entrance in the direction of the city gate. The sound of footsteps pounding on dirt and stone came from every direction as backup moved in. As he neared the gate, blinding light flashed in his eyes alerting him to the fact the way was blocked. He changed direction heading north wanting now to get outside the wall. Behind him, voices shouted for him to stop but he did not listen, well aware that if he were caught he was as good as dead.

He cursed to find his path to the outer palaces blocked and switched directions heading again to the central temple, he needed to find a place to hide, the only way he'd get past these guys was if he could take one of them out and slip past the net.

Ducking through the northern chamber, he entered the feasting hall and pulling up the tile in the corner entered the lower room. He was careful to put the tile back so that no one would notice the passage had been disturbed. There in the dark he sat and waited, praying he wasn't discovered.

31

"Stand down men, I know where the little mouse has gone," Hecate whispered, her brown eyes gleamed with amusement. It seemed Hermes didn't see all just yet, as he'd let a spy slip through his net. "I'll handle this personally," she assured security and watched with satisfaction as the guards disbursed.

As she lifted the tile to enter the lower chamber Hecate wondered just what the thief had been up to here in the dead of night, but figured the answer could wait. She'd been there herself trying to unravel what it was her ex-husband was up to, but had been distracted by the dagger she kept at her hip, it had begun to burn with warning and hunger as they entered the temple. Her only warning that they were not alone.

Her brown eyes ran over the dark chamber seeking him. She spotted him crouching near the altar at the base of the steps and smiled this would be too easy. Here was the perfect opportunity to get her hands on someone with inside knowledge pertaining to the dig site and Ian Broody's movements. Without Hermes knowing, all she had to do was play her cards right. "You can come out little thief, I'm not going to hurt you. I just want to know what you were after," she purred.

She watched as her prey blinked in the darkness and turned to look in her direction drawn by the power of her voice as their eyes met through the darkness, his name entered her mind.

"I swear to you Darrian, I mean you know harm. I am not one of Dr. Broody's people. I was sent by his employer to determine what is going on here? If you tell me what you know I will show you another way out of this place. One not even the guards know about." Hecate murmured pouring every ounce of her power and influence into her words willing him to listen.

Hecate looked on with interest as the man Darrian rose from his place beside the altar "Who are you?" he questioned before he began to move, with a stealth, that was shocking, towards her.

"I am but a servant of the man who is funding this dig," she answered as she watched him move closer. The knife at her hip began to laugh and she smirked. She allowed herself to be taken captive by the thief.

Felt an arm wrap about her neck as his other hand searched her for a weapon. She trembled as his fingers wrapped around the hilt of the dagger and the blade shifted from the madman's tool of torture to that of a warrior's dagger of old. He placed the blade to her neck

"Show me that this secret way exists and maybe we'll talk." Darrian demanded.

Hecate moved to the altar and with a steady hand placed her palm upon the trigger, it concealed the stone table slid away to reveal an opening in the floor. Using just a bit of her power she lit the torch below to reveal the path. "Here is a way out," she stated as his grip on her eased.

"Prove it," he demanded his voice cold and ruthless, his eyes gleamed with orange sparks and Hecate eased back into his hold upon her welcoming the war gods embrace.

"As you will," she murmured before she walked toward the opening to descend the ladder. Darrian released her and watched as she entered the passage below. He followed close behind and once inside, drew her back against him making it clear she was still his prisoner here and if she double crossed him she would suffer for it.

Hecate sealed the temple above concealing the corridor before leading him down the lit tunnel in the direction of the next leg of the secret passage. Hades would be pleased not only did she have a means to learn all that his rival knew but she'd managed to find him a suitable ally, all at once. With a little time Darrian would be ready to take his place at the underworld ruler's side.

32

Darrian followed the mysterious woman down the lit passage and watched as she pressed her hand against a tile in the stone wall before them. The wall slid away to reveal the inside of Hermes palace.

"This isn't out," he hissed with temper as he pressed the strange dagger more forcefully against her throat, aware the guards would be roused again.

"Patience, we've not come to the end of the secret paths of the lost city," she assured him before she moved to the opposite wall from him and once more opened another hidden corridor.

Darrian wondered how she knew so much about the place but didn't ask, not yet. He was still trying to sort out the strange blade he held. When he drew it from the sheath at her hip, he'd have sworn it was different. A strange curved and vicious blade meant to inflict great damage.

Now in his hand it was but a simple throwing dagger with a bejeweled hilt. But when he drew it from the sheath he'd envisioned not a knife or a dagger but a great long sword; battle worn and stained with blood. It felt old to him and part of his mind urged him to put it down. Something about it was not right.

Another part of him argued that, if he did, he'd lose his prisoner and any means of escape. The job he'd come to do was not yet done. Until the flash drive in his pocket was delivered, he didn't dare risk being found again. "No tricks," he warned his prisoner as he tightened his hold on her. The sense that, she wasn't quite what she seemed weighed heavy upon him.

"I wouldn't dream of it," she assured him as she entered the last leg of the secret path that would take them beyond the walls. "I have no interest in Broody finding me here either," she confided.

Darrian nodded, if she spoke the truth and she was there without the other man's knowledge her life was in just as much danger as his. Any doubt of her claim died as they came to the end of the passage and he found himself outside the city wall near the docks.

"Come on, I've got a boat waiting. Once we're off the isle I'll tell you what I know," Darrian vowed as he let her go.

33

Hecate eyed the man Darrian with amusement, while he'd released his hold upon her. He'd not returned the knife. It seemed Ares hold on this one was far stronger than it had been on the dead man. The killer had handed her his blade at every turn to do as she wished a sure sign that the war god was not set on using the mortal for his host.

"I look forward to hearing all you have to say as will my employer," Hecate said pleased as she slipped onto Darrian's boat and allowed him to take her from the isle.

She listened with fascination as Darrian laid out what he'd been up to at the temple and found it interesting that Broody's employees were unaware of the fact that certain projects taking place there were not under his control. She figured Hades would be pleased to learn that she'd foiled the thief's efforts to steal the data on the dragons and pass it off.

If she'd wanted, Hecate could have taken control back from Darrian with a thought at any time during their trip through the city; but she waited like a spider in her web for the fly to come to her. She had been aware that taking him from the temple would earn his trust. She'd build upon it just as she had with the madman and given a little time Ares influence on this one would grow. When it did, she'd be waiting. She'd turn him to her service and make him into a weapon to wield.

Hades sat aboard the private chopper of his host Magnus Halden bound for Athens. He was not far off from his goal now. Soon he'd be restored to his full power and then Hermes would be in for a rude awakening, there was much the winged footed fool didn't know and he looked forward to enlightening him.

At the thought of his brother's name unbidden, the image of the man's wife of old popped into his mind. Hecate. He wondered where she was now, and what the witch might be up to. The woman was ever careful to guard her secrets. Crafty and cunning much like a serpent in her nature, beautiful, powerful, ruthless and deadly. Not to be trusted.

As if the thought of her had conjured her, Hade's felt the press of her mind against his own.

"My dear lady, what news have you brought me now," he questioned, careful to keep his tone polite, aware that if she felt threatened she might turn on him in an instant.

"Much have I learned, oh lord of the underworld. The sword of Ares has picked a new wielder, one who would have disrupted your plans for the fire breathers' return."

"What?"

"A thief, my lord, who was hired by a yet unknown source to take the data on the genetics project," Hecate's mind whispered.

"I see, well then I'll just have to have my people look into this matter and tighten security around the team, it seems there must be a traitor in their midst. When I'm done, no one will be able to leave that site unmonitored again." Hades vowed before his eyes opened and locked onto Magnus's right hand.

"Russell, contact our security at the dig site. I want it clear: no one comes or goes unwatched."

"Yes, sir."

Hades smiled before turning his thoughts back to the informant. "Thank you my sweet, when next we meet I shall reward you with the pleasure of seeing your husband put in his place," Hades assured her before he broke the link and wandered once more into the dream realm in search of his chosen bride. Where was she? Why had they not yet met? Hades wondered as he fell back into the shadows to wait.

35

Zaharrah sank down on her bed, her body and mind weary. Her thoughts turned to her brother and she hoped wherever he was and whatever he was doing that he was safe. As her eyelids began to droop, she whispered a prayer for undisturbed sleep as a heaviness had been weighing on her mind of late. She'd not felt the like of it since Ithaca and knew what waited her on the other side of sleep, if she stepped through unguarded.

"Hades." She breathed the name with bitterness. The wretch had gotten a taste for her years ago and it seemed that Anna was right someone now possessed the damn candle she'd found in the god of the underworld's palace. The time of her peace was drawing to an end. Soon he would walk among them and, when he did, he would come for her.

It was yet another reason for her to get as far from the damn dig site as she could. No sense making it easy for him to locate her.

As Zaharrah slipped into sleep, she dreamed of happier days long gone and wished for the chance to go back. She wandered through a maze of questions that crowded her mind both in sleep and waking as she remembered a life she been forced to walk away from.

"Gunnar," she whispered the name in sleep that she dared not utter in the light of day. "Forgive me," the words fell from her lips as tears flowed from her eyes. In dreams, she embraced the man she still loved and the son she'd never known.

Zaharrah shifted in her sleep rolling onto her other-side and the image faded to the blackness of dreamless sleep.

36

Sam watched from the back seat of Terra's car, as the man Vince locked up the Brickskeller. He dragged his fingers through his hair in an old display of impatience. They were taking too much time to start the hunt. It had been at least twelve hours since Anna was taken. Every second that ticked by was one she didn't have. By now, Anna's plane must have reached her destination. She was probably on the ground; headed wherever Hermes had decided to call home. Sam just hoped she wasn't in Hermes hands yet. He hated to even think of what the fallen might do to her once he had her.

Sam closed his eyes, trying to change his focus from Anna to how to find her. Unbidden an image rose from the shadows of his mind to torment him. For a moment, he was back in the basement where he and Lance had found Catharine. He saw her again through the gauzy veil of fabric. Her hands and feet bound to the bed; naked, trembling with fear as the madman stood over her, touching her, delighting in her torment.

Then the nightmare shifted and he stood in the cursed throne room beneath Atlantis. The torches blazed with unnatural light. The graven images of the fallen and their lord looked down upon Anna stretched out upon the stone alter. Ian Broody stood over her touching her, his eyes lit with Hermes power.

Sam's eyes shot open and the image shattered. No! No, that wouldn't happen not yet, Hermes needed Anna alive. He needed the information she possessed concerning the mantels and the key. The fallen one couldn't afford to hurt her that way. Not until he knew what she did. Don't tell him anything doc, Sam's mind whispered as the car pulled away from the curb.

"Hey, Abrams, ya with us?" Terra's voice questioned breaking in on his thoughts.

"Huh?"

"I asked if ya had any idea where Miss Walsh is?"

"No, last time I saw her she was in Miami," Sam said coming out of his thoughts.

"Okay, then I guess we'll start there," Vince muttered.

"That's fine, there's someone there I want to talk to anyway," Sam stated as he sank back in his seat and tried to relax. They were moving, though he doubted in the right direction. Hermes wasn't going to be sitting in Miami overseeing the dig. He had what he needed from there for now. The fallen would be searching for the other mantles and the stone chests with a black palm upon them. Yet there was a good chance Zaharrah would know where to find him, seeing as she was his lead researcher.

As the trio sped toward the airport, Sam hoped Zaharrah would be more willing to talk in person. He had lots of questions for the clever tomb raider. The first being, where was Ian Broody?

37 ATHENS, GREECE

James Hardagen's plane landed on a private strip in Athens. He found a car waiting for him and his guests. Emily stepped off the plane and slid into the backseat. He moved back into his private quarters to collect his pretty guest.

With care, he lifted her from the bed and carried her off the plane. As he placed her in the car, she whispered Sam's name and James smiled as he wondered if her dreams were pleasant or a nightmare. The voice in his mind pressed him to let it look but James ignored it. For now there were more pressing matters to see too. Making sure Emily was okay first of all and then preparing to meet his host.

James still wasn't sure if he could trust this man Ian Broody or his promises. The voice within assured him he could; stating that a deal struck could not be broken.

"Where are we going James?" Emily questioned curious.

"To meet a friend," he replied easily.

"Why are we in Athens?"

"Two reasons. The first is the meeting. The second is to scout a shoot location for *Heart of Clay*."

"Oh. Then they found CJ?"

"Yes, love. She's working on the re-write now. When we get back we'll start the production again," James assured her.

"And her?" Emily asked eyeing the sleeping woman with question.

"Dr. Gallagher is an expert in Grecian history. She'll be helping to make the set authentic."

"I see. That's great."

"Yes, my dear, it is. Soon I'll be able to make the *Dark Heart* series into a masterpiece of the silver screen," James said with satisfaction. He closed the door and their car departed, speeding off for their final destination. With business settled, James closed his eyes and let his mind rest.

As the actor relaxed, Dionysus slid forward into control. Blue eyes opened lit with a violet glow. The wine god poured himself a sip of red wine from the bottle Hermes had provided and grinned, before leaning over to kiss the actor's pretty fiancé. She melted into his kiss, lost to his power over her. He lifted her hand to his lips in a courtly gesture long dead and then turned her wrist toward him.

Sharp teeth pierced tender skin drawing blood. Dionysus lapped at the injury drawing a wanton cry from his lover. "YES, MY SWEET, SOON," he vowed, before turning her hand so that the crimson elixir dripped from her veins to mingle with the wine in his cup.

Dionysus jostled the chalice combining the two tastes. He lifted the goblet to his nose and drew in the aroma; alcohol, the metallic taint of blood and lust collided, hitting his senses like a drug. He breathed on the cup and watched as the small measure grew; filling the cup to the brim and he laughed.

Finally, the cups' true power was being restored. Soon he would be at his full strength and then no one would be able to stop him. Turning he kissed the woman, James' bride to be, and bid her drink. When he came into his true power she would be the first to turn. She would be his queen of the Bacchae. In this new world he'd woken to, he could amass enough power to make a play for Zeus's crown. He needed only to bide his time.

38 Somewhere in the Bermuda Triangle, Atlantis

Dr. Brooke Silvers arrived at the dig site exhausted. Her heart was troubled. She'd received a text from Darrian last night informing her that he was making his move. She'd expected him to turn up some time in the early hours of the morning but he'd never come. It wasn't like him. She worried something was wrong.

Brooke passed the main temple, headed in the direction of the northern palace. She flashed her ID badge to security absent mindedly as she went.

"Dr. Silvers."

"Yes."

"We're going to need you to come with us."

"Is there a problem?"

"Someone broke into the site last night, we're still gathering evidence. Your crew is being asked to wait in the main temple."

"Okay," Brooke said with acceptance as butterflies began to dance in her belly. Darrian had been there. So where was he? Why no word?

Brooke stepped inside the northern entrance to the temple and passed through the strange chamber with a stone table to the central room where she heard raised voices. Stepping inside she found that the entire team was gathered here surrounded by glowing torches.

"Dr. Silvers, do you know what's happening," one of the crew asked.

"No they mentioned a break in."

"That's correct. Calm down people and all will be explained," a man's voice boomed over the crowd.

Brooke turned to see a blonde haired man in a black suit that she didn't recognize. His green eyes studied the group with an intensity that made her palms sweat. It was as if he was trying to look in their hearts and find the secrets they kept there. The crowd around her fell silent.

"That's better. We're going to speak to each of you separately about this incident, as the thief knew our security measures. All signs point to his having inside help."

Now the room began to buzz again with noise as Brooke's stomach rolled over with dread. The butterflies dancing in her belly stilled and turned cold as ice fear took their place.

"Dr. Silvers, this way please."

Brooke nodded. She turned and followed the mysterious figure from the main chamber of the temple into the eastern room. The statues of Ares, Hades and Chaos stared down on her as the massive fireplace came into view. She'd heard rumors that human bones had been found among the ashes. The glint of torch light off metal drew her attention to various weapons, instruments of torment and death.

A chill ran through her as ghosts from the past reached out to touch her mind with the secrets of history, images of pain and death. Brooke trembled under the darkness that lurked there. She was grateful when they stepped out into the daylight of the main square. She felt her fear subside a little as she walked along the cobblestone road after the man headed north. He turned through the eastern gate into the structure where security had setup.

It was strange to sit in the ruins of some old building and see the wall of TV monitors and other high-tech security implements. It almost felt wrong.

"Have a seat doctor." The man commanded.

Brooke did so, unable to stand. Her knees had gone weak under the feel of this place. A spirit stirred within this hall, blood thirsty and power mad. Something dark and dangerous and the ball of ice that had settled in her belly began to writhe like a snake.

The man flipped on a monitor and the screen lit with the image of a man dressed in black. He slunk through the corridors of the site, his path taking him to their work space. She watched as he gained access to the system and copied the files. Then fled only to be cornered in the temple and gunned down.

"What did the thief take?" Brooke asked as she fought back the urge to scream. Darrian was dead.

"The research on your project. We're not sure why he was after it but everything here points to an inside job. I hate to ask this but where were you last night?"

"I was out with Dr. Jackson at a bar until one. We were celebrating. The team had just finished stage one of a very difficult project."

"I see. And after the party broke up?"

"I went back to the hotel to get some sleep. I knew I needed to be ready to work this morning"

"Did anyone see you get in?"

"Yes, the receptionist. I requested an early wake up call."

"Okay. We'll check out your statement and get back to you."

Brooke nodded her understanding.

"Dr. Silvers, we probably won't get your workspace cleared for you today. Why don't you head back to the hotel and get some rest. You look tired."

"I will, thank you," Brooke whispered before she turned and left.

Relief filled her as she stepped out into the light of day once more. She wanted to cry but blinked back her tears. She couldn't. — not here, they'd see. Brooke drew a calming breath and tried to make sense of everything.

The video should have been blank. Darrian had known all the locations of cameras on sight. He'd learned their movement pattern to avoid being caught. So, how was it they had footage of his every move? Something didn't add up. As she made her way toward the dock, she reasoned the tape was a fake to scare them. If they'd really gunned down Darrian as the video showed they'd have the data and know who his accomplice was, it would be in the data.

No, they were bluffing. Something had happened last night but not what they'd shown her. Security was fishing, nothing more. Let them try. She had no intention of taking their bait.

39

James Hardagen rubbed his face against his soft pillow as awareness returned. Their car came to a stop. He blinked dazed trying to recall what he'd been doing since they stepped off the plane. He remembered explaining to Emily why they were there and then closing his eyes feeling very weary from the flight over. Then nothing. He was startled to find his pillow was in fact Emily's left breast. As he lifted his head, his fiancé's lashes fluttered and a mischievous grin curled her lips.

"My prince wakes. What was in that wine? It went straight to my head," She murmured as she stretched. It was then he became aware that one of his hands held his cup while the other was caught under her clothes.

"Mine as well it would seem," he said amused as he drew back from her. No sense being caught off guard in such a compromising position. He didn't want Emily embarrassed in front of strangers.

As the car door opened, he bid Emily get out before he gathered his sleeping guest in his arms and carried her from the car. He watched as the double doors parted behind them and a man with black hair and blue eyes emerged. Ian Broody's eyes sparked with excitement at the sight of James' burden.

"COME IN, MR. HARDAGEN. YOU ARE MOST WELCOME HERE," the man said cheerfully.

James smiled and, with Emily at his side, ascended the stairs to step through the door. He followed their host past a graven image of a winged figure into the room beyond. The circular chamber was clearly Ian Broody's workspace. Nine statues stood in the chamber all looked upon the large marble desk.

His host moved some papers aside. "PLACE YOUR BURDEN

HERE FOR NOW, AND WE'LL SEE TO OUR BUSINESS."

James did as his host bid as Pamela entered the chamber.

"MY DARLING, WOULD YOU BE SO GRACIOUS AS TO SHOW EMILY TO A GUEST SUITE. I IMAGINE SHE MUST BE TIRED AFTER HER TRAVELS."

"Of course. Come," Pamela prompted as she took Emily by the hand and led her from the room.

Once they were alone Ian crossed to his desk to study his prize. As he brushed a lock of her blonde hair away from her eyes, her lips parted and she called out the man Sam's name with need.

"YOUR PRIZE AS PROMISED, BROTHER. WHAT OF MY REWARD?"

Hermes smiled amused by the woman Anna's mental state. "I SEE YOU'VE BEEN PLAYING YOUR OLD GAMES, BROTHER. GO ON, CLAIM YOUR POWER. I HAVE NEED OF YOUR TALENTS WITH THIS ONE," Hermes said.

James crossed the room to where the graven image of a winged figure stood, hands outstretched, waiting. A crown of grapes sat upon his brow. In a daze, he set his cup in the open hands. As soon as the metal touched the stone, the taste of wine was on his lips and his blood burned with need of woman. James howled like a mad beast. His eyes falling shut. The sensation of a million hands touching him at once washed over him, their every caress flooding his body with pleasure.

His breathing became ragged and when he opened his eyes blue had changed to an unnatural red. A thirst clawed in his belly unlike any he'd ever known. His flesh burned with the need of a woman. His eyes landed upon the woman that lay still beside Hermes and he smirked. Her mind already burned with need of a man's touch. She would do but, from the look in Hermes eye, he wasn't likely to be parted with his prize so soon.

To quiet the hunger Dionysus picked up his cup and drank. When he felt the thirst begin to ease, he lowered the cup from his lips. His eyes dimmed to blue with a faint glow of violet. His skin paled and his hair lengthened to make him look more like CJ's Vampire Lord.

"HERMES, IT'S BEEN A LONG TIME."

"YES, I KNOW. I IMAGINE RIGHT ABOUT NOW YOU NEED A WOMAN, AND YOU'LL GET ONE, BUT NOT HER."

"I THOUGHT AS MUCH. I'VE QUIETED THE THIRST UNTIL I CAN GET BACK TO MY BRIDE. YOU SAID YOU

HAD NEED OF MY TALENTS, MY LORD."

"YES. I SEE YOU'VE ALREADY BEGUN TO WRAP YOUR POWER AROUND THIS ONE'S MIND."

"MERELY AN AMUSEMENT. A GAME REALLY. SHE AND TWO OF HER COMPANIONS," Dionysus said dismissively.

"YOUR GAME INSPIRES ME. THERE ARE THINGS SHE KNOWS THAT I NEED TOO, YET I CANNOT GAIN ACCESS TO THEM. SHE'S GUARDED THEM AGAINST ME. YOU ON THE OTHER HAND I CAN SEE HAVE SLIPPED PAST HER DEFENSES. YOU'VE PLANTED SOME SEED IN THERE AND ITS TAKEN ROOT," Hermes whispered.

"IT HAS, YES. EVEN NOW I CAN FEEL HER DREAMS STRENGTHENING MY POWER. I CAN SMELL HER LUST, IT CALLS TO ME; BEGS FOR MY PARTICIPATION IN HER FANTASY." Dionysus said as he approached the marble desk where the beauty in question lay lost in fevered dream.

"HAS SHE TASTED THE DRAUGHT FROM YOUR CUP, YET?" Hermes asked.

"NOT THIS ONE. SHE KNOWS ITS POWER SOMEHOW."

"I WANT YOU TO STAY HERE AS MY GUEST BROTHER. WORK YOUR WILL UPON HER, UNTIL HERS BREAKS AND SHE DRINKS, FOR THEN SHE WILL TELL ME EVERYTHING I WANT AND BEG FOR MY TOUCH. SHE'LL PAY PROPERLY FOR SPURNING ME SO."

"INDEED," Dionysus said with amusement. His eyes roamed over his charge, violet eyes began to turn red as the hunger for her reawakened.

"UNDERSTAND THIS, BROTHER: WHEN SHE BREAKS YOU WILL NOT TAKE HER. ANNA GALLAGHER IS MINE," Hermes hissed in warning.

"FAIR ENOUGH, YOUR FLOWER SHALL BE UNSPOILED," Dionysus relented as Pamela returned.

"Emily is settled in, my lord."

"EXCELLENT. PAMELA, MY DARLING, MEET MY BROTHER, DIONYSUS, THE GOD OF WINE AND DEBAUCHERY, AMONG OTHER THINGS."

"A pleasure," she whispered recalling their earlier tryst.

"BROTHER, I BELIEVE YOU KNOW MY WIFE, PAMELA," Hermes said amused.

"OH, NO. LADY, THE PLEASURE IS MINE," he assured her

with a wink.

"What do you want me to do with her?" Pamela asked glancing at the unconscious woman with distain.

"LEAVE HER THERE. I WANT TO SEE THE LOOK ON HER FACE WHEN SHE WAKES IN THIS PLACE," Hermes answered with a smirk.

Dionysus closed his eyes reveling in the feeling of his brother's lust. He felt his power swell and laughed, his brethren never understood that when they lost themselves in their lustful desire for human flesh in his presence that they too fed his power and gave him their worship. The lust of a god was more potent than any wine he could consume and made his own power stronger. It was with this taste of Hermes lust that Dionysus turned his mind towards Anna's, seeking entry.

He was pleased to find that the seed he'd planted there had indeed taken root and a vine had begun to grow. When he came to the shield that guarded her mind he pressed his hand upon it and let his power wash over it.

Cranberry lips parted and a moan issued forth in response as her lust intensified.

"LET ME IN, ANNA," Dionysus's mind whispered, his voice gentle and seductive as he nudged her shields again with his power. He was rewarded with a small gap in the layers and smiled. "YES, THAT'S IT, THANK YOU, ANNA," he purred with delight before slipping past.

He found her on the other side lost in the man Sam's embrace. Their body's pressed together so that not an inch separated them. Mouths locked in a fiery kiss.

"SWEET LADY, YOU'RE SO THIRSTY AND YET SO HESITANT. I'LL GIVE YOU WHAT YOU WANT," Dionysus whispered as he let his power lap at the edges of the dream.

He watched amused as her dream lover's hands moved from her waist to seize hold of her hips pressing his need against the center of hers. Hazel eyes flew open startled. Pupils dilated and eyes darkened with her desire. Her lips parted his.

"Sam?" She asked voice shaky.

"I WANT YOU, ANNA. NO MORE GAMES," Dionysus's mind whispered and her dream lover spoke them aloud. Their eyes locked and his hands took hold of her face waiting for her answer.

Dionysus watched as the vine he'd planted began to blossom and smiled as a trembling Anna kissed her dream lover's palm. He felt the touch in his own hand and repressed a groan. "YES, ANNA, THAT'S IT GIVE INTO YOUR LUST HERE," his mind urged. He was so close now.

"Sam, I want you, want this but--" Anna whispered. She licked her lips nervously and her voice was unsure.

"IT'S OKAY, ANNA. WE WON'T DO ANYTHING YOU DON'T WANT TO DO. I JUST WANT TO TOUCH YOU," Dionysus's mind whispered, giving her space to move and time to get used to the idea. Her dream lover's hands played over her body eliciting a needy cry as he spoke.

"Sam--"

"SHH, I'LL MAKE IT GOOD FOR YOU ANNA, I'LL SHOW YOU HOW A WOMAN DESERVES TO BE TREATED HERE," the wine god breathed making yet another pretty promise to draw her deeper under his spell.

"I want to Sam, but I shouldn't. He's here with us now; watching, waiting."

"Who?"

"Dionysus. I can't keep him out."

"FORGET HIM. WHAT CAN HE DO TO US HERE? THIS IS YOUR DREAM," Dionysus's mind whispered trying to get her to lower her guard further.

Her dream lover rubbed her back as he spoke; in an effort to sooth her spirit and ease her mind. Dionysus watched with satisfaction as Anna's eyes fell shut and she lost herself in Sam's touch. Beside him, a small sprig of grapes began to grow on the vine as another blossom opened up. His seed would soon begin to bear fruit.

40

Dionysus felt her mind ease under Sam's caress. She sighed with contentment as his request circled in the back of her mind. "I JUST WANT TO TOUCH YOU." He was doing that now wasn't he? There was no harm in it, she reasoned. As if he were aware of her acceptance, the small circles he'd been making on her back expanded. His hands moving lower brushing over her hips and thighs with a light touch that made her ache for more.

"I'LL MAKE IT GOOD FOR YOU, ANNA," his offer played over her mind and she bit her lip to repress a breathy cry in response to what his touch was doing to her. He'd spoken truth there as well; it was good. Talented hands were making her burn with need for more of him.

"Put your hands on me, Sam," she whispered having made her choice. She wanted this, wanted him.

Anna gasped at the feel of his nails biting into the flesh of her backside as he pulled her close to him once more. Her face, he pressed against his chest as he ground the evidence of his desire for her against her center. A jolt of hunger tore through her system at the contact and she moaned with pleasure. Anna blinked, dazed and before she could put the words together to slow him down, Sam had eased his grip. His hands slid along hips and thighs and back up her back.

Anna trembled in the circle of his arms overwhelmed by the contrasting sensations running riot through her nerve endings. She felt her heart begin to steady a moment before Sam made his next move. Gauzy silk fell away from her shoulders as warm fingers pushed the fabric aside and an eager mouth tasted soft skin in their wake.

Silk slid off her body to pool at her feet. Warm hands danced over heated skin in a subtle caress that left her desperate for more; teasing her senses with a taste of pleasure but not the full experience. He was holding back, making her crave what he offered now more strongly.

"Sam," she whispered his name, the single word a plea. An eager mouth trailed down her shoulder and over her collar bone to the swell of her breasts beneath her bra. Fingers pulled down the cups to give him better access. His mouth found a hardened nipple there and took hold of it. His kiss there had her eyes flying open, hands fisting in his hair, nail biting his scalp as a pleasant need became a dull ache. He tore through her reservations, making her forget everything but him.

41

Dionysus reveled in the feel of Anna's nails on his scalp. He couldn't touch her yet, but he was getting close. He gave her mind another nudge with his power and watched as her dream lover pulled off her bra and drew her deeper under his spell.

Her partner used his hands to entice her, teasing her with the promise of more as his mouth destroyed her resistance; drugging her with pleasure. Making good on his word, his every action making her feel good.

Dionysus felt each pull of her lover's hair as if it was his own. Felt her breath on his face and licked his lips with anticipation as he gave her another push. She was right on the edge, if he could just convince her to make the final leap, to accept this fantasy and give herself to her dream lover, then she'd be in his grasp. Her surrender here would make breaking her will in the real world that much easier.

The wine god looked on with bated breath as Anna's partner's hands slid down her midsection to caress her hips and thighs through the thin layer of silk that hid her from him. Fingers played over the part of her he longed to fill tormenting her with the friction created by fabric against her flesh and his touch.

Anna's arms fell from his head unable to hold on as her head fell back. She moaned with pleasure unable to suppress her response. Her knees weakened and Sam used his other arm to steady her.

"I'VE GOT YOU," he assured her before he kissed her again, not letting her up for air, clouding her mind so she couldn't think. His fingers stroked gently over her panties along her inner thighs and over her hips waiting for her to relax and accept this new touch as his lips parted hers once again to taste her skin.

"Sam--" she called his name her words a plea though for what was unclear.

"SHH, NO WORDS NOW, DOC. I JUST WANT TO TOUCH YOU. THAT'S ALL, REMEMBER?" Dionysus whispered quieting her objection before it could be given.

Anna nodded, unable to speak, as her dream lover's caress became rougher, sending a jolt of pleasure through her. She pressed against him seeking more direct contact.

"DO YOU WANT ME TO TOUCH YOU, DOC, OR SHOULD I STOP?"

"Sam--"

"I TOLD YOU I'D MAKE THIS GOOD FOR YOU. I CAN MAKE IT BETTER," Dionysus offered. Her partner's hand moved up the inside of her thigh and over her belly, fingertips skimming along the waistband of her underwear.

Anna groaned in protest at his touches withdraw and that was all the answer he needed. A crafty hand slipped beneath elastic seeking her. Fingers that itched with the need to touch, pressed through rough, spiky, feminine curls to cup the center of her desire. His mouth captured hers, quieting her startled cry making her forget what he was doing to her. His fingers raked over her lightly, as before, allowing her to get used to his intimate caress.

Dionysus chuckled as he sipped his cup. Beside him, the small cluster of grapes turned blood red, ripe for the plucking. He couldn't wait to taste them. He pulled the fruit from the vine and lifted them to his lips as Anna's lover took his seduction to the next phase.

Lance woke to the buzz of his phone and groaned after getting back from his meet at the Brickskeller, he'd gotten little sleep. His mind running riot with possible scenarios of what had happened to Philip King and who was responsible. What they were after, was it Anna or something else. He'd reviewed all the case info twice and his gut told him this had not been Broody's doing.

Once he set the case aside his thoughts circled back to his guest, Catharine. He'd been tormented in sleep by images of her back in that basement in Central Falls. She was bound and bloody, naked in the dark. Kurt standing over her touching her and he couldn't reach her. Lance swallowed back bile as the nightmare tried to resurface. He picked up the phone, grateful for the reprieve.

"Hello," he said, his voice still thick with sleep.

"Detective, sorry for the early call, but I thought you'd want to know you were right. Philip King's office was broken into," his superior stated.

Lance sat up now wide awake. "What was taken?"

"A couple of personnel files."

"Whose?"

"Miss Gallagher's for one and a Dr. Ian Broody."

"I'm on my way," Lance said as he got out of bed. He hung up the phone and began the task of getting dressed. Once ready to go he stepped into the hall. His ice blue eyes settled on the door across from him and he wondered if he should wake his guest or not. She'd asked for full access to what he did but it had been a long night and if she was resting, he didn't want to disturb her.

Having made up his mind, he moved down the hall to leave her a note, only to find her sitting at the dining room table. Her laptop open, typing away; a cup of coffee beside her.

"Morning, I thought you'd be asleep," he breathed.

"Couldn't stay there, had too much of the changes for *Dark Heart* on my mind, I needed to get them out. And you?"

"Got a call from the chief, Philip King's office was broken into. The thief took a couple personnel files," Lance stated.

"Which tells you what exactly?"

"That we've got a third player in this crazy hunt."

"What makes you so sure?"

"One of the files was Ian Broody's. If he was behind the theft why take his own file."

"Throw you off his scent maybe," Catharine offered.

"Possible, but I have my doubts. I'm headed over there now did you want to ride along?"

"No thanks. I've still got a lot to do here and the sooner I get through it the better."

"When I get back we should get started looking into that information Sam needs about the crown."

"I'm already on it. I've got my computer running a search through my writing database. It's looking for any tales that contain references to the missing elements and particularly the crown. As soon as it's done, we'll have a list of titles to start looking through."

"Great. Thanks Catharine," Lance murmured with relief.

"No problem," she said with a warm smile and a wink.

"You're sure you'll be all right here alone?" He asked worried leaving her, maybe a mistake.

"I'll be fine detective. Go, fight crime," she said playfully before turning her attention back to her laptop.

"Yes, ma'am," he chuckled before brushing a kiss on her forehead and moving for the door. Her laughter followed him out.

43 Athens, Greece

Anna's eye's shot open as a startled cry fell from her lips. She jolted from sleep to waking, her flesh burned with lust and her mind whispered a prayer for strength as images of the dream played over her mind. She bit her lip, repressing a pleasured moan as she waited for her system to level out. Anna could almost feel Sam's touch upon her and it left her body aching with need of him.

She blushed with embarrassment. She hated to think of him walking in on her now in this state or worse, having come in while she'd been dreaming of him. Lifting her head, Anna blinked heavy lids and gasped as her eyes began to focus. Where was she? This was not the motel room he'd left her in earlier.

"Take this, don't open the door for anyone but me," his voice demanded again as she sat up confused and disoriented trying to see through the maze of lust filled images in her mind to recall what was going on. She'd had troubled dreams and woken to see-- James, no Dionysus. She'd drawn the gun and shot him. They'd struggled, then she'd fled-- started down the steps and then nothing. Darkness and the dream.

She'd been taken.

Hazel eyes scanned her surroundings only to have her fear rise up in her heart. All around her the graven images of the fallen stood watching her. She felt the press of darkness around her and stiffened as her eyes became aware of the spirits trapped within them. Dark shadows that writhed like serpents.

"AT LAST THE SLEEPER WAKES," Ares hissed with amusement.

"SHE'D HAVE BEEN BETTER SERVED TO GO ON DREAMING," Poseidon laughed.

"DIONYSUS WOULD HAVE GIVEN HER THE ILLUSION OF HER HEART'S DESIRE. HE'D HAVE LET HER ENJOY HER CLAIMING. NOW, SHE'LL SUFFER HERMES WRATH FOR HER REJECTION," Hades whispered.

"AT LEAST WE'LL GET TO BEAR WITNESS TO THE BATTLE," Ares breathed with anticipation.

"IT WON'T BE MUCH OF A FIGHT WAR GOD. OUR BROTHER'S TOUCH UPON HER MIND HAS LEFT HER FLESH WEAK. SHE'LL SOON BEG HIM TO TAKE HER," Poseidon whispered.

"HE'LL MAKE HER MOAN LIKE A WHORE, DESPERATE FOR HIM TO DEFILE HER, EVEN AS HER HEART WEAPS FOR HER DENIAL OF HIM BEFORE. HE'LL MAKE HER ENDURE THE TORMENT OF HER HUNGER UNTIL SHE'LL DO ANYTHING HE DEMANDS OF HER. WHEN IT'S OVER SHE'LL TURN TO ME," Hades boasted his eyes gleamed with eagerness of that moment.

"OH HOW THE MIGHTY HAVE FALLEN, BAUCUS HAS TAKEN ONE WHO WITHSTOOD HERMES DESIGNS FOR HER AND IN BUT A FEW DAYS ENSLAVED HER BODY TO HIS SPELL. HER MIND STANDS ON THE BRINK AND WHEN IT FALLS SHE WILL BE OUR NEW WHORE," they all crowed now mocking her as one.

"Never!" Anna cried out in defiance and a laugh joined the others. Torches burst to life around her to reveal two figures standing over her watching her with amusement.

"SHE'S RIGHT MY BROTHERS NOT ONE OF YOU WILL EVER LAY A HAND UPON HER. ANNA HERE IS MINE. I'D HAVE MADE HER MY BRIDE BUT SOON SHE WILL BE MY WHORE INSTEAD," Hermes whispered with amusement and pleasure. He brushed loose strands of her blonde hair away from her face thrilling in the feel of her skin beneath his fingers. His touch more like that of a master to a dog than a lover's caress.

"I will never surrender to you," Anna snapped with disgust.

"OH, NO, MY DEAR, MY BROTHERS ARE QUITE RIGHT WITH DIONYSUS'S AID, I'LL MAKE YOU BEG FOR ME AND BEFORE I GIVE YOU EASE, I'LL MAKE YOU DO ALL THE THINGS THAT PLEASE ME MOST. ONCE I'M DONE YOU'LL BEG FOR DEATH BUT IT WON'T COME. YOU'LL BE MINE FOREVER," Hermes taunted as his thumb traced her lower lip bruising it with his touch. Fingers skimmed down her neck and over bare shoulder raising goose-bumps in their wake.

Anna turned from his touch as she prayed again for strength disgusted to find her blood indeed stirred with desire at his touch. Her body burned with the need of a man. Her heart cried foul, wanting only Sam but her flesh argued for what he offered, after all it knew this man before her. She'd been given to him and pledged, long before she met Sam.

"You won't win here Hermes. Your palace will fall to the hands of another. All your allies will turn from your side. The child you need shall shrivel in the womb and your bride will be reduced to a whore before the war for the crown even begins," Anna breathed. The words that poured from her lips, she did not know the source of, or understand, but found she could not stop them.

Hermes hand flew in temper. The blow knocked her back so that she hit her head on the marble desk. Golden lashes fell obscuring hazel eyes as darkness surrounded her. As she lapsed into unconsciousness, she heard the laughter of the other fallen as they mocked their brother instead.

44

Hermes roared in fury as the others laughed at his failed attempt to intimidate his prisoner. Her words burned his mind as his brethren mocked him.

"YOUR POWER WILL FAIL YOU BROTHER. WE SHALL ESCAPE!"

"NO, YOU WON'T. EVERY LAST ONE OF YOU WILL FALL AS THE OTHERS HAVE. YOUR POWER WILL BE MINE. I WILL BE THE NEW KING OF THE GODS," Hermes roared. He drew his bride into his arms and his mouth claimed hers. Pamela gasped startled by his abrupt demand of her but melted into his embrace. She watched with pleasure as he shoved the woman Anna aside only to lay her upon the desk in her place.

He tore at her dress in his fury and skipped any kind of foreplay entering her body with a vicious thrust that drew a startled cry from her crimson lips. "YOU ARE MY QUEEN. YOUR BELLY IS SWOLLEN WITH MY CHILD. I SHALL SOON POSSESS ZEUS'S CROWN AND WHEN I DO, WE WILL RULE OVER THE MEN OF THIS WORLD TOGETHER AND THERE IS NOTHING ANY OF THEM CAN DO TO STOP IT," Hermes boasted as he burnt off his lust for Anna.

His bride answered his hunger giving him the release he sought before he slid out of her, his body spent. His eyes gleamed seeing the wine god guzzle back another draught from his cup.

"DIONYSUS COME, TASTE THY QUEEN. INDULGE YOURSELF IN THE FEEL OF A WOMAN. I KNOW IT'S BEEN A LONG TIME."

"My lord?" The wine god questioned with disbelief.

"A REWARD FOR YOUR SERVICES TO ME, YOU KNOW HER TALENTS."

"Hermes?" Pamela asked uneasy with this sudden shift of mood.

"RELAX, MY DARLING, ENJOY HIM. MY BROTHER WILL EASE THE STING OF MY RUTTING. MY APOLOGY TO YOU FOR SUCH ROUGH TREATMENT," he assured her. Pamela blushed at his gift and whispered her thanks.

Hermes scooped up his prisoner and walked out of the chamber leaving Dionysus to his games. He deposited Anna in a quiet corner of the house to be dealt with later. For now he had other matters to attend to. While the wine god enjoyed Pamela he would bed Emily. If he could get her with child as Pamela was then Hermes could keep his brother from gaining ground on any claim to the crown.

45

Lance's blue eyes scanned over Phillip King's office with a growing sense of disquiet and certainty. Ian Broody was not behind this robbery.

"Lance, you look a little green. What's on your mind?" His superior asked.

"This wasn't Broody."

"Why do you say that?"

"When Dr. Broody had Miss Gallagher's place searched after she skipped town it was messy. They trashed the place. Nothing was left untouched. This is too neat." "Okay. I'm with you, go on," the other man requested.

"Beyond that Broody was careful not to spill any blood. Whoever did this didn't care. King's secretary and security are both dead. It's someone else."

"You're sure."

"Yeah, look at the signs of her torture. Whoever did this knew what he was doing. He knew where to mark her to inflict the most pain, without killing her. The wounds are deep, cut by a steady hand, someone practiced in torture. Once he had what he needed, he delivers the killing blow quick and efficient. This guys a pro."

"Yeah, that's what the coroner said about King."

"I want to head over to King's place and take a look if that's okay."

"Fine. If they missed anything I know you'll find it."

"I'm gonna' try," Lance muttered.

"Oh detective, where is your writer friend this morning."

"At home writing," Lance grumbled.

"After you brought her to our meet last night, I cleared her to enter the sight today."

"Why?"

"Glad to see you out with someone not connected to work. Thrilled to have you back in homicide, figured if she'd re-sparked the interest, I'd not interfere. Thought she'd be riding your coattails."

"So did I, she's distracted with *Dark Heart*."

"*Dark Heart*. Damn. Wife loves that stuff, think I could get her an autograph."

"I'm sure Catharine would be happy to," Lance said amused before he headed for the door.

"Detective, all teasing aside, it's good to have you back."

"Thanks chief. It's good to be back," Lance admitted before he left.

Sam raced up the steps of Aqualina Resort and Spa and stepped into the lobby. He hoped that Zaharrah hadn't left yet for the dig or they'd have to wait until she got back. Long strides ate up the distance between him and the receptionist desk.

The pretty brunette looked up from her screen and smiled at the sight of him.

"Mr. Abrams, welcome back. Did you need a room?"

"Not today. I'm here to see Miss Lynch is she in?" Sam questioned as Terra and Vince joined him.

"Let me check," the woman picked up the phone and punched in the number for Zaharrah's room.

He listened impatiently to the one sided conversation waiting for news. When she set the receiver down she went back to looking at her screen.

"Well?"

"Oh, sorry. She'll be right down, asked that you wait in the lounge."

Sam nodded and turned in the direction of the hotel's lounge.

"Who's Miss Lynch?" Terra questioned.

"A colleague of your sister's, if anyone will know where to find Anna she will."

"And you know her how?" Vince asked curious.

"Met her when Anna brought me here."

The trio sat down in a booth to wait. Terra and Vince ordered drinks while Sam watched for their guest's arrival. He didn't wait long, the dark haired beauty strolled into the lounge, eyes searching. She spotted him almost as quickly as he had her. Brown eyes lit with questions at the others and he waved in greeting.

"Mr. Abrams, how nice to see you again, but who are your

friends, and where is dear Anna?"

"Miss Lynch, this is Vince Fenton and his wife Terra. Terra here is Anna's sister."

"I see. So, what brings you back this way?"

"I'm afraid Anna was taken and by now Ian must have her. I was hoping you might know where he is," Sam admitted.

"Dr. Broody left the dig several days ago. He could be anywhere by now--" Zaharrah began.

"I see, I'd hoped-- damn. We'll just have to find another way to locate him."

"I didn't say I didn't know Mr. Abrams, just that he could be anywhere--"

"Then you do know," Sam said in relief washing through him.

"I didn't say that either. If you'd quit interrupting me I'd answer you."

"Sorry."

"It's okay. One place you might try is Athens. He's got a house there."

"Thank you," Terra said grateful. She rose from the table to leave Vince at her side.

Zaharrah moved to follow and Sam grabbed her wrist halting her departure. "Not so fast there Miss Lynch, now that they're gone I've got a couple more questions."

"Such as?"

"How do you know Gunnar?"

"Gunnar was my husband. Now I want to know why a Masada warrior would send me to an American reporter for help. Who are you Sam?"

"I'm former military," Sam lied. "How did you know about the woman? About Hecate?"

"No, I don't think I'll tell you that Mr. Abrams."

"Why not?"

"Because you just lied to me. If you won't give me your trust then why should I give you mine?"

Sam cursed. He didn't have time for this, he needed to get to Anna but to do the task they'd been given he needed those answers and he needed them now. "I was an agent for the US government anti-terrorist unit. I met Gunnar when I got him and his team out of an Iraqi prison. He had Intel I needed on a man I was hunting a man by the name of Russell York. At the time we thought he was the head of a terrorist cell."

"He wasn't?" Zaharrah asked.

"No. Turns out he was working for another man."

"Who?"

"Magnus Halden."

"Shit!"

"What is it?" Sam asked startled by her sudden outburst.

"I know Magnus Halden," Zaharrah muttered.

Sam's mind reeled with the revelation but before he could ask how her phone rang. He watched as Zaharrah drew the irritating device from her pocket and lifted it to her ear.

"Hello." Zaharrah sat and listened to the voice on the other end before the word 'speaking' left her lips. It seemed whoever was on the other end had been unaware the number was Zaharrah's direct line.

Sam watched as his interview subject rolled her eyes at the person on the other end then went stiff. "What about him?"

"What is it?" Sam asked sensing a dangerous shift in the woman who sat across from him. She ignored the question, her undivided attention given now to whoever spoke on the other end of the line.

"I'm on my way," she muttered before hanging up. "I'm sorry Mr. Abrams, but I have to go."

"What about Magnus Halden and my answers? Sam said in protest.

"You'll get them as soon as I see to this."

"But Anna--"

"Go get Anna, your answers will wait," Zaharrah said before she got up and left. Sam growled with frustration before leaving money for their drinks and moving to join Terra and Vince. He was not happy at being left hanging but Zaharrah was right the answers could wait. Anna couldn't. "What took so long?" Terra asked exasperated.

"I had other things to talk with Miss Lynch about."

"And they couldn't wait?"

"No. it seems she knows Magnus Halden."

"What? How?" Terra asked stunned.

"I didn't get that intel. She got a call had to leave abruptly said she'd fill me in later," Sam stated.

"You should have--"

"What got into an argument, potentially alienated her and wasted more time your sister doesn't have. No, the answers will keep. Right now we need to get to Anna before Ian Broody hurts her," Sam muttered.

"Ian wouldn't hurt her. He adores Anna," Terra said with

disbelief at the notion.

"When was the last time you talked about him?"

"Just after she left him."

"Then your intel is outdated. I've seen the man. I know what he's capable of and I'm telling you he'll hurt her to get what he wants from her." Sam warned before he walked out of the hotel. The sooner they got to the airport the better.

47

Catharine's fingers flew over the keys in a wild rush of words. She'd been at it since long before dawn. Already she'd completed the changes to *Heart of Glass* and *Heart of Clay*. She'd written the alternate ending for the first movie and had made the changes to the second script. Her fingers were beginning to ache but she didn't care, she would complete the changes for Heart of Stone today.

Unsatisfied with the brief exposition within the pages on how Rachel came to live with the lady Mason, she'd written a short with the working title Heart of Ice. She was nearing the end of the changes for the series, to lay the ground work for the fourth book. She couldn't wait to get started. Finally, Serenity's nightmare would end, just as hers had. Ashella would be reunited with Davrik and maybe once Serenity was free of her monsters, Catharine would be as well, she mused.

Catharine hit the save button with excitement, the revision work was done. Now all that remained was to read the new content and make sure it fit with the original work. Catharine pressed control home returning to the beginning and began to read to herself.

"Serenity Mason sat in her favorite chair under the picture window in her father's library reading to herself, enjoying the warmth of the noonday sun on her skin as she tried to relax. Butterflies danced in her stomach in anticipation of the evening's festivities. A celebration was to be held in the grand ballroom.

A lavish party for her, in honor of her birthday. Tonight her father, the duke would present her to the families of the court for the first time. Her coming out party. She wished her mother was there to help her prepare, aware that this night she might very well meet the man she'd marry. It was a big step in a young woman's life, her lady had told her, turning sixteen it marked the change from child to adult. The manor was buzzing with activity and security was tight. Her protector had not been far from her side since she emerged from her chambers that morning…"

Catharine soon fell into the scene lost in her story.

Hazel eyes scanned the crowded dance floor. Her pulse raced aware that something unnatural moved among the guests. She felt the familiar sensation of Davrik's eyes upon her and her fear eased as she turned toward him.

Serenity found her ever present protector at the edge of the dance floor. He stood alone, a shadow in black among the brightly arrayed nobles strutting about her like peacocks trying to win her attention. His eyes met hers for a moment. Green swam with questions and concern, but he did not move. Serenity took a step in his direction but a gentle tap upon her shoulder had her turning away.

"Hello, my dear Serenity, and happy birthday," her guest said in greeting. He bowed low in a show of respect his blue eyes lit with an inner fire that demanded her attention.

"Thank you kind sir," she whispered as he took her hand in his and kissed it.

At his touch something inside her shifted and the ballroom faded away. She blinked, the sense that something was not right here heavy in her spirit. When her lashes lifted she found she now stood in a garden so beautiful it hurt to look upon. At her feet lay a lake so still it was like a mirror.

She stared at a face that was not her own and trembled as her heart began to pound. As she sought the knowledge of her own name, his hit her like a punch to the gut. "Dionysus," she breathed the name with discomfort as she drew free of his grasp. The garden faded and the ballroom bled back in the lake becoming a fountain. She turned to seek Davrik but Dionysus grabbed her wrist turning her back to him drawing her into his embrace.

"WHERE ARE YOU GOING? MY SWEET SERENITY DANCES WITH THE VAMPIRE LORD IN THIS SCENE IT SEALS HER FATE," Dionysus whispered as his hands roamed down her back enjoying the feel of her in his arms.

"I'm not this Serenity and you're not Syvarin."

"I COULD BE, OR IF YOU PREFER I CAN BE HER

DAVRIK," Dionysus teased as he shifted his appearance to match her beloved.

"It doesn't matter which mask you choose to hide behind I know the truth. You're but a shadow that's invading my dreams. One not welcome or wanted."

"PERHAPS YOU'D PREFER THIS FACE," Dionysus hissed before the heroes guise melted away only to be replaced by that of Kovrin's.

She trembled now fear tearing through her at the face before her. Serenity feared him more than any other. "No!"

"ARE YOU SURE? AFTER ALL YOU BROUGHT HIM BACK FROM THE DEAD TO PURSUE YOU AGAIN," he said amused. Slipping deeper into the guise so that he sounded like the werewolf.

"I never wanted him," she snapped in disgust as his comment about bringing the monster back clicked into place, her name. She was Catharine.

"OH, I THINK YOU'RE LYING TO YOURSELF PRINCESS. I THINK SECRETLY YOU LIKED WHAT HE DID TO YOU. IT FELT GOOD WHEN HE TOUCHED YOU AND YOU YEARNED IN YOUR HEART FOR HIM TO IGNORE THE NICETIES OF COURTSHIP AND TAKE WHAT HE WANTED. YOU GOT A THRILL IN MAKING HIM LOSE CONTROL," Dionysus muttered as his touch turned rough doing just that.

"No, get away," Catharine cried in refusal of him and his words.

"OH, SEE, NOW THAT'S WHAT I MEAN, YOUR LIPS SAY NO BUT YOUR BODY SAYS YES. I CAN SMELL IT ON YOU SERENITY, LUST AND AROUSAL. I BET YOU'RE UNDERGARMENTS ARE WET WITH ANTICIPATION. I'LL BET IF I GRAB HOLD OF YOUR ASS NOW AND PRESS YOU AGAINST ME YOU'LL MOAN WITH NEED."

"I never wanted Kurt," Catharine snapped giving voice to words she'd kept locked away deep inside her heart. Tears fell from her eyes and the wine god laughed.

"AH, THERE, TRUTH AT LAST. I KNOW IT SERENITY, I KNOW," he crooned his touch gentle now. "SHH, IT'S ALL RIGHT MY SWEET. IT'S OVER NOW, YOU'LL NEVER SEE THIS MASK AGAIN," the wine god vowed.

"Why did you do that?" What do you want from me? Why won't you leave me alone?"

"BECAUSE YOU'RE MINE SERENITY, AND I WANT YOU TO SEE THAT, TO UNDERSTAND IT."

"That's not true."

"YES, IT IS. WHEN YOU GAVE YOURSELF TO KURT, IT WAS MY INFLUENCE THAT HAD YOU SURRENDERING TO HIS EMBRACE. I WOOED YOU FOR HIM AS I DID LATER WITH TOM AS WELL," Dionysus whispered as he wiped away her tears.

Catharine felt her flesh begin to warm under his tender caresses. "I don't want--"

"SHH, OF COURSE YOU DO. YOU DRANK FROM MY CUP LONG BEFORE I GAVE IT TO YOU. EVERY TIME YOU'VE GIVEN YOUR HEART AWAY YOU'VE SOUGHT MY EMBRACE TO DO IT. JUST AS YOU WILL WITH YOUR DAVRIK NOW. YOU CAN'T REACH THOSE EMOTIONS WITHOUT ME."

"That's not true."

"AH, BUT IT IS, THE FEAR THAT LIVES INSIDE YOU WON'T LET ANYONE PAST THE GATE, ONLY MY CUP QUIETS IT LONG ENOUGH FOR YOU TO LOVE."

"No I feel something for--"

"FOR HIM," Dionysus prompted as he took on Lance's face.

"Yes," she said with a blush, it was strange speaking of these matters with the wine god. More unsettling to have his hands on her offering comfort when he wore Lance's face.

"BUT THAT FEAR'S ALREADY TURNING YOU AGAINST HIM. I'M SURE I NEEDN'T REMIND YOU HOW THIS LITTLE SCENE PLAYED OUT," Dionysus stated as the ballroom faded only to be replaced by a crime scene where he had just finished prepping her to enter.

"No, you don't."

"STEAMY AS IT WAS, HE WAS NOT AMUSED," Dionysus reminded.

"I know."

"FORGET ALL THIS," Dionysus entreated and the image faded. "TAKE MY HAND AND LET ME FREE YOU OF THESE CHAINS OF FEAR," the wine god whispered as the garden returned.

"Where did those chains come from?" Lance's voice whispered in her mind as the real Davrik moved to her side.

"I don't know,' she admitted.

"FORGET HIM CATHARINE, HE'LL ONLY HURT YOU."

"Don't you think you should find out before you listen to his offer of freedom," her guardian questioned. His face shifted before her changing to the real Lance. Catharine blinked, startled by the revelation. She hadn't allowed herself to consider who this new Davrik was.

"But I--" she began in protest wanting to be free of her fears.

"Do you really want to trade one sort of bondage for another," Lance questioned as he turned her chin so that her eyes met his.

"I'M NOT GOING TO ENSLAVE HER. I'M GOING TO FREE HER AND MAKE HER GREAT," Dionysus argued returning his appearance to his own.

"At what price?" Lance questioned his cops' eyes demanding an answer.

"Lance--" she began not even sure what she meant to say beyond that.

"Consider carefully the offer Serenity, if it seems too good to be true it usually is," He said skeptically. He kissed her forehead before he reverted back to Davrik and *Heart of Clay*'s ending ran through her mind.

"Be silent fallen one. In the name of Jesus Christ, my lord, and savior. I'll speak no further with you. Depart from here now or be cast out," Catharine warned as she turned away from him.

"I'LL GO FOR NOW, SERENITY, BUT WE WILL SPEAK AGAIN," Dionysus vowed before the dream world faded

Catharine blinked and found she still sat at Lance's table, her laptop open to the opening scene of *Heart of Glass*. "Maybe I should take a break," she muttered before picking up her coffee cup and moving in the direction of the kitchen as she walked, she asked herself; what was the root of this fear that plagued her mind.

48

Lance pulled up to the curb in front of the address listed for Phillip King and immediately noticed it was the same model as Anna's home: a two story brownstone. He wondered if it was a status symbol of the scientific community as a company car was for other jobs but dismissed the notion. He wasn't here to analyze Phillip King or even Anna, he was there to study the mind of a killer.

Deciding he'd stalled long enough, Lance stepped out of his car and started up the steps of the brownstone. Yellow crime scene tape sealed the door. Pulling out his switch blade Lance broke the seal before stepping inside. He noticed immediately that the front entry was untouched. Nothing here had been disturbed.

Moving down the hall he spotted what looked like a work room to his right. The similarity between it and Anna's was uncanny. Book cases lined the walls, a work space in the center, a few antiques and art. Moving on he found the stairs, noted the tape across the way and moved on. The living room also showed no signs of invasion. Whoever had been here, they were not part of Broody's security detail.

The place was too clean. Lance moved back to the steps. Ducking under the line of tape he started up the stairs.

Once on the second floor, he moved down the hall to the bedroom. Here he found signs of a struggle near the bed. He pictured the late Dr. King asleep in bed. The assailant entering the room undetected. He stands over his victim, watching him for a moment; amused maybe. Crosses the floor to the bed and then wakes his target abruptly; a slap to the face perhaps.

Phillip's eyes snap open, fear etches his face as he sits up. He blinks and recognition sets in. He knows the intruder and gets out of the bed. Maybe yells at the other for invading his home and tells him to leave. The assailant does not listen. Phillip gets in the intruders face, points his finger at the other man as he demands the intruder go.

Things shift now as his unwanted visitor grabs the finger pointed at him breaking it. Phillip retreats now afraid. The other man advances.

"If you're finished blustering old man, I've questions for you to answer. So, sit down and shut up."

The intruder at this point shoves Phillip who falls back on the bed. The doctor scrambles to get up aware now that he's not safe, but it's too late. When he tries to flee the assailant lashes out stopping him. Annoyed he ties Phillip to the dressing chair using the man's own ties to secure him.

From there the interrogation and torture had begun. Based on what had been taken from the office it was clear he'd been looking for intel on Broody and Anna. Since he'd broken into the office it would seem Phillip King had not provided the answers that he sought. Which raised the question who was the good doctor that he'd endured such torment without cracking.

Lance pushed the question aside, it could wait. Right now he needed to focus on the killer who was he? What did he want with Anna and Broody. If this was indeed about them, then whoever he was, his next move would be her place. Lance moved out of the crime scene and headed back out to the street getting in the car, he headed for Anna's.

49

Hermes moved through his palace with the smug satisfaction of a man who was about to face his enemy and knew he couldn't lose. He had the woman Anna in his grasp and soon the information he needed would be his. Thanks to his cunning of distracting Dionysus with Pamela, he'd ensured that the wine god's efforts to produce an heir with his bride would be fruitless, for the lovely Emily was already swollen with his child. With the statues here in his keeping no other god could rise to full power. He was the new king of his brethren, all he lacked to prove it now was the crown. But he'd have that soon.

As he entered his office Pamela stirred, rising from Dionysus's side, she covered herself and moved to meet him. She kissed him in greeting to assure him of her loyalty and he smiled.

"PAMELA, MY DARLING, I'LL BE LEAVING FOR A FEW DAYS. I TRUST YOU CAN HANDLE OUR GUESTS."

"Of course," she answered.

"GOOD, WHEN HE WAKES, SHOW MY BROTHER TO HIS CHAMBERS. YOU WILL SEE TO THEIR EVERY WANT AND NEED. BUT KEEP AN EYE ON HIM. I HAVE FORBID HIM TO TOUCH OUR PRISONER; IF HE TRIES I AM TO BE INFORMED."

"I understand."

"GOOD. I SHALL RETURN AS SOON AS I CAN, MY QUEEN," he assured her. Hermes kissed her deeply, sealing his vow to make it clear he'd keep it. Letting his lust tease her with promise of pleasure to be had and assure her that his desire for her had not waned. Assuring her she was still his lady. "Hurry home my lord," she entreated.

"I WILL," he murmured and then he left to see to the hunt. His work there was done for the moment. It was time to head out to Gomorrah and see if its temple held the same secrets Sodom had. With a little luck the knowledge he sought would be waiting there for him.

50

Magnus Halden's chopper touched down on a private landing site outside the city of Athens. As he and his crew stepped off the huey his recon tem leader approached.

"Well," Halden demanded.

"We located the compound its approximately ten miles North East of here."

"Well done. We'll prepare for the assault tomorrow at dawn."

"There is a slight problem."

"What is it?"

"Dr. Broody left the island an hour ago."

"I see. Alright then, we'll settle in here and wait him out. When I make my move he will be there."

"Understood."

As the choppers engine quieted, Magnus's phone rang. Taking it out he pressed the button to connect the call.

"Mr. Halden--" A familiar voice said hesitant to speak.

"What is it Russell?"

"I spoke with Dr. King but he was less than cooperative. Claimed he didn't know where Dr. Gallagher or Dr. Broody were. I pulled their personnel files. I'm afraid they won't be much help either. Best we can do is trace a call."

"It's a start get back to the fortress and get started on that angle."

"Yes, sir."

"I expect results Russell. I want you here in the next 48 hours with answers," Magnus stated before he severed the connection;

Miss Gallagher was proving to be more trouble then he'd originally anticipated. He needed the key and she was the only one who knew where to find it.

Lance pulled up outside Anna's brownstone, after getting out of the car he moved up the stairs past the front door and slipped inside. As soon as he walked in he was struck by the feeling that the place was absent of the killers presence.

Passing down the hall he noted the place was as it had been left. Nothing had been disturbed. No one had been there, since Anna skipped town. He wondered what that meant and reasoned that whoever the killer was they'd known that no answers would be found here.

If that was the case then they'd been in contact with Kedar, other than Ian Broody, there was only one person that fit the profile: Russell York. Lance took out his phone and punched in Sam's number as he made his way out of the house.

"Hello."

"Sam, thought you should know Russell York is definitely looking for Anna and Broody."

"You're sure?"

"Yeah, Phillip King's office was hit, the killer took Anna's file and Ian's but didn't hit her place. He knew it was a dead end."

"Kedar."

"Right."

"Thanks for the tip. We're in route for Broody's now with a little luck Anna will be safe by tomorrow."

"Well, watch your back, he's on the hunt."

"Will do," Sam assured him before breaking the call. Lance put up his phone and left. He needed to update the captain and then he wanted to get back to his place and see how Catharine was doing. With these tasks in mind he got in his car and sped away. "

52 MIAMI, FLORIDA

Zaharrah stepped inside the noisy coffee shop, her eyes scanning the crowd for a familiar face, she found it in the form of the pretty brunette with troubled eyes. She'd seen the quiet doctor a few times at the dig but couldn't recall her name.

"You called."

"Yes, I'm sorry for the vagueness of the matter but I couldn't be sure the line was secure."

"I understand. Now, why, don't you start with something easy, like your name and how you know Darrian?"

"I'm Brooke Silvers. I'm working on the dragon. Darrian is my fiancé."

Zaharrah blinked, stunned at the revelation, understanding why he'd kept it hidden. Darrian had seen first-hand what happened to her and Gunnar, he wouldn't want to risk the same. "Where is he? I'm sure he warned you against talking to me."

"I don't know. I asked him to do me a favor but something went wrong."

"Okay, what favor?"

"I asked him to steal my data and get it to the authorities."

"Shit."

"Yeah."

"How wrong?"

"I don't know they showed me a video of him being gunned down but it's off."

"Why?"

"Darrian knew where the cameras were, had learned their timing sweeps. Identified the holes in their line of sight. He never should have been seen. I think the tapes a fake to draw out his accomplice."

"Makes sense."

"If he's not dead then it's not safe for either of us to linger at the site."

Agreed."

"I can't leave."

"Why not?" Zaharrah asked surprised by the refusal.

"They've tightened security."

"Why, what is it they're working on?"

"I'll tell you everything if you get me out of here."

"I'll help you but first I want you to show me some proof you know my brother."

Brooke nodded and pulled the chain around her neck up to reveal a ring Zaharrah knew all too well. It was a family heirloom. One only someone who knew Darrian could have.

"Don't worry, I'll get you clear, then find Darrian," Zaharrah vowed before she turned and left.

53

Hades watched with trepidation and a mild interest as Hecate walked past Magnus Halden's men with a dark haired young man.

"MAGNUS, THIS IS DARRIAN. HE IS A FASCINATING YOUNG ADVENTURER THAT WAS WORKING ON THE DIG SITE IN ATLANTIS FOR DR. BROODY. IT SEEMS THEY HAD SOME SORT OF DISAGREEMENT AND NOW BROODY IS HUNTING HIM. I HELPED HIM ESCAPE AFTER HE SAVED ME FROM BROODY'S GOONS."

"I SEE. WELL, THEN I THANK YOU FOR YOUR AID AND HOPE THAT WE CAN SPEAK DIRECTLY ABOUT OUR COMMON FOE."

"Perhaps," Darrian answered his dark eyes lit with a hint of orange.

"AH, SO HE HOLDS THE WARRIOR'S SPIRIT THEN," Hades said now intrigued.

"YES, THE SWORD HAS A NEW MASTER," Hecate whispered.

"NOT FOR LONG," a familiar voice snapped in outrage as an arrow cut through the chamber striking Hecate.

"ARTEMIS!"

"I WON'T ALLOW YOU TO REVIVE THE WAR GOD; WITCH."

"YOU'RE ANGER IS MISPLACED GIRL! ARES DID NOT KILL YOUR FATHER. IT WAS HERMES; THE LIAR AND MONSTER YOU NOW BLINDLY FIGHT FOR," Hecate hissed.

"ARES SWORD FELLED MY FATHER!"

"BUT MY HAND DID NOT WIELD IT," Ares breathed from

within the man Darrian in defense.

Hades looked on as Artemis turned, bow string drawn back prepared to fire. "STAY YOUR HAND NIECE, ARES SPEAKS THE TRUTH," he snapped, not about to lose the war god's aid again so soon. He watched as Artemis eased her grip on the bow before turning to look at him.

"SPEAK PLAINLY, OH LORD OF THE DEAD."

"I WILL SHOW YOU," Hades stated before touching the huntress's brow and letting the candle he held burst to light.

Artemis cried out in distress as a flood of memories washed through her mind. Tears fell from blue eyes filled with hate. The blue darkened beginning to glow as her power raged within seeking to burst forth with the weight of her emotions.

"HERMES!" The name tore through the silence of the room like the sound of a cannon. The room shook as wind ripped through the chamber and lightening crashed.

"CALM YOURSELF NIECE. HE WILL PAY FOR HIS CRIME AND HIS DECEPTION."

"WHAT DO YOU WANT FROM ME UNCLE?" Artemis asked.

"YOUR SUPPORT IN MY CLAIM TO THE THRONE."

"YOU'LL HAVE IT. THE GOD OF KNOWLEDGE WILL PERISH," Artemis vowed. "FORGIVE ME ARES, I HAVE PERSECUTED YOU IN ERROR."

"THINK NOTHING OF IT LADY, I UNDERSTAND YOUR WRATH. I HOPE THAT WE WILL BE ALLIES NOW AGAINST THIS UPSTART."

"YOU WILL HAVE MY BOW," she assured him as she knelt.

"I THANK YOU FOR IT," Ares said pleased.

"WHEN DO WE STRIKE?" Artemis demanded.

"AS SOON AS HERMES RETURNS."

"WHY WAIT? I CAN GET YOU IN. YOU CAN CLAIM YOUR POWER NOW--"

"I WANT TO SEE THE LOOK ON HIS FACE WHEN I STRIP HIM OF ALL HE'S WORKED FOR," Hades replied before his candle dimmed. He smiled, pleased everything was falling into place. Soon the only thing missing would be his bride. Wherever she was, she couldn't hide from him too much longer.

54

Lance unlocked his front door and stepped inside. The place, he noted, was quiet, only the faint sound of fingers on a key board broke the illusion the place was empty. His feet carried him to the dining room where his eyes settled on the red head bent over the laptop sitting at the table working away. He smiled at the image before him. The writer at work. It struck him then that she didn't look much different than Dana had in his office slaving away at a case.

Lance blinked and tried to chase the picture of the pretty brunette lost to her work from his thoughts. Dana was gone, she'd chosen the job over him. Left him here with her ghost. He watched as blue eyes rose from the screen to look at him a smile on her pink lips.

"Hi, have you been back long?"

"No, only a minute," he assured her. "I thought you were blocked," he said recalling only a few days before she'd been unable to write a word.

'I was, but before--I--" Catharine paused unable to go on.

"Before you were taken," Lance prompted reminding them both of where she'd been only 24 hours before.

"Yeah, before that happened, I had a dream and it helped me figure out how to end Dark Heart."

"What does it matter now?" Lance asked confused.

"Hecate was looking to become Serenity and Dionysus will use Syvarin's name to gain power as well. All that worship will make them both stronger, but if I free Serenity by telling the truth about her then they can't use *Dark Heart* anymore."

"Won't that make you a target?" Lance asked concerned.

"For now no. Hecate has other games to play as does Dionysus."

"If they figure out what you're doing--"

"It's a calculated risk," Catharine stated as she saved her work.

"Calculated? You're playing games with a crazed goddess and a manipulative god who's already got you at a disadvantage. I don't think you've figured the odds correctly," Lance snapped irritated.

"Detective Roman--"

"Damn it, Catharine. Haven't you risked enough."

"No."

"How can you say that, after what you've just been through?"

"I gave up my name years ago, then my life. If I don't finish *Dark Heart* I'll lose my career also. If I do this I can take all of it back. I need to do this. I have to," Catharine said with a determination that shook Lance to his bones. He'd seen it once before on another woman's face. Catharine would finish the story or die trying.

"Okay, I'm sorry, Catharine. I just don't want to see you get hurt again," he whispered wishing there was some way he could convince her to let it go.

"I understand--Have you got a couple minutes?"

"Yeah."

"Do you think you could read the changes I've made to books 1-3? I need to make sure the voice is consistent."

"I'd be happy to."

"Thanks."

Lance crossed the room to take the chair beside hers and turned his eyes to the screen. As he fell into the scene he was aware of the sound of a pen scratching against paper as Catharine worked beside him, but it too faded from his awareness as he lost himself in the pages of *Dark Heart*.

55 GOMORRAH RUINS, JORDAN

Hermes stepped past the skeleton crew working at the minor dig and made his way into the main temple. His gaze skimmed over the line of statues that stood over the stone alter. Hestia the goddess of the hearth and family stood at the end alone, eyes wild with fright, her eyes cast to something beyond view. To her right was Iris the goddess of sea and sky. She stood before his image, her eyes transfixed upon him as he blew upon his horn.

Hermes smiled to himself as his mind recalled with amusement the woman she'd been. The first of his brides taken young and innocent, she'd been transfixed by his power. Had fallen at his feet before him and worshiped him. When he'd kissed her, making his intent known, she'd wept with joy and surrendered to him, humbled by his desire, just as Pamela had. He licked his lips at the thought of her, yes Miss Walsh was the perfect embodiment of his sweet Iris. Unbidden, Hermes thoughts turned to his prisoner waiting back home. ANNA! She, it seemed was crafted from the same mold as his ex-wife Hecate. No matter, he'd soon put her in her place.

Turning from his musing, Hermes returned his focus to the other statues. Eos, the goddess of the dawn stood next. At the center Helios, the lord of the sun embraced Cybele, the goddess of nature marking them the King and Queen which the people of Gomorrah had served. Hermes blinked as he spotted the whip clutched in his right hand for driving the golden chariot. There was the answer. The mantels were here in the graven images.

To his left was Hephaestus, god of the forge, his gauntlets prominently displayed, and a mallet in one hand a chain in the other. Poseidon, the sea king followed, in his left hand he grasped his trident while his right arm wrapped around the center of his bride Amphitrite. Beside her, stood Persephone, the only child of Zeus honored with a graven image. His child by Demeter and the goddess of spring.

Moving toward the images, he slipped behind them and using his power lit the torches behind them to reveal the narrow door that lead into the depths.

Hermes descended the stairs entering into the dark chamber. Stretching out his hand, he watched as torches burst to life illuminating the room. Like the room in Sodom a stone chest with a black hand lay within the rubble. The god of knowledge pushed the heavy lid aside to reveal the cuneiform tablet within and smiled.

Blue eyes ran over the clay writing, searching for the detail he sought. The resting place of Zeus's crown. But it was not here. A great many secrets were within the text but not the one he craved most. Lifting the tablet from its enclosure Hermes moved back upstairs. He'd take this piece of the mystery with him back to his home to study and think further on where his answers waited.

56

Sam unfastened his safety belt and grabbed his gear as Terra and Vince did the same. They'd landed on a military base of Grecian soil only moments ago and he wasn't wasting another second, now that they were on the ground. They needed to get going. Zaharrah had said Athens but not where. It would be up to them to figure that out.

Sam considered what he knew about his enemy and contemplated where the troublesome fallen one might have set up shop. He slid into the backseat of the jeep and pulled out his cell phone looking for points of interest in the city dedicated to the former king of the gods. Anna was here somewhere and the sooner he found her the better.

Lance looked up from the laptop and blinked as he noted the time. Three hours had passed since he started reading. Catharine had managed to completely capture his imagination with the changes to *Dark Heart*. He'd made himself stop as he came to the beginning of Heart of Stone. He'd yet to read the third book and until he did, he'd not read on. "It's good."

"You're done already?"

"No, just the changes for *Heart of Glass*, *Heart of Clay* and the short. I haven't read book three yet."

"I'll make you a copy of the file so you can read all of it including the changes."

"You don't have too--"

"I want to. A test reader is helpful."

"If you're sure."

"I am."

"How goes the search?"

"It's still compiling. I'll let you know when it's done."

"Okay."

"What did you learn about your case?" Catharine asked.

"Broody is not behind it. I told Sam he's got a third party involved in this madness."

"You're sure?"

"Yeah, they knew Anna was gone."

"Someone connected to Broody but not," Catharine asked curious.

"Exactly. You'd have made a good detective."

"Thanks. I'm sorry I missed out on everything. I'm sure it would have been fascinating."

"Next time perhaps," Lance offered.

"Yeah, that sounds great," Catharine said enthusiastically.

"How are you?"

"I'm fine, nearly ready to start writing book four."

"No, how are you?"

"I'll be okay."

"Can we--"

"Not yet, please don't push Lance."

"Okay, when you're ready," he relented before rising from the table. He brushed a kiss on the top of her head before moving down the hall to his office to work.

58

Hermes sat aboard his plane, his mind wrestling with the lack of information within the stone tablet. Where was it? Why hadn't the answers laid waiting as the riddle had? The sister cities should have held all the kings secrets--unless. The plains cities had not been two but four, even the map room had revealed as much.

Perhaps the missing clues lay still buried under the sand of the Jordan. If that were the case it meant starting further digs without his backer's knowledge. Pulling out Ian Broody's cell phone Hermes pulled up the number for his best researcher.

"Hello," Zaharrah's voice came over the line laced with irritation.

"Miss Lynch, I'm sorry to interrupt your work but I have a project that requires your expertise."

"Something new, Dr. Broody?"

"Yes."

"I'm listening."

"Head back to the dig site near the Dead Sea determine the locations of the other plains cities and take a small crew to begin uncovering them."

"I thought they were deemed inconsequential," Zaharrah stated curious.

"They were, but I feel that there was perhaps something missed or overlooked by neglecting these sites. I want you to handle their exploration personally."

"What are we looking for Dr. Broody?"

"Similarities with Sodom and Gomorrah proof the four are indeed linked."

"What about Dr. Gallagher's research?" Zaharrah questioned.

"I'll see to that myself. I have a feeling Anna's secrets will soon be revealed to me," Hermes said with a smug grin as he pictured the woman in question laying within her prison slowly succumbing to Dionysus's spell.

"Okay then, I'll get right to that," Zaharrah said before breaking the call.

Hermes put the phone away and smiled. He turned in his seat and moved his focus to his newest member of the dig team.

"Mr. Elwood, I trust you're prepared to work under strenuous circumstances?"

"I am."

"Good. The work you do on the dig will go a long way toward gaining you the final credit toward your doctorate."

"Thank you for the opportunity."

"No need for thanks, your peers speak very highly of you. I've no doubt you'll make a great addition to the team."

"No one there knows I'm coming?"

"That's right."

"Good."

"I take it you're hoping to catch a certain associate of mine off guard."

"Something like that."

"I'll be sure to arrange a meet once we've landed," Hermes said amused.

"That's not necessary."

"I insist," Hermes whispered as he picked up the other man's thoughts and got a flash image of the reserved Dr. Chase lost in the throes of passion. He was looking forward to getting a better look at Dr. Robin Chase. It wouldn't be long now. After he indulged in the spectacle of their unplanned reunion he'd head home. Perhaps when he reached his palace Anna would be ready to speak. Then all the pieces would at last fall into place and his rise to power would be complete.

59

Zaharrah drew a breath to steady her nerves. Her conversation with Broody changed things. She had no time to get Dr. Silvers clear of there. She needed help. The noose was tightening faster than she'd anticipated. The desert waited and with it death.

Hands shaking; she punched in Sam's number and muttered a prayer he was able to speak. The phone rang twice before she was greeted with a curt hello.

"Mr. Abrams, I need your help."

"Miss Lynch, what can I do for you?"

"I've got a friend here that needs out of Miami fast. I told her I'd help but I can't. Dr. Broody has pulled me from the dig to start hunting for the other plains cities."

"Which leaves you with no time to get your friend clear. I'll arrange departure for her, provided you answer my questions."

"I'll tell you everything I know Mr. Abrams, when next we meet," Zaharrah vowed.

"Good. Now tell me, who are we pulling out?"

"Her name is Dr. Brooke Silvers--"

"The geneticist?"

"You know her?"

"We met, briefly. She had concerns about the scoop of her project which she shared with Anna."

"Well, things have escalated. I don't know the details but it's not safe for her here."

"She'll have a way out."

"Thank you." Zaharrah hung up the phone with that and began making arrangements to leave for Israel.

60

Hermes led his guest towards the main door of his Palace, as they walked a second vehicle pulled up in front. The car door opened and out stepped the pretty red head that his associate was so eager to see.

"FOX I BELIEVE YOU WANTED TO SEE DR. CHASE," he stated as he stepped aside giving the other man a clear path to the newcomers side.

"Robin," he said with excitement.

Hermes watched amused as the woman blinked, he saw the flicker of recognition and in that moment got a glimpse inside her mind. Robin Chase was swept away in a memory of a time when they'd been together. She was lost in the thrill of his touch in one minute and in the next felt the sting of pain of waking up to find him gone, the terror of learning she was pregnant and the grief of loss as that child died. Then there was nothing.

"I'm sorry, have we met," she muttered coolly acting as if none of it had ever occurred.

"ROBIN CHASE, MEET FOX ELWOOD THE NEWEST MEMBER OF THE TEAM. I WANT YOU TO GET HIM CAUGHT UP ON THE PROJECT ON THE WAY OVER TO THE DIG SITE. YOU'LL BE ASSISTING ZAHARRAH LYNCH WITH WHATEVER TASK SHE ASSIGNS," Hermes said amused before he turned and walked in the door leaving them to themselves.

61

Robin cursed Dr. Broody mentally for leaving her alone with Fox. He was the last person on earth she wanted to see again. But here he was before her now and she felt her heart race as she looked upon him. Get a grip girl he's no good, she reminded herself as she shouldered her bag and walked in the direction of the plane without a word. She heard his footsteps behind her and prayed he didn't have any ideas about talking to her. As far as she was concerned he'd given up the right to do so the night he left her bed in the middle of the night and never came back.

"Robin…"

"It's Dr. Chase," she said crisply as she stepped on the plane.

"Dr. Chase, it's good to see you again."

"Get on the plane Mr. Elwood, we've got lots of work to go over," she muttered.

"Right."

Robin set to the task of bringing him up to speed covering every detail she could think of, keeping him preoccupied with work. With a little luck she'd not be done till they landed and could keep him from small talk because she wasn't about to fill him in on the past year nor did she care to know where he'd been since he left, she told herself. But she knew she was lying, one look at him brought it all back like a flood and damn him, despite how he'd hurt her she was afraid that if he decided to try and pick things up where they left off she just might let him which made her an idiot.

62

Anna's eyes shot open as her mind rose from the blackness of unconsciousness. Pain exploded through her head as she woke. She blinked to find herself in strange surroundings. The room with the statues was gone and for a moment she wondered if it had just been a nightmare. But the voices of the other Fallen washed through her mind crushing the notion.

She'd been taken from her hotel room by James Hardagen and given to Hermes in exchange for Dionysus's freedom. The wine god was restored to his former glory. His power pressed against her mind now seeking to break her will. He worked now to enslave her completely with his touch. His goal to get her to lose herself in her passions and drink from his cup so that all she knew would be his for the taking.

She had to get out of there.

Anna lifted her head from the lone piece of furniture within the room: an oversized bed that took up most of the space within. She noted a small door to her right and stepping through cursed to find only a small bathroom. There was no way out of her prison. No visible door, which made the room she was in, a secret one.

By the look of it there was no way to open it from her side. The only way the door would open was if her captors entered it or let her out. Neither of which would end well. She was trapped.

63

Hermes strolled in the front door of his palace and smiled. His prisoner was awake. He couldn't wait to see her again, now that her head was clear and the reality of her situation had begun to sink in. At his side Ian Broody's spirit cried for the right to bear witness to her downfall.

"YES, YOU SHALL BE PRESENT WHEN SHE BREAKS AND YOU WILL STAND WATCH. DIONYSUS IS NOT PERMITTED TO HAVE HER. IF HE TRIES YOU WILL NOTIFY ME," Hermes commanded. Using his power he drew the graven image behind him as he made his way through the throne room and into his personal chambers.

Hermes found his wife resting and was careful not to wake her as he opened the door to the hidden chamber that lay in the southern wall. He stepped inside as the woman within turned to face him, hazel eyes lit with fear as the door slid shut behind him.

The graven image slid silently into the corner near the opening. Its eyes fixed on the bed. "MY TROUBLESOME LADY, I'M GLAD TO SEE YOU'RE FIRE HAS COOLED SINCE LAST WE SPOKE. YOU MUST NOW UNDERSTAND THE GRAVITY OF YOUR SITUATION."

"I'm a prisoner," she stated.

"YES, YOU ARE, MY DEAR, AND THERE IS NO MEANS OF ESCAPE. NO ONE WILL BE COMING TO YOUR RESCUE THIS TIME. MY BROTHER'S TOUCH WILL ROB YOU OF YOUR MIND IF GIVEN ENOUGH TIME. ONE WAY OR ANOTHER YOU WILL SUCCUMB TO ME, ANNA. I WILL KNOW ALL YOU KNOW AND THERE IS NOTHING YOU

CAN DO TO STOP THAT," Hermes whispered as he closed the distance between them.

He watched with amusement as she trembled before him. An effect of his brother's spell "YES, THAT'S RIGHT, YOUR FLESH KNOWS THIS BODY," he breathed.

"I may know that body, but I know not you, oh Fallen One, and I never will," Anna answered with conviction as Hermes grabbed her by the arm and drew her to him.

"WE SHALL SEE," Hermes challenged before his mouth fell upon her lips claiming them. Anna struggled in his grasp and he thrilled in the feel of her body and mind warring against each other. She was so close to breaking.

The man Ian laughed from within his prison and urged his keeper to push on, whispering secrets, he knew of the ways to please her, to make her burn faster. As the spirit lost itself in fantasies of how it would break her Hermes broke the kiss and stretched out his hand to the statue.

"COME, YOU SHALL BE PART OF THIS," Hermes commanded. He watched as the black vapor poured forth from the image to land in his open hand. His eyes moved to his prisoner. Anna stared at the mass of darkness unblinking.

"Ian no," she breathed with disbelief and horror. Hermes smirked as he saw that for a moment she felt the man Ian's mind press against her own as he played out some fantasy of what he wanted to do to her. She cringed and Hermes trembled with anticipation as the black vapor slithered from his hand to wrap around her leaving a trail of goose flesh and a wild hunger within in its wake that left her feeling sick.

The god of Knowledge's eyes lit with power as the spirit wound itself around her thighs intent on proving she still wanted him. Without warning, it was ripped back as Hermes closed his hand around the lingering piece of the spirit in his hand. Ian screamed as inhuman nails tore his spirit. Anna cried out startled at the abrupt touch of cold on her flesh as the god's power washed over her to replace the familiar touch of her past lover.

"NOW IAN BROODY, YOU ARE MINE," Hermes crowed before he lifted the tainted spirit to his lips and blue eyes blazed brighter as his power grew, his lust swelled with the taste of his favorite fruit upon his lips and he turned his full attention once more to his pretty prisoner.

"TIMES UP ANNA, WHICH WILL YOU HAVE A LUST FOGGED FANTASY WITH THE PROMISE OF PLEASURE OR

THE HARSH REALITY THAT WILL BEAR ONLY PAIN AND TORMENT?" Hermes asked as he wiped a stray tear from her face. He lifted it to his lips and tasted it. A groan rose from the back of his throat at the taste. Pain, fear they were a potent drug second only to lust.

Anna turned from his touch, giving her answer, though she could not speak.

"SO BE IT," he growled more than ready to end this battle of wills. He drew her to him once more. His mouth devoured hers as his hands tore at her clothes seeking her flesh.

Nails tore at him, hands fisted as she fought in vain for escape. She backed away only to have her knees hit the edge of the bed. There was nowhere to run. No place left to hide. Hermes pressed her back so that she lay trapped beneath him on the bed. His lips parted hers as he stared at her. She was shaking in her fear, powerless beneath him; helpless to stop him.

"No, God no," Anna cried her voice desperate.

"SAVE YOUR DENIALS WOMAN; THEY CAN'T HELP YOU NOW," Hermes mocked, as he tore open the front of her gown revealing her to his hungry eyes. "I WILL KNOW YOU AS IAN DID," he crowed in victory as he lowered his head to taste her.

Hermes froze just above her racing heart as the man James Hardagen's voice rose in his mind with a shout of warning. "WHAT NOW?" Hermes hissed in rage at the interruption before getting to his feet. "WE'LL FINISH THIS LATER," he vowed before departing abruptly.

64

Magnus Halden stepped through the double doors his team had just breached. It seemed Ian had not planned for the contingency of a military breach. Hermes had thought his secrets too well guarded for anyone to get this far; which made him a fool. No secret was ever safe from his reach. Hades mused as his eyes glowed with his power. He moved through the parlor and into the throne room. His eyes skimmed over the nine statues of him and his brethren and noted the mortal spirit trapped within Dionysus's image.

"GO, TELL YOUR MASTER AND HIS LORD I HAVE COME," Hades commanded. He heard the spirit's cry and waited.

Hermes emerged first, his eyes lit with fury at the intrusion. Good, he'd interrupted him at his games. Magnus produced the stolen candle and set it upon the outstretched hands of the image of the god of the underworld. The room shook and the spirit of James Hardagen wailed in horror. Magnus Halden's mind receded and Hades poured forth from his graven prison to fill the mortal vessel.

"DESTROY THEM," Hades commanded of Halden's men as he drew the two mortal spirits trapped in stone forth to claim them as his own. He was the keeper of hell after all. He watched as machine gun fire destroyed one image after another. He left only two standing; one was that of the war god the other his brother Poseidon.

"HERMES, YOU WHO ASPIRED TO BE KING, LOOK NOW UPON YOUR RUIN. PAMELA, MY DEAR, COME FORTH AND BRING YOUR GUEST WITH YOU," Hades demanded.

"HOW DARE YOU ORDER MY QUEEN," Hermes roared in

outrage.

"YOUR QUEEN WAS MY WHORE LONG BEFORE YOU MET HER," Hades mocked. He looked on with satisfaction as Pamela came out of the master suite with Emily in tow, Dionysus followed after his lady his eyes weary. Good the wine god knew his place here. Soon Hermes would also.

As Pamela came to his side Hades lay his hand upon her abdomen. He felt the child growing within her and smiled.

"YOU'VE BEEN BUSY BROTHER, BUT NO MATTER. TO UNDO WHAT HAS STARTED I NEED ONLY PLUCK YOUR FRUIT BEFORE ITS APPOINTED TIME AND IT WILL WITHER," Hades hissed and to prove his point he let his power wash over Pamela. She moaned in protest as Hermes stepped forward to aid her. Hades power slammed into him full force dropping him to his knees as the god of the dead worked his will, powerless to stop him.

Pamela crumbled to the floor in pain as Hades stepped forward to lay his hand upon Emily.

"YOU CAN'T, SHE'S MINE," Dionysus cried in objection.

"I CAN AND I WILL, FOR THE CHILD SHE BEARS IS NOT YOURS BROTHER, BUT HERMES. HE GAVE YOU HIS QUEEN TO ENSURE YOU'D NOT BE ABLE TO PRODUCE AN HEIR AND STOP YOU FROM RISING ANY FURTHER IN POWER," Hades muttered as he repeated the work of destroying Hermes would be heir.

"YOU BETRAY ME AFTER WHAT I'VE GIVEN YOU!" Dionysus raged.

"SILENCE FOOL," Hermes roared in fury not about to reveal his prisoner's identity, knowing if Hades got a hold of her he'd have the crown as well.

"YES. THE TIME FOR TALES WILL COME LATER. FOR NOW, OH GOD OF KNOWLEDGE, YOU WILL WATCH AND LEARN YOUR PLACE," Hades snapped as he drew Pamela from the floor where she lay. He breathed on her and watched as her whiskey colored eyes flew open. His mouth captured hers and she kissed him back with a hunger that left Dionysus drunk from its potency and had Hermes raging. Hades paid neither any further mind as he lost himself in the thrill of bedding his rival's wife.

65

Hermes looked on dumb struck as Hades took his bride. His thoughts drifted back to Anna's words spoken earlier in the heat of anger as she'd lain upon the marble desk, his alter. Her words had proven true, all of them. In a matter of minutes he'd seen his claim to the throne reduced to ashes.

"POOR HERMES, ALL YOUR WORK UNDONE," a familiar voice whispered.

"HECATE?" He asked as his eyes moved beyond his brother to the woman entering the room.

"YES, MY HUSBAND. IT IS I THAT HAS BETRAYED YOU AND IF YOU WISH TO BREATHE ANOTHER DAY YOU WILL FLEE NOW BEFORE THE HUNTRESS COMES FOR YOU."

"ARTEMIS?"

"KNOWS ALL."

"WHY?"

"BECAUSE I NEVER WANTED YOU OR ANY OF THIS. I LOVED ANOTHER."

"NOW, YOU'RE NOTHING BUT HIS WHORE," Hermes raged pointing his finger to where Hades was still lost in bedding Pamela.

"NO, I HAVE NOT SHARED MY BODY WITH ANYONE," She roared in defiance as Ares puppet entered the hall. Outside lightening split the sky. Thunder crashed breaking windows and shaking the house.

"RUN LITTLE GOD, BEFORE YOUR PET GETS HOLD OF YOU," Hecate urged again.

This time he did not hesitate. Hermes turned and fled. He saw now that the only way to make good his claim was to return with Zeus's crown upon his brow. Until then he was no match for the others.

66

Hecate watched with amusement as Hades finished the act of claiming Hermes's bride as his own. The would-be-king had fallen and soon Artemis would hunt him down like the dog he was. Dionysus was in his place and Ares stood near his true power as well. Only one remained. Poseidon, the sea king. She would see to him as well, but first there was the matter of revealing Hermes final game.

Hecate whispered a call for aid to her lover in unraveling her ex-husband's secret and her mind was filled with the image of the woman trapped within the walls of the palace. The key to all lay locked in her mind.

"HADES, NOT ALL WITHIN THESE HALLS STAND BEFORE YOU," she whispered. She watched with pleasure as the god of the dead rose from his whore at her voice.

"WHO ELSE IS HERE? WHY HAVEN'T YOU BROUGHT THEM FORTH," Hades demanded as he glared at Pamela.

"SHE KNOWS NOT WHERE HERMES PRISONER IS KEPT, MY LORD, BUT I DO. COME AND YOU SHALL SEE HERMES GREATEST TREASURE," Hecate murmured before she left the room entering the master suite aware Hades followed her.

67

Sam turned his focus from the points of interest list.

"Head for the Parthenon."

Terra nodded and turned the car in that direction.

"Who was dat on the phone earlier?"

"Miss Lynch."

"What did she want?"

"A favor. A mutual acquaintance needs a ride out of Miami."

"She tell ya about Halden?"

"No but she told me she would."

"Fine. We'll see ta her friend, but once it's done she tells us everything."

"It's already been agreed to," Sam assured her.

"I'll make the call."

"Thank you."

"I'll take yur' aid in rescuin' mi sister instead of yur' thanks."

"You'll have it. Let's just hope we reach her before anything else goes wrong," Sam muttered as they approached the hill where the Parthenon was. As they got closer he spotted a house under the hill and felt the hair on the back of his neck lift. This was where Hermes had set up camp. Every instinct in his body cried out in warning.

"I've got him," Sam muttered.

"You're sure?"

"Positive."

"Okay then, we'll take a look at the place closer over the next several hours," Terra said.

"We'll move in when it's dark if you're right," Vince stated.

"Sounds good," Sam said with approval.

"Let's get this dealt with," Terra said before she pulled out her phone and made the call to set everything in motion.

68

Hades stepped through the opening of the secret door to find a small chamber on the other side with a large bed. A familiar young woman rose from the bed her hazel eyes wide with alarm as she wrapped her dress about her.

"DR. GALLAGHER, WHAT A PLEASANT SURPRISE," He said amused.

"Hades," she whispered with terror.

"DIONYSUS, RELEASE YOUR HOLD ON OUR GUEST'S MIND I'D LIKE TO SPEAK WITH HER CLEAR HEADED," Hades requested.

He was pleased when he felt Dionysus ease his grip on her mind. He heard the wine god's steps retreat, leaving the room and Hades, to do with her as he liked.

"BETTER?" Hades asked.

"Yes," she breathed as she blinked relieved to be free of the wine god's influence if only for a moment.

"GOOD, I WANT YOUR HEAD CLEAR BEFORE I SPEAK."

"It is," she assured him as she clung to the ruined pieces of her dress hiding herself from him.

"PLEASE DOCTOR, RELAX, I ASSURE YOU I HAVE NO AMOROUS INTENT FOR YOU," Hades said amused and to prove his point he touched her shoulder and the gown mended itself. Once the gown was fixed he drew back from her.

Anna blinked. Her body relaxed.

"EXCELLENT. NOW DR. GALLAGHER, AS I UNDERSTAND IT, YOU POSSESS THE KNOWLEDGE OF

THE LOCATION OF A CERTAIN ARTIFACT.

YOU'RE GOING TO TELL ME WHERE IT IS NOW."

"No."

"ARE YOU SURE YOU WANT TO SAY THAT? I MEAN YOU CAN IF YOU LIKE BUT THEN I'LL JUST ANSWER WITH THREATS. DO YOU REALLY WANT TO GO THERE?" Hades asked his voice civil.

"What sort of threats?"

"OBVIOUS ONES ANNA. YOUR FAMILY, FRIENDS, ANYONE YOU CARE ABOUT I'LL CUT THEM DOWN LIKE THAT," Hades stated as he snapped his fingers.

"I can't--"

"SAM IS CLOSE BY. I'LL LET HIM WALK IN HERE AND TAKE HIM OUT IN FRONT OF YOU."

"No."

"IF YOU WANT THAT TO BE AVOIDED THEN ANSWER ME."

"I don't know where it is now. I had Zaharrah Lynch arrange to have it stolen for me."

Hades smiled amused by the news. "HECATE, MY DEAR, GO GET US THAT KEY," he urged and watched as she departed.

"THANK YOU, DR. GALLAGHER, YOU'VE BEEN MOST HELPFUL.

NOW I'LL LEAVE YOU IN DIONYSUS'S CAPABLE HANDS. I TRUST YOUR SAM WILL TRULY APPRECIATE THE IRONY OF YOUR STATE WHEN HE FINDS YOU. IT WILL MAKE THE SECOND TIME I'VE HARMED HIS BELOVED BUT SPARED HER LIFE," he mocked before he turned and left.

69

Artemis turned to go after Hades, not pleased with his decision regarding the prisoner.

"Hades, a word."

"WHAT IS IT NIECE?"

"I want you to give the woman Anna to me."

"WHY?"

"You got what you needed from her sire, she's not a threat anymore--"

"IT'S NOT HER THAT'S THE THREAT IT'S THE MAN SAM ABRAMS THAT'S THE THREAT. SHE SUFFERS; TO CRUSH HIM."

"I gave you Hermes palace now I'm asking you for the woman as payment."

"I THOUGHT YOU WANTED APOLLO BACK?" Hades said curious.

"I do, but I'm asking for her as well. I won't, no I can't watch her suffer so. Give her to me."

"VERY WELL, IF SHE MEANS THAT MUCH TO YOU, YOU WILL HAVE HER BUT FOR THE FAVOR I WILL EXPECT ONE IN RETURN."

"What is your price Uncle?" Artemis asked.

"FIND HERMES AND END HIM."

"With pleasure."

"GOOD. NOW GO SAVE YOUR PET BEFORE SHE'S BEYOND YOUR AID," Hermes demanded before moving on.

Satisfied Artemis turned and headed back to the secret room.

70

Zaharrah shoved the last of her shirts in her suitcase before closing the lid and zipping it shut. Her personal things were ready to go. She had only to pack up her work in preparation for leaving. Most of her notes and research were still on the isle. She'd have to collect them when she went over tomorrow.

Her flight wasn't leaving until Friday she hoped it would buy her enough time to get Dr. Silvers clear. After Friday the desert waited and she was not comfortable with the notion. All her dreams over the last five years told her one thing waited for her in that sand, Death. Hades was coming, she could feel him now at odd moments, on the edge of her awareness trying to peak in. She feared going to the desert was like giving him an engraved invitation.

As she fretted over the matter her phone rang. Pulling the cell from her hip she drew a breath seeing Sam's number.

"Hello."

"Miss Lynch, tell your friend her ride will be there on Wednesday. She'd best be ready. You should be sure you have an adequate alibi for the evening."

"Understood."

"Where do I find you once I'm done here?"

"Israel."

"See you there."

"Good luck, Mr. Abrams."

"To you as well, Miss Lynch," Sam answered before he hung up.

Zaharrah punched in Brooke's number and waited for an

answer.

"Hello."

"Dr. Silvers."

"Speaking."

"Your departure has been arranged. You'll be out of here by Wednesday."

"Understood. Thank you."

"All I want from you Brooke is an explanation for why Darrian is missing."

"You'll get it," Brooke assured her before she hung up.

"Darrian, where are you?" Zaharrah muttered with annoyance before she turned and left the room. Her feet carried her to the docks. Within moments she was on the ship headed into the Bermuda Triangle and away from her thoughts, she needed her work to distract her from the desert ahead of her. She wasn't ready to face Hades yet.

71

Anna flinched as the secret door opened expecting to see the wine god. She was puzzled to see the woman Artemis instead.

"IF YOU WISH TO REMAIN SAFE YOU WILL COME WITH ME," Artemis commanded.

Anna rose from the bed unsure but grateful to be leaving the inescapable prison. As she followed Artemis through the master suite and down a short hall to her left, lay the throne room to the right a door. Dionysus emerged from the throne room stopping her.

"WHERE ARE YOU TAKING MY TOY HUNTRESS?" The wine god questioned in temper.

"HADES GAVE ME THE WOMAN. SHE'S UNDER MY PROTECTION," Artemis answered.

Anna stepped closer to the goddess having no desire to be anywhere near Dionysus again now that she understood his power.

"HER FLESH IS MINE HUNTRESS, AND HER MIND NEARLY SO. SHE SUFFERS FOR WANT OF ME."

"NOT ANYMORE," Artemis challenged.

"YOU WANT HER?" Dionysus asked amused.

"I DO."

"WHAT WILL YOU GIVE ME FOR HER?" Dionysus asked.

"I'LL GIVE YOU PASSAGE TO HADES WHORES," Artemis offered.

"NOT INTERESTED. I'VE SAMPLED MISS WALSH'S FRUIT. I CRAVE SOMETHING EXOTIC."

"TAKE ME INSTEAD," Artemis commanded. Anna blinked stunned by the goddess's offer.

"YOUR WORD ON THE TRADE," Dionysus demanded.

"YOU HAVE IT," Artemis assured him.

"DONE. YOU HAVE FIVE MINUTES TO SEE TO YOUR PET, IF YOU'RE NOT BACK BY THEN DEALS OFF," Dionysus muttered.

Anna watched as Artemis nodded before turning and leading her on to a set of double doors. The goddess threw open the doors and Anna stepped inside.

"NO MATTER WHAT, DO NOT OPEN THIS DOOR."

"Why are you doing this?"

"I DON'T KNOW."

"Thank you."

"IF YOU WANT TO THANK ME, DO AS I SAY. STAY HERE," Artemis commanded before touching Anna.

Anna gasped as she felt a jolt, when it passed she found her body and mind were free of the wine god's influence. Before she could comment Artemis turned and walked out of the room. The heavy doors slammed shut behind her. The lock was secured and a magic seal pulsed over them. Anna settled into a chair and whispered a prayer of thanks for her protection and deliverance from Dionysus's touch.

72

Artemis moved down the short hall and stepped into the throne room. Dionysus stood before the marble desk that substituted as an altar and she drew a breath. Here then it would seem, before the eyes of the remaining gods. She swallowed as she shed her bow and quiver of arrows, in a show of good faith. Slowly she made her way to his side.

Violet eyes glowed faintly as he studied her with an intensity that made her tremble. "ARTEMIS, YOU'VE MADE A BARGAIN THIS DAY THAT YOU DON'T UNDERSTAND," he taunted as he poked her forehead with his index finger.

She groaned as his power touched her mind making her skin burn with desire as a million images of what he would do to her filled her mind.

"THERE, NOW YOU KNOW YOUR PET'S TORMENT FIRST HAND," he mocked as he trailed his finger down her face to skim over her lips. Bruising them under his touch. She imagined drawing it in her lips to tease him and was powerless to stop herself from acting it out. The wine god drew free of her lips; his moist finger skimmed down her neck toward her shoulders.

"THIRSTY MY LITTLE HUNTRESS?" Dionysus whispered as his hand stilled over her pounding heart.

Artemis nodded as she licked her lips. Her mouth felt as dry as a desert and she craved a drink. He obliged her lifting his golden goblet to her lips. The crimson liquid hit her system like a sledge hammer leaving her drunk with the first drop. The taste ripped through her like a tornado, it made her body more needy and aware of his touch. She felt the mild dose of lust that he'd touched her with arrow through her blood like a tidal wave that made her ache with want of him.

Artemis drank deep now from the cup hesitation gone. She was unable to resist its drugging draught. She drank down every drop and groaned with protest when it came up dry. Dionysus laughed.

"ALLOW ME HUNTRESS," he whispered and then his mouth was on hers drinking in her unique flavor. Artemis moaned overwhelmed, drowning in his kiss, when his mouth left hers to follow in the wake of his fingers. She found the cup was indeed full once more and drank greedily as she lost herself in the pure delight of its taste.

She cried out startled as his teeth sank into the flesh of her neck but then his tongue slid forth to caress the hurt and she groaned with the shock of pleasure she felt tear through her at the sensation. She felt his hands slide down her body to take hold of her hips and then she felt him.

Hard and ready pressed firmly against the center of her need. Though they were separated by layers of garments she felt the heat of his flesh and gasped at the feel of it burning through her clothes and against her over eager flesh.

For a moment she felt cool marble beneath her before his hands were over her. Fingers seized hold of delicate silk forming fists that tore the fabric apart. Goose bumps rose on heated skin as the cool air played over it. Only to be burned by the heat of his breath and skin as the wine god worked his spell over her.

Seducing and enticing making her unspoiled body tremble beneath him with want of more. And he gave it. The haze of the drink lifted only when he penetrated her virgin flesh. Her startled cry died out as teeth pierced her left breast marking her a second time.

Blue eyes flew open to find her uncle stood in the room watching, waiting though for what she didn't know. Anger bubbled up inside her as she realized Hades had known her request would bring her to this. Lost in the embrace of the wine god desperate, wanton in her need of a man; reduced from princess to one of his lowly whores.

As Dionysus released his bite Artemis began to go cold. "FORGET HIM HUNTRESS, FOR NOW, YOU ARE MINE," he whispered and to prove it he sank his fangs in her throat once more as he drove her over the edge to release. She cried his name desperate for him to follow her but he did not, instead he eased out of her body to accommodate his master as he curled up behind her and entered her forbidden passage and began to move.

Artemis cried out with ecstasy at the sensation as one hand fondled her breasts and the others groped her feminine core. She pressed back against him as her eyes fell shut. Artemis lost herself in the drugging effect of him and before she knew what she was doing she was begging for him to take her harder to take her any way he wished to teach her his arts.

She gasped overwhelmed as his hand withdrew she begged for him not to leave her. Blue eyes shot open with shock as she felt her body invaded once more and she screamed as sweet seduction became horror as she found herself faced with Hades. The god of the underworld smirked as he began to move within her.

73

Terra lowered her binoculars with disgust. "I think we have a problem."

"Meaning?" Sam asked not caring for her look of revelation.

"I don't see Ian Broody. I don't think he's the one calling the shots in there."

"Damn it. Magnus Halden, you're sure?"

"I've never seen him before but Yeah, pretty sure."

"If he's here, he'll be far more dangerous. We can't move until he leaves."

"Why not?" Vince asked.

"Yeah, he's only a man. We can take him."

"No, if we go in there now it'll end badly."

"What makes ya so sure? Not that god nonsense?"

"It's not nonsense. If we want Anna alive we'll wait until he leaves."

"Fine," Terra muttered as she looked back to the house. She was glad to see Magnus seemed to be done with the woman. Having risen from her to dress. Relief washed through her as blue eyes opened; not Anna.

"What's happening in there?" Vince asked.

"Nothin'," Terra lied no point in dwelling on what she'd just seen. She lowered her spy glasses again to wait. She prayed, wherever Anna was in that place, she was beyond Magnus Halden's reach.

74

Artemis crawled down from the altar careful not to disturb the sleeping wine god. She picked up her ruined gown and pulled it on. With her power she mended the fabric restoring it before reclaiming her bow and quiver. She crossed the throne room to the parlor to inspect her image in the mirror. She smoothed out her hair before accessing the extent of the damage Dionysus had done. She found his mark displayed upon her neck and cursed. He'd bitten her and more than once she recalled with disgust now that her head had cleared again.

He'd marked her as one of his Bacchae. After this she would be bound to him, forced to return once a month when the moon was red. As she wrapped a silken scarf around her throat to hide his mark Hades emerged from the shadows and rested his hands upon her shoulders.

"POOR LITTLE ARTEMIS, YOU GAVE UP YOUR PURITY TO A DEVIL AND YOU'RE BOUND TO HIM," he mocked.

"You knew what would HAPPEN!"

"OF COURSE I KNEW. I NEVER DREAMED YOU'D MAKE SUCH A FOOLISH DEAL TO KEEP HER."

"WHY?"

"BECAUSE THAT WOMAN IS OUR ENEMY. THE MAN SHE LOVES A THREAT TO US. I NEEDED HER BROKEN TO DEFEAT HIM. YOU SHOULD HAVE WALKED AWAY."

"SHE DIDN'T DESERVE WHAT WAS DONE TO ME!"

"SHE IS A DAUGHTER OF EVE, THEY ALL DESERVE TO SUFFER. NEVER FORGET YOU ARE NOT MORTAL. YOUR PLACE IS BESIDE US; THE GODS. IF YOU CONSORT

WITH THE ANIMALS YOU'LL BE TREATED AS SUCH," Hades hissed as his hands played over her body, groping her reminding her of what he'd done.

"STOP!"

"DO NOT EVER INTERFERE IN MY AFFAIRS AGAIN OR I WILL PUT YOU IN YOUR PLACE GIRL. I'LL MAKE YOUR LITTLE TRIP INTO DIONYSUS'S VINEYARD SEEM LIKE A FAIRY TALE UNION BY COMPARISON TO THE NIGHTMARE I'LL LAY BEFORE YOU," Hades growled as his touch became more invasive changing from simply fondling to molestation.

"UNCLE, PLEASE," she cried desperate, aware that in his display of power and rage he'd stirred up his own lusts for the flesh. His mind beyond mere punishment to his desires.

"GO! TAKE YOUR VENGEANCE NOW, OH HUNTRESS, BEFORE I CHANGE MY MIND. YOUR PET WILL REMAIN UNSPOILED," Hades vowed as he let her go.

Artemis turned and fled the palace grateful to escape her uncle's wrath and lusts. Rage filled her at his words. They were monsters all of them, not one worthy of her father's crown. She'd see to it no more emerged from their prison and ensure none of them ever found Zeus's crown. No king would ever rise to rule over the gods or mortals again.

75

After stepping off the boat Zaharrah made her way back to her work space. She began the task of packing up her things. She shoved Anna's research in her bag and began gathering her equipment. She found her pen had been moved and froze, someone had been there. Picking up the pen she noted the stack of memos she'd written looked disheveled and picked them up. Flipping through she felt her heart constrict as there in the middle, she found a short message in a familiar hand.

Darrian. He'd been here. Careful to seem unaffected by the pile she read the note to herself.

"To those worthy, knowledge is given. Walk in the steps of the hunter and seek the heart of the poet. Follow the flight of the arrows path and the eyes of the goddess will show you the place where your secret waits."

Zaharrah blinked surprised by the cryptic nature of the message but reasoned that whatever it was he left for her to find he didn't want anyone else to discover it. She considered the opening line and reasoned it referred to Artemis and Apollo. She'd seen a text referring to the twins on one of the shelves as she worked through the records. Turning she moved in that direction.

When she located the text she noted that the image of an arrow was poised ready to fly. Doing as the note said she walked on down the row until she found the image of a peacock. Lifting the text she found, beneath it a small thumb drive which she pocketed.

"What secrets do you have for me?" Zaharrah whispered before returning to her workspace. Whatever they were it would have to wait until she was clear of the island.

It wasn't until the sun had set that Lance next saw Catharine. She was exactly where he'd left her six hours earlier and it left him uneasy.

"Hey, ready for a break?" He asked curious.

She blinked dazed like a woman coming out of a trance. "Yeah, I just need one more minute," she answered distracted as her fingers kept working.

"Are you hungry?"

"No."

"Something to drink maybe?"

"I'm fine."

"No, you're not, it's been six hours since I left you to work, you haven't moved from that spot. Did you eat anything at all today?"

"No."

"Catharine, ignoring yourself isn't going to help matters."

"I'll eat just as soon as I finish the chapter."

"Fine, but we're going out for a bit. It's not good for you to be here like this all day," Lance muttered.

"What makes you think you know what is or isn't good for me?" She snapped.

"I don't, all I know is I watched Dana do this same thing after she lost Heather. Try to bury herself in work to forget. It didn't work. She killed herself unable to deal with the grief."

"Damn it, detective, would you stop; please. I'm handling this the only way I know how to. Just let me finish the chapter and we will go, but, don't you stand there and compare me to a dead woman, I never met. I can assure you I have no plans to kill myself," Catharine snapped with disgust.

Lance flinched. Her words hit him like a slap in the face and he drew a breath looking for calm. He didn't want to fight with her but at the moment it felt like that was what she wanted. It was what she knew. Fight, apology, sex, quiet and fight again. A vicious cycle of abuse that had become her normal even when she'd been single she'd had Bryan to fight with.

"I'm not going to fight with you Serenity. I won't play that role for you. If you want to fight you can fight with yourself," he murmured as he took out his keys and got ready to go.

"Chapter's done okay, just give me a minute to save and freshen up," Catharine requested.

"Sure."

"Thanks, I'm sorry. I don't want to fight with you either I don't know why I said that it was cruel."

"Don't worry about it," Lance assured her. He watched as she saved her file and rose from the table before moving off down the hall. Lance eyed the laptop with curiosity wondering what she'd written but hesitated to look. It was her work he had no business poking through it without her knowing.

"You can take a peek if you want," Catharine's voice called from down the hall with amusement almost as if she knew he'd been thinking about it,

"Thanks," he answered before sliding into the chair she'd abandoned.

'Green eyes studied the dead with disgust as a sense of relief washed through him. It wasn't his Ashella before him but whoever was killing these women was clearly hunting her. Each victim had her same general appearance. Each wound, a brand, the killer then sliced out. His mark; which meant they knew of his claim but didn't care. They meant to make Ashella their own even if it killed her.'

Lance blinked as he came to the end of the last page. It wasn't long before he understood. Catharine had brought Ashella and the others into the present. Davrik has been searching for her since the end of the events in Heart of Stone as have others but no one has been able to find her. Now someone has taken to killing look-a-likes to draw her out. It was brilliant.

Lance wanted to go back further to see where the story began but wouldn't do so, he wanted to finish Heart of Stone before he read more.

"Well?"

"It's good so far," he said as he closed the laptop. He noted

Catharine had changed and it looked as though she'd brushed her hair.

"Here this is yours. I hope you'll like it," Catharine stated as she handed him a thumb drive.

"Thanks. I'll read it later. For now, let's see about dinner," Lance prompted he shoved the drive in his pocket and led her out of the house to his car. Serenity could wait for a little while.

77

Anna lowered shaking hands from her ears as all around her fell silent. The cries of pain and pleasure had ended. Whatever Artemis had been forced to endure for her sake had come to an end. She heard Hades earlier, his words though unclear had been laced with anger. The only thing she was sure of was that Artemis had left.

The unsettling silence was broken by the sound of feet shuffling outside the door.

"I WOULDN'T TOUCH THAT IF I WERE YOU," Hades voice warned.

"WHY NOT? THE HUNTRESS IS GONE I'M WITHIN MY RIGHT TO HAVE HER PET."

"SHE SEALED THE DOOR AGAINST US. IF YOU TRY TO ENTER YOU'LL BE POWERLESS WHEN YOU TOUCH HER."

"DAMN YOUR NIECE. WHY HAS SHE INTERFERED?"

"I DON'T KNOW, BUT I FEAR SOON SHE'LL BE DEAD TO US."

"I WANT WHAT'S MINE!" Dionysus raged.

"THE DOCTOR IS NOT YOURS YET BROTHER," Hades snapped.

"MY INFLUENCE UPON HER HAS BEGUN TO BEAR FRUIT. SHE IS AS MUCH MINE AS EMILY, SHE WILL DRINK FROM MY CUP; JUST AS HER MASTER DID."

"REMEMBER, ARTEMIS ONLY DRANK TO SATISFY YOUR DEMAND. SHE WOULD NEVER HAVE TAKEN THAT CUP ON HER OWN. I GAVE YOU THE PRINCESS AND YOU WILL KEEP HER SO LONG AS YOU REMAIN LOYAL TO

ME. IF YOU EVER THINK TO PLOT AGAINST ME AS YOU
DID HERMES I WILL DESTROY YOU," Hades hissed.

"WHAT OF THE WOMAN--YOU SAID--"

"YES, I KNOW WHAT I SAID. I WANT HER BROUGHT
LOW BEFORE HER PROTECTOR SHOWS UP BUT UNTIL I
CAN FIND A WAY TO GET AROUND THAT BARRIER
NEITHER OF US SHALL TOUCH THOSE DOORS."

Anna sank down on the bed relief sweeping through her mind.
They couldn't reach her. For now she was safe. .

Lance sat across from Catharine in the quiet corner of his favorite restaurant. He watched with a growing disquiet as she picked at her meal. She'd barely touched it since she got it and had said even less. She was lost in her own thoughts and her silence was deafening.

His gaze moved from her plate to her face settling on her bandaged cheek. "Does it hurt?" He muttered realizing perhaps the act of eating as he'd requested might be uncomfortable for her.

"What?" she asked as if brought back to the moment suddenly by his voice.

"Are your cuts causing you discomfort?"

Catharine blinked as if coming out of a daze. She lifted a bite to her lips and chewed wincing a little as she did. "A bit yes," she confessed.

"I'm sorry. We could have gone someplace where the food--"

"Don't this is fine I just didn't consider that what I ordered might upset my injury. I should have gotten something softer."

"You still can," Lance offered.

"No, I wanted steak and I'll eat it, just maybe not right now," Catharine muttered.

"We'll take it with us."

Catharine nodded turning her attention to her baked potato instead. Lance finished off his salad trying to ignore the strange silence that had settled in between them. Before she was taken they'd not been able to stop talking now there was this awkwardness between them as if they couldn't find the words to speak around what had happened. The strange sexual tension that had surrounded them had diminished. It seemed with Dionysus no longer in close proximity his influence had abated. The realization came as both a relief and disappointment.

It was nice to know they were both clear headed and she wouldn't be troubled with illness induced by a wine she'd not tasted in days, but on the same token he'd liked feeling that strange burning in his blood around her. He'd not felt that kind of desire in some time. The brief but violent jolt of the true taste of lust had left him keenly aware of his maleness. The nudge reminded him he was human and he had needs for companionship he'd ignored for too long.

A companionship he'd begun to think of exploring with her but though she sat mere inches across from him her mind was miles away, beyond his reach. Just as Dana's had been after her path crossed that of the killers. A chill ran through him as he wondered if Kurt would claim his final victim from beyond the grave.

For a moment he saw a flash of the madman standing over her, a hand on her naked body tormenting her, lust drunk mind with the promise of what he would do to her, but not giving it. He saw those haunted eyes that graced the cover of her novels and curled his hand in a fist at his side as rage washed through him.

No! He wouldn't let the madman claim her as he'd claimed Dana. He'd keep Catharine close. Watch her, make sure she didn't finish the slide into madness she'd begun with *Dark Heart*, he'd help her to finish the transformation she'd begun and draw her back from the darkness when she got too close. Keep her grounded in reality, Lance vowed.

If he was going to do it though he'd have to walk away from the current case. The chief would understand, Lance reasoned as he finished his meal. When she was done eating he'd take her home and see her to bed then he'd call the captain and inform him of his intentions before turning in himself. Perhaps in the morning things would look better.

79 Miami, Florida

Zaharrah fell into her bed after stepping in the room and dropping her bag. She was asleep as soon as her head hit the pillow. Exhaustion from the day's events having overtaken her.

Her mind slipped into dreams almost immediately. In her dream she stood upon a sea of sand dunes.

Sand stung her eyes and wherever she looked there was no end to the desert in sight. Her lips were rough and cracked, caked with dried blood. She'd been wandering for days with no water left. If she didn't find shelter and water soon she would die out here before she found what she was looking for.

Zaharrah blinked as she tried to recall why she'd come there but the heat had long since fried her mind, all she knew for sure was that someone pursued her in this cursed place. Looking back the way she'd come she saw him atop the furthest dune looking down on her, a dark figure poised ready to strike.

She turned and fled running further from him, keenly aware that for each step she took away from him, he'd taken a dozen toward her. Zaharrah trembled at the feel of his icy breath on her skin. Death. He'd found her at last, here in this sand sea just as she'd foreseen all those years ago. As she trudged on she saw footprints in the sand ahead of her and cursed knowing she was running in circles and going nowhere. Her steps only brought him closer.

Looking down she saw her hiking boots had been replaced by golden sandals, her normal attire replaced by a Grecian gown. An icy hand touched her shoulder and her heart skipped a beat. She was just outside his dream realm, one more step and she would see him.

"ZAHARRAH, COME TURN AND FACE YOUR GOD," his voice whispered a soothing balm that eased the pain she felt from the deserts heat.

"No."

"LOOK AT ME MY LOVELY ONE, AND I WILL GIVE YOU WATER TO QUENCH YOUR THIRST," he offered.

Zaharrah licked dry lips craving nothing more than a drop of water to wet her tongue but she did not turn. She knew her time to face this monster had not yet come.

"Only the creator's son can quench this thirst," Zaharrah breathed. "Father if it is your will let my thirst be eased," she whispered as she shrugged off the Fallen One's grasp and the wind stilled. She walked beyond his reach as rain fell from the heavens to give her ease.

"THIS IS NOT DONE YET ZAHARRAH, YOU WILL BE MINE," Hades hissed as the rain carried her beyond his reach.

80

Hades roared in rage as his mind was thrown out of the dream realm. He'd come so close. He'd seen her if only for a minute. Spoken with her. Been close enough to touch her. She lingered right at the border between sleep and the dream realm. Lost in the desert of Tartarus near the edge of the river Styx on the edge of life and death. If she'd accepted the water he'd offered her she'd have been bound to him just as his Persephone was. At the last she'd cried out to the Father.

Hades smashed the mirror in the bed chamber at the thought. Always his Father embraced these flawed mortals and refused him for his part in the rebellion. These men who betrayed him and misused him and spat in his face time and again. For them God had forgiveness no matter how they wronged him. Why were they so special? Hades felt fury roll inside him. He hated mankind with a passion that no other knew.

Had he been given free rein to use his power without discrimination, he'd cut every last one of the spineless worms down in some horrific fashion, but his power was bound. Shackled by the candle's flame and the scythe he wielded, only when the appointed time came could he strike unless the soul he followed answered his call.

Zaharrah had answered his call years ago and would again soon. Somewhere in the desert their paths would cross and then at last she would be his. He would bind her to him and make her his queen and with Zeus's crown upon his brow they would rule over all the earth. The hell, God had prepared for him and his brethren for their rebellion, he would make sure she tasted when her time came so that he would never be left alone ever again. He would know love in that pit and it would bring him ease.

Lance emerged from his room after a night of fitful sleep hoping to find Catharine still in bed instead he found her sitting once again at the dining room table, typing away.

"Detective--I'm sorry, did I wake you?"

"No, I--How long have you been at it?"

"Since a little after midnight."

"Did you sleep?"

"A little."

"Nightmares?"

Catharine said nothing more, simply turned back to her laptop.

"Can I get you something to eat or drink?"

"I don't want anything at the moment."

"You're sure, little sleep, nothing to eat you'll burn yourself out."

"Let me finish the chapter," Catharine requested.

Lance nodded before moving into the kitchen to prepare something. When it was ready he'd interrupt her again. He just needed to keep his eye on her and she'd be fine," he assured himself as he tried to relax but the warning signals in his mind would not be silent. Every instinct in him told him this was just the calm before the storm. When the flood let loose it would be bad, enough even to drown both of them, if he wasn't careful.

82

Catharine finished the current chapter and saved, trying to quell her mounting irritation at Lance's interruptions. She understood he was trying to look out for her, but she didn't appreciate it. She knew what she was doing. Burying herself in her work had always been her way of dealing with her problems. The more she worked the easier it was to dismiss her nightmares. If he'd just let her be she'd get through this latest horror the same as the others before.

He meant well, she told herself as she put down the lid and waited for him to return. He only wanted to make sure she was okay. After breakfast she'd be free to work uninterrupted as he'd be busy with his case and by the time he got back she'd make sure she was in her room. Whatever his concerns, he'd not invade her personal space. She'd be free to work without further distractions.

At the rate she was going she'd have Serenity in the woods running from her pursuer by the end of the week.

Catharine smiled at the thought at this rate she'd have the last novel done in time for Christmas. She pictured herself sitting at a table signing copies. Could hear Bryan's voice in her head as he stood over her commenting on sales and she froze.

Suddenly without warning she was cold and scared. She felt the bite of rope tearing into her wrists and ankles as that same voice spoke of cuts and tears. She felt the cool bite of steel on her skin as she was stripped bare and trembled.

Her eyes shot open as she ran from the image. Bryan was gone. She'd never see him again. He'd never really existed Kurt had made him up as a way to watch her.

"Hey, you okay?" Lance asked as he came back in the room.

"Yeah, I was just thinking about the book and imagining the response, for a minute I was picturing Bryan's reaction and then--"

"You remembered he's gone," Lance said as he set down their food.

She nodded. "He was the closest thing I had to a friend--"

"I'm sorry Catharine," he whispered as he drew her into his arms to comfort her.

"He was going to rape and torture me to death unless I became his accomplice. He wanted me to kill for him. Thought I could, because of Nivali but I couldn't." She pushed him away not wanting his comfort; feeling unworthy of it.

"He never really knew you Catharine," Lance assured her as he brushed her hair away from her eyes.

"When I wrote Nivali for the first time I put the pen down, she scared me so bad. That she had come from my mind--" Catharine swallowed, unable to go on, she turned away from him unable to face him. He made his living catching killers and she had one lurking in the shadows of her mind.

"She came from your imagination Catharine. She's not you. She's the polar opposite of who you are," Lance stated as he drew her back against his chest; refusing to let her go as she desired.

"He wanted me to bury a knife in Gale's heart for him and I wanted to if only to end her suffering, but I knew if I did Hecate would have taken over my body. She wanted me to kill so she could become Nivali."

"You're not a monster Serenity, you never were."

"But it's in me and if I were pushed, if I snap--"

"If it didn't happen then, it won't. Don't torture yourself that way. You could never be Nivali. It's not in you."

"How can you say that? You barely know me," Catharine snapped in fury as she moved out of his embrace.

"I'm a cop Serenity, a homicide detective. I know the warning signs. I have instincts that warn me against potential threats to me or society at large. You're not one of them. The only person I'm worried about you hurting right now is yourself."

"I told you detective, I'm not contemplating ways to kill myself," she hissed in outrage.

"Maybe not, but you're not taking care of yourself either. A couple hours sleep here and there and a meal; when I ask you to come up for air; isn't healthy."

"That's not fair! It's only been a day--" she blinked stunned over twenty-four hours had come and gone since Lance saved her from the basement. Trouble was when she wasn't writing it felt like only a minute.

"I know, a little over twenty-four hours, but how many hours of hell did you face before I got there Serenity? What nightmares did you endure that are keeping you from sleep now?"

"Detective--"

"I know you're not ready and I'm sorry for pushing but your silence scares me Catharine. I've walked this road before and I don't want to see that madman win because he claims his final victim from beyond the grave."

"That won't happen," Catharine assured him before sitting back down at the table. She took the plate he set down and grabbing a fork and spoon began to eat. She watched as he sighed before sitting down to do so as well.

83

Zaharrah woke with a pounding headache and groaned as she wondered why. She reached up to brush her hair away from her face and found that most of it was still tied back. She growled as she pulled it down. "Well, that would be the reason," she muttered as she opened her eyes. Zaharrah's next oddity of the morning was to find she still had on her boots. She hissed as the night before came back to mind; she hadn't done anything when she got in last night.

Crawling out of bed she found her bag still laying by the door. It was with the thought of work that she remembered her brother's note and the flash drive she'd discovered. Now wide awake and annoyed with herself to boot Zaharrah pulled the drive from her pocket and loaded it in her laptop.

When the device was open she clicked on the file it held and cursed as a password prompt covered the screen. She tried Darrian's birthday, then her own, their parents anniversary, her anniversary, his name in numbers, her name, their last name, their mother's maiden name, his favorite weapon, his favorite movie, book but nothing worked.

Finally, she tried Brooke's name with his and still nothing happened. Zaharrah growled in irritation and shut the drive. "All right, brother, what is it?" she asked the room but found no answer. With a sigh she set it aside she'd think on the matter and try again later for now, she'd turn her focus to Anna's notes and see if she could sort out what Ian wanted from the other lost cities.

84 Athens, Greece

Sam gazed through his binoculars into the picture windows of Hermes palace through the front parlor and into what he figured had been Hermes throne room. He noted several piles of rubble along the walls riddled with gun fire and reasoned Hades was responsible. "Why destroy them?" Sam muttered to himself puzzled.

"Why destroy what?" Vince questioned.

"The statues."

"Not and art fan," Terra suggested with disinterest. Sam ignored them both studying his enemy, the man Magnus Halden he knew was no more. The figure before him was the god of the underworld: Death, himself in the flesh. At the moment Hades was studying desert maps of the middle-east marking locations on them. The first point he recognized as the location for Sodom, having been there. The second he assumed would be Gomorrah as Hades marked the third and the fourth points after circling Zoah, Sam wondered why Death seemed so interested in the locations of the other plains cities.

"Well, what is he doing?" Terra demanded impatient. She'd been slow to give up watch and seemed anxious since her last watch. He wondered what she'd seen but if asked, she said nothing. He didn't believe her but figured if he was going to keep her cool, he best answer her.

"Studying a map," Sam turned his own question over in his mind trying to sort out his enemies mind. The only thing Broody had been interested in was the key and the crown. If Hades was looking at the lost cities-- Sam pulled out his phone and punched in Zaharrah's number.

"Hello."

"Miss Lynch, do you know if when they explored Sodom and Gomorrah they found the kings remains."

"Why do you ask?"

"A hunch."

"Let me check Anna's notes."

Sam waited for his answer while Terra looked at him in question.

"According to Anna's notes, no. The king was not found at either sight. What's on your mind Mr. Abrams?"

"I'm thinking the reason no one has found the scepter or the crown is because they were given to the missing king who must be at one of the other still missing cities."

"That's why Broody's sending me out into that god forsaken desert."

"Maybe. I'll let you know if I get confirmation from my research team. For now watch your back because I suspect your Mr. Halden is headed that way too."

"Yeah, I know."

"Dreams," Sam muttered.

"Visions," she corrected.

"He starts turning up in your dreams be on guard."

"I'm well aware."

"How?"

"All will be revealed at the appointed time," Zaharrah said before the phone went dead.

Sam cursed. Her answer was about as cryptic as his winged friend's. Turning his focus back to his target, he watched as Hades poured sand on the two points of the map then touched the first one. His fingers sank through the sand and into the page a green glow surrounding them. He repeated the process with the other and when he was done a smile curved his lips.

Sam jaw tightened it was a good bet Hades had his destination. He watched as the lord of the underworld blew the sand off the map and looked up. His dark eyes glowed green as they locked with Sam's. Lips parted. "I see you Mr. Abrams," he said clear as day though Sam could not hear his voice.

Sam lowered his binoculars startled. Hades knew he was there. He wished the annoying Fallen One would leave and go get his damn crown. As he stood and watched, Sam was aware of Terra's voice asking him questions but he ignored her as he handed the spy glasses off to Vince. Death was waiting but for what he didn't know.

85

Anna woke to the feel of a physical darkness around her and swiped her hands over her skin to tear it away. She blinked as she found herself not in the secret prison but Artemis's chambers. She was safe here at least for now. The darkness she felt was Hades power not in here but beyond the door being used. Her thoughts turned to his threat the night before the one that had her revealing her deal with Zaharrah to steal the key.

"What sort of threats," she heard herself ask again.

"Obvious ones Anna. Your family, your friends, anyone you care about I'll cut them down like that." Anna heard his fingers snap in her mind and jumped. "Sam is close by, I'll let him walk in here to save you and then take him out in front of you." his words brushed over her skin like a cold touch.

Her thoughts drifted to Hades argument with Dionysus later that evening. Sam was a threat to his plans. If he really was close by she had to get out of there or Hades would use her as bait to kill him. Anna moved for the doors and the seal pulsed. Artemis's parting words washed through her mind.

"NO MATTER WHAT, DO NOT OPEN THIS DOOR."

Anna froze taking a step back, the moment she opened the door they would know it and everything Artemis had sacrificed would be meaningless. She could go nowhere until Artemis returned. "And what if she doesn't return? What will I do then? What will happen to Sam and the others?" Anna wondered as fear began to creep in around her.

86

Artemis walked through the ruins of the greatest of the king's four cities in the direction of his palace, none of the workers paid her any mind thanks to her disguise, she blended right in. She stepped into the temple and walked past the graven image to study the map. Hermes may not remember the location of her Father's crown but she did. She recalled all too well the day her Father's mantle was lost and where.

As Artemis studied the map of the king's domain her mind drifted to that fateful day.

Artemis walked behind her uncle Hades through the gate into the heart of Admah, the people around her fell before his feet as he passed on his way to the palace they sang songs of praise and offered pledges and tokens of their loyalty. As they entered the palace the king bowed low.

"My lord we are honored at your presence."

"AS YOU KNOW MY BROTHER, OUR KING HAS FALLEN, AS IS OUR LAW HIS CROWN COMES TO YOU FOR SAFEKEEPING AND TO HONOR HIS TREATY WITH YOU. WITH IT I PRESENT AS WELL ARTEMIS'S HAND AS A TOKEN AND PLEDGE TO UNITE OUR PEOPLE FOREVER."

Artemis blinked and the memory faded. "WE'D HAVE ALL BEEN BETTER OFF IF NONE OF THOSE CURSED THINGS HAD EVER SEEN THE LIGHT OF DAY AGAIN," she muttered before she turned from the map and left. As she walked past the fresco of the gods she nudged it with her father's power and watched with satisfaction as it fell from the wall and shattered into a million pieces. These petty gods would not rise again to rule men.

87

Hermes watched with interest as Artemis walked out of the ruins of the ruined city. He'd been watching and waiting for the woman Zaharrah's arrival, instead he found himself looking upon an angry huntress and wondering what she was doing there. He considered for a moment following her to see where she would lead but then thought better of it. If she saw him, she'd kill him with one of her arrows. No, better to send a spy. Maybe a servant to make a treaty, after all he still had in his possession the answer she sought most. The location of her twin.

He'd send a spy first if she spared it then a messenger would follow. Perhaps if he restored Apollo to her she would let the rest go, or at least allow him to live long enough to locate his crown. Once he had it, her power would diminish and no one could dare oppose him again. Then he would take back his palace and make Hades would be bride his whore and his prisoner, well she'd take her rightful place at his side as queen of the earth.

88 Miami, Florida

Zaharrah sat reading over Anna's notes, contemplating, forgetting Ian Broody's request to go back to Sodom and find the location of the missing plains cities. She wasn't a member of the Black Hand anymore. It wasn't her responsibility to keep the mantles safe. That task had fallen to Sam and Anna, nor was she responsible for the stone tablets, that was Darrian's duty. If she wanted she could just hop on the plane and leave this place. She didn't have to go to the desert.

Didn't have to meet Death face to face. She could run. Yeah, and the moment she did, he'd chase her. He'd enjoy it she imagined as every myth she'd ever read had the old gods chasing after some woman till he found her. They always found their woman and managed to trick her into their bed. Running would prove pointless. In the end he'd find her.

Member of the order or not she felt obligated to do the job. Her brother was missing and Anna captured. She was the only other person on the face of the earth who knew what was happening and could stop it.

Zaharrah sighed and counted herself a fool. She was going out to that desert and was walking straight for a meeting with Death. She hoped when the time came she'd be able to walk away as well.

Her morose thoughts were interrupted by the ringing of her phone. "Hello."

"Miss Lynch, your friend's ride has arrived they want to meet tomorrow at one to go over the plan."

"Tell me where."

"Pawn shop, two blocks from your hotel, they'll be waiting."

Zaharrah heard the familiar sound of the line disconnecting and closed her phone. Everything was set, there was nothing more she could do now but wait.

89

Catharine cursed as the page she was working on was covered by another screen that read task complete.

"What is it?" Lance asked as he looked up from his own laptop to her. She'd forgotten he was sitting there. After breakfast he'd informed her he was going nowhere. If she wanted to work that was fine, he could read but he would be dragging her up for air from time to time to eat and she better get used to the idea.

"The computer finished running my search. It just blocked my page in the middle of an intense scene," Catharine muttered.

"The search on the crown?"

"Yeah."

"What did it find? I'm nearly done with Heart of Stone I can get started on that," Lance said with a yawn.

"Don't you want some sleep first?" she asked recalling he'd not been to bed. When she'd balked at the notion he'd stayed up with her and kept right on reading.

"Were you going to turn in?" he countered.

"Where are you at?"

"Rachel is facing Nivali."

"You are almost done."

"Yep. So what did your search give us to read?"

Catharine clicked on the box and it took her to the minimized search window. One book."

"Just one."

"Your Mr. Abrams isn't going to like this."

"What is it?"

"Old tale out of Zoah pertaining to the fall of the plains cities a story about a festival in which the king of the plains was presented the crown of a god."

"Oh, hell."

"Yeah."

Catharine watched as Lance pulled out his phone and dialed Sam. She closed the search and returned to her book. Knowing there was nothing more she could do.

"Sam, it's me we found your crown but you're not going to like it." Catharine pictured the other man on a green hillside somewhere staring at a large house demanding to know where.

"According to a myth out of Zoah it was given to the king of the plains. Did Anna mention if they found the king's remains?" Lance paused again as Sam answered him. "Then it must still be under all that sand somewhere," Lance muttered. Silence settled again only to be broken by Lance once more. "Have you found Anna?"

Catharine lifted her head to study her companion, the grim look on his face told her he didn't like the answer. "Right. Be careful. I mean that's Death you're dealing with and given his host it's a good bet he knows who you are." "Yeah, you to." Lance answered after another short pause before hanging up.

"Did he find her?" Catharine asked.

"Yeah, in some house near the Parthenon, trouble is--"

"Hades is in control there not Hermes."

"Yeah."

"They're waiting for him to go." Catharine said with understanding.

"Exactly."

"You're worried."

Lance nodded. "He was Magnus Halden before--"

"So, Hades knows about Sam the real Sam I mean," Catharine stated.

"Right."

"Puts him at a disadvantage."

"If he knows who he is why not just kill him," Lance muttered voicing the question that troubled his mind. "Why toy with him?"

"Maybe he can't," Catharine offered.

"What do you mean?"

"What if his power is bound somehow?"

"Meaning?"

"Well, when death was unleashed as a plague it was limited striking only the first born of those who were not marked."

"Okay."

"Perhaps he's still bound so he's only able to take those whose time is up."

"Then why bluff?"

"I don't know," Catharine confessed.

"Maybe if you believe the lie it becomes real," Lance muttered.

"Could be, so now what do we do?"

"What do you mean?"

"The crown has been located, but Sam can't go after it not until Anna's safe."

"Well, we can't go get it. Broody's team will never let us near the dig site."

We can't just leave it for Hermes or Hades to find," Catharine argued.

"Sam will handle it."

"So we do nothing?" Catharine asked incredulous.

"We pray," Lance muttered.

"Great plan detective," Catharine groused, her voice thick with sarcasm.

"You got any better ideas, I'm willing to hear them," Lance snapped.

"I'll think of something," she muttered before turning her focus back to her laptop.

"Well, while you think, I'll see about breakfast." Lance sighed before saving his place and closing the laptop.

90

Artemis stood upon the top of a sand dune in a sea of them, in her mind's eye she could see it as it had looked in its glory days. The crown jewel of the kings cities Zeboim. The one where his queen resided. Artemis sneered at the thought of the other woman. The king's beloved had been nothing precious at all. The scepter she'd been given was no gift but a bribe, the price at which she'd given her body to the sea god.

Artemis pictured the cursed thing in her mind and drawing upon her power called it forth. It rose out of the sand to rest in her hands a golden scepter bejeweled with pearl and lapis lazuli. "You shall not ever wake Uncle," Artemis whispered before she snapped the scepter in two. Artemis felt a jolt as the sea kings power wrapped around her and filled her. She dropped the pieces to the sand. She turned ready to move on to the king's city and the crown but found her path blocked by a servant of the creator.

"Artemis, peace."

"What do you want here messenger?"

"I bring words of warning. The witch has found your father's key, she cannot be allowed to take it to your uncle."

"Then stop her!"

"I am but a messenger, as you said, but you are more, go, now stop her yourself and then see to the crown, it cannot be destroyed."

"Then what do I do?"

"When the time comes you will know," he answered, he touched her brow and vanished. The location of the key filled her mind. She looked across the sand in the direction the crown lay and hesitated. It shouldn't wait. A shadow passed overhead and Artemis cursed as she spotted the small falcon.

"Hermes!" she roared the name in rage before lightning struck the bird killing it. The crown would wait for now, or Hermes would follow her to it. She'd see to the key as the messenger bade. Her mind made up Artemis left the desert.

91

Hades roared in fury as he felt Poseidon's power shatter. "ARTEMIS!" Death bellowed in outrage, aware the only explanation was that the Huntress had turned on him. She alone beside him knew where the scepter and her Father's crown lay. If she'd broken one the crown would follow he had to reach it before that happened. The problem was his spirit told him the time to go was not yet upon him. Zaharrah was not in the desert yet. He couldn't leave until she was on the move. It was why he lingered here. Their paths were meant to cross in the desert it was then he would hold all he sought. Until she entered the desert he was forced to wait.

"MR. YORK!"

"Yes, sir," the frightened mortal answered aware somehow that the man before him was no longer his employer, despite the fact he'd not been present to witness the change.

"BEGIN PHASE TWO."

"Me sir?"

"YES, I WANT YOU TO SEE TOO THINGS IN THE DESERT PERSONALLY. IF YOU SEE ANY TRACE OF IAN BROODY I WILL BE NOTIFIED."

"Understood and what of the other matter?"

"MISS GALLAGHER'S LOCATION HAS BEEN DETERMINED. I'LL HAVE THE ARTIFACT SOON," Hades replied.

"I see."

"GO. MY CHOPPER IS WAITING."

"Now, but I just got--" Russell York began with objection then froze. "As you say," he answered hastily sensing the danger his words brought.

Hades watched as the man left before turning his gaze to a pile of rubble in the room. "COME BROTHER, HE'S GONE."

Dionysus emerged from the shadows eyes weary. "YOU CALLED, MY LORD."

"YES, I'VE BEEN PONDERING OUR LITTLE DILEMMA OVER THE DOOR AND I WANT YOU TO RESUME YOUR ASSAULT ON DR. GALLAGHER'S MIND."

"TO WHAT END?" Dionysus asked intrigued.

"WORK AT LURING HER OUT OF THE ROOM. AFTER LOOKING AT THE SEAL CLOSER IT SEEMS THAT IF SHE CROSSES THROUGH IT WILLINGLY THE GOOD DOCTOR WILL BECOME FAIR GAME ONCE MORE."

"I SEE. IT WILL BE MY PLEASURE," Dionysus said with a laugh.

"I'LL LEAVE YOU TO YOUR WORK THEN," Hades said before he withdrew to his chambers. As he sank down on the bed a warm body turned toward him, fingers brushing over his chest. Hades seized Pamela's hand removing it from him. "DIONYSUS IS IN THE THRONE ROOM LADY, GO SEEK HIS TOUCH IF YOUR FLESH HAS NEED. I'VE NO DESIRE OF YOU HARLOT, MY BRIDE IS CLOSE NOW," he said with dismissal.

"My lord? I thought--"

"YOU BELIEVED I'D TAKE YOU AND MAKE YOU MY QUEEN AFTER YOU POLLUTED YOUR FLESH WITH NOT ONE BUT TWO OF MY BROTHERS' SEED. FOOLISH WOMAN. KNOW YOUR PLACE, YOU HAVE BEEN DIMINISHED BY YOUR ACT; NOT A QUEEN, BUT THE WHORE OF THE FALLEN," Hades hissed and he watched with satisfaction as she crawled out of his bed and slunk away to seek his brother.

Once alone he closed his eyes and lost himself in his plans aware that the time to act was drawing near .

92

Zaharrah stepped inside the Miami pawn shop five minutes until one and began to browse. As she was studying the assortment of hand guns in the back case she heard the approach of booted feet. Checking the reflection in the mirror to her left she got a glimpse of her contact. At least she reasoned it was him. To an untrained eye he looked like an ordinary Joe who'd wandered in off the beach. Blonde hair, brown eyes, a full tan, but she knew better. Under the playful smile and easy nature; was a killer. He was large intimidating and well-muscled. Ex-military maybe.

"Miss Lynch?"

"In the flesh," she answered.

He smiled at that amused. The flicker in his eyes told her it wasn't what he'd expected.

"Follow me."

Zaharrah turned and followed the man around the counter into the back and through a door.

On the other side five others sat around a table. A nondescript bunch of men and women some like her contact looked like they came from the beach, others like they had fled from Central American persecution. Not one looked out of place in the area. More like locals than outsiders.

"Miss Lynch, my crew. Best extraction team on US soil," the gentleman boasted.

"And you are?"

"Who I am is of no concern. We are the wolf pack."

Zaharrah blinked at the name knowing it. She'd heard Gunnar mention them a couple times.

"You're familiar with the name," the commander said pleased.

She nodded.

"Good. Then you know we can help your friend."

"Her name is Dr. Silvers," Zaharrah said as she tossed a photo of the woman on the table. She works in the northern end of the dig. That is where you'll extract her," Zaharrah added before tossing a photo of the dig site down beside the first.

"Why not the hotel?" A woman with dark hair asked.

"The staff is on Broody's payroll. We want to get her away clean without witnesses. We go in at night when she's working and there's a skeleton crew on staff. Fly her straight out so no one can follow."

"What do you mean we?" the commander asked.

"I'll be assisting you. There is Intel I've been promised once she's clear."

"We can deliver it," another man on the team argued.

"No. No one talks to her but me," Zaharrah snapped.

"Commander--"

"You heard the lady, she rides along. If you're going Miss Lynch, I suggest you be sure you can keep up."

"I can," she assured him before the group began to discuss at further length the plan she was presenting. Things were in place but it did nothing to ease her mind. She felt the cool chill of Hades touch upon her and knew he was seeking her yet again in the dream realm. He was aware that their time of meeting was now close at hand.

93

Dionysus rose from Pamela's side his power strengthened by her amorous desires. He crossed the throne room to the double doors that barred his way to Artemis's pet and probed her mind gently looking to see what her current state was. He found her resting and smiled. The wine god pushed his power beneath the door toward the sleeping woman. He pictured it in his mind settling over her like a thick blanket of fog. The woman Anna stirred in her sleep turning from her side to her back.

"RELEASE," he whispered and the mental block he'd set in place to do as Hades bid crumbled. The mist sank into her flesh as his power washed over her and through her.

Dionysus sent a second wave of power at her and as it sank into her, his mind slipped through the crack in her mental guard to look within. The wine god smiled to find that the small vine that had begun to grow had gone wild as his power swept through her anew. His influence had taken root and was beginning to bear fruit.

As he moved deeper, he found her lost in a nightmare; Hades threats had shaped and wrought. One she sought to escape. Dionysus plucked a grape and indulged in the taste, if she wanted an exit he'd be more than willing to give it. The wine god drew upon his power and let it wash over her again.

"ANNA, COME FORGET THIS DEATH AND EMBRACE THE PLEASURE LIFE HAS TO OFFER YOU," he whispered entreating her to come to him in a quiet corner of her mind and find peace.

94

Anna heard the faint whisper offering her escape and knew instantly she was not alone or awake.

"I'm dreaming," she whispered with relief and understanding. The nightmare faded and her surroundings altered. She was no longer in her prison but outdoors somewhere in the midst of a small vineyard. "I will not come to you Fallen One. Your peace would bind me in chains. Take your fruit and be gone from me."

"OH, MY SWEET, NAIVE LADY, THIS IS NOT MY VINEYARD IT'S YOURS," Dionysus whispered as he emerged from the shadows.

"Mine?" She asked with stunned disbelief.

"MY TOUCH PLANTED A SEED IN YOUR MIND. ONE YOU'VE DWELLED UPON AND LET TAKE ROOT. IT'S GIVEN ME PASSAGE HERE. I SAW IT BLOSSOM AND BEAR FRUIT THE LAST TIME I ENTERED HERE. FRUIT I'VE TASTED. YOU YEARN FOR YOUR LOVE IN A WAY THAT LEAVES ME REELING AT ITS TASTE," Dionysus murmured.

"Anna," a familiar voice called from somewhere in the distance.

"He's not real," she muttered to herself.

"HE CAN BE AS REAL AS YOU WANT AND YOU CAN HAVE AS MUCH OF HIM AS YOU DESIRE HERE. HE'S WAITING FOR YOU. WILL YOU NOT ANSWER HIM NOW?"

"Not with you here."

"WOULD YOU PREFER THE NIGHTMARE THEN?"

"No."

"THEN GO, FLY TO YOUR LOVE. WHAT HARM IS THERE IN INDULGING YOURSELF IN A BIT OF COMFORT IN THE MIDST OF YOUR CAPTIVITY. AFTER ALL YOU'VE SUFFERED DO YOU THINK IT WRONG TO SEEK EASE," Dionysus whispered.

"I don't want a dream," Anna said her voice weak, lacking conviction.

"Anna where are you," Sam's voice called again more desperate.

"Over here," she whispered unable to not answer.

"WILL YOU MAKE HIM SEEK YOU THEN?" Dionysus asked amused.

"Leave me Fallen One," she demanded, before she turned from him to go. She wandered through the vineyard alone and afraid. Afraid of the nightmare she'd walked out of, the harsh reality that waited for her upon waking and of herself. The wine god was right she did want Sam. As if the mere thought of him had conjured him, the dream image appeared before her. His blue eyes lit with relief and he moved to embrace her.

"No Sam, you're not real," she whispered as she prayed for strength. His arms enfolded her but had no substance as she turned her back to him.

"Anna?"

"You're a dream," she said closing her eyes. Tears fell from under her lashes.

"What's wrong?" He asked gently.

"I'm scared," she admitted.

"It'll be okay."

Anna smiled despite herself. "I wish you were here Sam," she whispered in confession as she closed her eyes.

"What do you want from me Anna?"

"Just hold me a while," she requested as she leaned back into his embrace. His chest became solid and warm, his arms wrapped around her shoulders; held her close.

"I've got you," he assured her his voice gentle as he held her close, offering her the comfort she sought.

95 SOMEWHERE IN THE BERMUDA TRIANGLE, ATLANTIS

Zaharrah tied her long hair back in a tight bun before pulling a black ski mask down over her face. She like the rest of her team was clad from head to foot in black. Zaharrah checked the clip in her gun to ensure they were blanks. For her plan to work and to leave Brooke above suspicion they had to make it look like she'd been taken against her will. As if the failed theft the other night had resulted in the person responsible deciding to abduct her instead.

The operation was a simple one but as she prepared, Zaharrah couldn't shake a growing feeling of unease. Her gut told her something here was off. Maybe it was the haste with which the rescue had been put together or the fact that Darrian had not surfaced but she got the distinct feeling they were walking into a trap.

Zaharrah looked over to the commander and considered voicing her concern but worried if she did they'd abort and she'd not be there for the next attempt. She cursed Broody's timing for pulling her from the main dig, aware she couldn't delay her departure any longer than she already had. He'd get suspicious. Zaharrah knew from Anna's little episode what happened if Broody got curious. She wasn't interested in having a constant tale. There were things about her time she wanted to keep hidden. In particular acts like the one she was about to undertake.

"Everyone ready?" The commander asked.

Zaharrah watched as one after another his team gave a good to go signal before nodding.

"Let's move," he ordered and the team exited their boat headed in the direction of the dig site. Zaharrah followed in silence. The time for hesitation had come and gone, the operation had begun. She hoped it went as smoothly as it should.

96

Hecate studied the corner flat across the road with interest. She'd known locating Zaharrah's residence would not be as easy as Hades seemed to think. The house in London had held nothing but here she could feel the echoes of the key's presence. She wondered how the lord of the underworld would take the news, his bride was living at times within but an hour's drive from her beloved. Hecate considered revealing the matter but decided it would be more amusing to watch the situation play out on its own.

Turning her thoughts from the matter, Hecate crossed the street and entered the building that contained Zaharrah's flat. As she walked down the corridor she let her gaze sweep over the walls and using her power looked within; knowing the place would be protected. Finding the various security measures in place Hecate switched off the silent alarm, removed the firing pin from the gun poised above the door and stepped inside.

Closing the door behind her she walked through the main room careful to avoid the switch plate under the rug. Closing her eyes she set her focus on the faint pulse of the key's power. It led her to a wall lined with records. Hecate ran her fingers over the cardboard covers until she felt a familiar jolt. Opening her eyes she pulled the cardboard out and tilting it on its side watched as instead of a vinyl album, a seven inch in diameter disk of metal and stone slid out. She noted with amusement that three of the five rings were missing.

It was no matter. Hades needed only the main piece to open the door in Atlantis. He need not know that pieces were lost and since there were a few gone there was no harm in her taking one as well. Hecate studied the ring closest to the crystalline core and smiled at the image. The scholars had not been able to sort out the meaning, but she knew the ancient marks well. The water sign sat at the top, next fire, wind and earth all surrounded by the branches of a tree.

Hecate touched the wind seal and watched as the symbols faded only to rise again wind on top, water next, earth and then fire as the gods marched in rank of their power. The ring fell off with a click and a clink to reveal more of the crystal form below. She lifted the ring off of the crystal. Here was her treasure the means to see her beloved again. She pulled the ring over her head to wear it like a necklace and placed the key itself in her bag. It was time to go.

"FREEZE WITCH."

"ARTEMIS."

"HAND OVER THE KEY OR I'LL PIERCE YOUR BLACK HEART WITH ONE OF MY ARROWS."

"WHAT NEED HAVE YOU OF THE KEY HUNTRESS?"

"I'LL NOT LET THESE DOGS CLAIM MY FATHER'S CROWN OR HIS POWER."

"YOU BETRAY YOUR UNCLE?"

"HE HAS BETRAYED ME. THEY ALL HAVE. YOU KNOW WELL THEIR TREACHERY."

"YES, MY DEAR, I DO."

"THEN GIVE ME THAT KEY AND SAY NOTHING TO HADES OF ITS FATE."

"AS YOU WILL," Hecate whispered and she handed over the disk. She watched as the huntress departed and smiled. Things were working out better than she ever could have dreamed. Let the angry little girl play at stopping these demons. When Artemis was done and the smoke cleared she would be the one holding all the cards.

Hecate departed from the flat careful to replace everything as she found it. No sense tipping off Zaharrah that her haven had been breached.

97

Artemis raced from the city into the desert, her eyes ever alert for Hecate's presence but she found no sign of the witch. Artemis wondered why Hecate had not resisted but figured the woman was more than happy to double cross Hades and his brethren. She had more reason to hate them than most.

She wondered if that made Hecate her ally but reasoned it did not. The witch was playing her own games. Spurring this nightmare forward somehow and to some unknown end. Artemis studied her prize and removed the final ring. The crystal mass below shifted taking shape and as it did Artemis understood the messenger's words. She knew exactly what to do with her Father's crown.

98

Brooke Silvers sat at her desk finishing up her notes on the days findings. She had another hour of study and research to finish before she could head back to the hotel for the night. She glanced to the pack of cigarettes at her right wanting a break but ignoring the impulse, as long as she remained in the lab area, security was staying clear. Instead she pulled out her late night snack. A pack of candy and a small thing of chips. Brooke ate in relative silence; only the sound of the bag crinkling as she reached for another chip; broke it.

She was lost in her thoughts contemplating the rest of her evening when her solitude was disrupted. A masked figure dressed in black entered the lab followed by two others. The first raised a gun from their side and pointed it at her.

"Dr. Silvers if you wish to live you will come with us," a masculine voice she didn't recognize demanded.

Brooke rose from her desk her hands raised to show she was no threat. One of the two figures took her hands and bound them behind her with a zip-tie. While the other grabbed her laptop. Whoever they were, they were after her research. Brooke considered shouting for help but before she had the chance she was gagged by her captors.

"Let's move people. Camera sweep in 5,4,3,2--"

They were out of the lab and in the city moving down cobblestone streets headed south for the exit. Two others joined them from out of the shadows, closing ranks making sure she was secure. Whoever they were they knew the systems in place; every cameras position and its blind spots. Brooke was in deep trouble and she knew it. Her only chance was that someone from security would decide to check on her when they noted she was missing from the lab and had left her smokes at the desk.

Brooke prayed for just such a break as they entered the temple through the northern chamber. The stone table loomed before her and she swallowed with discomfort as images of what it might be suited for washed through her imagination. It wasn't a table but an altar. One large enough to hold a grown man or woman. She saw now it could be used for ritualistic human sacrifices of blood, death, or worse.

"Keep moving doc," the man hissed as he led her past the altar and into the central chamber. As they entered the feasting hall, all hell broke loose.

"Dr. Silvers," A familiar voice questioned calling into the darkness.

Brooke tried to cry out in warning but it was too late. Two of her abductors opened fire as the other three led her on in an attempt at making their escape. She heard the guard call for back-up before he was taken down.

The trio led her out the southern doorway and down the steps toward the city gate as more gunfire sounded around them. The man who had been barking orders took control of handling her as the others split off to deal with security. He prodded her with the barrel of his gun forcing her to pick up her pace. Guiding her through the city gate and away from the docks into the shadows.

Brooke ran before him blindly through the dark, stumbling on the occasional rock or loose clump of earth. As her eyes adjusted to the darkness she spotted a chopper looming ahead of her on the horizon. She swallowed with a growing sense of dread. If he got her on board Brooke figured she was as good as dead.

"That's far enough doc, don't want to lead security to our exit," the man muttered as he jerked her to a halt. Brooke turned to face her captor as she considered her best move. "Alone at last. It's nice to finally meet you Brooke. A shame we won't have time to get to know each other," he grumbled.

Brooke blinked surprised to find that he seemed to know who she was. She wondered how that could be. Brooke jolted at the loud echo of a gunshot and dropped to the dirt on her hands and knees as her captor returned fire.

"Stay down," he commanded but his voice was muffled as if far away. Around her the night grew darker.

99

Zaharrah cursed as she ducked behind the cover of a stone pillar near the gate. Something had tipped security but what she had no clue. All she knew was the commander had taken Brooke beyond the gate alone and the plan had been shot to pieces. Of the six who entered she and the commander were all that remained and unless a miracle happened she wasn't going to survive the night either.

Brooke's machine had been blown to bits, but it didn't matter. If she could manage an escape she had a copy of the doctor's research courtesy of Darrian, wherever he was. She questioned for the first time if maybe the video Brooke had seen was correct and her brother was dead. Wondered if she had Magnus to thank for that. Had Death grown tired of waiting for her and selected another or was he unaware of the goings on here. As her thoughts wandered over these dark paths a shadow emerged from the temple like an avenging spirit cutting down her adversaries.

Using the distraction for cover Zaharrah made her run for the gate. She felt the burning pain of a bullet as it tore through her flesh and bit back a scream of agony as she raced for the chopper. In the distance she spotted the commander down on the ground beside Brooke and cursed. All their efforts it seemed had failed. As she reached the pair Zaharrah dropped to her knees. She checked Brooke first. No pulse, or breath. She rolled the doctor on her back to begin CPR and froze a bloody stain bloomed over her left breast. A bullet to the heart. Brooke was gone and with her any answers she might have given.

Zaharrah turned her attention to the commander and found a weak pulse. The man lived. She began the task of reviving him. If they were going to get out of there alive she needed him. Zaharrah could drive a great many things but a helicopter wasn't one of them. Looking back she saw the dark form approaching and swallowed. "Come on," she snapped with impatience as she shoved a hypodermic needle with epinephrine into the commander's chest. She didn't have time for him to come around on his own.

She had her suspicions on who was coming and she had no intention of facing a damn god that night; not with Brooke so newly dead and her own life slipping away. She might just make a fools deal of desperation.

No, she'd meet Death in the desert, not before.

Relief flooded her mind as the commander came to. They moved for the chopper in a rush. Slamming the door shut. Zaharrah heard the blades begin to spin as her dark eyes fixed on the dark clad figure coming closer. He got smaller with each passing second as they rose off the ground and took to the air. Zaharrah settled back in her seat as the sound around her began to fade away. She cursed before falling into unconsciousness.

100

Orange lit eyes watched with regret as the chopper took to the air. He'd come too late. Zaharrah was gone. He hoped she was in safe hands. The fire in his blood cooled and his eyes became brown once more. Darrian blinked trying to recall where he was and how he'd gotten there. As his eyes scanned his surroundings his heart constricted.

"Brooke," he gasped. The name torn from his throat was more like a sob. He dropped to his knees at her side and lifted her into his arms. He kissed her with regret as he tried to understand what had happened.

A voice within his mind whispered to him telling him not to fret that there was someone who could help him, but Darrian refused to listen. He carried Brooke's body away from the wretched city as he considered where to bury her. Darrian rest his head against her brow and closed his eyes.

When they opened they were orange once more. War looked back at his handy work and smiled. The man Darrian was a far more skilled fighter than his last host but he lacked the rage Kurt had possessed. He'd been hoping to pass his power onto the man with Zaharrah but had missed his chance. Now he'd have to wait and bide his time, a thing he didn't have.

Hades was free as were Hermes and Dionysus, if he stood any chance at winning the crown Ares needed a host he could turn immediately. The detective, Hecate had presented him would have been perfect if he could have pushed him just a little further. Damn Artemis and her bad timing. When he was free she would pay dearly for her interference.

War studied the man Darrian's love and contemplated his next move. Perhaps if he could convince Hades to restore her then Darrian would be more tolerant of his presence and a more accepting host. His plan in place Ares departed the city of the gods to return to the palace in Athens. If he got there fast, just maybe Darrian's pretty doctor would live again to become his.

101

Hades jolted from sleep to waking as his spirit urged him to move. Zaharrah had departed the Atlantis ruins. At last the time to act was upon him. He rose from the bed where he'd lain in slumber and walked through Hermes self-styled throne room. His gaze fell to the door where his prisoner lay waiting. Anna would wait. She was nothing to him in the grand scheme of things. If Dionysus managed to bring her forth so be it. The wine god would see to her punishment and in doing so would crush his adversary as well. Sam Abrams would fall, then there would be no one to oppose him.

His crown was waiting for him in the desert in the king's city. Even if Artemis reached it first it would not stop him. Zeus's crown could not be broken. He'd take it from her cold dead hands if he had to. There wasn't a place on earth she could hope to hide it from him and she knew it.

102

Sam watched with relief as Hades walked out the front door in the direction of a car and sped off into the night. Whatever game the god of the underworld had been playing he'd apparently grown tired of. Only Dionysus remained within.

"We go in tonight," Sam said as the sun began to rise. They'd need the cover of darkness to begin the assault.

103

Zaharrah woke with a start as adrenaline filled her veins.

"Easy Miss Lynch, you're safe," a familiar voice breathed.

"Commander?" She asked confused.

"Yeah."

"What happened?"

"I don't know, I was hoping you'd tell me," he groused.

"We were ambushed. Security--the teams dead, Dr. Silvers as well."

"How did you manage to escape?" Her pilot questioned with suspicion written on his face.

"Another intruder-- Took security out, I used the distraction to escape."

"Who?"

"I don't know. Never saw his face."

"Well, until we figure out who and just what the hell went wrong you're stuck with me."

"I have duties to see to," Zaharrah protested.

"Yeah, well, I have deaths to answer for," the commander snapped with irritation.

"I'm sorry."

"Where to?" he asked ignoring the apology having no interest in the words. He'd only be satisfied when he got his answers.

"Airport at Miami. I've got a flight to catch."

"A flight out to Tel Aviv," he said recalling her destination.

"Right."

"Why?"

"I've got to get back to my real job before my employer gets suspicious," Zaharrah muttered as her phone rang. "Hello."

"Miss Lynch, where are you?" Ian Broody's voice questioned with impatience.

"Getting ready to check out of my hotel," she lied easily.

"What's taken so long?"

"Earliest flight I could book was tonight. I'll be in Tel Aviv by Friday," she assured him.

"I understand."

"Sorry for the delay Dr. Broody."

"It's all right Miss Lynch, I know some things are out of your control," he replied before hanging up.

"You were saying?" her chopper mate prompted.

"He's impatient to get me started on his new project," Zaharrah said annoyed.

"I see."

"Look, if you want to ride along with me to Israel that's your business but you can't be seen with me once we land."

"Understood."

"Just get me to Miami so I can get on my way."

"You got it Miss Lynch," the commander assured her as he flew towards land.

104

Lance yawned as he finished reading the tale of the crown. He'd finished Heart of Stone hours earlier and had moved onto the tale to pass the time. Fatigue was setting in now and Catharine showed no signs of fading. She'd stopped only to eat when he prompted her and to use the restroom. Sleep seemed far from her mind.

"Why don't you get some rest detective, you look tired," she stated.

"I'll sleep if you do," he answered.

Catharine nodded. "Let me wrap this up? "She requested. Lance gave her an okay and set the book she'd given him earlier, aside. He watched as she shut her laptop and rose from the chair.

The pair moved down the hall together and Lance watched as she stepped into the guest room. He bid her good night then moved into his own room and sank into the bed but left the door open. If she came back out again he'd know it. Satisfied she would not be able to return to her work he closed his eyes and fell into sleep.

105

Catharine sighed seeing he'd left the door open. She'd not be going back to the laptop again until daylight. Opening her purse she pulled out a bottle of sleep meds and shook out two.

If she was going to sleep she was going to make damn sure she didn't dream. Catharine swallowed the pills without water and laid down in the bed finding it ironic she owed the thanks for having them to Dionysus. She'd bought them to help her combat his lust filled dreams. Now she found herself using them for an entirely different reason. As her eyelids began to fall the haunting image of a candle lit basement filled her mind.

Catharine opened her eyes and curled up on her side as she willed the drugs to take effect. Her eyes fell shut again as lack of sleep caught up to her. She felt the sting of rope biting into her wrists and ankles as a cold blade cut her dress from her body. The sting of it tearing the skin beneath her eye before its cool edge brushed over her naked body in a twisted caress.

She bit her lip drawing herself out of the nightmare and flipped on the bedside light. She pulled out pen and paper. She'd write until the drugs dragged her under; Catharine reasoned as she lost herself once more in *Dark Heart*.

106

Dionysus stood before the doors barring his way to Anna silently. His eyes were closed, his mind within the room watching his prey. Anna lay upon the bed lost in slumber. She'd retreated from their harsh reality into a quiet corner of her mind where she hid. He'd found her there now on a couple different occasions seeking comfort in the arms of her Sam.

His efforts to move her along had thus far been unsuccessful. She clung to Sam but would not seek ease of her lust with him. She never forgot he was but a dream image that Dionysus had created to use against her. The wine god grew weary of waiting; this was his hour. He would break her will this time and when he did Anna would open the door and come to him willingly.

107

Anna lifted her head from Sam's shoulder where she'd been resting. The sound of footsteps echoed through the vineyard and her hazel eyes sought the intruder out. She spotted him at a distance studying her with amusement. A bunch of grapes were in his right hand. The left held a single berry at his lips poised to taste.

She'd seen him do so twice before. Always when he came he watched and waited as he indulged in the fruit he'd already managed to cultivate. Each time he came she felt the press of his power against her and the hunger rose. Her blood burned with longing for Sam's embrace to shift from comforting to demanding.

Anna remembered the feel of his hands upon her body, teasing her, seducing her, making her ache with the desire to feel him inside of her, to forget if only for a moment that he was only a dream.

"What's wrong?" Sam asked.

"He's back," she whispered.

"Forget him, he's no concern of yours here," Sam whispered as he brushed a kiss on her cheek.

"He brings his power here to destroy my peace. Makes me want things I shouldn't," Anna argued.

"No, he reminds you of things you already desire," Sam corrected.

"Sam--" Anna said in protest to his response.

"Do you think that I don't feel your pulse rise as I hold you? That because I'm a dream, I can't understand why your skin burns in his presence."

"Sam, I can't--"

"Yes you can. You already have. I get the same glimpses as you do when he comes," Sam revealed.

"That's not possible--"

"Why, because I'm only a dream? I'm as real as you are here and you know it. Damn it Anna I can feel you in my grasp aching, straining, seeking my touch," He whispered as his hands stroked her arms reminding her of his caress.

She sank back in his arms and her eyes fell closed as Dionysus's power washed over her. Her mind sank into the images the wine god liked to torment her with; as Sam's hands skimmed over her hips and down her legs.

"Shh, relax Anna, I've got you," Sam whispered his voice light gentle urging her to stay calm.

"Sam," she breathed the name in surrender his feather soft touch working his will upon her, making her forget.

"Tell me what I'm doing to you," he requested his voice thick with desire as he continued to stroke his hands over her body.

"You're touching me," she murmured voicing what he was doing in that moment and in the image that ran through her mind due to the wine god's power.

"That I am love," he said amused as his own eyes fell shut indulging in the memory as well. His hands slid up her legs and along the inside of her thighs. Anna stretched against him moving closer. He wrapped one arm around her waist holding her still as the other brushed over the center of her desires. She moaned, a startled and desperate cry that had him going hard instantly. He had touched her as the image suggested. He'd had her all but naked in his arms once before begging for him to touch her.

"Sam--" She called his name to stop him.

"Hush doc, let me touch you, let me make the aching stop," he whispered. She groaned as his hand cupped her sex through her clothes.

Anna trembled in his embrace wanting to lose herself in his touch but knowing she couldn't. She didn't dare allow herself to leave reality so far behind.

"Anna please, our time here is drawing to a close. You have to go back. When you do they'll be waiting. Let me touch you before they do. Let me love you once before death takes us."

"Sam no, don't talk like that please, I'm not ready to go back to face that nightmare," Anna cried out in protest.

"You know I'm right. You can't hide here with me like this forever. Dionysus will grow impatient. He comes for the fruit, what will happen when there is no more to eat?" Sam asked.

"I don't know."

"If he can draw you into the dream world doesn't it stand to reason he can force you out as well?"

"No, this is my dream," Anna cried in protest.

"Dreams end Anna," Sam whispered.

"I'm not ready to go back," Anna whispered before she turned and kissed him.

Sam's mouth came alive under hers devouring her lips like a starved beast as his hands tore at her clothes seeking her flesh, desperate to touch her. Anna gave no more protests if this would allow her to linger with him if only for a little while longer she'd allow it; after all she could stop it whenever she liked. It was her dream.

108

Dionysus smiled as more grapes began to grow. Some were already ripe, ready to eat. He watched as Anna's dream lover stripped off her dress to touch her as they both desired. The wine god crept closer as he let his power wash over the pair. The seduction before him now was much faster than last time. Already Sam's hand was toying with the waistband of her panties. Anna was more than ready for Sam to touch her.

It was a shame to disrupt them now when she was poised to leap but now Dionysus needed her to chase after that desire. He needed her to answer her lovers call. The wine god watched them for a moment longer. Saw the moment Anna felt her lovers touch where she wanted it most. Was witness to the sight of her back arching closer to her lover as a talented finger sank into her hidden depths to tease her with the promise of what she now craved most.

"Sam," Anna cried her lovers name in fear and need. Dionysus broke the spell around the pair and her dream lover vanished. She blinked dazed. "Sam?" she called her voice trembled with fear but the tone was laced with frustration.

"Anna," his voice answered from somewhere in the distance.

The wine god watched with pleasure as she turned and ran in the direction of her lover's voice without a moment's hesitation. Her mind was all but won. All that remained was to draw her from the dream to waking and get her to come forth to seek her lover there as well. As Dionysus mused on these matters Anna found her dream lover once more and surrendered to his embrace. Losing herself in his touch. The wine god crept closer, slipping into her lover's form. He coaxed and teased her leading her back to that point of desperate need. Thrilling in the feel of her body beneath his hands begging for more. As his wicked fingers played over the center of her raging lust he trembled fighting with his own need to sink his teeth into her throat and mark her as he tasted the passion in her blood.

It wasn't time not yet.

Now he needed her to accept his touch and pursue it.

Dionysus toyed with her secret parts coaxing her towards release and then as before he broke the spell around her leaving her alone and aching with need of her lover.

"Sam?" She called desperation in her voice now.

"I'M HERE, ANNA," the wine god whispered and was rewarded moments later by her throwing herself in his arms. Her mouth crashed against his claiming it.

"Touch me, Sam," she demanded as she put her hands on him.

"WITH PLEASURE MY LOVE," he answered and began the seduction again wrapping his spell more completely about her. His hands played over her eager and willing flesh giving her what she asked and delighting in her thirst for what he offered. She'd soon be his.

109 SODOM RUINS NEAR THE DEAD SEA, JORDAN

Zaharrah moved through the city ruins in the direction of the king's palace. After landing in Tel Aviv she'd sent her bags to the hotel and gone straight out to the dig. She was looking now for the map of the plains cities, she had to locate the other cities. If Broody was after the crown there was a distinct possibility he'd found the tablet but she couldn't look into the matter now. That would have to wait until nightfall. For now she had to study the map.

As she stepped into the king's temple Zaharrah noted the broken relief and wondered at it for a moment before turning her attention to the map wall. She wrote notes on her setting and took a couple photos.

"YOUR KEY HAS BEEN TAKEN."

Zaharrah turned to find herself faced with a blonde woman she didn't recognize.

"My key?"

"YOU KNOW OF WHICH I SPEAK. IT IS SAFE FOR NOW."

"Who are you?"

"ANNA KNOWS ME. YOU SEEK THE MANTLES. FORGET THEM, THEY ARE A CURSE, NOT A GIFT."

"I know it well."

"THEN WHY PURSUE THEM?"

"For now I must play the role I've been given."

"GOOD LUCK TO YOU THEN MORTAL. I PRAY YOUR EFFORTS ARE FRUITLESS," the blonde said before she turned and left.

Zaharrah pulled out her phone to call Sam figuring he'd know who her mysterious visitor was but she forgot her reason for pulling the phone as she found she'd missed a call from Darrian. Going to her voice mail she found a message.

"Go back to the source of our woe, it holds your key." Zaharrah turned off the phone and blinked two mysterious messages in a matter of minutes. What was this all about?

110 DESERT OF JORDAN

Artemis stood in the midst of a cluster of sand dunes and focused her power on her father's crown. It rose from the depths to rest in her hands.

"NOW NONE OF YOU WILL EVER BE KING," she hissed before departing again. So long as she stayed ahead of them she'd survive this madness.

111 ATHENS, GREECE

Hecate walked inside Hades palace and made her way through the throne room to the room where his prisoner lay trapped within. The wine god stood before the doors his mind wandering within.

"DIONYSUS," she whispered the name and nudged him with her power to draw him back.

"MY LADY, TO WHAT DO I OWE THIS MOST UNEXPECTED VISIT," He asked.

"I NEED YOU TO CHECK ON MISS NICHOLS FOR ME WINE GOD. I FEAR SOMETHING IS AMISS WITH DEAR CATHARINE AND WE BOTH NEED TO KNOW THAT *DARK HEART* IS MOVING IN A DIRECTION WE WILL APPROVE OF."

"INDEED."

"WILL YOU HELP ME?" Hecate asked.

"OF COURSE. MY FIRST FAVOR IS FREE LADY, BUT THE SECOND WILL COST YOU," Dionysus cautioned before closing his eyes once more he eased his hold on Anna's mind and sank deep into the dream realm to seek Catharine. He soon found her lost in a nightmare. As she struggled with her tormentor he slipped into her mind and poked through her memories.

"YOUR CONCERNS ARE MERITED. SHE'S BEGUN TO WRITE THE FOURTH BOOK AND IS WORKING TOWARDS FREEING SERENITY."

"THAT CAN'T BE ALLOWED TO HAPPEN. YOU MUST STOP THIS," Hecate hissed.

"I'LL TAKE CARE OF IT BUT I WANT YOU TO DO SOMETHING FOR ME."

"WHAT FAVOR WOULD YOU ASK?"

"OPEN THE DOOR THAT ARTEMIS SEALED. ALLOW ME PASSAGE TO HER PET AND I'LL MAKE SURE SERENITY'S FATE IS SEALED."

"IT WILL BE DONE AS YOU SAY WHEN I'M SATISFIED HER MIND IS ALTERED."

"CONSIDER IT DONE," Dionysus said before he slipped back into Catharine's mind to do as Hecate requested.

112

Dionysus found Catharine where he'd past her moments before, trapped in a memory induced nightmare. She was bound to a bed surrounded by candles naked and afraid. Her captor stood over her, a man she knew. A shadow from her past held at bay by the war god.

"YOU'RE SO WILLFUL SERENITY, YOU MAKE IT HARD FOR ME TO NOT TREAT MYSELF TO A REAL TASTE OF YOU. I'VE NOT HAD A BRIDE THAT PLEASED ME SO COMPLETELY IN OVER TWO THOUSAND YEARS AND I WANT TO TAKE MY TIME WITH YOU BUT THE MORTAL WHOM I'M SHARING THIS BODY WITH WANTS ALL OF YOU NOW AND IN THE WORST SORT OF WAYS IMAGINABLE, " Ares whispered as his fingers slid down into the valley between her breasts.

The wine god watched as the pretty writer trembled both with fear and need due to his influence upon her as Ares touched her. Catharine turned her eyes away from her captor and Dionysus moved closer.

"SERENITY, FORGET HIM AND THIS PLACE OF PAIN. HE CAN'T HURT YOU ANYMORE UNLESS YOU ALLOW IT," the wine god whispered. He watched as her blue eyes moved past her captor to lock with his and the memory faded. The basement reverting back to his garden. She was dressed now in her green Grecian gown.

"Twice now you've invaded my mind and set me free from some inner fear tormenting me. Why?"

"I DESIRE ONLY TO SEE YOU FREE OF YOUR TORMENT. YOUR MIND IS NOT ONE I'D SEE LOST TO DARKNESS. YOUR IMAGINATION IS ONE I TREASURE. YOU'VE GIVEN ME A GIFT IN *DARK HEART* SERENITY, AND

I WILL PROTECT THAT AND YOU WITH IT."

"What do you want?"

"I WANT TO SEE SERENITY FIND HER PASSION AS MUCH AS ANYONE BUT NOT IN THIS FAIRY TALE YOU'VE BEGUN TO BUILD."

"Hecate sent you."

"NO, I CAME TO CHECK ON YOU, TO SEE IF YOU'D CONSIDERED MY OFFER."

"I've had other things on my mind."

"AS I CAN SEE BUT YOU'RE LETTING THEM CLOUD YOUR JUDGMENT. YOU SAID IT YOURSELF, SERENITY AS YOU'VE WRITTEN HER IS A MONSTER NOW, YOUR EFFORT TO REDEEM HER IS JUST YOU CATERING TO YOUR FANS. IT'S NONSENSE AND YOU KNOW IT. IT CAN'T WORK."

"I think it can."

"YOU'RE LYING TO YOURSELF SERENITY, JUST AS YOU ALWAYS HAVE. WHAT HAS HAPPENED BEFORE CANNOT BE UNDONE. YOUR SERENITY MUST FIND A WAY TO LIVE WITH WHAT SHE HAS BECOME JUST AS YOU MUST LEARN TO DEAL WITH THIS NIGHTMARE THAT PLAGUES YOU," Dionysus whispered.

He waved his hand swiping away the image of a redeemed Serenity and they stood now together in the shadows of that candle lit basement looking upon the image of her as she'd been with Ares standing over her his hands on her.

"I CAN CHASE THIS AWAY FOR YOU AS I HAVE EVERY OTHER FEAR THAT'S TROUBLED YOU. I CAN GIVE YOU THE COURAGE TO EMBRACE YOUR NEW COMPANION, YOU NEED ONLY ASK IT OF ME AND I WILL GIVE IT," Dionysus offered as he held out his cup for her.

"I'll not bind myself to you, fallen one, blindly. You offer freedom but at what cost? No, be gone. I'll deal with these troubles on my own," Catharine hissed.

"SO BE IT, YOU NEED ONLY CALL UPON ME TO BE RELEASED IF YOU GROW WEARY OF YOUR STRUGGLES," Dionysus hissed and then he was gone from her side and she was once more bound and naked upon the bed with her jailor standing over her, his hands upon her.

Dionysus shoved his power into the dream in a fit of rage. It rushed over the nightmare like a tidal wave and Serenity screamed as the war god began the act of the second cut she'd born witness to. She'd chosen the nightmare and now she would face it completely for she alone knew the madman's ritual and though he'd never completed it with her, here she would endure all of it until she cried to Dionysus for aid or she woke up.

113

Catharine woke screaming. The nightmare was still fresh in her mind. She'd been trapped in a candle lit basement with Kurt, only Lance had never found her. She'd endured cut after cut just as she'd seen Gail endure. Until her mind couldn't take anymore. She trembled now still feeling Kurt's touch on her. She crawled out of bed and crossed to the door.

Lance stood in the hall his hand poised to knock.

"Sorry, nightmare," she muttered with disgust.

"You okay, do you need to talk about it?"

"I'll be fine. I just want to get cleaned up," Catharine muttered.

Lance nodded and allowed her to walk past him.

"Breakfast will be waiting when you get out," he stated.

Catharine mumbled a thank you before closing herself in the bathroom. She stripped off sweat soaked clothes and stepped into the shower turning on the hot water. She grabbed the soap and scrubbed at her skin desperate to wash away the feeling of Kurt's touch upon her. As she closed her eyes the nightmare resurfaced.

Her eyes flew open and she switched off the water. She needed to get back to work. Stepping out of the tub she wrapped a towel around her and crept down the hall back to her room. Catharine pulled on fresh clothes picked up her pages and headed for her laptop.

114

Lance watched from the kitchen as Catharine sank into the chair in front of her laptop, put a stack of pages on the table and went right to typing. Her nightmare must have been worse than he figured. He cracked an egg open and set it in the skillet letting it sizzle. He pictured her in his mind, in a candle lit basement naked, bound to a bed and swallowed. It wasn't too hard to imagine what she'd been dreaming about, given his own nightmares, finding her too late. Ares still inside her as he stole her last breathe before driving his knife in her heart.

He'd gotten sick upon waking, only to be ripped from his peace as the dream abated, by her screams. He'd been ready to break down the door until his rational mind returned. He'd prepared to knock but she'd emerged her eyes haunted and tormented. He had no idea what she'd seen during her captivity but he had no doubt whatever it was she'd been back in that basement enduring it all.

Lance swallowed back a growl at the thought and turned his attention back to his eggs. He cursed, finding he'd ruined them. Switching off the stove, he decided cooking was a bad idea. Maybe they both needed to get out of there for a while.

Looking back to his house guest he doubted she'd be interested in leaving. So he crossed to the fridge to look for something he couldn't ruin.

115

Catharine's fingers flew over the keys as she worked to finish the scene she started before falling asleep.

'Serenity raced through the woods aware someone was out there chasing her. Fear wrapped around her heart and threatened to stop her in her tracks. She wheeled abruptly tired of this endless nightmare.

"Show yourself you coward. I'll not flee before you another step. You hunt Serenity but you'll not find her I am

Nivali and I will end you."

"Ah the sheep has fangs, after all," a familiar voice mocked.

"Syvarin--" She gasped with alarm and disbelief. "How?"

"Did I survive? By staying in the shadows the same as you. Did I find you? Simple I never lost you. We are bound one to the other."

"Why?"

"Seek you now… to warn you. Kovrin is alive and searching for you."

"But Davrik--"

"My son is dead. Kovrin was only too happy to put him out of his misery after he understood you were beyond his reach."

"You lie!"

"He died trying to save you."

"From what?"

"You don't know?" Syvarin asked.

"Know what?"

"Kovrin when he couldn't find you, he began hunting others

like you. He's killed half a dozen so far."

"No."

"I'm afraid it's true. Look for yourself," Syvarin said as he handed her a stack of crime scene photos.

"Oh, god."

"He's never forgotten his taste for you Serenity. He'll not rest until he has you back. I sought you out to warn you and to offer you my protection if you wish it."

"Why would I come back after what you did--?"

"I made mistakes with you Serenity, I know it but I loved you, still do. I let my jealousy cloud my judgment. It incensed me that you chose my son over me. Let me make right now the wrong I did you in our past."

"Syvarin--"

"Give me a chance Serenity. Let me love you as you deserved. Let me protect you from him. Together we can defeat him," the vampire lord entreated as he offered her his hand.

Serenity looked from his hand to the bloody photos. Memories long forgotten rose from the dark recesses of her mind. Terror filled her. "What token do you desire to seal this pack?"

"Give me my heir Serenity, take your rightful place at my side once more."

"My life spared his wrath at the cost of my life," she said with disgust.

"No, your life protected for your company."

Serenity took the outstretched hand unwilling to face the were-wolf lord again alone.

"You've made a wise choice," Syvarin whispered and he drew her into his arms and kissed her with a passion that stole her breath away.

His hands were everywhere, making her burn with desire as her mind was swept away in a million memories of a time when she'd been his. Her heart raced as her body prepared itself for him. As his hands found the part of her he wanted most he growled to find her wet and ready. His fangs sank in her throat as he entered her body to breed.'

Catharine's fingers fell still as she lost the thread of the story. This was not where she'd planned the scene to go and though she could see the sordid love scene and knew her fans would eat it up she couldn't see what was to happen next. She considered where this turn would lead but found nothing. Frustrated she saved her work and slammed down the lid.

"You okay?" Lance questioned clearly surprised by her abrupt turning from her work.

"Yeah, just stuck. Can we get out of here for a while?"

"Sure," Lance answered putting the food away. We'll grab breakfast," Lance offered as he moved out into the dining room.

"Great," she answered with relief before they left the house.

116

Dionysus laughed at the way things had played out.

"WELL," Hecate asked with impatience.

"SHE STOPPED WRITING FOR NOW, WHEN SHE COMES BACK TO IT I'LL MOVE HER ALONG AGAIN. WHEN IT'S DONE SERENITY WILL FIND HERSELF BOUND TO THE VAMPIRE LORD SYVARIN AND THIS UPSTART DAVRIK WILL VANISH INTO OBSCURITY. SATISFIED?"

"NO. I WANT YOU TO ENSURE THAT SHE NEVER WANDERS BACK TO THE ORIGINAL PLOT. FOR THAT TO HAPPEN WE BOTH KNOW YOU HAVE TO GET RID OF THIS INTERLOPER. THE COP. DRIVE THEM APART."

"AS YOU COMMAND," Dionysus relented. Closing his eyes once more he sank into the dream realm to do as she bid. He slipped back into Catharine's mind and found her wrestling with her nightmare.

"SERENITY, COME FORGET THIS PLACE OF DESPAIR."

"I'm trying but every time I step away from the book--"

"IT COMES BACK HERE, THAT'S BECAUSE YOU GIVE IT NOWHERE ELSE TO GO. THINK OF SOMETHING PLEASANT TO DISTRACT YOURSELF WITH, OR SOMEONE."

Catharine blinked at his words surprised he'd not come to offer her escape once more but to give her a solution. "What are you playing at?"

"DOES IT MATTER? YOUR COMPANION IS RIGHT IF YOU DON'T CHANGE THIS WAR WITHIN IT WILL DESTROY YOU AND I CAN'T ALLOW SERENITY'S CREATOR TO FADE TO NOTHINGNESS."

"Why? Serenity is but one in a million of characters as are the rest, they could be forgotten overnight."

"BUT ARE LOVED NOW. AS YOU SHOULD BE. YOUR COP OFFERS COMFORT," Dionysus stated as Lance's form stepped forth from the shadows of her mind.

"I know."

"TAKE IT. EMBRACE HIM NOW, LET YOUR TROUBLED MIND REST. MAKE A NEW THOUGHT ON WHICH TO DWELL. SOMETHING PLEASANT AND OF YOUR CHOOSING," the wine god urged as the image of Lance drew her into his arms and held her close to him.

Catharine wrapped her arms around him and clung to him for dear life. Dionysus smiled. His mind retreated from Catharine's to seek out her companions. A nudge there was needed as well something far more subtle and yet just as pointed. He'd drive them together and then their budding romance would fall apart.

117

Lance unlocked the passenger door for his guest and opened it. He waited in silence as Catharine moved past him and settled into the seat. The smell of whatever soap she'd used filled his lungs and he sighed as he closed the door. It was a pleasant scent. One he found he liked.

Uniquely feminine but not overly so. It wasn't flowery or sickly sweet like some that reminded him of candy. Nor was the smell of some tropical fruit that got a man thinking of an island paradise, it was something subtle and far more inviting. A mystery. Something he knew but couldn't quite place.

As he rounded the hood of his car his gaze moved to the woman within. She was in the process of fastening her seatbelt. Her hands drew the safety strap to the buckle at her hip. He blinked as blue eyes met with his brimming with impatience. She wanted to get moving. He lingered a moment longer studying her face.

Catharine was a rare beauty. Her red hair still damp from her shower, curled around her face. Drops of water clung to her peaches and cream skin, a few running down her swan like neck. Unbidden his mind turned to the memory of their time together in LA.

"Stop that." Lance muttered interrupting her.

"Stop what?"

"Stop acting like we've just met and are no more than a couple of strangers, I don't like it," Lance warned.

"But we have only just met detective and in all honesty you're little more than a stranger to me," she reminded.

"You know that's not true," he challenged, the desire he felt for her began to stir inside him once more.

Unbidden the memory of their kiss flooded his thoughts and made him ache with the desire to feel her mouth hot and wild against his own. He burned with the need to touch her as he mentally undressed her with his eyes. He cursed, aware he was losing his carefully managed control. If she kept pushing him there was no telling where it might lead to.

"Do I detective?" she questioned with amusement as she pushed him a little more. She knew he was on the edge and the troublesome vixen was toying with him. Waiting for his control to snap, knowing when it did he'd forget his promise to not press her. That he'd take what he wanted from her and what she now seemed to desire of him.

"Catharine," he breathed her name; the word both a plea and a warning.

"Detec…"

She didn't get to finish the taunt as his lips were on hers cutting it off muffling the rest. His kiss was hard and demanding, bruising her lips. His fingers fisted in her hair, holding her in place for him as he stole her breath away.

His hand slid out of her hair to brush over her wanton flesh. She stretched and moaned under his caress encouraging him begging for more.

Lance's lips drew away from hers breaking the kiss. He licked them reveling in the taste of her that still lingered there and she smiled knowing he was lost to her now. His eyes opened to look at her. The pale blue orbs were no longer cool but a blazing fire of lust waiting to combust. They raked over her body with an intensity that made her tremble.

Lance blinked startled by the sudden reminder of their passion. He swallowed, his mouth watering for a taste of hers. He drew a breath to steady himself and his eyes fell shut. The moment they did his thoughts ran right back to her.

Catharine moaned with a fevered hunger as Lance's hand slid beneath her panties. He repressed a groan as his hand slid over feminine curls to find her more than ready for him but drew back.

"Damn it Catharine, I want you, I'm not going to lie, I want you so much it hurts…" he gasped struggling to ease back.

"Then take me," she demanded lost to him.

Lance's eyes flew open as the reminder of their time together tore through his system heating his blood as the desire he'd felt then began to awaken within him once more. His heart pounded wildly and he felt his body respond to the image.

Lance drew his eyes from her and got in the car. Slamming his door and shoving his seat belt into place as he berated himself for his thoughts. Catharine wouldn't appreciate them nor was she in any state to deal with his interests. She'd been-- Lance shoved the reminder of just where she'd been and in what state from his mind, having no desire to see the nightmare again. He put the key in the ignition and pulled away from the curb.

"You okay?" Catharine asked.

"Yeah, just got a lot on my mind," he muttered. His eyes moved to her for a moment. His lungs filled with her scent as it surrounded her and her close proximity made his hands itch with the desire to touch her. He looked away from her as he grabbed the steering wheel in a tight grip to ignore the impulse.

The truck fell into silence as an unsettling sound that left him aware of only two things the beating of his own heart and their breathing. It allowed his mind to wander and at the moment it seemed to have set upon her.

To combat this sudden hunger for a second he pictured her naked in his arms, body shaking, heart pounding with fear as he carried her to safety reminding himself of the harsh reality of what she'd endured but even this was not enough to quench the fire that had begun to burn inside him.

The image shifted and fear was replaced with desperate need as he held her close to him, their lips locked in a wild kiss. His hands on her, seeking bare skin. Lance switched on the radio to break the silence, needing a distraction as the sound filled the background the image in his mind faded.

Catharine sighed in her seat beside him. Lance glanced over at her and he found her eyes were closed. She looked peaceful and blissfully unaware of his gaze. Lance's eyes were drawn to her mouth and she whispered his name. He wondered what she was dreaming about even as he pictured himself leaning over and waking his sleeping faerie from her repose with a kiss. As his mind played out the scene he was reminded yet again of a time when he'd kissed her before and of their taste, one he'd enjoyed.

Lance turned away from her returning his attention to the road as the song on the radio changed to Meredith Brooks crooning about what might happen if she kissed some mystery guy. It wasn't helping him. Reaching over he changed the station. The current song ended and the new one wasn't much better. He muttered a curse under his breath as his passenger slept away unaware of his sudden madness.

118

Catharine dropped into sleep as soon as the car started moving. She fell into the dream she'd left earlier. Wrapped in Lance's embrace the world around her quiet. His hands stroked over her back and along her sides each pass widening the area he touched.

She whispered his name and he froze as if suddenly aware of what he was doing.

"Catharine, I'm sorry. Are you okay? I didn't mean to--"

"Shh, it's fine detective, that feels nice," she confessed her voice held no discomfort.

"Are you sure? I--"

Catharine kissed him to quiet his fears. "Its fine," she assured him.

"Good, you'll let me know if I--" he began trying to make sure that she was comfortable and would remain so but she cut him off kissing him again to silence his fears. When she drew back from his lips he didn't follow and she smiled.

"Of course," she whispered before she kissed him once more. He got the message loud and clear as his mouth came alive under hers and his hands became bolder in their exploration.

Catharine trembled under his touch as her mind swam with the memory of what it felt like to have his hands on her directly. She sighed with contentment at his caresses knowing she wanted to feel that way again. She longed to feel his fingers play over her secret places and make her ache with the need for more. She desired to feel him for a while if only to forget Kurt's uninvited touch.

She found that Lance seemed more than willing to do just that. It wasn't long at all before she felt his hand rubbing her where she wanted him through her clothes testing the waters to see what she could handle. When she answered by seeking more he gave it. A warm hand slid inside her jeans to paw at her over thin cotton.

"Lance," she breathed his name before her nails marked his back. His response was to end his teasing. A rough hand brushed through feminine curls to press against heated flesh. She bit his shoulder at the feel of him where she wanted him most and was rewarded by the sensation of a thick male finger pressing inside of her.

"Better now?" he asked his voice both amused and aroused.

"Yes," she murmured as her eyes fell shut lost in the sensation of his touch.

"Good, I want you to enjoy this," he breathed before he began to stroke her towards release.

"Lance--" his name left her lips her voice rough with passion begging though what for she didn't know.

"What do you desire of me, Serenity?"

A flash of memory ripped through her mind for a moment she saw a candle lit basement and she felt fear claw at her. Catharine opened her eyes looking at her lover. She bit her lip at the sight of him before her. His hand down her jeans still waiting for her answer. The finger inside of her buried deep rubbing against secret parts making her ache. "Help me forget," she whispered wanting the nightmare to fade from her thoughts. Longing only to think of him.

"You will," he assured her before his mouth fell upon her skin tasting her as he pleasured her further.

119

Catharine woke as the car stopped moving. She opened her eyes dazed and blinked heavy lids. As her mind unclouded she became aware of her bodies state. Her flesh was tingling with delight, her nipples hard begging for attention. She glanced down self-consciously and was relieved to find it wasn't obvious.

Her gaze moved to the man beside her in the car and she was grateful he seemed unaware that she'd woken. Catharine looked away from him quickly not wanting to draw his attention her way needing her system to level out but the quick peek in his direction had only heightened her sexual awareness; she was wet now ready for him. Why? What had she been dreaming about? Catharine wondered as she shifted in her seat trying to ease her discomfort.

Unbidden the image of the detective standing in front of her his hand down the front of her pants filled her mind and the feel of him pressing inside her washed through her. Her body tightened in response and her eyes flew open. Catharine blushed with embarrassment as she thought of what she'd been dreaming of him doing to her. She bit her lip to try and cool her raging hormones.

"The sleeping beauty wakes," Lance's voice whispered with amusement interrupting her solitude.

"Yeah, I'm up," she stated referring both to her being awake and her current physical state.

"Hungry?" Lance questioned.

"Famished," she replied though at the moment what she hungered for most was him.

"Good, let's go eat," Lance muttered as he got out of the car. He rounded the hood and opened her door for her to let her out. Catharine unfastened her seat belt and pictured herself grabbing hold of his shirt collar and dragging him back into the car to kiss him. She blinked, stunned at the image and swallowed before getting out of the seat and moving past him to head for the cafe door.

Catharine heard the door slam behind her and tried not to jump. He wasn't mad at her, she told herself even as her mind flashed back to another scene where he'd been angry and pinned her to a wall, and he'd kissed her and touched her taking that which he desired as he prepared her for him.

"Get a grip girl," she muttered to herself; that had been a bit she'd written; it wasn't real.

"You okay?" Lance questioned as he opened the door for her.

"Yeah," she said trying to do as she'd suggested and get a handle on her lust. She took a seat opposite him in a booth in the back and grabbed the menu; not to study it but to take her eyes off him.

"What's on your mind?" He asked, his voice made it clear he was aware she was uneasy about something.

"Nothing," she lied not wanting to discuss their growing-- relationship, infatuation-- carnal passion, ah she didn't know what to call this thing between them.

"No *Dark Heart*?" he asked surprised.

"I'm stuck. Please don't say that so loud, I really don't want--"

"Sorry, not used to this. My chief was wondering if you could sign a copy for his wife." Lance said his voice was sheepish.

"Sure," Catharine answered amused before turning her attention back to the menu.

"He likes you."

"Who? Your chief?"

"Yeah, he had the way cleared for you to be on the sight yesterday," Lance related.

"Really?" Catharine asked looking over the menu at him.

"Yep."

"I'll have to thank him for that," she said finding herself ridiculously pleased to hear it.

"The signed copy will be enough," Lance assured her. Catharine lowered her eyes to the menu once more but her gaze was drawn back to him again as he spoke again. "Do you know what you want?"

"I think so," she replied.

"Good, now if we could just get a waiter--"

"What's the rush detective?" She asked curious.

"Nothing," he answered a little too quickly telling her it was a lie.

"Same as mine I bet," Catharine muttered as the waiter appeared. The pair made their orders and then fell into an uncomfortable silence.

Catharine felt his eyes on her as they waited on more than one occasion. He was watching her even now and with some of the heat she'd felt while they were out in LA. Her thoughts drifted to their time together out there and she smiled before lifting her gaze from the table to look at him. His icy blue eyes met with hers and for a moment she saw in them the same hunger she felt stirring inside her before he looked away.

"What's on your mind detective?" She asked curious though she had her suspicions.

"I-- was just thinking how beautiful you looked in your dress the other night. It was a hell of a party I'm kind of sorry I missed it."

"Believe me it's better you did. A million people would have wanted to know who you were and how we met--" Catharine stated.

"Yeah, and a hundred other details that wasn't there business," Lance added.

"Getting close to me will have its drawbacks," Catharine warned.

"Getting close to you?" Lance asked his voice held curiosity and desire.

Before she could answer the waiter returned with their breakfast. The two again lapsed into silence as they ate. Each one lost in their own thoughts. It wasn't until the bill came that they were forced to face one another again as they both reached for it.

Catharine felt a pleasant jolt at his touch that had her skin heating and the rest of her aching to be near him. Their eyes locked and the look in his gaze had her biting her lower lip in anticipation. The sexual tension between them was so thick she could all but imagine the cloud they were surrounded by under them in place of the floor.

"I've got it," Lance stated.

"No, this one is on me," Catharine countered before sliding her card into the tray. She watched as the waiter took it away.

"I could have--"

"Yes, you could but I insisted on going out."

"We needed to; I burned the eggs."

Catharine laughed at the admission as the waiter returned, she sighed for the meal and collected her card. The pair made their way to the door. Lance opened it for her, along with the car. She climbed into the seat and waited for him to close the door. Instead he grabbed her seat belt and dragged it across her body fastening it. Before she could react he closed the door.

Her body hummed with delight at the gentle touch and she closed her eyes thinking of another time he'd touched her with more intent. She felt his eyes upon her and opened hers slowly. Lance stood in front of the car watching her intently. He was probably wondering how she'd reacted to his unexpected move.

Catharine batted her eyelashes at him playfully and smiled. She was rewarded with a laugh before the detective rounded the hood and got into the car behind the wheel. He closed his door and put the keys in the ignition. She watched as his wrist flexed to start the car. Lance froze letting the keys go and turned to look over at her.

"What did you mean before about getting close to you?" he asked unable to let the question go unanswered.

Rather than speak Catharine grabbed his face in her hands and kissed him. She smiled to find she'd caught him off guard and enjoyed sipping slowly at his lips; savoring the taste. When she let him go he opened his eyes dazed.

"Why'd you do that?" he asked his voice thick with desire.

"I had to know if you really tasted as good as I remember."

"Do I?" He asked curious and hungry.

"No," she said curtly her voice cool and serious. She watched as he swallowed. Disappointment was on his face and she smiled unable to maintain her rouse. "It was better than I remembered," Catharine whispered before she kissed his nose.

"You're killing me Serenity," he breathed as his hands slid into her hair before he kissed her. Their mouths met, the pressure hard demanding, the other yielded. There was nothing slow or gentle now, only two fierce hungers wild and desperate to find their fill.

Catharine leaned forward to draw him closer only to find herself jerked back by the seat belt and she cursed. Lance's lips came away from hers and he chuckled.

"No Serenity, not yet," he whispered before he fastened his own seat belt. He kissed her then indulging in a slow and gentle tasting of her mouth. "You're right though it is better than I remembered," he confessed before pulling out of the lot.

Catharine sat back in her seat and blushed aware that if not for her seat belt she'd have forgotten where they were and let him do as he wished in a parked car in broad daylight for anyone to see.

"I like that look on you," Lance teased.

"What look?" She asked confused.

"Dazed, a little mussed, lips kiss swollen, skin flushed. You look good enough to eat," he muttered.

"Keep your eyes on the road detective," she chided as she grinned unable to maintain her stern tone. She was absurdly pleased with his interest in her.

"I'm trying Serenity, but you're biting your lower lip and it's distracting me."

Catharine released the lip and laughed. It felt good to laugh, nice to be wanted and even better to find she could desire another, that she could just for a moment forget what she'd seen in a candle lit basement hours earlier and what had been done to her. "Sorry, is that better?" she asked turning to look at him as they hit a red light.

"Much," he answered before he turned and kissed her. They indulged in this meeting of lips until the light changed and he again turned his focus to the road. His fingers ran over her face and down her neck. Catharine purred under his touch and leaned into it wanting to get closer. She wanted out of the car and in his arms. Wanted his mouth on hers as his hands made her burn for him.

120

Hecate laughed at the scene playing out in the car with amusement as she broke her link with Catharine.

"NOW I AM SATISFIED WINE GOD. GO, CLAIM YOUR PRIZE. WITH HADES AND THE HUNTRESS BOTH GONE, NOW IS YOUR TIME TO STRIKE," Hecate commanded as she drew upon her power and shredded the barrier barring Dionysus's entrance to Artemis's chambers. When the barrier gave way the lock turned and the doors flung open wide to reveal the woman asleep within.

Sweat sheened her brow, her skin was flushed with passion, body trembling with need. Dionysus stepped over the threshold into the room before closing the doors behind him and locking it to ensure he was not interrupted.

Hecate touched the wooden doors and with her power unlocked the doors setting the stage as Hades desired; perhaps Sam would become War before the day was out. Whatever the outcome she didn't care. Her business now was in Washington DC. She would see to it that Catharine never threatened her power again.

121

Artemis hissed at the feeling of Hecate's power shredding her seal. The witch it seemed was not done playing games. She'd just given anyone within the palace access to Anna. She'd pay for interfering, Artemis vowed. She'd not endured the wine god's passion only to see Anna suffer the same fate. Drawing upon her own power Artemis worked to mount a defense. She summoned her protector to Anna's aid. The mortal woman would not be left unguarded as Artemis made her way back to the palace. Her sentinel would stand watch over Anna until she arrived. With this step taken Artemis did what she could to hasten her return.

122 ATHENS, GREECE

Ares arrived at the Grecian palace Hades had taken from Hermes control only to find his brother gone. He lay the woman Brooke down upon the marble desk and sent a mental summons for the lord of the underworld, aware that time was running out for the lifeless beauty before him and his host was growing impatient. As the man Darrian grieved for his lost love, Ares contemplated his next move, it wouldn't be long before his host became too willful to be of any use to him.

123

As the last light of day faded Sam, Terra and Vince crept silently toward Hermes palace. The place was still, appearing deserted but Sam wasn't fooled. Somewhere within Dionysus waited and Anna was being held captive. They had to be careful. This raid had to go off without a hitch or Anna would pay dearly for their mistakes.

Terra worked the lock and in seconds they were inside. Sam pushed into the throne room and found a lone figure standing over the altar, a dead woman lain upon it. He raised his gun at the other man.

"Where is Dr. Gallagher," he demanded in a low whisper. His voice was fierce hinting at a barely contained fury. The man's head lifted, dark eyes lit with an orange glow. Ares! He'd miscalculated the number of gods gathered here.

"YOUR LADY IS THROUGH THAT HALL. DIONYSUS IS WITH HER, GO QUICKLY," Ares commanded before brown eyes fell back to the broken woman. Sam didn't hesitate, he turned in the direction indicated even as he wondered what the War god was playing at. He heard Terra and Vince behind him as he prayed they weren't too late.

124

Dionysus crossed the floor to the bed where Artemis's pet lay lost in the dream he'd slowly fashioned for her. He sank into her mind once more and found her lost to her lover's touch. The wine god smiled with amusement and felt his body respond to her pleasure. It was time for the dreamer to wake. He slipped into her lover's skin and eased his fingers out of her. Hazel eyes flew open stunned.

"You can't," she gasped outraged to be thwarted so close to bliss.

"SHH, I'LL MAKE IT RIGHT," he vowed as he pulled off her clothes. He used his mouth then to please her, tormenting her flesh with the promise of things he could do for her, to her if she just asked.

"ANNA," he breathed her name as he rest his cheek against her breast, lost in the sound of her racing heart.

"Sam--I want--but not--"

"HUSH LOVE, OUR TIME'S NEARLY UP. LET ME SEND YOU TO WAKING SATISFIED," he whispered before his mouth closed around a hardened peak begging for his attention. Anna's eyes fell shut as her fingers fisted in his hair, nails pricking his scalp. He gave her more as she demanded, as he freed himself from his pants. He drew her naked body closer to him letting her feel the heat of him pressed against her. When she made no move to retreat from him he ended the seduction filling her body with his aroused flesh with a hard thrust that had him buried inside her to the hilt.

Hazel eyes flew open with shock as her body trembled with instant release. Her lips parted on a strangled cry as he began to move inside her. Her vision darkened as the dream world she'd been hiding in began to melt around her and reality threatened to crash in.

125

Anna's eyes flew open as the dream faded. She kicked off her blankets to find herself burning up. Her skin was slick with sweat and her body burned with the need of Sam's touch. She trembled as she recalled the dream and found she could almost swear she felt him still. The sudden need to strip herself bare to ease her bodies discomfort washed through her and she reached for the shoulder straps of her dress to do just that but froze. Something inside her, telling her she wasn't as alone as she believed.

As she looked about the darkened room she gasped startled to discover that Dionysus stood at the side of the bed watching her. His violet eyes darkened becoming red and she swallowed with fear as he moved closer. The wine god drew in a breath and smiled.

"YOU'RE READY FOR ME ANNA," he whispered with delight as he reached out to touch her.

Anna tensed afraid but his hand never got to her; a cat leapt down from the head board and hissed before biting him. She used the distraction to rise from the bed.

"DAMN YOU ARTEMIS, I'LL NOT LET YOU KEEP ME FROM WHAT IS MINE," Dionysus hissed as he swatted the cat away. He rounded the bed to where Anna stood. "NO MORE GAMES ANNA," he murmured as he advanced toward her.

Anna trembled with fear and anticipation as he drew closer. She was mortified to find he was right her body was so ready for a man she wondered if she'd do as she had in the dream. Fly apart, reaching peak at his first touch. She heard the sound of the cat licking blood from its lips and she pictured the wine god licking the sweat from her body.

"OH ANNA, YOU ARE A BAD GIRL AFTER ALL," he murmured with delight. "YOU'LL HAVE WHAT YOU DESIRE," he assured her as he came closer.

"Oh God," she began in disgust as she felt her body begin to itch with demand that it be touched.

"FORGET HIM ANNA, HE CAN'T RELIEVE YOU NOW. YOU'VE INDULGED IN MY EMBRACE, NOW ONLY I CAN SCRATCH THAT ITCH FOR YOU," he breathed as he moved closer.

"That's not true--" she said in denial.

"OH, YES, YOU'RE RIGHT, YOU COULD OR EVEN YOUR SAM BUT IT WILL KEEP COMING BACK, THIS NEED TO BE PLEASURED UNTIL YOU FEEL MY TOUCH," Dionysus stated.

"I'll never let you near me," Anna said with conviction.

"FOOLISH WOMAN, YOU ALREADY DID. DO YOU THINK I WASN'T THERE IN THAT DREAM AS YOU PARTED YOUR LEGS FOR HIM TO TOUCH YOU? I SLIPPED INSIDE HIS SKIN AS EASILY AS I ENTERED THE PINK SLIT BETWEEN YOUR LEGS AND FELT YOU QUAKE IN MY ARMS AS YOUR FEMININE PARTS TIGHTENED ROUND ME, DRAWING ME DEEPER, BEGGING FOR ME TO STAY INSIDE YOU AND FILL YOU WITH MY LUST."

"No!"

"YOUR DENIAL IS POINTLESS. YOUR BODY KNOWS THE TRUTH. IT CAN STILL FEEL ME, BECAUSE IN THAT REALM I'M STILL INSIDE OF YOU, MOVING, PRESSING YOU TOWARDS YOUR NEXT RELEASE AND YOUR FLESH IS BEGGING FOR A TASTE OF WHAT YOUR MIND ALREADY KNOWS I CAN GIVE YOU. THE TASTE OF THE DRUG YOU NOW CRAVE," the wine god stated as he grabbed her by the wrist and drew her to him. Behind him a fierce roar rumbled in warning as a black panther stalked toward him to insinuate itself between them.

Dionysus roared back at the cat in reply, it turned and Anna flinched as the large head moved closer, she felt its breath on her skin and waited for it to attack. Anna watched as the cat turned away moving into the shadows. It vanished. The god of wine grabbed hold of her once more and drew her against him.

"NOW THAT WE'RE ALONE AT LAST I WILL HAVE WHAT IS MINE." He breathed the words before his mouth fell upon hers claiming it. Anna struggled in his grasp but only for a moment. For his power wrapped around her once more. Her mind fell back into her dream as he began the act of seducing her for real.

As the dream image moved inside her Sam's face melted away to reveal the one whose touch she'd surrendered to. "Dionysus," she said with shock and dismay.

"YES LADY, NOW YOU SEE. WE ARE BOUND," he breathed before he sank his fangs in her neck sending her to a violent orgasm.

Anna's eyes flew open to find she was clinging to the wine god to stay on her feet as his hands played over her body driving her mad with want of him.

"No," she cried out with alarm as she let him go.

"HUSH ANNA, WE BOTH KNOW YOU WANT THIS," he whispered as he pressed his hand against the center of her lust. She trembled at the feel of him there her body screaming for him to touch her directly. Demanding he tear off her clothes and take her.

"No. God no. Please," she whispered the words mortified but he silenced them with another drugging kiss that left her shaking inside because she knew he had her. "God, help me," her mind whispered as she begged for forgiveness for wallowing in her lust filled dreams.

126

Lance pulled in his drive and unfastened his seat belt as he cut off the engine. He drew Catharine to him and kissed her deep. A meeting of lips that stole his breath and had his body tingling from head to foot with the need to feel her. She reached for him and again her seat belt snapped her back denying her.

Lance eased back as she tore at the buckle with impatience. No, not in the car he told himself and he opened the door stepping outside into the morning air as Catharine freed herself. He opened the door for her and took her hand in his before heading for the apartment. He fought with the lock and once it gave way he stepped inside. He heard the door shut behind him and turned. His arms wrapped about her in a second and his mouth met with hers as he locked the door.

Catharine's arms wound around his neck and he pressed her back against the door as his hands slid down her body. She moaned into the kiss and he deepened it knowing now what she'd meant about getting close to her. CJ Nichols, no Serenity wanted him. Lance's hands slid over her body experimentally testing her limits and found none, her fevered pace only grew more rapid with the contact. Her hands tearing at his clothes looking for his body.

Lance reveled in the feel of her even as he wondered what they were doing. Forty-eight hours earlier she'd been-- the images flooded his mind and he froze. She'd been as good as dead, now she was in his arms alive. Trembling, seeking to have him and he wanted her. Wanted to hold her, touch her, taste her and then fill her. He wanted to surround himself in her presence until he drowned in it. Wanted her naked against the door screaming his name. Lance blinked no, not against the door that might be unpleasant for her. He wanted, no needed for her to be comfortable, to enjoy their union, but more than that he needed for her to be ready to take this step and she wasn't, not really.

This sudden hunger they felt tearing at them was not natural. Dionysus was playing with them. The notion turned his stomach even as his fingers found their way inside her jeans. He hissed finding her warm and wet. His eyes fell shut as her hips bucked against him pressing him inside her.

His eyes opened. Ice blue met with cobalt and saw the all too familiar gaze, that haunting mix of fear and desperation that confirmed his suspicions, she wasn't ready. He'd wanted to be wrong. To see no fear there but it was unmistakable the wine god was at work here. Lance groaned in frustration, he'd begun to think Dionysus's influence upon them was gone now that they were no longer with in an arm's reach of his host but he saw now he was mistaken.

Lance eased back from Catharine breaking their kiss and drawing his hand out of her clothes.

"Lance?" Her voice held hurt and confusion and he swallowed unsure if he could endure it. He kissed her forehead as he drew a breath to calm down.

"You're not ready for this Catharine--" he stated knowing he needed to explain.

"How can you say that? You touched me. You felt--" she began with disbelief. He kissed her to quiet her, unsure if he could resist the writer painting the image of what he'd felt with her words.

"I did, but you're not, it's too soon after--" Lance swallowed unable to go on. He watched as she blinked as if coming out of a daze. The harsh reminder doing a considerable job of cooling her blood. She drew her hands from him as if burned.

"God--Lance, I'm sorry. I didn't mean to--I was going to use you to forget-- I can't believe--I think I'm going to be sick," she said ashamed.

"Don't hate yourself Serenity, neither of us are quite ourselves. Dionysus--"

"Shh, no need to explain-- I get it-- thank you," she said before turning away from him unable to meet his eyes.

"Look at me Catharine," he requested.

Blue eyes lifted to meet his gaze once more.

"It's not that I don't want you Serenity, so don't think that even for a minute. I do want you more than you'll ever know, but not with him in the middle of this. I want us to be clear headed when I touch you but more I need for your eyes to be free of fear when I have you," he stated as his hands brushed over her hips, his fingers caressing her inner thighs to tease the center of her desire.

Catharine gasped at the caress reveling in it and startled by it. His hands stilled, easing back. She licked her lips nervous now. "I don't know if that's possible," Catharine admitted.

"I'll wait." he assured her.

"Why?" She asked with disbelief.

"I love you Serenity, and you're worth waiting for," he whispered. He kissed her brow before turning to move down the hall.

"Lance--"

"I need a cold shower love, give me a little while to level out and we can talk further if you want," he stated before moving on.

127

Catharine moved away from the door and on stiff legs headed in the direction of her laptop. She flipped up the lid and opened a blank document. She set her fingers to the keys and set to typing, clearing her lust clouded mind by putting her thwarted desire in scene. When the work was done she closed the file without saving and drew a breath.

"I love you Serenity," his words echoed in her mind and left her terrified. He couldn't, they'd just met. It was too soon. Catharine swallowed knowing it was true, but more frightening was that she found she returned his feelings. Despite her vow to never love again she'd fallen blindly, hard and fast for the cop in his shower down the hall.

Part of her wanted to go after him and finish what they'd started, another part felt her stomach roll with illness and knew he was right Dionysus had been playing them, a third part wanted to throw open the door, turn, run and never look back. Knowing it was safer.

Catharine rose from the table and headed for the guest bathroom. She'd deal with the aftermath of Dionysus game and when her head was clear then she'd sort out what to do about Lance and her feelings for him.

128

As Sam reached the end of the hall the double doors ahead of him flew open before him. Thrown open by a strong wind. What he saw before him made his blood boil with fury.

"YOU GET HER OUT OF HERE, I'LL DEAL WITH THE WINE GOD," a familiar feminine voice commanded.

Sam blinked. Artemis. What was she doing there? Why help Anna? He didn't know nor did he care. He didn't hesitate though to do as she bade, aware he needed all the help he could get. Sam watched as the huntress pulled Anna from Dionysus's embrace before his fangs could pierce her throat. The wine god roared in rage as Anna moaned in protest at the loss of his touch.

Red eyes met with the huntress's blue ones. "SHE WANTS ME. I'M WITHIN MY RIGHT HERE."

"SHE WANTS HIM, AND YOU'VE TWISTED THAT," Artemis corrected as Sam gathered Anna into his arms. She trembled in his embrace and protested as he led her away from Dionysus.

"Anna, come on doc, it's over," he murmured as he tucked her head under his chin and held her close to him. His fingers brushed the straps of her dress back into place covering her body to conceal it from her captor and the others around them.

"Sam?" her voice questioned weak and unsure.

"Yeah, doc, it's me. I've got you. We're getting out of here," he assured her.

"Is this real?"

"Yes it is sister dear, now come on," Terra muttered with irritation as she watched the bizarre events transpiring within.

Anna wept with relief and whispered her thanks to the heavens as Sam led her from the room. As soon as they were clear of the doors he heard them slam shut and lock. Artemis was making it clear she would face the wine god alone. Sam didn't care right now he just wanted Anna as far from this place as he could get her. He wanted her safe before Hades returned. As they entered the throne room, gun fire greeted them and it was clear getting out would prove more difficult than getting in. Terra and Vince returned fire as Sam moved Anna behind him and drew his weapon. It was going to be a long night but at least the War god wasn't in the fray.

129

Zaharrah sat in her hotel room at the King David studying the map of the old kingdom working to glean the location of the other cities from the modern map beside it. As she tried to make sense of it her eye lids began to droop with fatigue.

She'd gotten little sleep since Brooke's call and what sleep she'd managed had been troubled by dreams of the desert she was about to enter. Hades was close now, she could almost feel him watching her. She had to be ready to guard her mind against him. This was her last conscious thought before she dozed off and slipped into dreams.

Chocolate eyes blinked as her mind woke on the other side in the dream realm. Zaharrah cursed knowing where she was. Her normal attire replaced by a Grecian gown of blue. She sat up and a hand reached down, it grabbed her by the wrist and drew her to her feet so that they stood face to face.

"ZAHARRAH, MY DARLING, IT THRILLS ME TO MEET YOU AT LAST," he whispered before raising her hand to his lips and kissing it. Zaharrah drew her hand free of his grasp breaking contact quickly.

"You waste your time here Hades, I will never be yours."

The god of the underworld laughed at her words as he drew her to him again. "MY DEAR LADY, YOU'VE BEEN MINE YOUR WHOLE LIFE. THE VOW YOU SPOKE IN YOUR YOUTH AND THE ONE YOUR PARENTS MADE WHEN YOU WERE DEDICATED TO THE ORDER BOUND YOU TO ME FOR LIFE. JUST AS THE DAY YOU BROUGHT GUNNAR'S

CHILD INTO THIS WORLD SEALED HIS FATE."

"I walked away from them as you bid and have never looked back. I severed that tie. You have no right to touch them so long as I never set foot in that door again," Zaharrah snapped in outrage.

"YES, BUT SOON THE EVENTS UNFOLDING WILL LEAVE YOU WITH NO CHOICE. YOU'LL GO BACK AND WHEN YOU DO THEY WILL BE MINE, UNLESS--"

"Unless what?"

"UNLESS YOU SURRENDER TO MY WILL HERE AND NOW," Hades muttered.

"Even if I consent here you cannot force my hand out there. I have to give myself willingly in desire, not swayed.

"YOU KNOW MUCH, I'M GLAD. THEN YOU SHOULD KNOW I WILL NOT BE TURNED AWAY," Hades hissed as his hands roamed over her curves.

"Yes, as I know the power you wield is capable of carrying out your threats so long as one bound by blood believes. I will not run from you Fallen One nor will I fight you here. If it is this dream form that will stay your hand I will give you my body here in this place as you demand but only in this place. My heart and soul you will never touch."

"WE SHALL SEE," Hades murmured as he drew her into his arms so that no space was between them. "OH MY DEAR, SWEET LADY, ZAHARRAH, THE DESERT BLOSSOM, LONG HAVE I AWAITED THIS NIGHT. YOU WHO ARE MOST LIKE MY BELOVED PERSEPHONE OF OLD, NOW AS THEN YOU GIVE ME A PART OF YOURSELF AND WITH TIME YOU WILL SEE THAT A PART LEADS TO ALL," he whispered before his lips fell upon her claiming them and he took greedily that which he was given. .

130 ATHENS, GREECE

"OUT OF MY WAY WOMAN," Dionysus roared as Artemis blocked his path to pursue Anna.

"Never. She is my charge, you'll not touch her again."

"SHE WANTED ME, EVEN YOUR PET CONCEDED THE FACT IT COULD SMELL HER DESIRE ON HER."

"You've manipulated her mind. We both know it wine god. She wants that mortal and you cannot bed an influenced mind and hope to have an heir and we both know it. Leave Hades games to him. Forget Anna she will never be yours. Forget her and have me instead. An heir of Zeus's blood would strengthen your claim to the throne," Artemis whispered.

"YOU MAKE A GOOD POINT."

"Release her and I will be your queen," Artemis bargained.

"WHAT OF YOUR ALLEGIANCE TO YOUR UNCLE?" Dionysus asked curious.

"He lost it the moment he entered my body," Artemis hissed in rage.

"SO ANGRY, MY HUNTRESS IS. I WILL GIVE YOU BLISS AND TOGETHER WE WILL CRUSH THOSE WHO OPPOSE US MY QUEEN," he whispered.

"RELEASE HER," Artemis commanded again. She watched with satisfaction as Dionysus poured out the wine in his cup and drank water instead. He grimaced at the taste and spat out the rest cleansing his palate of the wine made from Anna's lust. "Promise me that you will never sip from that cup again," Artemis requested.

"I SWEAR IT."

"THEN COME OH BAUCUS, LORD OF DEBAUCHERY, COME AND CLAIM THY BRIDE," Artemis commanded. The wine god closed the distance between them and embraced her. His form twisted and bent revealing the true face of the beast beneath the facade. She kissed him in acceptance of his real form though the mortal blood in her veins screamed for her to run.

Artemis then turned her head to the side exposing her jugular for him. Giving him the right to taste her blood. She felt the sting of his fangs followed by the sudden rush of pleasure as he licked her skin. Using the intoxicant in his bodies' secretions to draw her under his spell.

Fierce nails tore her dress apart before cutting his own wrist for her. Artemis took the offered drink and lifted it to her lips. She licked the wound tentatively expecting to be turned away by the metallic taste of blood but found not the unpleasant tang of blood but the familiar taste of a wine she knew well. She gasped as it went straight to her head. She wrapped her lips around the wound and drank deep as its flavor ran through her making her burn with need of him.

His fangs sank into her breast and she cried out in agony and ecstasy as he drew her deeper under his spell. Her fingers fisting in his hair, holding him to her, begging for more. She felt her knees bump into the end of the bed and his lips parted her flesh as she fell back on the bed lost in the haze of passion. She was numb, aware that his bite had sent her over the edge, her womb was clenching with her first release.

She'd barely recovered from the first storm when his fangs pierced her inner thigh along the femoral artery. She moaned as his feeding built her need of him again the ache between her legs became painful now not even his bite would ease it. If he didn't take her soon she feared she'd die for want of him.

Artemis squirmed moving more of herself onto the bed weak from the blood loss but not caring, all she wanted was him inside her. Dionysus settled over her and offered her his neck. She bit him driven by instincts not her own and drank desperately in her thirst and need. She felt his fangs pierce her breast again as he gave her that which she wept for.

His body entered hers with a long, slow thrust that had her body arching toward him trembling in instant release. His eyes met hers as he lifted his head from her breast. "NOW LITTLE PRINCESS, YOU ARE MINE," he whispered before he kissed her and began to move.

His stokes were long and hard. Each time he drew back he left her body completely empty exiting slowly so that she felt every inch of him. Every penetration was fast and brutal burying him to the hilt so that his balls pressed against her teasing her forbidden entrance with the promise of its own chance at being filled so. His every advance left her quaking with the next peak of her pleasure and his retreat had her begging for more desperate to have him back inside her.

That was his power, he gave pleasure on a level that drove one mad for whatever he gave. Artemis cried out with shock at the heat of his seed filling her womb and trembled as her body tightened around him squeezing every drop and taking it deeper. She lay beneath him eyes nearly black with her passion as he drew out of her, pressed his still swollen member against her belly. His form reverted back to the man. "BREATHE HUNTRESS, AND DRINK WE'RE JUST GETTING STARTED," he whispered as he offered her his wrist, she drank as he bid and lay still as he sought his own enjoyment.

131

Sam and the others moved into the throne room, Magnus's men now dealt with. Terra and Vince headed for the door as Sam brought up the rear Anna between them. As he moved to go Ares lifted his head and orange eyes met with his.

"WILL YOU LEAVE WITHOUT DEFENDING YOUR LOVE'S HONOR? I THOUGHT YOU A WARRIOR PERHAPS I WAS WRONG."

"Artemis will see to the wine god," Sam said with confidence recalling how she'd dispatched the War god's previous host.

"IS THAT WHAT YOU THINK?"

"She dealt with you."

"YES, SHE DID AND YET HERE I STAND BEFORE YOU. IF A BATTLE RAGED I'D FEEL IT MORTAL. I'D KNOW. MY POWER COMES FROM WAR. THERE IS NONE IN THIS PLACE. THE HALLS REEK OF MY BROTHER'S WINE, AS YOUR WOMAN DOES. ARTEMIS ISN'T FIGHTING BAUCUS SHE'S FUCKING HIM," Ares mocked.

Sam froze. "You're lying."

"SHE GAVE HERSELF TO PROTECT YOUR LADY, AND NO DOUBT HAS AGAIN TO ENSURE HER SAFE PASSAGE. DIONYSUS IS GETTING EXACTLY WHAT HE WANTS. A WILLING WOMAN TO GIVE HIM AN HEIR AND YOUR LEAVING, MEANING THAT HE'S NOT ONLY GOING TO GET AWAY WITH WHAT HE'S DONE TO YOUR WOMAN, HE'S GOING TO HAVE A BRIDE OF ROYAL BLOOD. AFTER HADES LITTLE DISPLAY HE'LL BE IN PLACE TO CLAIM ZEUS'S THRONE."

"Your war is not my concern."

"DO YOU THINK THAT DRUNKEN WOMANIZER WILL EVER REALLY LET YOUR WOMAN GO? DO YOU

HONESTLY BELIEVE SHE'LL EVER BE FREE OF HIS POWER? THE MOMENT HE HAS MY BROTHER'S CROWN HE'LL BREAK HIS VOW WITH THE HUNTRESS AND FINISH WHAT HE STARTED. HE'LL MAKE HER BEG FOR HIM TO TAKE HER. YOU SAW HER AS DID I, SHE WAS NEARLY DESPERATE TO BE BACK IN HIS ARMS."

"Enough!"

"OH, I SEE THERE IS SOME FIRE IN THOSE VEINS YET. SHE'LL TURN THAT PRETTY HEAD FOR HIM AND HE'LL BITE HER THROAT. HE'LL GET DRUNK ON THE TASTE OF HER LUST. THAT BITE WILL DRIVE HER MAD. SHE'LL SURRENDER HERSELF TO HIM THEN, DRINKING HIS BLOOD AS HE TAKES HER."

Sam was by the marble desk in an instant unaware of when he'd begun to move or how he'd gotten there. His fist flew striking Ares host in the face. "I said that's enough," Sam hissed.

"THERE, THAT'S BETTER. RAGE, WRATH, HATRED I KNEW YOU HAD IT IN YOU. HERE, TAKE MY SWORD. CUT DOWN YOUR ENEMY," Ares whispered as the man he possessed held out a knife to him.

Sam stared at the blade wanting it. Wanting, to do as the War god said. Dionysus was his enemy and a threat to the woman he loved. Every fiber in his being demanded he kill the wine god. Knowing that Dionysus was not being punished as he'd imagined but growing in power made his mind rage for vengeance.

"Sam no!" Anna cried out in distress as she moved toward him. He reached to take the knife prepared to do what Artemis had not. "SAM! You can't I won't lose you. If you take that sword you'll be his," Anna shouted as she came to his side.

"ANNA go! This has to be done."

"NO! It doesn't. Forget this madness. Once you cut down Dionysus then what? You'll just put down the sword."

"Yes."

"Don't lie Sam. He'll whisper in your ear set you to killing Hermes and then Hades and any other he can convince you is a threat to me. One taste of blood and he'll have you. You'll put that knife in his hands and your soul will be his to devour. Once you're gone who will protect me from him? Nobody will be able to. He'll be in your body!"

Sam blinked seeing the image she painted in his mind and knew it to be true. If he took that blade now and acted out his vengeance they'd both be lost.

"I'LL RELEASE YOU WHEN YOU'VE SLAIN HIM. I CAN FIND ANOTHER HOST I ALREADY HAVE, TWICE," Ares assured him.

"No, Anna's right. I'll not play your puppet war god. I'll not hand you the key to your freedom, a bride and the crown in one second for revenge. God will see to him and you as well," Sam hissed before he took Anna's hand and turned to walk away.

"I KNOW YOU SAM ABRAMS, AND I'LL NOT REST UNTIL ALL YOU LOVE IS DEAD. YOU WILL TAKE THIS KNIFE NOW OR IT WILL TAKE YOU."

"Then it will take me. Find another soul to take Fallen One you won't have mine," Sam stated before he led Anna from the room. Ares roared in rage behind him as his host refused to act upon his command to kill them.

132

Zaharrah woke to the loud blare of her alarm clock and the unpleasant memory of having spent her sleeping hours within Hades embrace in the dream realm. Explicit images of what she'd endured through the night at the lord of the underworld's hand flashed through her mind and her stomach rolled in disgust as she rose from the table where she'd been working.

As she moved about she found her body ached and she wondered if Hades spirit had indeed visited her while she slept and violated her as the old legends claimed. She could feel him watching her now, his scent lingered in the air. His power was all around her and she could swear she felt his touch upon her still.

Disgusted by the sensation she entered the bath and washed. Hot water beat down on her flesh and she scrubbed at her skin. She lingered in the shower until the water ran cold and still her mind tormented her with what she'd allowed him to do. She felt no change in her physical state. Her skin was raw from washing and she didn't feel clean. As her mind flashed, the image of him over her naked moving inside of her, Zaharrah lost the battle with her stomach and wretched in the toilet. She rinsed out her mouth clearing away the sick taste. Grabbing a towel she dried off her skin and got dressed.

Returning to her workspace she compared the king's map of his realm to a modern one and fixed her first destination for the missing lost cities. As she packed up her gear her phone chimed with a text. Zaharrah glanced over at the message and groaned it seemed the commander had made good on his threat, he was there in Jerusalem and wanted to know when she would be free to meet again.

She sent him a quick response explaining she'd be out in the field for the foreseeable future and that meeting was an impossibility, if he needed to talk to her he'd have to maintain contact via text. With his questions answered and the path before her identified, she grabbed her gear and left the hotel setting off for the desert. She prayed her path would not cross with Hades that morning for she wasn't ready to face the consequences of last night's actions yet.

133

The commander read Zaharrah's reply and cursed, he considered following her but his phone chirped signaling another incoming text; he read the message to himself and dismissed the notion.

"Back off Miss Lynch's trail she's well in hand."

All right then, he'd play the game as Miss Lynch had dictated. Send messages for now, so that she didn't question his silence and perhaps once her work here was done they'd meet again to determine just what the hell had gone wrong at the dig site in the Bermuda triangle and why his team was dead.

134

Catharine groaned as she re-read the most recent content she'd written for her book. She was still stuck and none of her normal tricks for getting through the block seemed to be working.

"Problem?" Lance asked as he stepped into the room to check on her. They'd kept their distance since he finished his shower, careful not to get too close. She'd tried to write and he'd read in the other room.

"Yeah, are you done yet with Heart of Stone?"

"I finished it yesterday," he said pleased with himself.

"Would you mind reading what I've got on the new one? I'm stuck and can't seem to write my way out of it. Maybe a fresh perspective will help me." Catharine explained.

"Sure, in the meantime why, don't you, take a break? Watch a movie or something else enjoyable for you?" Lance suggested.

"It couldn't hurt," Catharine muttered. She saved her work and hit control home to return to the beginning of the document then rose from her chair. As she walked out of the room Lance walked in to take her place. They passed each other without a word, careful to avoid eye contact, fearful of setting off a spark that might reignite the fire Dionysus had stirred up between them earlier.

Catharine drew a breath trying to settle her nerves and the smell of fresh soap flooded her senses as they passed. Unbidden the words he'd spoken earlier raced through her mind. "I love you, Serenity," They echoed around in her brain and once she was in the hall Catharine looked to the front door, her mind screaming at her to run away. Falling in love never ended well for her. She was better off not trying again.

But she couldn't just leave, not yet anyway, she'd just put her book in his hands and until she got it back; she was stuck. Catharine's gaze moved to look down the hall in the direction of the living room and instead of walking out as her instincts cried she moved further into the house. Entering his living room she grabbed the remote and flipped on the TV. Catharine sank down on to the couch to wait him out. When he was done then she'd be free to go.

135

Zaharrah's thoughts ran back to her strange visitor and her brother's strange message. She considered what it might mean but the knowledge escaped her. She pulled out her phone to call Sam Abrams instead and ask him about the woman. She paused in her efforts to dial and cursed finding she'd missed another call during the night. She wondered if it was from the commander and figured she better check. Pressing the button for her voice mail she punched in her pin number and waited for her message.

"Zaharrah, to obtain the key you seek you need to go back to the root of our family tree, the source of our woe," Darrian's voice whispered before the line went dead.

She checked the number for the incoming call but didn't recognize it. Darrian was alive and now thanks to his second clue she could open the files he'd left her on the flash drive. Zaharrah pulled over on the side of the road and pulled out her laptop. She turned it on and waited impatiently for the system to boot up. When it was done she popped in the thumb drive and pulled up the file. The password prompt came up once more to block her from gaining access and she typed in the word 'Pandora' and hit enter. The prompt went away and a number of documents opened.

Zaharrah skimmed over them, most of it was Brooke's notes and research concerning the project. Genetics jargon way over her head but a brief document buried in the middle of them was clear enough.

"Operation Firestorm to commence. Beasts bred and on line. Target 31° 46' 48" N / 35° 13' 48" E."

Zaharrah ran a net search on the quadrants and froze as the true meaning of the words sank in. Understanding now why Brooke had hired her brother to steal the data. Why Darrian had left it with her, when he couldn't get out clear? Why Brooke was now dead and what Hades had meant last night in the dream about things being in motion that would take her back to Gunnar's door. Hades was planning to have a dragon attack Jerusalem. She had to warn him.

No, not yet. She couldn't go home, her job wasn't done. But she had other options. Zaharrah linked her cell phone to the laptop and copied over the files. She then punched in Sam's number and prayed he would answer.

136

Sam pulled out his cell phone to call Lance and let him know Anna was safe as they reached the airport. Before he pressed the button to dial out, it rang. The caller ID indicated it was Zaharrah and he pressed the button to connect the call.

"Hello."

"Mr. Abrams, thank God."

"You sound relieved to have caught me, Miss Lynch."

"I am. I'm sending you a file. I need you to get it to Gunnar in Jerusalem as soon as you can."

"Why? What's going on?"

"I found out why Brooke Silvers was murdered and it's big. I'd fill him in myself but I'm headed into the desert to find the remaining plains cities on Broody's orders."

"Damn it. That is not good news."

"Why?"

"My research team found records that point to the crown being in one of the two remaining cities."

"So that's what he's after; which is all the more reason for me to go. I'll do my best to make sure he doesn't get it."

"Zaharrah, Hades left here. He's headed that way too."

"Yeah, I know." Zaharrah muttered. She sighed and the image of her visitor popped into her head. "Oh, some blonde woman with intense blue eyes warned me to stay clear of the other mantles. She said they were a curse not a gift. Who else is out on this twisted treasure hunt?"

"That would be Artemis."

"Is she a friend or foe?" Zaharrah asked needing to know.

"Not sure. Friend maybe," Sam replied considering the matter.

"Okay. Thanks for all your help. I'll meet up with you in Jerusalem as soon as I get clear of the desert and fill you in on all that I know," Zaharrah promised.

"We'll be waiting to hear from you," Sam said before he hung up. "Change of plans gang; we're headed for Tel Aviv and then Jerusalem."

"Do I even want to know why?" Terra asked, her voice made it clear she hadn't cared for the odd exchange she'd just witnessed.

Sam opened the file Zaharrah had sent and cursed. Before handing it over for her to look at.

"A dragon? What?"

"How the hell are we going to stop a bloody dragon?" Vince asked.

"We kill it," Sam said though how one did that he had no clue.

"How? It's not like I've got a sword or lance handy," Terra muttered.

"Ah darlin', ya' disappoint me, I thought ya' had a full arsenal with ya 'at all times," Vince said with a wink.

"So, we'll find something," Anna said amused by the pair.

"Oh no, not we. I'm trained for this, you sister dear are going back state side--" Terra snapped.

"The hell I am. The minute I go home is the same moment I get caught again," Anna muttered with disgust.

"Anna's right, if we send her back she's as good as caught. Broody, Halden, or Hardagen any one of them might pick her up."

"Why? What is this all about yank?" Terra demanded.

"I'll let Anna explain it to you, in the meantime I'm going to give my research team a call. They'll come up with some kind of dragon lore for killing this thing," Sam muttered before he took back his phone and punched in Lance's number.

"What do you mean you're trained for this? You're a DJ," Anna snapped and Sam chuckled. Yes, those two had a lot to talk about. He'd give them a chance to do it before they got on the plane.

137

Lance cursed as the sound of his cell phone ringing broke into the scene he was reading. He glanced at the clock and groaned who was calling him at three in the morning anyway.

"Catharine, can you get that?" He called not wanting to stop reading, he was nearly done.

"Yeah." Lance turned his attention back to the laptop but her voice drew him out again. "Oh, hello Mr. Abrams, did you find Anna?" Lance heard her ask. "Yeah, that's great."

They'd gotten Anna back, finally some good news.

"So are you headed back?"

"Catharine, put him on speaker phone I want to hear what he has to say," Lance requested. The book could wait for a minute.

"No, we're headed to Jerusalem," Sam's voice came through the room as Catharine made her way from the living room toward him.

"Why?" Lance asked surprised.

"We've got a message to deliver there."

"Okay," Catharine said, her voice was full of curiosity and he could see the writer's mind working to sort out what that might mean.

"Look, I know it's late but can you do us a favor?"

"Sure," Lance muttered figuring he'd be up a while yet at this rate anyway.

"Get together as much information as you can on dragon slaying," Sam answered.

"On what?" Lance asked with disbelief thinking maybe he'd heard wrong.

"You heard him right," Anna's voice chimed in. Lance let out a breath, as relief washed through him, she sounded fine.

"Okay we're on it," Catharine assured them before he could

respond.

"Thanks," Sam said before he hung up.

"Dragon slaying?" Lance asked his voice incredulous.

"Slide over," Catharine commanded as she rounded the table to start the search. Lance did so still not believing the request. He watched as Catharine opened another program and typed in the words 'dragon lore means of slaying' then pressed enter. The word 'searching' filled the screen and she minimized the prompt going back to her book. She skimmed the page looking to see where he was. "Almost done," she said pleased.

"Yeah, that's why I wanted you to take the call."

"I'll leave you to finish."

Lance moved back to his seat as she got up and turned his focus back to the scene. "Dragons." he muttered,

"Is that so difficult to accept, given the fact we've been face to face with an old god?"

Lance blinked, when she put it that way; maybe not.

"You have a point."

"Go back to your reading detective, the computer is doing our research when it's done we'll see about the answers Mr. Abrams needs," Catharine said amused before disappearing back down the hall.

Once he was alone Lance fell back into the scene he'd been reading before their phone call interrupted him.

'Serenity raced through the woods aware that someone was out there chasing her. Fear wrapped around her heart and threatened to stop her in her tracks. The same fear that had been eating away at her for centuries. She roared in fury at the pressure and turned abruptly to face whatever came at her. She was tired of the endless nightmare.

"Show yourself you coward! I'll not flee before you another step," she shouted in defiance. "You hunt Serenity but you'll not find her, I am Nivali and I will end you," she hissed in challenge and threat as her hazel eyes searched for her enemy.

"Ah, the sheep has fangs after all," a familiar voice mocked.

"Syvarin--" she gasped the name with alarm and disbelief. "How?"

"Did I survive? By staying to the shadows the same as you. Did I find you? Simple, I never lost you. We are bound Serenity, one to the other."

"Why--"

"Seek you now-- to warn you Kovrin is alive and searching for you."

"But Davrik--"

"My son is dead. Kovrin was only too happy to put him out of his misery after he understood you were beyond his reach," Syvarin revealed.

"You lie!"

"He died trying to save you."

"From what?"

"You don't know?"

"Know what?"

"Kovrin, when he couldn't find you he began hunting others like you. He's killed half a dozen so far."

"No," Serenity said with disbelief and fear.

"I'm afraid it's true. Look for yourself," Syvarin said as he handed her a fistful of crime scene photos.

"Oh God."

"He's never forgotten his taste for you Serenity. He'll not rest until he has you back. I sought you out to warn you and to offer my protection if you wish it."

"Why would I come back after what you've done to me?" Serenity asked her voice held disbelief and anger.

"I made mistakes with you Serenity, I know that now, but I loved you, still do. I let my jealousy cloud my judgment. It incensed me that you chose my son over me. Let me make right now the wrong I did you in our past."

"Syvarin--" She said overwhelmed by his sudden gentleness.

"Give me a chance Serenity. Let me love you as you deserved. Allow me to protect you from him in my son's absence. Together we can defeat him," the vampire lord entreated as he offered her his hand.

Serenity looked from the extended hand to the bloody photos. Memories long forgotten rose from the dark recesses of her mind. The smell of Kovrin's breath on her face, the feel of his hands on her as he pressed her body, enticing her to surrender to him. The sensation of him moving inside her as she begged him to stop. Terror filled her and Serenity moved to take the vampire lord's hand, but caution woke once more within her as she was reminded of his tricks of old. Anything Syvarin offered came with a price.

"What token do you desire to seal this pact?"

"Give me an heir Serenity, take your rightful place at my side as my queen once more."

"My life spared from his wrath and lust at the cost of my life?" she asked with dismay.

"No, your protection for your company," Syvarin corrected.

Serenity nodded her understanding before she took the offered hand with hesitation. Though she did not love him she was unwilling to face the werewolf lord again alone. She knew in her heart if she did; she'd not survive it.

"You've made a wise choice," Syvarin whispered pleased and he drew her into his arms. Serenity trembled at being so near him again but did not turn away as he kissed her. His lips met hers with a passion that stole her breath away. Tears fell from her eyes at the feel of his hands on her once more. Her heart cried out in denial of his touch, longing for Davrik even as her body began to burn with desire in the wake of his caresses. His hands were everywhere pawing and groping making her ache as a million memories swept through her of a time long ago when she'd been his.

Her heart raced in that strange yet familiar rhythm of fear and anticipation as her body prepared itself for him. Shame hung over her as she moaned in pleasure at the feel of his hands within her clothes touching the part of her she knew he desired most.

She trembled in his arms defenseless against the wave of pleasure that tore through her as a finger slipped inside her and felt her stomach twist with disgust knowing what he'd felt there. Her skin was warm for him, her passage wet and ready, weeping for him, begging to be filled. Serenity cursed Kovrin knowing it was his fault her body so quickly betrayed her heart. He'd taught it to respond when stimulated.

Syvarin growled in response to having touched her, aware of her state and she knew she was lost. Serenity felt the sting of his fangs as they sank into her throat, it came in unison with the sensation of his violent penetration as he entered her body to breed.'

Lance blinked having come to the end of the scene and licked his lips that had gone dry. He saw why Catharine was stuck. Her fans wanted to see Serenity happy and with the step she'd just taken that couldn't happen. Serenity was dying in this scene in that very moment. The only way she could end this was in death.

"I'm finished," he called trying to figure out what to tell Catharine to do. Worried it might reflect her own mind. Did she think she was alone?

"What do you think?"

"It's good, but I see why you're stuck."

"Any ideas what I should do?" Catharine asked.

"I'd drop that last bit with Syvarin. You've left Serenity in a place where this can't end well for her."

"I know, and I've tried to change it but it keeps writing itself this way. I've added more detail, emotion but it's always Syvarin who turns up for her here."

"Maybe it needs to be."

"What do you mean?"

"The way you've written her, Serenity always chooses the man to save her regardless of the consequences that follow. Maybe she shouldn't take his hand. She's not alone-- You're not alone Serenity. I'm here."

"I know…I just got scared."

"So you kill her off. You told me you weren't thinking suicide remember. This isn't helping your case."

"I remember and you're right, I'm just struggling with what happened more than I anticipated. I can't get it out of my head. Not this time and well Dionysus paid me a visit. He offered--"

"You a way out. Embrace him and he'll help you forget-- and you're considering it?" Lance asked with disbelief.

"Yes, no-- I don't know. He said some things about me that have got me all messed up."

"What things?" Lance asked trying to understand how she could write something that was basically her admission of surrender.

"That I've never been able to love someone without his influence over me. I lack the courage to give away my heart on my own."

"That's not true. You loved--"

"It is. I never wanted Kurt. He used alcohol to get to me. I didn't let Tom close until I'd had a couple glasses of champagne. It was the same with my artist friend. Hell, I haven't touched you, not once without Dionysus influence over me."

"That's not true you kissed me before LA."

"Never with intent, curiosity, maybe a little bit of desire but every time I've been ready to tear your clothes off its been his doing."

Lance blinked as her words sank in.

"When you told me before--"

"That I loved you," Lance finished seeing she couldn't say the words herself.

"I nearly turned and ran out the door I was so scared."

"I'm sorry, I didn't mean to--"

"Don't apologize. It's not your fault Lance. It's me I'm scared to love."

"Why?"

"All it's ever brought me is pain," Catharine stated.

138

Catharine swallowed her mind troubled with a storm of chaos brought on by all this talk about her feelings. "I mean Kurt claimed to love me and then he made me watch as he raped and tortured another woman just to slap at you for daring to come near me. He wanted me to kill her for him to prove my devotion. When I refused he--" Catharine's words died out as her throat grew tight. Tears welled in her eyes that she refused to let fall, as the images of what she faced filled her mind. She wanted it to stop; was aware in that moment she'd give anything to make it all go away.

"He what, Serenity? Talk to me. Tell me what happened in that basement. What did he do? The not knowing may drive me mad," he confessed seeing her turmoil, aware she was near the precipice and if he didn't draw her back he'd lose her as he'd lost Dana.

Catharine wiped her eyes and drew a breath. She bit her lip as she considered his request. He waited now with baited breath wondering if she would answer him or refuse again. Her lips parted and she swallowed past the lump in her throat.

"The act of killing them was a ritual for Kurt. The first cut marks the beginning of her first pain. He cut off the victims clothes with his knife and once she was naked then he teased her body with the feel of the cold blade against her skin, like some twisted caress. The more she moved to resist the wandering metal the more nicks the knife left against her skin. With the second cut the blade was replaced by his hands. He ran them over the victim's body to make clear what was to come tormenting her with the knowledge her body would be violated."

"That's what he was doing when I came in," Lance said with disgust.

Catharine nodded. "He spoke to me as he did these things breaking his pattern indulging in the taste of my blood. He needed their pain to help him with the rape. But not mine. I could see it in his eyes as he spoke."

"What did he say to you?" Lance asked needing her to stop telling the events like a third party observer. She needed to face it directly or it would only haunt her.

"You're so willful Serenity, you make it hard for me to not treat myself to a real taste of you. I've not had a bride that pleased me so completely in over two thousand years. I want to take my time with you but the mortal whom I'm sharing this body with wants all of you now and in the worst sort of ways imaginable," she quoted with disgust.

Lance tensed recalling the words from when he entered that foul place. He'd managed to block them from his mind somehow. "As he was doing that, saying those things, you knew what would come next when he was finished touching you," Lance said with mortification as he pictured it from her position.

Bound bloody, naked without any means of defense, laying there as a man who claimed to love her took liberties with her body he had no right to anymore; knowing the horrible things he would do to her before he ended the game and began to rape her.

"Yes. That's why I can't sleep at night. When I close my eyes he's there in the dark waiting. I feel it all again, only you're not there to stop him. I'm forced to endure all of it. Every cut, every pain, until he drives his knife into my heart and steals my last breath. I can't wake up until he's done and then when I do it's to the sick reality that because I foolishly drank from Dionysus's cup that I'm all hot and bothered. My body is crying for someone to fuck me," Catharine said with disgust.

Lance swallowed back a scream that threatened to tear free. Things were worse than he'd feared. The scene was a clear image of her mental state, she would either accept Dionysus's offer or kill herself given enough time. He cursed knowing he couldn't let either happen; he'd not survive it.

"Do you know how sick that is? To have seen the things that monster did to her, to dream he's doing it to me and wake up to find I want it," Catharine shouted in outrage and self-loathing.

"You don't want what he did to her, Serenity--" Lance began trying to reason with her.

"Yes, I do. I want to feel that blade cut beneath my eye marking me with a third tear. I want to know what it's like to have his mouth, any mouth hot and eager tasting my flesh. Licking the blood he's drawn from me with his knife. His teeth tearing my skin to indulge in more, where he wants. Followed by the bite of that god awful knife as he marks my face with a fourth tear.

The prick of golden fangs as he winds the first of his serpents around my arm from my wrist to my elbow marking me as his. I want the next one to prick my jugular and form that twisted choker then the feel of the fangs as he set the crown of serpents on my brow--"

"Catharine stop," he said not sure if he could listen to anymore, her words painting the image in his mind making his stomach revolt.

"The knife follows marking the fifth tear and its then you're aware of the smell; the fire burning. Watching helpless as he draws the first of his brands from the flame to press it against my arm. Screaming in a disturbing mix of pleasure and pain waiting for the next brand to mark me finding that I want it too, feeling somewhere inside that I deserve it, this pain tearing through me and making me ache for more. The knife tears my skin making the sixth cut and it's then he tattoos the dog on my foot. Making it clear your place here in this, you're his bitch and nothing more."

"Serenity--"

"The Seventh cut comes and he beats me. It's at that point I can't stand it anymore I want him to rape me and get it over with but the pain hasn't ended yet. The eight cut he turns his victim on her back and cuts the wings into my skin. He's careful to keep the slices shallow so it can't kill, he tastes the wounds licking at the blood like a cat laps at cream. His hands fist on my hips pressing his body against me letting me feel how my pain is effecting him. Making it clear that when he does use me, I won't know which way it'll be."

"That didn't really happen," Lance whispered trying to reach her. She'd not heard him once since she started this blow by blow relating of what she born witness to as Kurt had ended Gail Blackwood's life.

"The ninth cut he turns me back over and it's now he makes his first invasion of my body, fingers slamming deep inside me clawing at my hidden parts making them burn and ache with pain as he prepares for the real act to begin. The last cut is the worst, he puts needles in my flesh one after another all at major pressure points, when he's done he electrocutes me. When its' so much I feel like I'm blacking out he makes it stop-- waits for me to recover and then the final act begins."

"He rapes you," Lance said his voice weak as he struggled with the emotions warring around him.

"No it's worse than that. He uses my body for his pleasure one way after another defiling me in ways that are so vile I can't even describe them. By the time he's finished the first I want him. Want him to use me as he pleases until I'm all but dead. Then he picks up the knife lets me see it, asks me if I want it and has me begging to feel that blade pierce my heart and send me to the peace of oblivion after enduring all that pain and pleasure," Catharine roared; the words coming out of her like a cobra's venom.

Each image she painted was a blow to his heart that tore through him. Rage welled up inside him for what she'd been forced to see. For what she'd endured and what Dionysus had done to her that she could think she wanted that.

"No, you don't. You want only to be loved," Lance corrected.

"Yes, and that is how he loves."

"You said it yourself you never wanted Kurt. You don't want that. Look at you. The very thought of it disgusts you," Lance said trying to reach her now.

"But I wake up aroused," she said with shame and dismay.

"Dionysus's work. That's not what you want. You want a man who will love you as you deserve. One who'll treat you with kindness and stand by you. One that doesn't ask you to do anything that would damage your heart," Lance assured her.

"How can anyone want me after I've loved a monster," Catharine asked giving voice to a fear that weighed heavy on her heart.

"Because you're not what you've loved. You're not a monster Serenity. You are a beautiful faerie that's forgotten how to fly," he whispered as he drew her into his arms to offer her comfort.

"A faerie?" She asked amused.

"Yes, love. A wild, vibrant faerie princess lost in the woods unable to find her way out," he whispered and he kissed her hair.

"Thank you."

"You want to thank me change that scene and promise me you'll never accept Dionysus's offer."

"I promise."

"Good, I don't want to lose you to him, to any of them," Lance murmured as he held her close.

"You won't. Just be patient with me detective, all this love talk scares me."

"It scares me to Serenity," he confessed as he held her close.

139

Zaharrah pulled off the road and got out of her car as the rest of her team began to unload their gear. She skipped the tools and moved out into the sand to take a look. As her eyes scanned the area she noted the sand around the site had been disturbed. Something was off here.

She picked up a handful of dust and let it fall through her fingers. It was tainted by power. Not one she recognized but power none the less. There was nothing here. She needed to move on.

"You guys get started here, Mr. Elwood, Dr. Chase I'm going to drive on to the other location and scout it out," Zaharrah said before she turned and headed back to her car.

As she opened the car door she heard Fox mutter something about grandstanding tomb raider before heading into the desert. Zaharrah sighed as she got behind the wheel. Let him think what he wanted, she didn't care. Her phone beeped signaling a new text and she noted the commander had sent her a response. She'd look at it later she had a job to do.

140

Russell York watched as Zaharrah drove away, he stepped out into the sand to see what she'd seen. As he walked around he noted the sand seemed as if it had been disturbed recently. He moved to turn back to follow her and froze. In the distance the sunlight glinted off something. He moved towards it as the archeology team began setting up to start searching.

He found lying in the sand two pieces of what had been a golden scepter with pearl and lapis lazuli accents. He bent down and picked up the pieces then headed back to his car. Mr. Halden had told him to watch the dig, he'd go after Zaharrah but the gold was his. Severance after ten years of service when this job was done he was getting out before it was too late.

141

Catharine closed her eyes as her mind found ease in Lance's embrace. As he held her, an image began to form in her mind, the way to work out the mess she'd put Serenity in. The way to fix the current scene and get back to the outline she'd written. She opened her eyes and eased back.

"You okay?"

"Yeah, I just broke my wall. Let me go detective, I need to get back to work."

"You did?"

"Yeah, I'll let you read it when I'm done with the scene," she said as she moved back to her chair.

"Deal."

"Good, now go, you distract me," she said with a smirk before she put her fingers to the keys and began typing.

"I'll go for now," he answered before dropping a kiss on her head and walking away.

Catharine backed up the scene to just before Serenity took Syvarin's hand and began to type the changes she'd envisioned.

142

Sam drove across town in the direction of Gunnar's home as he tried to raise him on the phone, but he got no answer. He hoped Gunnar was in the mood for visitors because his home was about to be invaded by three US agents and one tenacious American archeologist. His eyes moved to Anna and he felt a kick to the back of his seat.

"Eyes on the road agent," Terra muttered.

The *Rogue* was less than pleased that her sister was there. If she'd had her way Anna would be far from them. It had taken some effort but Anna had convinced her of the danger they were caught in the middle of, if not all the full insanity. He didn't blame Terra for her temper, part of him wanted to leave her and Vince here to handle the matter and take Anna as far from this place as possible. It was the same part that had been listening to Ares words. The warrior that demanded he protect what was his.

Sam blinked as he turned his focus back to the road. Anna was not his. He punched in Gunnar's number and waited for an answer. When it went to voice mail this time he left a message. "Gunnar its Sam we need to talk, headed your way. Be there in about fifteen minutes, call me."

"Still no answer?" Vince asked.

"No."

"Maybe we should wait?" Anna suggested.

"No time," Sam muttered as he tightened his grip on the wheel. His mind was still wrestling with the strange impulse to protect Anna as if she were his. His mind drifted back to the weird exchange with the angel last time they spoke.

"Thank God you're here, help her. Take his curse away."

"Is that's what you really want, for her to no longer desire you? For her eye to fall upon another," the angel asked.

Sam blinked. Why was it his choice? If it meant she'd have peace yes, his mind answered but a part of him deep down cried out in protest.

"That's what I thought. No, this is not something that can be taken away." The angel stated.

"I didn't say anything," Sam objected.

"Yes, you did," the angel corrected.

He still didn't understand why the decision had been given to him to make or why the angel had acted as if he'd given an answer when he'd said nothing. He considered the question as he asked him again and froze as their meaning sank in.

He'd been given a choice to let her go. If he'd allowed it Anna would have forgotten him and found another. She'd have fallen in love with another, married and had his kids. Sam tore the mental image apart not liking it. If he'd let her go would he have forgotten her as well he wondered and again he rejected the idea, he didn't want to think about his life without her.

Anna--was his.

"Sam?"

"Yeah," he answered distracted.

"You okay?" Anna asked.

"Fine, just got a lot on my mind."

"How much further till we get to Gunnar's?"

"Five minutes," Sam answered,

"What's wrong?"

"Nothing."

"Sam--"

"What's with all this Sam business Annalynn? I've never known ya' ta' be overly familiar with anyone beyond the family," Terra inquired curious and uneasy.

"Mr. Abrams prefers to be called Sam," Anna said with a blush.

"I see. It took ya' a year to call Dr. Broody by his given name."

"Why the sudden interest in my habits?" Anna questioned not caring for the sudden interrogation.

"I don't want ta see ya' get hurt again sis and the reality is that Mr. Abrams is not--"

"Not what?" Anna asked her voice warning of temper.

"I'm not safe to be around Anna. My work makes anyone around me a target," Sam stated finishing her sister's warning for her, not caring for the intrusion in their business.

"And you are?" Anna asked her voice incredulous.

"Which is why ya' rarely see mi," Terra countered.

"I don't understand, you told me love isn't safe, it's a leap and now when I'm ready you--"

"Yes, it is but not this one Annalynn he's a spy, he'll be gone all the time, ya' won't know where he is, what he's doing or who he's with. Ya'll spend most of your nights unable ta sleep wonderin' if he's ever comin' back or if ya'll' get a phone call informin' ya' he's dead."

"I was a spy," Sam corrected his temper rising. He didn't care for the conversation around him one bit, they were talking about him as if he wasn't there.

"Do ya think they're goin' ta just let ya go again after this? Ya wanted back in, yur in; they won't let ya walk again Mr. Abrams," Terra snapped.

"What are you saying he's not worth the risk? You don't know him," Anna said with disbelief.

"I know his type Anna, he'll hurt ya."

"He'll hurt me; so don't jump? Should I run back to Ian then?" Anna asked with fury.

"No, I'm not sayin' that--"

"It's what it sounds like to me Terra-Anne," Anna challenged.

"Don't ya take that tone with mi Annalynn Darcy Gallagher."

"How dare you use my full name you're not my mother," Anna snapped.

"Terra we both know it doesn't have to be like that. She could go with him."

"Are ya honestly suggestin' mi baby sister become an agent Mr. Fenton. Have ya gone daft; she's a civilian."

Sam saw the other man flinch and then draw a breath.

"Aye she is, but so were you once and she seems quite resourceful."

"I don't believe mi ears. Are ya defendin' them then? I thought ya were supposed ta be on mi side, yank."

"I am on your side, love."

"And yet ya defend this foolishness."

"Foolishness," Anna asked hurt.

"Careful Terra--" Vince pressed.

"They're throwin' the word love around lightly, the both of them and they barely know each other, its madness."

"Terra, I'm just playin' devil's advocate."

"Well, bloody stop it. Do ya expect mi to sit by and watch while they blow kisses back and forth until he marries her?" Terra asked with fury.

"Yes, because it's my bloody choice," Anna snapped.

Sam's mood lightened at that and he chuckled amused by their spirit and the argument, immensely pleased to know if he asked; Anna would marry him.

"Are you not going to defend yourself Mr. Abrams?"

"No, you're doing just fine love," he said amused.

"You find this funny?" Anna asked her temper flaring.

"No-- not at first anyway, it was irritating."

"Then why are you laughing now?" She asked furious.

"Because your spirited debate has left me with a clear picture of where I stand in your estimations."

"And where is that exactly Mr. Abrams," she said reverting to miss prim and proper to push his buttons, the way he was pushing hers.

"Marriage material."

"I never said--" Anna began with alarm.

"I'm afraid ya did lass," Vince stated.

Sam watched amused as she blinked replaying the argument in her mind.

"I did," she said stunned, as she blushed with the boldness of her words.

"Ya stay out of this Mr. Fenton. Don't ya go givin' her any crazy ideas."

Sam's mind turned over the entire argument and his own realization of what Anna was to him, and though his logical mind told him it was too soon, his mouth opened and he asked a question he never thought to utter again. "What do you say Anna, will you marry me?"

"Sam-- I hardly know you," she said stunned at the question.

Terra kicked the back of his seat again. "That's enough Mr. Abrams, you've taken your joke too far now."

"I'm not joking. it's like you said our lives are unpredictable, short even. I love her, why not ask her to share my life. I'm not asking you to marry me tonight Anna, tomorrow or even a month from now. I'm asking you if at some point in the future when you're ready you'll be my wife Anna."

"You're mad," Terra said stunned.

"Maybe," Sam admitted. "What do you say Anna?"

"Yes."

"You will?" Sam asked a mix of joy and fear washed through him.

"The hell she will. I'll kill ya first."

"You will not. I love him sister and if I hear another word against it I'll never speak to you again."

"What will Mother and Father say when ya bring home a man who makes his livin' takin' punches?"

"I don't care," Anna said before she leaned over to kiss Sam's cheek.

Her sister blinked stunned by Anna's answer. "Well, haven't ya got anythin' ta say about this?" She asked Vince.

"Yeah, congratulations."

"Ah, you're as mad as them."

"I'd have ta be."

"Why's that?" Anna asked amused.

"I married your sister," Vince muttered,

Anna laughed at the response.

"Yeah, how did you two meet?" Sam asked.

"I'll tell ya another time," Vince promised.

143

Zaharrah slowed her car as she neared the point on the map, she'd marked as the sight for the fourth plains city Admah. Before even stepping out of the car she noted that the sand here looked disturbed as well. Someone had been here. Climbing out of her vehicle Zaharrah approached the shifted sand and gathered a handful. As it slipped through her fingers she found the same magic taint and cursed. Was she too late? Had they found what they came for?

"IT AMAZES ME HOW SUCH A BARREN WASTELAND CAN HIDE SUCH ASTOUNDING SECRETS," a man's voice murmured. It was one she had never heard and yet knew all too well.

"Hades," she breathed the name without turning, having no desire to look upon him. Her knees trembled with the need to run.

"HERE YOU ARE AT LAST IN THIS PLACE OF SAND AND DEATH SO LIKE TARTARUS. A BEAUTIFUL DESERT BLOOM, JUST LIKE MY SWEET PERSEPHONE," he whispered.

"I'm not your wife," Zaharrah hissed.

"OH, WELL I KNOW IT. PERSEPHONE WAS A TITLE GIVEN TO MANY A WOMAN IN THE PAST, NOT ONE WOMAN. THE NAME BESTOWED UPON MY BRIDE AND QUEEN. IT WILL SUIT YOU WELL."

"I'll never answer to it."

"HUSH, LADY, LET'S NOT FIGHT, JUST YET, COME I WILL SHOW YOU THE DESERT'S SECRET. BEHOLD ADMAH, THE CITY OF THE KING," Hades declared as he drew upon his power to unearth the city. Parting the sands like the Creator had parted the Reed Sea.

Zaharrah studied the ruins and noted it was laid out in much the same fashion as the others. She started through the gate beside him, though she wanted nothing to do with him, her feet compelled her to keep his pace.

"HERE THE KING'S SUBJECTS BUILT A TEMPLE DEDICATED TO US THEIR GODS. WE TEN STAND ALONE AND IN RANK WITHIN TO ACCEPT THEIR OFFERINGS. IT WAS HERE AFTER ZEUS WAS SLAIN THAT I BROUGHT HIS CROWN TO BE PRESENTED AS A GIFT TO HONOR THEIR KING. ARTEMIS CAME WITH ME THAT NIGHT FOR IT WAS MY INTENT TO GIVE THE GIRL TO THE KING AS A BRIDE. A PLEDGE TO MAKE THESE PEOPLE OUR OWN. A LINE OF THE FALLEN. HUMAN BUT MORE, THEY WERE TO SERVE US, WORSHIP US AND FEAR US. ONE'S WHO WOULD SPREAD OUR NAMES ON THE FOUR WINDS NEVER TO BE FORGOTTEN. IT IS HERE MY PRIZE WAITS."

"Why surrender the crown at all?" Zaharrah asked puzzled.

"OUT OF RESPECT. ZEUS WAS OUR KING. IT WAS NOT RIGHT TO SQUABBLE SO SOON AFTER HE WAS SLAIN OVER HIS THRONE. IT WAS AGREED ZEUS'S THRONE WOULD SIT EMPTY UNTIL THE KING'S THIRD GENERATION HAD PASSED."

"You were more concerned with maintaining order among your sheep," Zaharrah muttered with disgust.

"NO, NOT ORDER THAT WAS NOT OUR DESIGN, WE LOOKED TO PRESERVE THEIR WORSHIP."

"Your source of power."

"RIGHT."

"Then how is it you have power now? Your old names are but myth today."

"YES, BUT THE LOVE OF WHAT WE REPRESENT STILL BEATS STRONG IN THE HEARTS OF MEN, AS DOES THEIR FEAR," Hades said amused as they reached the king's palace.

Stepping inside he made his way to the temple and Zaharrah noted that here was the difference that marked this city unique. The wall carving in Sodom and Gomorrah was missing; in its place stood statues of the gods in a half circle gathered around a stone table, at each end stood two goddesses waiting.

As she moved deeper into the room the images became clear. On the right hand side of the altar stood Hera and Demeter side by side, the goddesses of power and fertility, on the left Aphrodite and Cybele goddess of love or passion and the wild. A symbol was carved on the stone; one that made Zaharrah tremble with fear. The image for Persephone.

The gods stood in ranked pairs, Helios at the far left followed by Hermes, Zeus and Poseidon, Hades stood in the middle overlooking all that took place within the chamber with Chaos at his side. Ares and Hephaestus together and Eros and Dionysus at the far right. As her steps brought her closer to the table Zaharrah understood why he'd brought her there. Why it was here they were destined to meet?

"THIS IS MY CITY ZAHARRAH, AND THIS IS THE KING'S TEMPLE. EVERY SACRIFICE HE EVER OFFERED WAS IN THIS CHAMBER. HIS WORSHIP WAS GIVEN TO ALL THE GODS BUT I GOT THE LION'S SHARE OF IT FIRST. THIS PLACE STILL HOLDS GREAT POWER FOR ME, IT ECHOES IN THE ROOM. EVERY BRIDE I WAS GIVEN WAS OF ROYAL BLOOD, CREATED IN THIS VERY ROOM," Hades revealed as he ran a hand over the stone reveling in the echoes of the acts performed there, drawing power from it.

Zaharrah tensed feeling it now, his taint all around her. The reason for her inability to turn away from him was the ground itself had cast a spell upon her, drawing her here to this place. They'd met here; because here he had the advantage.

"YOU ARE ONE OF PRIVILEGE ZAHARRAH; YOU CAN NOW BOAST THAT YOU WERE FOUND TO BE THE EQUAL TO A QUEEN OF ROYAL BLOOD. A TRULY HIGH HONOR FOR A WOMAN TO ACHIEVE. YOU WILL BE MY QUEEN."

"No."

"OH, BUT YOU WILL. ONCE ZEUS'S CROWN IS UPON MY HEAD WITH THE POWER I HOLD YOU WON'T BE ABLE TO RESIST ME," Hades whispered as he combed his fingers through her long dark hair. He moved from her side towards the map wall and she spotted them, Erebus and Hecate, standing facing each other their hands outstretched, a pillar between them. It sat bare, but she could picture it in her mind a golden crown had rested there bejeweled with the stones of all the gods marking them subservient to his power.

Zeus's crown was gone. The mantle that marked the king of the gods was missing. Its pedestal was empty and Zaharrah laughed.

"It looks like you were gloating too soon, Fallen One. Your prize is gone. Claimed by another and despite what you say we both know my hand is not free for the taking," Zaharrah hissed as she took a step away from the altar, Hades' spell upon her having broken with the discovery he didn't know all. His power like the others was limited.

"YOU LEFT THAT LIFE BEHIND ZAHARRAH. IT DOES NOT GIVE YOU THE RIGHT TO DENY MY CLAIM," Hades snapped in warning. The torches around her blazed higher, their light blinding her. "YOU EMBRACED ME JUST LAST NIGHT FREELY IN THE DREAM REALM," he reminded in temper his voice closer now. Zaharrah threw up her hands to shield her eyes as she instinctively took another step back away from the stone table knowing it was there he meant to bed her. That the power it held would make her defenseless against him. She had to get out of that room.

"YOU WERE BOUND TO ME IN THAT PLACE FOR HOURS; IN THIS REALM, THERE IT IS LIKE DAYS. YOU GAVE ME PLEASURE AND TOOK IT IN RETURN," he challenged like a prosecutor arguing his case before a judge. His voice was close now as she took another step back her eye beginning to adjust as soon as she could see she would turn and run she vowed.

Images of the night she'd endured with him to fulfill their bargain rose in her mind at his words. The strange ache she'd felt upon waking began to settle over her again and she cursed as she felt his power wrap around her leaving a trail of phantom caresses on her skin that had her hissing through her teeth at the unsettling sense of pleasure and discomfort they brought her.

"YOU FELT ME UPON WAKING, AROUND YOU AND IN YOU," he murmured. Zaharrah trembled at the feel of his breath upon her skin. "AS YOU DO NOW, ZAHARRAH, YOU CANNOT DENY ME," he breathed as he took hold of her wrist and drew her to him. "WE ARE ONE, YOU AND I," he told her as his body molded against her own. He wrapped around her like a death shroud leaving her with no room to breathe as his power ran over her around her and through her, preparing her for him.

"I will never be yours," Zaharrah hissed in defiance even as he moved her back toward the altar. She swallowed in fear knowing if she didn't do something now that nothing could save her from his designs for her.

"WE'LL SEE," Hades countered amused by her spirit.

Zaharrah gasped at the feel of cold stone as it hit the back of her knees. She felt a jolt of power tear through her like a lightning bolt splitting the sky and her spirit cried out in desperation for defense against her plight as Hades mouth slanted over her own to claim it. His kiss was hard, cruel and demanding. Bruising her lips then splitting them as his teeth pulled at them forcing them apart so he could taste her breath.

His hands pulsed with power and when he touched her clothes they withered and aged falling from her; leaving her naked before him. Zaharrah trembled in his arms frightened and aroused, his kiss clouding her mind with images of the night. As her body was assaulted by the phantom echoes of those acts making her want him, pushing her to forget any other. She felt cold stone beneath her as a warm hand ran over her petting her making her ache for a thing her heart cried she didn't want.

Tears fell from her eyes as his hand fondled her lower mound. His touch there woke her mind from its haze. She saw in her mind a man's face. Kind eyes, dark hair, Gunnar. She was Gunnar's wife not this fallen one. The image of herself in a hospital in labor filled her mind. They had a son. One she'd never seen directly since that night but he was hers none the less. She watched him in secret. Watched them both.

"No," Zaharrah breathed the word it was barely a whisper.

"HUSH MY LOVE, IT'S TIME," he whispered as he kissed her tears away tasting them.

Zaharrah cried out in protest and pain as he entered her. More tears fell at the intrusion.

"AH, THERE YOU ARE AT LAST, MY DARLING PERSEPHONE. YOU KNOW IT WAS MY HOST THAT FIRST INTRODUCED ME TO YOU. HE WAS FIXATED; YOUR MAGNUS HALDEN. HE WANTED THE PRIZED LADY OF THE BLACK HAND. HE DIDN'T SURRENDER HIMSELF TO ME UNTIL YOU PROMISED YOUR HAND TO ANOTHER. I TOLD HIM I COULD GIVE YOU TO HIM AND THE FOOL BELIEVED IT. WHEN I SAW YOU I KNEW I'D NEVER SHARE YOU WITH HIM. I KNEW YOU WOULD BE MINE," he revealed as he began to move inside her, rutting like a beast seeking only to mate and reproduce.

"No!" Zaharrah screamed. The loud cry more an inhuman roar that tore her vocal chords. It ran on until she could not make another sound. But the word echoed in her mind a constant and tortured word as the god of the underworld raped her.

144

Hermes retreated from the king's temple unnoticed and tried to forget the image of his brother's mating. The crown was gone. It had been before either of them got there. As he touched the earthen walls with his power he demanded the land give up it' knowledge to him and in his mind's eye he saw Artemis standing upon the sand calling forth the crown. The huntress had taken it to prevent its discovery. No matter. He'd find it, but first there were other secrets to be recovered.

Heading back to the main temple he focused his attention on recovering the cuneiform tablet below. It and the one waiting in Zeboim now held his key to ascension and none of the others knew anything of it.

Hermes smiled as he walked past the graven images of him and the others. Let Hades screw his bride it would not help him to claim Zeus's throne. The crown was gone, beyond their reach. A bride could not help him now. No the only path left lay within the passage he held. Within one lay the key that would ensure his victory. He'd claim his bride later once his power was cemented.

145

Sam pulled the rental car to the side of the road and got out. When the others moved to follow he held up his hand to stop them. "Wait here, Gunnar doesn't take kindly to strangers. Hell, he's protective of his private life. I didn't even know he was married. No sense pissing him off," Sam stated before he crossed the street to approach the man's home.

He was half way up the walk when the door flew open and a dark haired man with sun bronzed skin and the dark eyes of a predator emerged gun at the ready. Brown eyes blinked at the sight of the figure before him with recognition and Sam relaxed knowing he wasn't going to be shot after all.

"Mr. Abrams?" the Masada agent questioned with disbelief.

"Yeah, Gunnar. I tried to call first--"

"Phone's off I'm off duty, no interruptions."

"I understand, sorry to intrude but the matter is urgent."

"Who is that in the car with you?"

"Fellow agents."

"Three. What has your government sent you here on this time?"

"Not the government, a contact." Sam corrected as a boy no older than five ran to the door. His face was Gunnar's but his eyes were his mother's.

"Who?"

"Zaharrah Lynch." Sam watched as the Israeli tensed and paled before he bid the boy go back inside.

"You lie! Zaharrah has not made contact with me in five years," Gunnar snapped. His finger tightened on the trigger and Sam flinched maybe he was going to get shot after all he muttered to himself as the sound of a car door opening and closing echoed behind him. He watched helpless as Gunnar trained his gun on the new comer.

"He's telling the truth. Zaharrah is a colleague of mine, they met in Miami--"

"A colleague-- she's not an agent. Explain," Gunnar demanded.

"Dr. Gallagher is an archeologist. Miss Lynch is as well. I accompanied the lady to a dig as protection. I met your wife--"

"Zaharrah is not my wife, she left me years ago," Gunnar said with disgust and regret.

"I met Zaharrah there. She called me two days ago said that you had told her if she ever needed help to call me."

"That is true."

"When I asked her how she knew you, she said she was your wife."

"She did?" Gunnar asked shocked.

Sam nodded and watched as the other man eased his hold on his gun. "She called me this morning asked me to deliver a package. Said we'd meet here," Sam explained.

"Zaharrah's coming home?"

"I don't know she said it would be here in Jerusalem next we meet."

"I see. Come in, please. Forgive my rudeness but I must be careful with Caleb, not many know of him. Zaharrah said not to let anyone of her kin see him. I've been careful to keep him hidden."

"We understand, got ta protect home and kin," Terra said as she joined them followed by Vince. Gunnar lowered his weapon and showed them inside. Once the door was shut Sam handed over his cell phone for Gunnar to see.

"This is unbelievable," the Masada agent said startled.

"What can we do?"

"We've got a team researching how to handle the problem for now, we wait and pray."

146

Zaharrah rose from the stone table her movements slow, her steps silent. She covered her body with the only thing available Hades shirt. She didn't bother with the buttons, simply slipped her arms in the sleeves and crept away as the lord of the underworld lay in the drugged slumber of physical release. As she slipped out of the king's temple her pace became a fast walk, each step carried her further from him and the center of his power in this place. As she passed the city temple Zaharrah began to run knowing the gate was near. Her car waited beyond and escape.

As she passed under the stone arch she felt the beginnings of his phantom caresses and cursed knowing she was running out of time. His mind was in the dream realm now with her if she closed her eyes she'd see him, feel him and he'd know what was happening. She had to keep him blind to her actions here for as long as she could manage so that she could get away from this vile place and to somewhere safe.

Zaharrah's hands shook as she took hold of the steering wheel. She could feel that unwanted ache between her thighs begin and growled. Hades was impatient, pressing her to join him in her mind and she knew she could delay him no longer. As she sped her way across the desert road she let her mind fall into the dream world and his waiting arms the longer she could keep him there the better her chance of reaching safety.

147

Catharine smiled as she pressed the icon to save her work. Her eyes danced with amusement and success. As she backed the document up to the beginning of the scene, message prompt came up with the words search complete. She flipped over to the list and wrote the titles down once Lance finished reading the scene it seemed they were headed for her place in New York. Most of the books on the list were rare or hard to find, but she knew they were in her library. She hoped the detective would be up for a road trip.

"I'm finished with the scene, detective have a look and tell me what you think," she called. Catharine watched as Lance emerged from the living room and noted he looked weary. Perhaps a short nap was in order before they hit the road. Neither of them were alert enough to be behind the wheel.

"What's that?"

"List of books on dragons."

"Already?"

"Yeah, more specific, request less time."

"Okay, well maybe we should--"

"It's six am. There is no place open yet besides these are rare books. I have most of them back home, but they'll wait."

"Sam needs--"

"I know, but we need to get there in one piece and neither of us is fit to drive. We've been up nearly twenty-four hours. Read the scene detective tell me what you think and we'll see about a nap."

Lance nodded and then sank down in the chair in front of the laptop. Catharine picked up her notebook and sat down at the end of the table to review her notes so she knew where the story was headed next.

148

Lance studied Catharine for a minute and noted she seemed less tense. It seemed that their talk earlier had done her some good. The scene he figured would tell him more of her mental state. That she'd suggested a nap seemed like a good sign maybe she was coming back from whatever corner she'd been hiding in.

"You're supposed to be reading detective," she muttered without looking up from her notes.

"Sorry," Lance answered before turning his focus to the screen, ice blue eyes skimmed back over the earlier part of the scene from Serenity's stopped flight to the vampire lord warning and offer. He switched to reading as he came to Syvarin's request.

"Give me a chance Serenity. Let me love you as you deserved. Let me protect you from him. Together, we can defeat him," the vampire lord entreated as he offered her his hand.

Serenity looked from the extended hand offered in alliance to the bloody photos, weighing her choice. Memories long forgotten rose from the dark recesses of her mind. The unsettling feeling of being watched. The fear of hearing a branch snap in the distance, the sudden awareness of being hunted. The pointless flight that found her trapped where he wanted her. The smell of Kovrin's breathe on her face as he moved closer. His hands on her body enticing her to surrender to him. The feel of him moving inside her as she begged him to stop.

Terror filled her and Serenity reached blindly to take the vampire lords hand, her own shaking, but caution woke within her and she paused as she was reminded of Syvarin's tricks of old.

How he'd used her affections for Davrik to turn her. He tricked her into killing his enemies for him and then used her love for his son to bed her and enslave her to his will. Anything Syvarin offered came with a price.

"What token do you desire of me to seal this pact?" Serenity asked.

"Give me an heir Serenity, take your rightful place at my side as my queen, once more."

"I was there not even a week before you bedded another. I saw it. You'll betray me again."

"No Serenity not this time. I don't want any other," he whispered.

"My life spared from his wrath and lusts at the cost of my life?"

"No, your protection for your companionship. I don't want a slave Serenity I want a partner," Syvarin corrected.

Serenity eyed the vampire lord with suspicion his words gave her mind ease and yet she knew she couldn't trust them. Syvarin was a good liar and he knew her well. Had access to her mind, could just be saying what she needed to hear. He had before. He'd done vial things to her in the past to enslave her. Her mind flashed to the image of herself on the cold stone floor of the vampire's court. Naked, bleeding, in agony as the men of his house had their way with her as punishment for her failure to kill his son.

She saw Syvarin enter the hall to join in her debasement and to claim back what he felt was his. He'd used her body in every way imaginable then withdrew again to watch as the others continued in their sport. She remembered knowing she was going to die there because she'd dared to love another.

Rage bubbled up inside her, followed by sorrow as his words sank into her mind like a splinter. Davrik was dead. Her beloved, her mate, the man who'd been sire to her child and the only one to love her as she'd dreamed of love in her youth. As her head fell in her grief, her hazel eyes settled on the bloody photos and her stomach churned with disgust.

Six young women were dead. Their bodies violated multiple times in every way imaginable. Four bites inflicted one at the neck, another at the wrist, the left breast and the inner thigh. Later to be cut out. A bloody cut left under the eye one for each time she was raped. It marked how long she lasted until he tasted her last breath and ripped out her heart to taste it. Then in her own blood the word 'whore' was written upon her brow. The bite spit out upon her face the rest of the heart taken.

As she stared at the photos she could feel Kovrin's breath on her skin and could smell its foul stench fill her lungs. His hands playing over her feminine curves stimulating her, waking her body for him to mate. She trembled as Syvarin spoke.

"Because of what you are you'll last for days, maybe even weeks," he whispered seeing the fear in her now and pressing his advantage.

Tears fell from her eyes as those phantom hands parted her thighs. She gasped and a sob broke free as she felt the echo of Kovrin moving inside of her and knew she couldn't bear to know that hell again. Davrik had spared her that pain once but he was gone. He couldn't protect her from the were-wolf anymore. Alone she'd never survive. Kovrin would find her, Syvarin was right about that and he'd use her until he killed her or until his anger died out and then he'd never let her go. She wasn't sure which was worse but she was sure of one thing she didn't want to endure either.

Serenity looked again to Syvarin's outstretched hand and swallowed. A brutal death at the hand of a sadistic rogue were-wolf unless she survived his wrath then she'd endure him forever or an eternity with Syvarin, which was worse.

"How many more will you let suffer so on your account. You know what he's doing to them. Do you think that will stop once you're gone? He's got a taste for it now." Syvarin stated giving her another nudge, knowing he almost had her.

"I have no choice then is what you're saying," Serenity said, her voice weak as she lifted her head to meet his gaze once more.

"No, I'm asking if you can live with that."

Nivali screamed at her to say yes and walk away, but Serenity could not do it. Her spirit had become the dominant personality in her time in seclusion. Serenity reached to take the offered hand.

"Ashella, no!" A familiar voice roared in her mind and she froze as her eyes lit in shock.

"Davrik?" she called with disbelief.

"You're mistaken Serenity. I told you my son is dead," Syvarin whispered as he pressed his power around her in an effort to block the mental link. He was so close to his goal.

"I could have sworn--"

"An echo from the past, a memory," Syvarin suggested as he sifted through her mind for one that fit.

She blinked as the image of herself poised to strike down her guardian entered her mind and Davrik shouted to stop her. "You're right, but why?"

"Grief does strange things to the mind," Syvarin answered.

"What do you know of grief?" she challenged.

"I've grieved your loss every day since the night you disappeared as I grieve my son."

"There was a time you bade me to kill him."

"Rage cools and jealousy fades with time as you know." Serenity nodded and placed her hand in Syvarin's.

"No! You're not alone," Davrik roared from the distance.

Serenity drew her hand from Syvarin's with outrage.

"You lied!"

"Of course I lied, my naive little Serenity. I'd have said anything to gain your pledge. You gave me your hand--"

"We have no deal devil. I'll not surrender my soul to you again," Serenity hissed.

"You already have," Syvarin whispered as he snatched her by the arm and drew her against him, "and it was a wise choice."

"Let her go father," Davrik shouted as he drew near them.

"She took my hand--"

"You deceived her. Used her own mind against her, the contract is void and you know it. Let her go."

"How dare you order me boy? You're no match for my power. Your mate is mine once more and she will remain so forever. There is nothing you can do to stop that now."

"Your power is weakening old man as mine grows. Your cloak serves me now; its power is mine. You couldn't keep me out of her mind."

"I have the ring."

"It does not serve you; it drains you. It is bound to the one who killed its master. To Ashella," Davrik argued as he drew Serenity free of Syvarin's grasp.

Lance blinked falling out of the scene as Davrik's words rolled around in his head. His words to Catharine. "Am I Davrik?" Lance asked shocked.

"Yes, I hit that yesterday. Scared me. I hadn't really thought about who he was when I started writing him," Catharine admitted. "Are you okay with that, I can change him--" she began worried she might have upset him again. Lance put a finger to her lips quieting her as he pictured the character in his mind. He felt a pleasant dose of lust wash through him as he recalled the one love scene between the two and smiled.

"No need to, I can live with knowing he's me. I kind of like him. Mated huh? Is that how you see us?" he asked as he brushed her hair away from her eyes.

"More or less," she replied with a blush and she bit her lip nervously.

"So, does Davrik get the girl?"

"You'll have to read it and see," Catharine whispered.

"It can wait I think," Lance said as he closed the laptop and got to his feet. He took the notebook out of Catharine's hand and drew her to her feet.

"What are you doing?" She asked shocked.

"Taking you to bed," he answered before he brushed a kiss on her cheek.

"To bed--" she stammered with disbelief.

"Relax, Serenity, you can trust me," he assured her as he started toward the back of his apartment. He was pleased when she followed him, hesitant at first but then more at ease. He smiled amused as he wondered what sort of ideas she had running around in her head at the moment as he opened his bedroom door and led her to his bed. He turned down the sheets and gave the mattress a pat calling her to him.

She sank down on the bed and he knelt by her feet taking off her shoes. As he got up he saw her tense no doubt wondering what he'd take off of her next. Instead he lay her back and tucked her in. She blinked and he laughed as he took off his own shoes.

"You rat you had me--"

"I never said anything to imply I meant to touch you. In fact I told you I wouldn't until I was sure you were ready. Did you think I was lying?" he asked as he sank down on the bed beside her.

"No."

"Then why would you think I was bringing you in here for anything other than sleep?"

"I guess I thought with your seeing Davrik for who he is and that scene I wrote that maybe you'd come to the conclusion I was-- it could be looked at like reading a page out of a diary-- I don't know," she said with a laugh feeling foolish now.

"Relax Serenity, you're safe here," he assured her before he drew her back against his chest to hold her close. He kissed her hair and closed his eyes before giving into sleep.

149

Hades trembled as he slid out of his bride and kissed her.

"OH MY DEAR, ZAHARRAH, YOU PLEASE ME BETTER THAN ANY PERSEPHONE BEFORE. YOUR BODY IS EXQUISITE AS IS YOUR MIND HERE, IT EXCITES ME SO I CAN FEEL MY BODY STIRRING ALREADY, BURNING FOR YOUR FLESH. WHEN I WAKE I'LL HAVE YOU AGAIN, I WON'T BE ABLE TO STOP MYSELF," he whispered as his hands skimmed over her tormenting her with the promise of more.

"Stay here yet a while," she entreated as she turned toward him pressing her body more firmly against his. Teasing his mind with the feel of her.

"YOUR MIND'S DESIRE IS INSATIABLE MY LOVE AND YET YOUR HEART STILL REFUSES ME."

"I've spent five years in exile my body denied another's touch my mind barred from lustful pleasures. It craves what my heart refuses," she whispered.

"I'VE FED YOUR MIND LOVE, LET ME EASE A COLD BODY WITH MY HEAT NOW; IN TIME YOUR HEART WILL LEARN TO ACCEPT OUR UNION AS WELL," Hades whispered as his touch became more demanding.

"You were rough with me before, allow my body time to recover," Zaharrah requested.

"YOU'VE HAD ADEQUATE TIME," Hades breathed as he pressed inside her once more and began to move. "I KNOW IT BECAUSE I CAN FEEL YOUR FLESH BURNING WITH WANT OF ME, AS I BURN FOR IT. DO NOT LET YOUR HEART DENY THIS," he turned as she trembled beneath him in release.

"I'm not ready," Zaharrah confessed.

"WE'VE LINGERED HERE LONG ENOUGH," Hades hissed

now impatient.

"Don't."

"I'VE BEEN GENTLE WITH YOU IN THIS PLACE, PATIENT NOW YOU TRY THAT PATIENCE. I CAN BE CRUEL," Hades warned as he caressed her brow and filled her mind with unpleasant ways he could use her body here for his own gratification and leave her aching for him only to be denied.

"No," she whispered with dismay as she turned away from him.

"I CAN AND I WILL, AS IS MY RIGHT AS YOUR GROOM," Hades warned as he pressed his aroused flesh against her rear in threat.

"Do you wish me to leave?" she asked outraged.

"YES, RISE FROM THIS DREAM WITH ME AND MEET ME IN THE FLESH."

"I--"

"YOU WHAT? WHY DO YOU WAIT? DO YOU THINK THAT BY KEEPING ME HERE YOU CAN PREVENT ME FROM HAVING YOU OUT THERE?" Hades asked in suspicion as he began to suspect her intentions here. He'd thought her attention a sign of her submission but now he had his doubts.

"No--"

"LIAR! YOU DO. YOU MEANT TO KEEP ME HERE TO DELAY OUR MATING AGAIN, TO AVOID MY EFFORTS OF FILLING YOUR BELLY WITH MY CHILD! YOU MEANT TO STOP ME FROM MOVING FORWARD WITH MY PLANS!"

"No--I--"

"MY MIND CAN BE HERE ZAHARRAH, FUCKING YOU ONE WAY WHILE MY BODY HAS YOU ANOTHER," Hades hissed as he drove inside her forbidden passage and began to move.

Zaharrah cried out in pain and alarm at the feel of him moving through her there, it was undesired.

Hades laughed at her pain as he felt his own pleasure grow. His body reached for hers in reality set on doing just as he said to find her gone.

Hades roared in fury as he rode her mind harder. "WITCH! I'LL FIND YOU AND DRAG YOU BACK TO MY BED YOU CAN'T ESCAPE ME!" His hand closed round her throat nails biting as he punished her.

Her fingers tore at his grip trying to get free.

"YOU WERE BLESSED WITH MY KINDNESS WHEN NEXT I HOLD YOU, YOU WILL KNOW MY WRATH," Hades snarled as she vanished from the dream.

He woke with fury and dressed to go after her. Grabbing his phone he punched in the number for Magnus's right hand.

"Hello."

"YORK. OPERATION FIRESTORM IS A GO."

"Understood."

Hades hung up the phone as he walked out of the king's temple. "RUN TO YOUR BELOVED ZAHARRAH, YOU'LL GET TO SEE HIM DIE AS HIS CITY BURNS. THEN WHEN IT'S OVER, I'LL DRAW YOU FORTH FROM THE ASHES AND FLAME AT MY DOOR AND TAKE YOU BACK. YOU WILL BE MY PERSEPHONE!"

150

Russell York disconnected the call and pressed the two on his speed dial. When the line connected he spoke.

"Proceed as planned," with the command given, he broke the call and moved to leave, he was done here. When the boss returned he'd be long gone. He looked to the man standing by the desk and decided to warn him.

"It's all gone to hell, the boss is in a wrathful mind, if you're wise you'll leave the woman to appease him and make yourself scarce."

The man said nothing he simply turned and left. York put down his phone beside the woman then turned and walked out.

151

Artemis woke to the whisper of Ares mind bidding her flee. She rose from her bed and began to dress.

"WHERE DO YOU THINK YOU'RE GOING, MY DEAR?" Dionysus asked as he grabbed her by the arm intent on dragging her back into the bed to continue in their mating.

"ARES BID US LEAVE. My uncle is coming and he is in wrath. He'll have little tolerance for us. WE MUST GO."

"INDEED, LUCKY FOR YOU I HAVE A WAY OUT OF HERE," Dionysus answered. He let her go and followed suit.

"Yes, I know."

"AND A PALACE TO GO TO."

"Is it wise to return to your host's life?"

"I'LL LEAVE YOUR UNCLE AN OFFERING HE WON'T BEGRUDGE ME MY FREEDOM."

"Where do I fit in that world?"

"YOU WILL PLAY THE MOST IMPORTANT ROLE OF ALL. YOU WILL BE MY SERENITY."

"I'm not an actress."

"NO, YOU'RE NOT, BUT YOU CAN PLAY THIS PART AND YOU WILL MY. LADY, OR YOU'LL FIND OUR LIFE TOGETHER A LIVING HELL."

"As you say my husband."

"COME IT'S TIME WE WERE OFF."

"I need to make a stop on the way. I'll meet you in L.A."

"WHAT STOP?"

"One to keep Hades power from growing too greatly."

"HOW?"

"I will slay his beast."

"GOOD HUNTING THEN."

"Thank you. I trust you will honor our agreement. The mortal Anna--"

"WILL NOT BE TROUBLED BY ME FURTHER," Dionysus assured her. "COME WE HAVE A STOP TO MAKE BEFORE WE DEPART."

"My lord?"

"THE TEMPLE ABOVE. WE WILL MAKE OUR MARRIAGE OFFICIAL."

"As you will," Artemis answered and the pair departed Hermes Palace leaving it all but abandoned.

152

Catharine woke from sleep with a jolt. The arm around her waist tightened and she sank back against the warmth of Lance's chest and sighed. Her mind began to ease even as she tried to recall what had roused her. She'd been dreaming but not the nightmare that had been haunting her sleep. As she sought her memory for what she snuggled closer to the detective seeking the comfort of his embrace.

Lance whispered her name in his sleep as if aware of her distress and she smiled. Before she'd dozed off he'd assured her she'd be safe there and she knew it was true. He loved her, but his love was safe. He'd never force her to do something she didn't want or ask her for something she couldn't give. Catharine turned to face him taking the opportunity given to study him at rest.

He looked in sleep free of worry or care. Like one bound by enchantment. A sleeping prince waiting to be brought awake by a kiss. She considered doing just that but figured the moment she did that, the waking would not end with a simple kiss. His appearance here was deceptive he was not as unaware as he seemed. All his senses were alert and honed for the first sign of distress. He was the warrior of old at rest ready for battle at the first hint of danger.

Catharine blinked as the image of the knight faded and out of the depths of her mind rose the image of a beast, dark scales, leathery wings and breathe of flame. It descended from the heavens setting the earth ablaze. Out of a building Sam and another spilled forth to take on the terror. A dark figure emerged, he challenged Sam and killed him. The beast was impervious to the other man's weapons. The city was destroyed.

"Lance wake up."

"Huh?"

"We have to go."

"What about a nap?"

"You can sleep in the car. Sam and the others are running out of time," Catharine said as she got out of the bed.

"What?"

"I'll explain on the way," Catharine assured him as she headed for the door.

153 JERUSALEM, ISRAEL

Zaharrah gasped for air as her mind returned from the shadow realm. Her eyes blinked as her sight returned to the world around her. When she fled the desert her intent had been to head for her place in Jerusalem but her eyes told her she was within a block of Gunnar's place.

She made the final turn that would take her home as trembling fingers reached out to touch her neck. They came away warm and tacky with blood and she swallowed as she wondered if she'd find it was bruised as well. What other marks did her flesh bear as a reminder of where she'd been and what Hades had done to her. She didn't know and there was no time to worry about it.

Zaharrah pulled up across the road and after shutting off the engine worked at buttoning her shirt. The task was difficult because she couldn't get her hands to stop shaking. She finger combed her hair and wished for more time to wash and change but Hades knew she was gone and he'd know where she was headed, which meant his dragons wouldn't be too far behind her.

She hesitated wondering what Gunnar would make of her appearance but told herself it didn't matter either. She'd stalled as long as she dared. Opening the door she took two wobbly steps toward the house and cursed. She was in worse shape than she'd figured. Her vision faded as the door opened. Zaharrah screamed as Hades power tore through their mental link to inflict pain upon her.

154

Gunnar stared at the dark haired figure coming up the path with disbelief. He blinked thinking that when his eyes opened she'd be gone but she remained.

"Zaharrah?" he whispered the name still unsure. She looked weary and broken. As he moved toward her she cried out in torment before collapsing. Gunnar's mind snapped and he was by her side in an instant catching her before she hit the ground. He held her close for a moment indulging in the feel of her before gathering her into his arms and carrying her inside. He walked past his guests without a word to lay her down on the couch.

"Zaharrah," he murmured wanting her to answer him but she was silent and still. He studied her with wonder and concern. It had been five years since he last saw her. He wondered where she'd been and why she'd left. What brought her back now?

"Is she okay?" Anna asked concerned.

"I don't know. Look at her… what has happed to her? She looked so scared. My Zaharrah was never afraid." Gunnar said confused.

"Will you let me take care of her?" Anna asked.

"Yes," Gunnar said. His voice was thick with emotion as he fought for calm. "I need to see to my boy."

Anna nodded then turned to gather what she needed to take care of his wife.

Gunnar brushed a kiss on Zaharrah's brow and whispered several Hebrew words of endearment before he turned to seek out their son.

Anna passed him in the doorway and he closed off the room to ensure the boy not see his mother in her current state. As he walked Gunnar fought back his temper as he wondered who had dared to put their hands on Zaharrah to kill her.

155

Anna put the set of clothes she'd grabbed for Zaharrah down on a chair and set the rag, water and soap on the coffee table. After wetting the cloth and ringing it out she dabbed at the cuts on the tomb raider's neck. With care she then washed them.

Zaharrah flinched and Anna watched as other marks began to appear on the other woman's flesh.

"Shit," Anna muttered with irritation. While she didn't know where Zaharrah had been since they last met or what had happened to her, one thing was clear, somewhere along the way the tomb raider's path had crossed Hades.

"Come on Zaharrah, snap out of it before he kills you," Anna commanded. Zaharrah moaned in her sleep as her skin paled. Whatever was happening on the other side it was killing her. "Damn it! Crazy tomb raider call for aid and wake up; your family needs you. I need you," Anna hissed.

"She can't hear you," a familiar voice whispered.

"Help her!"

"I cannot interfere," her winged companion answered.

"Then why come?" Anna snapped in frustration as she looked up at the angelic being.

"Because you called. You can interfere."

"Me?"

"You can intercede on her behalf."

"I don't understand."

"You can stand in the gap for her, face what she does and attempt to lead her out."

"Why didn't you tell me that?" Sam asked in temper as he entered the room.

"You weren't ready then."

"Is this dangerous?" Sam questioned.

"Potentially."

"Then she's not doing it," Sam stated in a voice that said he'd hear no argument.

"Sam if I don't do this; Zaharrah will die," Anna whispered.

"Anna…"

"Please, I have to try. I know what's happening to her in there. No one deserves that kind of abuse."

Sam swallowed and nodded. Anna knelt beside Zaharrah and lay her hand on the other woman's brow as she began to pray. The angel touched her and Zaharrah, easing Anna's spirit and healing Zaharrah's body before he vanished.

Sam muttered with annoyance before moving behind Anna. She felt his arms wrap around her and draw her back against his chest offering her warmth and comfort. Words fell from her lips she was aware they were not English and yet she understood them. Her voice moved at a pace that should have left her breathless and she felt no need of air. Only spoke on, her voice raising from a low whisper to a more conversational tone, at times she nearly shouted as tears fell from her eyes. Her spirit pleaded but for what her mind did not fully understand.

For a moment she felt Sam's hand wiping away her tears and in the next she was no longer in the living room of Gunnar's house. She instead stood in an all too familiar garden of brilliant color. She looked down expecting to see her own clothes gone but found they were not. She blinked and began to walk. There was no time to ponder why; she had to find Zaharrah.

"Guide my steps lord," she whispered into the emptiness and a path appeared before her where an endless sea of grass had been. Anna followed it. The path led her into a dense wood of dead trees and ended in a clearing. In the midst of it she found her.

Zaharrah lay upon the dusty ground naked and bleeding. Her feet blistered, her lips dry and cracked as if she'd been wandering in a desert and could go no further.

Anna raced to her side and fell to her knees. She brushed away Zaharrah's hair from her face with care. Brown eyes opened wild with terror, then eased at the sight before her.

"Anna?"

"Yes, it's me," she whispered as she dabbed at the tomb raiders frightened tears.

"How?"

"It doesn't matter I've come to take you away from here."

"Away?"

"Out of the dream."

"Dream?"

"None of this is real Zaharrah, your dreaming," Anna whispered. Before she could say more Zaharrah groaned as if in agony.

"Run!"

"What? Why?"

"He's coming," Zaharrah answered with dismay as she curled in on herself.

"Get up Zaharrah," Anna commanded.

"Why I can't run anymore," Zaharrah said her voice full of despair.

"I'm getting you out of here," Anna answered.

"To what end I can't hide from him he can feel me. Wherever I go he will find me." Zaharrah said distraught. "Go, save yourself."

"I won't leave you here to die," Anna argued as she whispered for help. The harsh light of the sun was shaded by clouds and the heavens parted rain falling from the sky. It quenched Zaharrah's thirst and cleansed her body healing her wounds. Anna gave thanks before grabbing the other woman by the arm. "Come, we must go now."

"Too late," Zaharrah muttered.

Anna watched in horror as a green and black dragon appeared in the heavens and descended landing in the clearing before them. It roared at the sight of her and she closed her eyes praying for peace. When her lashes lifted she saw not the beast he meant to terrorize her with but the man. He eyed her with interest and amusement. His green eyes glowed with his power as he began to weave another spell around them.

"HERE YOU ARE PERSEPHONE, AND WITH A GUEST. HELLO ANNA, I CAN'T TELL YOU HOW THRILLED I AM TO HAVE YOU HERE. I'VE BEEN WAITING FOR A CHANCE TO SEE YOUR WILL BROKEN. IT SEEMS THAT I'LL NOW GET THE CHANCE TO DO SO MYSELF."

"I'm not here to mix words with the likes of you Fallen One. I came for her."

"YES. I KNOW."

"You are killing her," Anna warned.

"I AM AWARE."

"Surely you don't desire her death. What good is a bride to you who lay in a grave?"

"INDEED YOU ARE RIGHT LADY, BUT SHE'S EARNED

MY WRATH AND UNTIL IT COOLS SHE WILL REMAIN HERE."

"Let her go."

"NO, SHE MUST PAY FOR HER DECEIT!"

"She'll not survive anymore."

"SO BE IT. IT IS THE PRICE SHE WILL PAY FOR HER CRIME. TREASON IS ALWAYS REWARDED WITH DEATH. IT IS NO DIFFERENT FOR A BRIDE."

"Let me stand as her whipping boy," Anna requested.

"WHAT?"

"You wanted the chance to break me, here it is. Let me endure the rest of your wrath in her stead."

"NOT INTERESTED," Hades lied.

"Anna no!" Zaharrah cried in warning.

"Consider your answer carefully oh god of the underworld I'm here in the spirit protected from your reach. You can't lift a hand against me as I am and you know it. I'm offering you the opportunity to conquer your brother's greatest foe and to strike out at your nemesis. Sam is on the other side with me, he'll bear witness to my fall." Anna taunted.

"YOU'RE A FOOL WOMAN, BUT SO BE IT," Hades whispered with delight.

"I won't let her," Zaharrah yelled in defiance.

"YOU HAVE NO SAY HERE. BE GRATEFUL FOR HER ACT IF NOT FOR HER YOU'D BE DEAD," Hades snapped. "SHE'S RELEASED," Hades stated and shackles that bound her to him fell from her wrists and ankles. A gown covered her body and sandals were set upon her feet. "DEPART FROM ME, PERSEPHONE," he commanded and Zaharrah vanished.

Anna watched with dread as he turned toward her, his eyes gleaming with excitement. "NOW, LADY GALLAGHER, YOU ARE MINE," Hades murmured. At the pronouncement of the final word golden shackles closed around her wrists and ankles.

Anna flinched at the feel of the cold metal on her skin. It was like ice freezing her blood and yet it burned like a brand of fire marking her. She cried out at the strange mix of sensation and had barely adjusted when the next torment began. The cruel bands bit into her flesh as he pulled them roughly. Anna's mouth went dry as he drew her towards him. His green eyes gleamed with an inner fire that blazed with his wrath and fear washed through her.

The deal was done.

She'd taken Zaharrah's place. That rage that until a moment ago had been directed at the tomb-raider was now pointed at her and there would be nothing to shield her from it. The angle had made it clear he could not interfere she would endure all that was to come.

Anna flinched as his cold hand closed around her wrist and drew her the last few feet so that only mere inches were separating them. She felt his breathe on her skin and the heat of his flesh. She turned away from his gaze not wanting to stare into those cruel eyes aware that in that moment he was merely toying with her to awaken her fears further.

"LOOK AT ME ANNA," he commanded and against her will her head lifted hazel met that sickly green and he smirked. She trembled as his hands closed on her hips and drew her flush against him pressing his body roughly against her so that she felt him. "THIS WILL NOT BE QUICK. IT WILL NOT BE SIMPLE, OR PLEASANT. YOU WILL FEEL NO PLEASURE AND YOU WILL REMEMBER ALL OF IT. A WHIPPING BOY IS WHAT YOU OFFERED AND MY WRATH IS WHAT YOU WILL KNOW. THERE WILL BE NO MERCY. YOUR TORMENT WILL GIVE ME GREAT PLEASURE AND WHEN YOU BREAK FOR ME, WHICH YOU WILL, MAKE NO MISTAKE IN THAT HE WILL KNOW IT." Hades mocked before his head lowered to capture her lips. His nails bit into her ass and when she screamed his tongue pressed inside her parted lips to taste her breathe.

156

Sam knew the moment Anna's mind entered the dream realm. He felt her body tense and her skin go cool as her spirit stilled. He wondered what was happening on the other side as she was silent and motionless. He wished he was there with her but understood it wasn't possible.

Sam watched as Zaharrah became still once more and drew a deep breath. Whatever it was she had gone to do had begun. Zaharrah's eyes flew open and she gasped as if she'd come back from the dead. Her brown eyes found Sam and she sat up.

"Where am I?"

"You're at home."

"How?"

"You showed up about five minutes ago. Collapsed before you reached the door. Gunnar brought you in. You had us worried."

"Hades had me…"

"We figured as much."

"Anna…"

"Not back yet," Sam said his voice held concern. Worry became fear as the woman in his arms jolted and cried out in pain. Whatever she'd done it was beginning. Marks now began to appear on her flesh and Sam closed his eyes. He brushed his hands along her body to sooth her but she was beyond his reach.

He whispered words to comfort her that fell on deaf ears. Words became prayers as she grew weak. He prayed she be able to endure the torment and asked for his strength to be passed to her even as he begged for her pain to end. As her cries went on, Sam feared he'd go mad, even found himself wishing for a moment that he'd taken Ares sword the night before and ended them all. Then repented the notion, well aware if he had, Anna would have wound up as Ares bride not his. He'd have been lost and she with him.

157

Hazel eyes shot open as Anna's mind emerged from the shadow realm. She gasped and clean air exploded into her lungs as strong arms tightened around her.

"Easy doc, I've got you," Sam whispered as his hands slid down her shoulders to sooth her.

"Sam," she breathed the name with relief and sank back against him.

"Yeah, you're back."

"Thank God."

"What happened?"

"I don't remember," she lied not wanting to dwell on what Hades had done to her in his wrath.

"Nothing?"

"All I remember was thinking I was going to die and then feeling this flood of new strength... your strength. Thank you."

"I wish I could have done more. Sitting here listening to your pain, powerless to help you; it was torture. Please, don't ask me to do that again."

"I won't. Can you give us a couple minutes to take care of our injuries and for Zaharrah to change?"

"Of course," Sam answered and he kissed her gently before letting her go and moving to the door. He paused and looked back at her worry in his blue eyes. She smiled.

"I'll be right out," she assured him and watched as he turned and left closing the door behind him.

158

Why did you lie to him?" Zaharrah asked puzzled.

"About what?"

"Remembering. Hades would have made sure you couldn't forget."

"Because Hades wants to destroy Sam. The fastest way to turn him is me. If Sam knew what was done he'd seek vengeance if he takes it he will become the one he kills."

"What?"

"The act of blood-shed gives them claim to the body." "
Shit," Zaharrah muttered with discomfort.

"I lied to protect him as you'll do to protect Gunnar."

"What makes you think…?"

"When Hermes had chains on me it was my wrists. Hades had two sets and given his fury I'm willing to bet that means he's gained access to more than just your mind. What happened out there in the desert Zaharrah?"

"Broody sent me to find the other two plains cities when I arrived at the first sight it was clear someone had already disturbed the sight. I left the interns and moved onto the other site. When I got there he was waiting. He uncovered the city with his power and then entered it. I knew who he was but I couldn't go. I followed him through the city into the king's palace. When we reached the temple I understood why. The land itself had cast a spell. Everything there was like the other cities but the king's temple."

"How was it different?" Anna asked curious.

"The carving was gone. In its place were statues of the gods and an altar was there as well. To the right of it stood
Hera and Demeter."

"A request for their blessing upon the offering. The desire for the one presenting to be blessed with power and the desire for his offering to be fertile." Anna stated.

"On the left of the altar stood Aphrodite and Cybele."

"An invocation seeking to make the act wild and passionate," Anna said not liking the ramification of the goddesses being petitioned. It didn't bode well.

"The table itself bore a brand."

"What was it?"

"The seal of Persephone."

"Oh, no."

"Yes, you begin to see it. Admah was his city." Zaharrah said with disgust.

"The images gathered round the altar," Anna prompted waiting for the full picture to develop in her mind.

"Hades and Chaos stood together in the center. They were who the king served. Hades gloated over his victory then turned to claim his prize."

"The crown," Anna asked her throat going dry with dread as she whispered a silent prayer that the god of the underworld had not claimed it, fearful of what that would mean for them and the world as a whole.

"Was gone."

"Oh thank God."

"I think it was Artemis's doing. Seeing it was missing I laughed."

"You didn't."

"I did, and the spell broke."

"What happened?"

"I tried to leave but it was too late…" Zaharrah stated.

"I'll say nothing about it as long as you do the same for me."

"What if Hades says something?" Zaharrah asked pointing out the flaw in Anna's plan.

"We'll cross that bridge when we come to it," Anna replied as she got to her feet.

"What are you doing?"

"I thought I'd go, let you get dressed."

"Thanks."

"You're welcome," Anna answered before she left.

Zaharrah picked up the kakis on the chair and pulled them on. She peeled off Hades shirt and tossed it in the corner. If she got the chance she'd burn it, Zaharrah vowed as she pulled on the tank-top Anna left for her, grateful to be dressed.

She drew a breath and tried to relax knowing she'd soon have a million questions to answer.

159

Gunnar stood in the living room having slipped in as Zaharrah pulled on a fresh shirt.

"Where have you been Zaharrah?"

"A lot of places," she replied vaguely and his temper flared, but he reigned it in, she was in no shape for a fight.

"Why did you leave?" he asked letting the previous question go for the moment.

"To protect you from my job," she muttered.

"I thought you were a librarian."

"I was and I wasn't."

"I don't understand."

"I'll explain it soon," she promised.

Gunnar reached out and brushed his fingers over the mark on her neck. "What happened here?"

"I got into a fight with someone," she said simply.

"This man, he tried to kill you?" Gunnar asked with disbelief.

"Yes, occupational hazard."

"This man did he defile you as well?" Gunnar asked his voice going cold as he recalled her lack of clothes upon arrival.

"It's not your concern," Zaharrah said as she stepped away from him, just out of reach.

"How can you say that Zaharrah? You were my wife. If he abused you in such a fashion it's my right to avenge your honor," Gunnar reminded as he held up his hand to show her he still wore his wedding band.

"Don't talk that way. It's my matter. I want you to let this go."

"Let it go…a stranger assaults you and you ask me to forget it."

"It's not that simple…" Zaharrah began.

"Did you seek him out?" Gunnar asked with irritation.

"No."

"Did you invite him?" He questioned raising his voice.

"Of course not," Zaharrah snapped with outrage that he could even think that.

"Then you have been wronged Zaharrah, in the worst way a woman can be. I'll not stand by and allow it." Gunnar said with patience.

"Nothing you do now can change what has happened. Promise me you won't kill him."

"Why? Do you love him?" Gunnar asked confused as jealousy woke in him again.

"Never."

"I don't understand this Zaharrah…"

"He's not human. If you kill him you will become him."

"Zaharrah…"

"I know how that sounds but I'll explain it; just not yet."

"Why not?"

"I only want to have to say it once."

"Very well."

"Gunnar, can you ever forgive me for what I've done to us?"

"That depends."

"On what?"

"On your answer to my last question," he said.

"Fair enough."

"Did you ever love me Zaharrah?"

"Yes, I'm sorry if I've made you doubt that."

"You did?' he whispered his voice held relief.

"Gunnar, I never stopped loving you," she murmured.

"Then I can forgive you, my love," he breathed as he brushed her hair away from her eyes. Zaharrah turned into his caress and took comfort in his touch after so long apart. "I never thought I'd see you again," Gunnar confessed his voice weak with emotion as he drew her into his arms.

"I've missed you every minute of each day that passed since we parted," Zaharrah admitted as she buried her face in his shoulder.

"I'm glad you are here Zaharrah, regardless of the reason," Gunnar stated before he kissed her.

Tears fell from her eyes as years of banishment came to an end. Gunnar held her close as the weight of sadness he'd carried fell away. Zaharrah was back in his arms where she belonged. His wife had come home at last.

160

Hades walked into the main hall of Hermes' palace to find it deserted. Ares and Dionysus had both fled. His prisoner was gone as was Magnus's man. York it seemed after giving the order for the strike had departed as well. No matter, it was past time he left this place. It held nothing more of interest for him.

"Pamela, bring our guest," he commanded sensing the other woman's presence as he entered the throne room. He found a surprise waiting for him on the altar a tribute from the war god and smiled, pleased to know that at least for now, Ares and Dionysus allegiance lay with him. "BROOKE," Hades whispered as he skimmed his fingers over her broken body. Tapping into his power he mended torn flesh before he lowered his head. His lips sealed over hers and he blew a breath into her lungs his power washing through her.

Lashes fluttered as her mouth came alive to feast. He answered her passion with a wrath driven demand, that had her crying out in distress as he used his power to strip her bare. Hades looked up from his new play thing as Pamela entered the room with Emily at her side. The pretty model was Dionysus's token of loyalty. Her mind was completely lost to the wine god's influence, she craved one thing only, pleasure. He'd see to it she got it, but first he'd see to Brooke.

He'd always found that a woman he called back from the river Styx was a less restrained lover. Willing to let him do as he wished. "BROOKE," he breathed her name again as his eyes locked with hers. "KNOW YOUR LORD," he commanded as he entered her body. She pressed her head back against the marble as her lips parted on a silent scream. Her hips rose to meet his and he took hold of them using them for leverage as he began to move.

Hades closed his eyes picturing Zaharrah beneath him as he

pressed her harder, hands bruising, teeth marking, drawing blood. Nails tearing, punishing her even as he drove her mad with ecstasy. Hades opened his eyes as he felt her tremble with release. "TAKE MORE," he demanded as he pressed her further. His gaze moved from Brooke to lock with Emily's. She watched him her eyes glowing with a hunger of her own. As he drove Brooke over the second peak he followed her into bliss filling her with his seed. The act complete he rose from her and crossed the floor to his avid spectator.

Hades spoke no words simply drew her against him and took control of her mouth. At his touch her clothes melted away. He pressed her back against the wall and she moaned with delight as she felt the fire of his lust upon her.

161

Zaharrah and Gunnar emerged from the living room and made their way in the direction of the kitchen, where the others were gathered. Neither had said anything more. They'd let each other go reluctantly but in silent agreement that there were other matters to see to. Things she knew had to be shared. Duty would for now, stand before their reunion.

As she stepped in the kitchen four pairs of eyes settled on her and she swallowed. Zaharrah didn't like to be the center of attention. It went against her training. As a member of the order she was taught not to draw other people's focus on her. She was supposed to blend in, be forgettable. She sighed as she admitted she'd never been good at that.

"We're waiting Miss Lynch," Sam prompted with impatience and she nodded.

"I was born of a blood line weighed down by a heavy burden of responsibility. You ask how I know Hecate and my answer is simple, we share the same blood."

"You're her descendant?" Anna asked shocked.

"Not direct as you're imagining doctor. Hecate or Pandora as she was known in life had a sister. I am descended from her. The box Pandora opened possessed the mantles, she gave them to her husband Hermes as a present. When the gods were bound, her lover bestowed power upon her. Her rage didn't die out with their imprisonment it grew. She went mad taking up the name Hecate and spread chaos on her lord's behalf. She moved in and out of time as a myth until one of her sister's offspring came to possess the sword of Ares. Your myth calls him Arthur. He with the help of his sister managed to bind Hecate with the sword. It was left to their children to ensure that the sword never surfaced again."

"Then how is it a madman came to possess it?" Sam asked with disgust.

"Magnus Halden was one of our number. He learned the truth about the nature of the sword and other details pertaining to the mantles. He left the order and has been working to one end ever since, to locate the other mantles and claim their power for himself. Kurt Dryden was born Kurt Halden, He's Magnus's brother. Magnus led his brother to the sword as an experiment to see what would happen. He didn't know that when Kurt took the sword it would free Pandora as well."

"Were you at the dig for the mantles?"

"No, I left the order to be with Gunnar."

"Then why did you leave me?"

"After Ithaca I had a dream. In it Hades killed you to get to me. I couldn't let that happen. I left because I understood he was coming for me and he'd kill anything that stood in his way. I left because I loved you too much to let him kill you and I wanted our child to live a life free of my family's curse."

"He's my son."

"Born of my blood, if the order or even my parents had known about him they'd have taken him to make him one of their number."

"How did he find you then? Sodom wasn't unearthed yet, the clock wasn't ticking?" Anna said confused.

"Magnus told him everything."

"How?" Sam questioned.

"Before Gunnar and I married he wanted, no felt he'd earned the right to my hand. Hades told him he'd give it to him."

"He was behind the bombing," Anna said with understanding.

"You're all mad," Terra muttered.

"Why do you say so?" Anna asked.

"Because you spout nonsense about gods like they're real."

"You'll have to excuse my sister, she's yet to encounter one of the fallen directly," Anna stated.

"Then she shouldn't be here," Zaharrah snapped.

"I'm not leaving mi baby sister ta face a known terrorist," Terra hissed.

"If she doesn't believe she's at risk," Zaharrah warned.

"She'll adapt," Sam assured her.

"She better."

"We know Hades is coming but what if the others come as well?" Anna asked.

"What others?" Vince asked.

"Ares or Dionysus," Sam muttered.

"How many of these bleedin' gods are there then?" Terra demanded.

"Four so far, there were ten originally but some have been absorbed," Anna replied.

"Dionysus turns up, you take your sister and get clear," Sam stated.

"The hell she will," Terra argued.

"I won't have either of you here for him to play with," Sam muttered.

"I'll get her clear," Anna assured him. "But if Ares turns up you have to stay clear of him," she countered.

Sam nodded.

"Now that we're all up to speed what are we going to do about our problem?" Vince asked.

"My research team is on it, but perhaps Zaharrah you're people kept records on how to slay a dragon."

"If they did it will be in the archive. I could go look into it, but that will be Hades first stop on the way here," Zaharrah stated.

"So, going is a gamble," Vince stated.

"Aye," Terra answered.

"It's my risk, the council won't allow outsiders," Zaharrah muttered.

"You're not going alone," Gunnar said vehemently. "It seems to me these people should be notified of what is happening though. They know of me I will go."

Zaharrah nodded. "Let's hope we get there first."

162 ATHENS, GREECE

Hades fixed his clothes putting them back into place and with his power restored Emily and Brooke's garments.

"COME LADIES, IT'S TIME WE LEFT THIS TOMB."

"We're not staying?" Pamela asked shocked.

"NO, OUR ENEMIES KNOW WE'RE HERE. WE CANNOT STAY INSIDE HERMES PALACE ANY LONGER BUT WORRY NOT, I HAVE A FORTRESS OF MY OWN HIDDEN FROM OUR ENEMIES WE WILL GO THERE," Hades stated as he headed for the door. The trio followed after him. Once they were outside the walls Hades turned his power to the structure and tore it down. Leaving Hermes palace in ruins, the only thing he left standing was the final statues of his brethren.

163

Lance moved through the living room of Catharine's two bedroom New York apartment with fascination. The space held numerous book cases, art and collectables.

"Grab a seat on the couch; I'll bring over the books," his hostess called as she moved about the shelves.

Lance nodded as he crossed the floor to the furniture. He found it interesting, she lived off Central Park and wondered if she walked there on days when she needed to think. He tried to picture her at work in the space around him but it didn't fit. The space was not readily designed for her laptop use. No outlet near the table.

"It's down the hall on the right."

"What is?"

"My work space."

"How did you know?"

"You were looking for an outlet. This room is where I go to unwind."

"I see."

"Did you want to see my work space?"

"If you don't mind."

"Knock yourself out, you showed me your office," she stated as she pulled another book.

Lance changed directions heading in the direction she indicated. There were two doors side by side on the right side of the hall. He opened the first room and flipping on the lights found it was the room in question. The walls were painted with unique murals that told a story. The desk set with her back to the windows. A door led from the room he was in to the one next door. He wondered what her room looked like but ignored the impulse to walk through. He instead turned after switching off the light and returned to the living room.

As he reached the couch Catharine set a stack of books on the coffee table.

"This is everything."

"Okay then, let's get started," Lance said as he grabbed the book on top of the stack and started reading it was going to be a long day.

164

Sam turned his attention from thoughts of dragons and old gods to that of his fiancé and how he'd managed to rescue her.

"Where are you counting Artemis on the battle grounds?" he asked.

"I'm not sure. I mean her actions of late have been odd," Anna muttered.

"When this started she was our enemy," Sam stated.

"No argument there. She was hunting us at Hermes command until Ares surfaced," Anna replied.

"Then she was helping Hades for a split second before she stepped into protect you. Why?"

"I don't know. Even she didn't know why she was helping me, but she did and then came back to rescue me when Hecate broke the seal on the door," Anna muttered.

"Sounds like an ally." Sam offered.

"Yes and when you add to that she took Zeus's crown before Hades reached it the belief sounds reasonable and yet I don't know that we can count on her to be standing up against this thing or the others when the time comes," Anna admitted.

"So, she's not on their side but you're not sure she's on ours either," Sam concluded.

"Exactly. I think at the moment we share a common foe but how we handle that and how she does may differ.

"A wild card. Never was fond of them," Sam muttered.

"We'll, worry about her if she turns up. For now, I think we should keep our eyes on what we know is coming and prepare for it," Anna said as her sister came back into the kitchen.

"Perimeter is secure."

"Good I'll see about helping Vince with our inventory check. One of you ladies should go check on Gunnar's kid," Sam suggested.

Anna nodded and satisfied things were in hand, he stepped out of the room.

165

Anna rose from the table to go check on Gunnar's son but Terra stopped her.

"Annalynn I want ta apologize for how I reacted before about ya gettin' mixed up with Mr. Abrams. You're right I did tell ya before love is a leap, I just didn't think ya'd be leapin' toward someone like him. I don't wanna see ya hurt again."

"I know Terra-Anne and I appreciate your concern but I've made my choice. Sam is a good man and if not for him I wouldn't be here to argue with. He stood as my protector in this mess though he didn't know me."

"Grateful I am of that but marriage…"

"I love him Terra, more than I ever thought it was possible to love another, when I'm ready I will marry him."

"Do ya understand the risk?"

"Does he? I've got three old gods pissed off at me for one reason or another," Anna muttered.

"Oh lord in heaven, please don't start spoutin' that rubbish again. It makes mi head spin. Really Annalynn ya were always the more logical minded one of us since when do ya believe in old gods?"

"Since I met one face to face. Hermes, god of knowledge – I watched him possess Ian Broody and devour his soul. Feeling the effects of Dionysus's touch upon my mind was also a bit hard to ignore. You saw me. Have you ever known me to behave so?"

"No, but the fact ya were doesn't make him a god."

"Then how do you explain it?" Anna challenged.

"He could have drugged ya."

"Then why am I clear headed now. Why didn't I try ta throw myself at Sam or Vince?"

"It was wearin' off maybe…"

"We both know there were no drugs."

"Perhaps ya were drunk then."

"I was drunk but not on liquor."

"Anna…"

"Fine, see what you want but when we face him in the days ahead you'll see the truth," Anna muttered before she moved off to check on Gunnar and Zaharrah's son.

166

Catharine looked up from the book she was reading and set it aside. Nothing particularly helpful was within the pages. It only held vague references to knights slaying beasts of old. She glanced over at her associate and found that Lance had dozed off. Catharine took the book he'd been reading from his hands and set it on top of the stack. She rose from her seat and crossed the room to a closet where she pulled out a blanket.

Catharine covered her guest, careful not to disturb him, then leaned down and brushed a kiss on his forehead. "Good night detective," she murmured before returning to her seat. She picked up the book he'd been looking at and began to read from the page he left off on. When he woke he could start on a new one.

167

Lance heard a scream from somewhere ahead and ran after it. His heart pounded with every step he took. Fear held him captive as he drew his weapon and scanned the area ahead. His path led him into a giant hedge maze and he hesitated. Was this really where the scream had originated from? He wondered.

As if in answer to his unspoken question a second scream came from within the labyrinth. This one he noted sounded familiar to him, though why he wasn't sure. Lance moved into the elaborate maze and started down the trail toward the center but he found the path was changing around him, leading him away from his goal and into one of the many dead ends.

When he came to the corner he found that he was no longer in the labyrinth but in the middle of a cemetery and resting on a grave under the eyes of an angel was a familiar sight. Dana kneeling beside a body garbed in a red Grecian gown, a crown of serpents on her head. As he began to slide into the scene a scream echoed in the distance. He blinked turned and tried to correct his course.

The next dead end he encountered was like a gut shot that left him reeling. He was in his own home. Laying on the floor in a pool of her own blood was Dana. Unable to face the scene again he turned and fled wanting out of the maze. He couldn't find a way out and soon ended up in yet another dead end. Waiting for him here was the hotel suite of Kim Frasier. She lay dead upon the bed under the watchful eye of cherubs; that look of pain and desire on her face that Serenity was famous for. A scream echoed from the distance, a cry he now knew.

Catharine.

He had to reach her before Kurt could hurt her again.

168

Hecate slipped inside the woman Catharine's dwelling and smiled to find her spell held the woman's protector in place. She stepped into the room where the pesky writer sat studying her books, hard at work searching for answers to Hades most recent game. Hecate let the task go on. What Catharine discovered or didn't was of no consequence to her. No the thing that troubled her was *Dark Heart*. If Catharine was allowed to finish it as it was now planned it would destroy everything she had been building. Serenity could not be set free. Nivali had to live on.

It was time that Catharine got a dose of reality. Time she was reminded that all men were monsters and love was a prison. With this thought in mind Hecate poured out her power and let it wrap around the unsuspecting woman.

169

Catharine blinked as the lines on the page blurred. A sudden wave of exhaustion washing over her. She looked up from her book with the sudden awareness she was not alone and cursed at the sight before her. Hecate stood but a few feet away, coming in behind her was Dionysus and Ares.

Her lips parted to cry for aid but too late as she felt the wine god's power wrap around her as well; as Ares stood silent, watching, waiting.

She felt reality fade as she was drawn into the dream realm powerless to stop it. The pair had come to stop her from freeing Serenity, just as Lance had feared, she'd miscalculated the odds and now she would face the consequences. As her mind began to cloud over with the dream wrapping around her Catharine clung to one truth: none of this was real.

When she opened her eyes next it was in her personal version of hell. Around her a million torches blazed. Above her the graven images of angels and death looked down. She felt two pairs of hands shove her so that she fell onto the bed surrounded by gauzy layers of fabric the color of flames. She scrambled to get up but too late. A powerful arm was already securing her left wrist to the headboard. As her right wrist was secured the third intruder moved closer. Her eyes black as coal.

"YOU KNOW WHAT WILL HAPPEN NEXT."

"I do," Catharine admitted as Ares bound her right leg to the footboard.

"I CAN MAKE IT STOP, CATHARINE YOU NEED ONLY ASK IT," Hecate whispered.

"It's not real only a dream," she answered.

"NAÏVE MORTAL, THIS IS MORE THAN A MERE DREAM. THE SPELL AROUND YOU IS MORE POWERFUL

THAN ANY CAST BEFORE," Hecate whispered as the war god bound her other leg. Once she was fully restrained Ares drew his sword and began the task of cutting her clothes off her body. As he exposed her flesh Dionysus's hands played over it, his magic stirring within her blood, making her ache for a man's touch. By the time she felt the first cut her body was warm and ready for whatever the vile trio had planned.

As Ares blade began to skim down her body in the twisted caress Dionysus's hand began to slide up the inside of her legs making her tremble with fear and anticipation for the moment when he touched the center of her lust, which he'd begun to stir up.

"I don't want this," she told herself willing it to be true.

"I KNOW SERENITY, SAY THE WORD AND IT WILL ALL STOP, YOU'LL NEVER HAVE TO FEEL THIS WAY AGAIN," Hecate assured her as Ares blade brushed over her belly the two sensations coming dangerously close to each other making her hyper aware of them both. She was both relieved and frustrated when the wine god withdrew his touch just shy of her feminine mound.

"OH SERENITY, MY DEAR YOU'RE SO READY AREN'T YOU, BUT THE EASE YOU DESIRE WILL NOT COME SWIFTLY," Dionysus taunted as Ares blade slid down her left leg slowly.

Catharine endured it in silence until she felt the bite of the second cut when her lips parted on a scream.

170

Lance froze as the most recent scream echoed around him. The heart of this horrid maze lay just ahead. His nightmare was drawing to a close and he was glad of it. Lance knew what was waiting for him. He wasn't looking forward to it, he realized he'd rather remember Dana's death than watch helpless as Catharine endured Kurt's tormenting her. As the corridor around him became that dark basement, he wondered if now that he knew the rest of the ceremony, if like Catharine had described, he'd be forced to watch the rest.

Darkness gave way to a candle lit room and within he saw not two but three figures looming over a naked, trembling, bloody Catharine. Hecate stood near the foot of the bed studying the scene as it played out with amusement. Dionysus stood at her left drinking from his cup eyes eagerly watching as the man Kurt ran his hands down Catharine's neck and towards her breasts.

His fingers lifted to his lips to taste her blood upon them and his eyes glowed orange with the madness induced by the war god's sword.

"Let her go," Lance demanded as he stepped into their midst. He lifted his gun ready to shoot as the curtains around them became a ring of flame.

"HERE YOU WILL FIND THAT WEAPON A USELESS THREAT. THOSE TWO WILL HAVE HER NOW DETECTIVE, AND THERE IS NOTHING YOU CAN DO TO STOP IT NOW. SHE'S THEIRS HAS BEEN SINCE THE DAY HER MOTHER GAVE HER OVER TO HER BOYFRIEND IN HER YOUTH. YOUR PRECIOUS SERENITY KNOWS EACH ONE MORE INTIMATELY THAN YOU EVER WILL," Hecate taunted.

Lance watched as Ares puppet put his hands on her breasts fondling her in such a way that had her crying out for more.

Dionysus muffled her cry as his lips claimed hers. His kiss leaving her drunk and desperate. The wine god sank his fangs in her left wrist indulging in the taste of her growing passion as the war god's hands moved lower. Dionysus gave the wound a parting lick before his mouth moved onto her neck. She hissed as tongue brushed against her jugular in greeting as Ares hands slid down her hips and thighs.

"Enough!" Lance roared as he cocked his gun ready to fire.

"YOU DELUDE YOURSELF DETECTIVE, THEY'RE JUST GETTING STARTED WITH YOUR SWEET SERENITY AND SHE KNOWS IT. AS SHE KNOWS YOU'RE HERE. SHE DOESN'T CARE SHE WANTS THEM AS SHE WANTS YOU."

"She wants none of this," Lance argued.

"WATCH AND LEARN."

Catharine turned her head giving Dionysus better access to her throat and he watched as her blue eyes filled with that strange mix of fear and desire as the war god's hands slid down to the inside of her thighs, fingers teasing her mercilessly. She moaned in pleasure as the wine god's fangs pierced her neck and Ares fingers entered her feminine depths. As the moan faded her lips parted whispering words of demand, begging her captors to finish what was begun.

The pair laughed at her. Ares moving to stand beside her head as Dionysus's hands took up the task the war god had begun. Using his considerable skills to drive her towards release even as Ares readied his knife to inflict the third cut.

Catharine screamed as Lance fired killing the man Kurt before he did any further harm to her. He swung his gun around to take aim at Dionysus. "Back away or join him," Lance hissed as he cocked his weapon ready to fire.

"AS YOU SAY," the wine god breathed with amusement. His hand slid out of the woman before him and she whimpered in protest to being denied the bliss of release. Lance circled the bed to where his enemy lay dead picked up the knife prepared to cut Catharine loose and bring an end to this vile dream.

171

Catharine watched as Lance came toward her and understood what game the old gods were playing at as he stood over her, knife poised not to free her as was his intent but to finish what Kurt had begun. His mind now enslaved to the will of the knife. His body being slowly possessed by Ares.

"No, stop this," Catharine cried out in dismay.

"YOU WISH IT TO END THEN YOU STOP IT, YOU KNOW HOW," Hecate hissed even as she moved to Lance's side. Her hands played over his body coaxing him with the promise of pleasure.

"Dana," he whispered with recognition and Hecate smiled.

"YES LOVE WE CAN BE TOGETHER AGAIN SOON YOU NEED ONLY FINISH WHAT YOU'VE BEGUN," she whispered as she ran her hand down his chest and towards the proof of his arousal.

Catharine turned her eyes away with disgust even as Dionysus skimmed his hands up her belly towards her breast. She screamed as the wine god's fangs pierced her left breast in the same moment, she felt the sting of the third cut as Lance did as the witch bid him. Catharine felt warm breath on her skin and her stomach churned with disgust knowing the witch wasn't bluffing, if she remained silent the dream would go on. She'd endure the rest of the ritual with Lance in the roll of the killer.

Hecate would twist the truth until she hated him. She'd make her believe he was a monster.

"Let him go witch," Catharine hissed as Dionysus's fangs left her flesh.

"THIS WILL ALL END IF YOU SAY THE WORDS I DESIRE," Hecate countered as Lance's mouth covered hers. Her gaze met his; ice blue eyes pled for a moment for forgiveness before they blazed orange as Ares took control stealing her breath with the intensity of his kiss as the wine god sank his fangs into the flesh of her inner thigh.

"All right enough. You are Serenity," Catharine shouted in desperation as Lance's teeth sank into her right wrist to follow in Dionysus's act. The wine god touched her mind to show her what was yet to come.

Hecate smiled and Catharine faded from the dream even as Lance's fangs pierced her neck.

172

Lance felt his stomach role with disgust as he cut the fifth line under her right eye. He looked down at the naked woman she trembled eyes full of fear and desperate longing the wine god had worked his spell well. His prisoner was eager and willing at times she whispered words in an effort to move him along begging for him to take her.

His own blood burned with desire as the war god drove him on. He wanted her, this woman. Desired her in a way he hadn't any other. He struggled against Ares wanting to not hurt her but he couldn't put the knife down, He'd watched helpless as the ritual went on. The war god torturing her as Dana looked on with excitement.

Not Dana.

Dana was dead. He'd lost sight of that for a moment, she was Hecate and the woman before him was Serenity, not the vampire but the real one, the writer and creator of *Dark Heart*. This wasn't real. He was dreaming. It was some sort of sick, twisted nightmare. Dionysus and the others were playing with him, maybe with both of them. He wasn't sure; all he knew was he'd had enough.

173

"NOW MY SWEET SERENITY, AT LAST YOU ARE MINE," he heard the war god whisper before he gave them both what they desired as he filled her body with his aroused flesh. Lance groaned at the feel of her. She was wet and ready for him. She wept beneath him with relief as her body shook in orgasm. Her eyes opened to meet with his and they were black as coal.

"AH, THERE YOU ARE, NOW I HAVE YOU," she whispered as she turned the tables on him no longer bound and in his control. He found instead that it was him that was restrained and she hovered over him lifting her body from his she sat up and began to ride him driving him towards release using his body to please herself.

"What do you want with me witch?" he said his voice was thick with passion as she was getting to him. Her face switching from Dana's to Catharine's to Serenity's, giving him his pick of the form she wore.

"I WANT YOU LANCELOT," she breathed as she dragged her nails down his chest.

"Stop this Devil's whore I don't want this," Lance growled willing it to be true.

"OH, BUT YOU DO LANCE, YOU'VE DREAMED OF LITTLE ELSE SINCE YOU MET HER. PERHAPS YOU'D PREFER THIS," Hecate whispered as she blended the images of Serenity and Catharine together becoming his faerie princess.

Lance closed his eyes against the image as he groaned with pleasure drawing near the edge. "I don't want her this way: without a will of her own," he argued.

"YOU WANT HER WITHOUT FEAR. SHE IS NOW AND WILL STAY SO," Hecate murmured.

"You're not Serenity."

"OH, BUT I AM," Hecate whispered, "JUST AS YOU HAVE BECOME WAR," she added as she cut his arms free with Ares knife. His hands seized hold of her hips taking control of her body pressing her harder on him so that she too began to ache as he did. His eyes glowed orange once more.

"WHAT DO YOU WANT OF ME WITCH?" The war god hissed as he raged inside of her driving her to the same peak she'd been pushing his host's flesh toward.

"YOUR SWORD FOR THE PAIR. HER FLESH TO USE AS YOU DESIRE AND HIS BODY AS YOURS, SO LONG AS YOU STAY OUT OF MY WAY AND PROTECT ME FROM YOUR BRETHREN."

"DONE," Ares agreed as he pushed her into ecstasy and followed after. He thrilled in the feel of her, Hecate had not been touched by any of them since Zeus, that she gave herself to him now spoke volumes of where she felt her best interest lie.

"I'M GLAD WE'VE REACHED AN AGREEMENT," Hecate said as she rose from the bed. She ran her fingers through her tussled hair and her body was covered once more.

"WHAT OF ME?" Dionysus whispered as he moved to her side his fingers skimmed along her neck reminding her of his part in their game.

"YOU'LL GET TO KEEP YOUR POWER GENERATOR. SERENITY'S JOURNEY WILL BE YOURS TO TELL," Hecate assured him as she touched his cup and watched it fill to the brim.

Dionysus sipped from the glass and his eyes glowed at the potency of the powers draught. "EXCELLENT, LETS FINISH THE GAME," the wine god said with excitement as he let his power wash through Lance Roman's mind once more. It was time the man woke to take his place among their ranks.

174 CAIRO, EGYPT

Zaharrah stepped inside the ancient library with a boldness she'd not felt since Ithaca. Gunnar was at her back. His eyes skimmed over the space looking for any threat. Trying to make sense of what his eyes told him was a simple library, yet she stated was more. Zaharrah made her way to the staff only door and punched in her code. The door opened and she stepped through with Gunnar hot on her heels. Her path was barred by a security door before the council hall and she cursed.

"Zaharrah, what is the meaning of this? You know our laws. No outsiders," the gate keeper hissed as the corridor behind them closed as well.

"I've come with a warning and he is here to back my claim. I will see the council and they will tolerate his presence or you will all suffer disaster for your failures."

"Speak plainly girl."

"What I say will be for the council and no other."

"You know the penalty for daring--" the gate keeper began.

"Let them pass," An elderly man's voice commanded and the doors before them parted allowing them passage.

Zaharrah stepped through aware that Gunnar was right behind her.

"What news do you bring that you risk death?"

"Magnus Halden has betrayed you. He has become Hades and now moves to destroy us and Israel as well," Zaharrah stated.

"These accusations are grievous, what proof do you offer?"

Gunnar stepped past her and handed over a printed copy of the intel Darrian had provided her with.

"Is there anything further?"

"Pandora is free," Zaharrah stated.

"How can that be?"

"Magnus led his brother to the sword. When he took it she was unsealed. She is moving among the shadows. The fallen are among us, what will you do about these matters?" Zaharrah asked her voice full of anger and challenge.

"We will investigate these claims and if they prove true we shall act."

"Investigate them. Do you think I would make something like this up?"

"You are not one of us any more child, remember you walked away."

"Yet you allow me to come and go as I please from this place. Your words are hollow. You know I speak truth and yet you hesitate. I suggest you not hesitate too long. Abandon this place soon. Hades will come." Zaharrah warned.

"No one would dare invade this hall--"

"You're fools. The archives have been raided, Hades will come to destroy any knowledge that he deems a threat to his plans.

"You speak of matters you know nothing about."

"I know more than you think. If there is anything within the vault on dragon slaying I would request access to it."

"Your request is denied. Depart this hall now and never return."

"Sir--"

"Be gone! And be grateful to have your lives."

Zaharrah turned and marched out Gunnar at her back.

"Old fools."

"You tried."

"This was a waste of our time. I hope Sam's researchers have better luck," she muttered as they got in his car. While they were pulling away from the curb Zaharrah watched as Hades stepped out of another vehicle and pointed a finger at the library. His eyes glowed green as he drew upon his power. The library's roof caved in as the walls began to crumble.

"Is that--" Gunnar began in question.

"Yes, drive!" Zaharrah ordered interrupting him as the ruins burst into flames.

Lance woke with a jolt to find himself no longer in that god forsaken basement but instead on Catharine's couch. His eyes scanned over the room taking in his surroundings as he tried to sort through the mess in his head. He'd been dreaming the last image he recalled was feeling Catharine's body quake beneath his in completion and then her eyes opening to find they were coal black. Hecate.

Lance shoved aside the blanket over himself, sitting up, terrified he'd find that Catharine was missing once more. He was relieved to find her resting in the chair directly across from him but his ease dissipated as he noted the figure standing behind her. Dionysus. His fingers were combing through her red hair, his eyes closed as he touched her mind. Hecate sat in the seat beside her also motionless. Ares was poised near the door blocking his way out. Even if he'd had any notions about escape it was clear they were pointless.

"RELAX DETECTIVE, WE JUST WANT A WORD WITH OUR SWEET SERENITY," Dionysus stated as his eyes opened. The dim violet glow marking his power as fading as they reverted back to blue.

"If all you wanted was to talk then why the mental attack?" Lance challenged with disgust.

"WE WEREN'T SURE HOW YOU WOULD RESPOND TO US BEING HERE," Hecate whispered as Gail Blackwood opened her eyes, only rather than brown they were coal black.

"What do you want from us?" Catharine asked her blue eyes lit with alarm.

"WE WANT YOU TO END DARK HEART OUR WAY," Dionysus answered.

"Why can't Serenity end up with Davrik, he's Syvarin's heir, he's the next vampire lord," Catharine argued.

"THEN WHAT?" Hecate asked amused.

"Then whatever. Blood war Begins. Kovrin falls and maybe Syvarin vanishes in to shadow to find his own mate," Catharine muttered on the fly.

"COULD WORK," Dionysus said amused. "I COULD HAVE YOU WRITE ME A SPIN OFF SCRIPT FOR SYVARIN, EVERYONE WHO COUNTS GET THEIR HAPPY ENDING," he stated pleased and then sipped from his cup.

"What about him?" Lance asked pointing at Ares not caring for his presence so near to him.

"ME, I'VE NO INTEREST IN THIS *DARK HEART* NONSENSE," Ares said with disgust. "QUITE HONESTLY, I'VE NO INTEREST IN THIS WORLD AROUND ME. WAR IN ITS PUREST FORM IS DEAD. GONE ARE THE DAYS OF HEROES AND SWORDS. THERE IS NO POWER IN YOUR WARS FOR ME, NO EMOTION BEHIND IT. I'M HERE BECAUSE OF YOUR CURRENT PLIGHT. MY BROTHER HAS BROUGHT BACK HIS BEASTS AND YOU SEEK A MEANS TO DEFEAT THEM. I HOLD A SOLUTION, BUT IN THESE HANDS IT CANNOT BE WIELDED. MY CURRENT HOST IS TOO TAINTED WITH HADES BRAND TO BE OF ANY USE," Ares said with frustration.

"You're here for me," Lance said with understanding.

"YES, AS WE STOOD FACING EACH OTHER IN THAT CANDLE LIT BASEMENT I FELT IN YOU A SPARK OF POWER FROM MY WARRIORS OF OLD. A FIRE THESE OTHERS LACKED."

"And you thought that filling my head with images of my harming her under your control would somehow make me more willing to submit to you?" Lance asked incredulous.

"NO, THAT WAS HER GAME. I SIMPLY PLAYED THE PART SHE ASSIGNED," Ares corrected as he pointed an accusatory finger at Hecate. "SHE WANTED TO CONVINCE SERENITY THAT SHE COULD TURN YOU AGAINST HER TO GET WHAT SHE WANTED. WANTED TO GIVE YOU A TASTE OF MY POWER AS WELL."

"Why?" Lance questioned confused.

"I DON'T KNOW THE OLD WITCHES PLANS NOR DO I CARE TOO. I WANT YOU TO TAKE MY SWORD AND USE IT TO SLAY HADES BEAST."

"So, you can possess me like some disease and claim a willing bride. No thanks," Lance answered with disgust.

"I'VE NO INTENTION OF TAKING YOU OVER DETECTIVE, AND AS FOR HER I'LL NOT INTERFERE WITH YOUR COURTSHIP. I'LL EVEN GO SO FAR AS TOO HAVE DIONYSUS HERE RELEASE HER OF HIS INFLUENCE."

"So you say but how can I trust the words of a fallen one?" Lance muttered, knowing not to listen but unable to ignore the war god's words completely. If he were serious what he offered was indeed tempting.

"DO YOU WISH A VOW THEN DETECTIVE, PROOF OF MY CLAIM?" Ares asked amused.

Lance nodded.

"WINE GOD--"

"WHAT DO YOU WANT WAR LORD?" Dionysus muttered annoyed at the deal being made.

"RELEASE YOUR HOLD ON HIS WOMAN," Ares commanded.

"WHAT DO YOU OFFER IN EXCHANGE FOR HER?" The wine god asked eyeing him with curiosity now.

"A FAVOR TO BE GIVEN UPON THY REQUEST," Ares replied.

"WHAT SORT OF FAVOR?" Dionysus questioned.

"ANY YOU DESIRE."

"VERY WELL," Dionysus relented knowing the payment was indeed worthy of the request.

Lance watched as the wine god poured out the contents of his cup and replaced it with water. He drank with a grimace and muttered "twice in one week," in agitation before spitting out the remaining taste of Catharine's lust.

"YOUR WOMAN IS FREE OF HIS POWER. I SWEAR BY HEAVEN I WILL NOT PRESS TO ENSLAVE YOU OR HER TO MY WILL AND I SEAL THAT VOW WITH MY OWN BLOOD," Ares stated as he pricked his finger with the tip of the knife. He then held the blade out to Lance.

"That thing is evil, Lance it's tainted with the blood of a god. Its power is stronger than any other for turning the hearts of men," Catharine warned terrified.

"If I do this she releases her hold on Serenity and none of you come near her again, ever," Lance hissed as he pointed a finger at Hecate.

"WE'VE REACHED A COMPROMISE ON *DARK HEART* I NO LONGER NEED HER," Hecate assured him.

"I mean it one dream, one stray thought not her own and--"

"WE UNDERSTAND DETECTIVE, AND AS SOON AS THE DEAL IS DONE I WILL MAKE IT CLEAR TO HADES AND HERMES AS WELL," Ares assured him.

"Lance you can't--" Catharine cried in protest.

"IF HE DOESN'T YOU AND YOUR FRIENDS WILL DIE, NO MEANS YOU POSSESS CAN DEFEAT HIS BEAST," Ares snapped in interruption Catharine swallowed. Lance saw in her eyes that what Ares said was true. She was afraid for their friends.

Lance took the knife from the other man's grasp and it became a sword once more. The man Darrian fell to the floor unconscious as Ares spirit left him.

"Time to go," Lance stated.

Catharine nodded. "Are you okay detective?" She asked her voice thick with concern.

"I'm fine," he assured her as he turned to go. "Our uninvited guests will leave after we're gone," Lance stated in a voice that made it clear they'd better as the two of them walked out.

176

Hecate laughed, as the door closed her and Dionysus in the apartment together.

"That was interesting," Dionysus said as he poured out the water and turned his thoughts to Emily. The cup refilled and he swirled it before taking a sip.

"It went better than I could have hoped for," Hecate said pleased.

"How do you figure? We both had to let go of our claim on Miss Nichols."

"Yes, but you still have a hold on him and Ares is now in their midst. Serenity will give us what we need and Hades grand entrance will be interrupted. The playing field is even. Go back to your palace in L.A. I'm going my way and Ares will go his. With a little time perhaps we'll take our rightful places in this game after all," Hecate whispered.

"Here's to an even battle," Dionysus said as he lifted his glass before swallowing down its contents.

"Indeed." Hecate answered before she departed. Her eyes glowed with excitement as she went. The evening's game had gone perfectly, now it was time to go claim her prize.

177

Terra sat silently at the Masada agent's kitchen table trying to mentally prepare for the conflict to come. She struggled with the notion that sometime in the future her baby sister was going to marry Sam Abrams, the spy she'd personally burned. Terra felt a headache begin to bloom behind her eyes and cursed.

Sitting here and waiting was not helping matters. Terra had always been a shoot first and ask questions later kind of girl. Vince was more the brains of their unit. She wondered what his take was on all this old gods nonsense and figured when she went back to check on his post she'd ask.

What she was sure of was that the quiet they'd been surrounded by since setting foot in this house was almost up. It was time she notify her employers of what was going on out here and what she'd learned about Magnus Halden. Taking out her cell phone Terra punched in the number for headquarters. After going through the codes and identification checks she was connected to her boss. Terra laid out all she knew to date in regard to their target. She was careful to leave out any notion of old gods or powerful relics, aware such talk would lead her employer to think she'd gone mad.

When she was finished with the report Terra hung up the phone and moved to seek out her husband. She found him and Mr. Abrams with their heads together talking in the front hall.

"Sorry to interrupt lads, but I'd like a word with me husband."

"No problem, I'll just go check the back half of the flat to make sure it's secure," Sam said before me moved off.

"What's on your mind Terra-Ann?"

"I was just wonderin' what you make of all this old god shite their spoutin' on about Mr. Fenton," Terra muttered.

"It's pretty absurd you ask me, except that it's your Annalynn saying it. From everything ya told me about your little sister I'd say if she's saying it there must be some truth in it and we best be on guard."

Terra nodded. "And your take on him?"

"Good man, loyal. If he's got your sister's back I'd say she's in good hands."

"I still don't like it," Terra muttered.

"I know Mrs. Fenton, but you'll get used to the idea just as ya got used to me," Vince teased before he drew her into his arms and kissed her.

178

Gunnar pulled up next to the curb outside his flat and switched off the engine. As he got out of the car his mind replayed the image of the man dressed in a black suit stepping out of a car. His hair back and red eyes like steel, lit with a green glow. Hand lifted in the direction of the library. The feel of the earth shaking beneath his feet. The roof of the building caving in as the walls crumbled, almost like in that instant the structure had aged centuries before his eyes. Then burst into flames.

He hadn't believed all that talk of old gods and ancient curses not really, he'd simply believed his wife that she'd left because she felt that she had to protect him and their son from harm. After meeting the council he'd seen why she wanted to keep Caleb from them.

Hades display of power had convinced him of the rest. His city was in danger and his superior needed to be notified. They had to be ready for the assault. Granted he didn't know if any of their modern weapons would be of use against a dragon but he was sure as heck going to find out.

Taking out his cell phone, he dialed the number for his boss and once connected relayed everything which he had been given, passing on copies of the pertinent files and informing his commanding officer of the team in place before requesting arms.

"Your request will be considered if your intel checks out with our American contacts, weapons will be deployed and waiting at your normal pick-up location.

"Understood," Gunnar answered before the line disconnected.

Catharine sat in front of her laptop finishing up an e-mail to James Hardagen as she typed her last line she read it back to herself.

"Mr. Hardagen,

Enclosed are the deleted scenes for Heart Of Glass as well as the completed script for Heart Of Clay, I trust you'll be pleased with the work. However with our recent selection for the role of Serenity gone, filming I fear will be delayed until I get back to assist with casting calls next week.

Sincerely,

CJ Nichols"

Satisfied the message was clear and she'd not let her general distaste for working with the wine god bleed through. So the copy going to her publishing house would convey she was making nice on their behalf. She attached the two files in question and sent the letter to the man producing her film James Hardagen.

She then copied the letter and created a new one to the publishing house.

"To whom it may concern,

Within you will find my most recent communications with our film producer regarding the *Dark Heart* project as well as the current script and my work to date on the fourth *Dark Heart* book with the working title Heart of Fire. I am also attaching my proposed changes to the current trilogy to make my vision for the fourth book possible. I have already begun discussions with Mr. Hardagen concerning the fourth book. He looks forward to doing the film. Please contact me if there is anything else you need with regard to the project.

Sincerely,

CJ Nichols"

With the letter done she attached the e-mail to James along with the other files mentioned and sent it off. She prepared to shut down her net connection but noted a reply from James and opened it.

"Miss Nichols,

I've already got the perfect woman in mind for the part. I trust you'll be satisfied. Filming is set to begin on Monday. I look forward to your return as well as reading the completed fourth instalment of *Dark Heart*. Be sure to bring your detective out with you as he was a fascinating house guest.

D"

Catharine forwarded his response to the house and then closed out of her e-mail and glanced up over the screen at her seat mate.

"Are you done?" Lance questioned.

"Yeah, business is attended to," she replied. Catharine licked her lips in a show of nerves. It was strange sitting across from him now when she was aware that Ares was in there looking back at her as well.

"Gonna work on the book?" Lance asked curious.

"No, I'll wait until we get on the ground. I've never been fond of working off battery power it's too easy to lose my work," she answered as she shut down her machine.

"Good, I've got you all to myself then," he said amused.

"Right--" Catharine said uneasy not sure how she felt about that.

"Are you okay?" He asked concerned.

"Yeah, are you?" She asked.

"Yep, fine," he assured her.

"Do you feel any different?"

"Not really, less tired maybe and more aware."

"What do you mean?"

"I can hear your heart beating, you're scared," he whispered.

"I'm sorry, knowing he's in there somewhere is making me edgy --last time--"

"He's not," Lance said interrupting her.

"What?"

"He's not in my head Serenity. He's in the sword."

"You shouldn't have taken it," Catharine whispered.

"It's done Catharine, these troublesome fallen will not bother you anymore."

"At what cost?" Catharine asked as she brushed his hair away from his eyes.

Lance took her hand in his and kissed her palm before curling her fingers inside his to kiss her knuckles in a courtly fashion long gone. "It doesn't matter. All I care about is that you stay safe, my lady," he whispered before releasing her hand. His fingers sank into her hair. Catharine blushed flattered and he smiled. "There, that's better. No more fear. It's just me Serenity," he assured her before he leaned closer and his lips captured hers.

Catharine's eyes fell closed and she lost herself in his kiss. When his lips came away from hers fiery lashes lifted to meet his stare. The same warm, playful gaze she knew looked back it was just him. Satisfied she rose from her seat across from him and sank down in the one beside him. She rested her head on his shoulder and closed her eyes. As she drifted into sleep the last thing she was aware of was a kiss laid against her forehead and Lance's voice whispering I love you.

180

Dionysus sat sipping a glass of wine as his eyes ran over the computer screen in front of him. After sending his reply to Catharine's e-mail he'd opened the new scenes to be added to the deleted scenes selection of the DVD release of *Heart of Glass*. The additions would be easy to shoot and the fans would love them. She'd even added a couple additional scenes with Syvarin to tie it all together. He couldn't wait to start filming again on Monday.

Now he was into the heart of the second script and his blood was humming with the promise of passion that was building. The story was darker, grittier, and the perfect follow up to *Heart of Glass*, picking up where it left off, but with the storm racing toward Serenity and Davrik. The shadows closing in on their heroine. Syvarin's turning her was a master stroke that would explode onto the screen and make him a god among CJ Nichols fans. The worship he craved would be given soon. The short to be included on DVD was a master stroke and would answer a lot of questions for the readers.

Dark Heart would become a smash hit taken beyond a dark fantasy romance to a masterpiece. Soon the names within the pages would be in the hearts, mind and on the lips of every soul on earth. With that kind of power none of the others would be able to stand against him.

181

Zaharrah sat in the living room lost in her own thoughts. In her mind she pictured the image of the library's destruction and tried to forget it. She wondered if anyone had made it out. Pondered who had been there. Were her parents--? Zaharrah derailed the question unable to even think of them as gone. Feeling responsible for what had happened. If she hadn't left--

"Zaharrah, I've brought you a visitor," Gunnar's voice said interrupting her musings.

She looked up from her hands to her husband to see a face that until that moment she'd only looked upon from a distance. "Gunnar no. Don't bring him near me," Zaharrah hissed with despair.

"Father?" the boy asked alarmed.

"Why not?" Gunnar asked confused.

"You saw what happened at the library that was my fault."

"Caleb, go wait outside I need to speak to our guest alone first," Gunnar requested.

The boy nodded and withdrew.

"That was not your fault."

"It was. If I'd stayed--"

"Do you think he'd have not struck down the library? You know that's not true. He knew your family was a threat to him. If you'd stayed or not he'd have destroyed it," Gunnar argued.

"But--"

"But what Zaharrah, everyone there was already dead; just as anyone missed soon will be. This isn't your fault."

"Even if it's not, the fact remains, if he knows who I am his life is forfeit."

"Where will you go when this is done? Back into the shadows, watching from a distance. Living some half-life; wishing for more but afraid to risk it."

"I can't stay."

"You can. I want you to. I want you to have faith in me.

I'm not so easy to kill."

"Our son deserves better than to live under the threat that his parents could both die like that," Zaharrah said as she snapped her fingers.

"He deserves to know his mother."

"He deserves the chance to have a normal life. Forget me Gunnar. Find another," Zaharrah said as she turned her back to him.

"I don't want another Zaharrah. I want my wife," he answered as he grabbed her by the arm and turned her to face him. His lips met hers and he held her fast as she struggled to push him away. Her fighting soon died out and she kissed him back unable to deny him.

"I'll never turn my back on you Zaharrah, we are one," Gunnar whispered as he held her close to him. "Stop running, come home," he requested as he wiped tears from her eyes.

"I can't--" she said with regret and dismay.

"Of course you can."

"He'll kill you both if I--" Zaharrah began with fear.

"No, he won't. I won't let anything happen to our family again," Gunnar vowed.

"You can't--"

"Yes, I can, have faith," he entreated.

Zaharrah nodded relenting wanting to believe.

"Good, now come, its time you met our boy," Gunnar said and taking her hand he led her from the living room down the hall to their son's room.

"Caleb," Gunnar called.

"Yes father."

"Come, I want you to meet someone."

"Okay," the boy answered. Zaharrah stood silent listening to the exchange, her heart melting. They were so close Gunnar and her boy. She wondered if they could ever be that close. Gunnar stepped aside letting Zaharrah in the room.

"You're the lady from the living room," the boy said nervously at seeing her.

"That's right," she said pleased by how smart he was. "I'm sorry if I scared you before," she murmured.

"Why are you so sad?"

"I've been away from my home too long."

"Oh--father, who is she?" The boy asked noticing the way

Gunnar had stepped closer to her to rest a hand on her back.

"Caleb, this is your mother,"

"My Mother?" the boy asked stunned as he looked at her with wonder and confusion. A million questions swam in his eyes and Zaharrah crossed the room to his side, she fell to her knees before him and drew him into her arms,

"I'm so sorry," she whispered as she held him tight unable to take her eyes off him. That she held him now was a miracle she'd never allowed herself to even dream of. She felt Gunnar's arms wrap around them both and tears unbidden fell from her eyes. Finally, after years of wandering in exile she was home.

182

Lance looked over at the sleeping beauty using his shoulder for a pillow and drew a breath. It was the first peaceful sleep she'd had in almost a week. He was grateful that so far Ares was keeping his word. He felt no press from the war god's mind to take over and Catharine's interest in him seemed to have cooled back to that of the curious writer studying a subject. There had been a hint of more in their kiss earlier but the fog of Dionysus's wine had cleared.

Lance felt a strange mix of relief and disappointment at the change. He was pleased she was free of the wine god's influence but disappointed to have lost her full attention. He'd liked the feel of her in his arms. Enjoyed the thrill of feeling her body respond to him in such a fashion. He wondered if he'd ever see that desire in her eyes for him again or if it had all been brought on by Dionysus's spell as she'd said. He found he didn't know and the uncertainty of it bothered him.

Turning his thoughts from the matter his blue eyes moved from the pretty writer to the sword at his hip. It had been a mere knife in the other man's hands in New York as it had been in Kurt's so why was it a sword for him? What did it all mean?

Ares had spoken of a spark in him the others had lacked. What spark? What made him unique? He wasn't by nature a particularly violent man. Heck he wasn't overly fond of war or bloodshed. So why had Ares bargained so strongly to put the blade in his hands?

What he'd told Catharine earlier was true. Ares was not in his head. The war god's presence was wrapped tight around the blade itself. He heard him whisper on occasion but other than that he seemed strangely silent.

"IF YOU ARE GOING TO BE ANY USE TO YOUR ALLIES YOU MUST KNOW YOUR DESTINATION UPON LANDING SOON. THERE WILL BE LITTLE TIME TO PREPARE UPON

ARRIVAL. HADES IS ALREADY EN ROUTE," Ares mind whispered.

Lance pulled out his cell phone and punched in the number for Sam. He hoped the other man would be free, forth coming with the location or everything he'd done might be pointless. As it rang he asked the question that had been troubling him since he took the sword: how was he going to slay a dragon.

"RELAX, DETECTIVE, I'LL SHOW YOU WHEN THE TIME COMES," Ares assured him as the line connected.

"Lance, man, tell me you've got something," Sam requested.

"I do. In route to deliver it. Where are you?" Lance listened as Sam rattled off the address and directions.

"What did you come up with?"

"I'll fill you in when we arrive, just be ready. We don't have much time," Lance said before he hung up. His eyes settled once more on Catharine and he wondered how much longer he'd have with her.

"YOU'LL SURVIVE YOUR ENCOUNTER WITH HADES BEAST, I'LL ENSURE IT," Ares whispered.

"What do you want from me?" Lance asked with concern and curiosity.

"PATIENCE DETECTIVE, ALL IN GOOD TIME," Ares answered as Lance's eyelids began to droop.

"PLEASANT DREAMS TO YOU LANCE," he whispered as the mortal fell into sleep.

183

Hecate stood next to the rail of the boat she chartered. Coal black eyes staring out at the distance, the isle of Atlantis lay on the horizon and her lips curled into a wicked smirk. So close now. It wouldn't be long until all she'd worked for fell into place. Her goal was within reach now she could nearly touch it. The smell of victory hung in the air. The sea breeze carrying her to the city of the gods would take her back to her beloved as well. After all this time they'd be together again at last. Her mission was nearly complete. Once she held the crown again it would be over. She'd be able to go home soon.

184

Gunnar eased his grip on his wife and their son at the feel of his phone vibrating at his hip. With caution and stealth he crept from the room to take the call.

"Hello."

"Gunnar, I have confirmation from our people in the US the package you requested is ready for pick-up."

"Thank you sir."

"Good hunting solider."

Gunnar disconnected the call and moved into the kitchen to update Sam and his team on the state of things.

"Gunnar, I was just going to come find you," Sam said.

"What is it my friend?"

"I just got word from my research team they got what we need and are in route."

"Good news. I just got off the line with my superior our claim has been substantiated, weapons are waiting I was about to see if one of your team would like to join me in a supply run."

"I'll go."

"Don't you mean we?" Anna challenged.

"Not this time doc, if Hades hit the library there's a chance he'll try again at the pick-up. I want you safe. Your sister will kill me if anything happens to you and she'd be right to do so. Stay here Anna for me," Sam entreated.

Anna nodded relenting. "Just be careful, Mr. Abrams," she requested.

"Always," he assured her, he then brushed a quick kiss on her lips before turning to go.

"Let's get going, the faster we get this done the sooner we can get back," Sam muttered.

"Get what done?" Zaharrah asked as she stepped into the kitchen.

"Weapons run," Gunnar answered.

"You meant to leave without me?"

"I want you here with our son. Keep him safe till I get back."

"You're fighting dirty," she hissed.

"Zaharrah, please."

She nodded and he kissed her before he and Sam left.

185

Lance woke from strange and disturbing dreams to find himself on Catharine's private jet bound for the airport in Tele-Viv Israel. Catharine was still sound asleep at his side safe from the dangers of the fallen who now moved upon the earth. Relief washed through him as he brushed her brow with a kiss. As he lifted his head away from hers he dropped a second kiss against her temple as trembling fingers brushed strands of red hair behind her ear.

He wondered what he'd been dreaming of before he woke but the images were shrouded from his mind. All he knew was that something had happened to her. It had been bad, bad enough to leave him shaken. He drew a breath to steady his nerves and was greeted by her scent. Lance's eyes fell shut as his lips pressed against her cheek.

In his mind's eye he saw her lying motionless on a stone bed her flesh cold with death. Skin white as chalk, stained by grotesque bloody tears. Her blue eyes wide but sightless, lips parted in a frozen scream silenced abruptly by the black silk tied tight around her throat. Looking up he saw Hades standing at a distance a candle in his hand still smoking from when he snuffed it out.

"You had no right she was mine," Lance roared in rage.

"DO YOU THINK A MORTAL SUCH AS YOURSELF CAN SLAY MY BEAST AND REAP NO CONSEQUENCES? YOURS, PLEASE. SHE WAS NO MORE YOURS THAN ANNA WAS." Hades laughed.

"I loved her."

"YES, I KNOW, THAT IS WHY SHE IS GONE. IF YOU STAND BEFORE MY DRAGON TO DESTROY IT YOU'LL NEVER KNOW A MOMENT'S PEACE AGAIN. YOU'LL WATCH AS EVERYTHING YOU LOVE MEETS A SIMILAR END AND BECOMES MINE," Hades hissed as he crossed to

Catharine's side and parted his lips to call her back a slave bound to his will.

"No!"

"IF YOU WISH THIS IMAGE TO BE UNDONE SIMPLY FORGET THIS FOOLISHNESS OF FIGHTING MY BEAST AND I'LL SPARE HER MY WRATH," Hades offered. The god of the underworld instead blew his breath upon her and before Lance's eyes the silk vanished and color returned to her cheeks as her heart began to beat once more his work undone. Catharine drew a ragged breath as golden fiery lashes fluttered. "Lance!" she called his name desperate as she threw her arms around his neck desperate and seeking comfort.

Lance opened his eyes to look at her once more, she was still lost in sleep blissfully unaware of the threat made against her. He didn't dare endanger her now, not after what he'd risked to ensure her safety.

"DO YOU THINK I'D LET HIM HARM HER WHEN I KNOW HER VALUE TO YOU?" Ares whispered amused.

"What can you do to protect her from him? You're not even in your full power?" Lance snapped.

"TRUE, BUT I'M NOT WITHOUT MY WAYS," Ares answered cryptically. "SLAY THE DRAGON AND I'LL SEE THAT NO HARM BEFALLS YOUR LOVE," Ares murmured.

"If she dies, so will you," Lance vowed.

"FAIR ENOUGH," Ares replied as Lance settled back in his seat and closed his eyes once more to rest. .

186

Ares smiled as the man Lance's mind slipped back into sleep. He could feel his power swelling around him in a way that neither the madman Kurt nor the warrior Darrian had been able to produce for him, the detective's wrath and anger coming in a form that the blade found more acceptable. It was pure and untainted. His emotions were like that of the raw material Ares had molded in the past to form some of his greatest leaders. It had cost him a considerable amount to achieve but his sword was in the detective's possession and it wouldn't be long until sword and arm came together to spill blood. Once that happened the game would shift.

187

Anna watched as Zaharrah took a seat at the table in front of her. She'd known the tomb raider for some time now and had known nothing about her. She couldn't imagine what it would be like to being coming home to a family she loved after being gone for years. The nightmare that must haunt her of knowing that an angry god was coming to destroy them. The same god who hours earlier had used his spell upon her to lure her into a trap with the intent of violating her to claim his new bride.

Anna shuddered at the thought. Zaharrah was made of sterner stuff than her. The memory of it all she figured would have driven her mad and fast Anna figured. "How are you holding up?" Anna questioned concerned.

"About as well as can be expected," Zaharrah muttered.

"How are you even still standing? I mean--"

"Gunnar and Caleb need me." Anna nodded her understanding.

"How about you?" Zaharrah asked.

"Still trying to see how this can end any way but badly," Anna admitted.

"Your friend said he has a solution."

"But how can they survive a dragon raid long enough to kill the thing?"

"They'll manage it," Zaharrah whispered.

"I hope so."

188

Sam stepped out of the SUV as Gunnar opened the storage unit. The two men began loading various crates into the trunk. Focusing on the task at hand as the moons light began to fade. Clouds moved in obscuring the night sky as they worked. The wind shifted signaling the approach of a coming storm and Sam swallowed; knowing that one was on the way that would rain down fire and death. He doubted anything he was loading would be a match for the beast or its master. He hoped whatever Lance had would do the trick and that it would arrive in time.

He slammed the trunk as Gunnar closed up the storage unit. Within moments they were back on the road but he wondered if there was anything he could do now to prevent the coming chaos about to be unleashed and if by some miracle they did survive it, what nightmare would wait in the other side.

189

Gunnar pulled his SUV up to the shed in the backyard and together with Sam unloaded surpluses of ammunition and hardware, careful to keep it concealed from his boy's curious eyes. When the work was done the team joined the others inside.

"Where's the boy?" Gunnar asked as they entered the kitchen to see Anna and Zaharrah sitting alone.

"Asleep," Zaharrah assured him.

"Good," Sam muttered.

"Equipment's in the shed. We're all set for when this god of yours turns up," Gunnar stated.

"Not quite, with a little luck Lance will turn up before Hades does," Anna added.

"At any rate there's nothing more we can do for now," Zaharrah stated.

"Right except keep watch," Sam suggested.

"Indeed."

"We'll take the first watch, you two should get some rest," Anna suggested.

Zaharrah nodded grateful knowing when the quiet ended she'd be caught in the heart of the storm.

"Wake us at first light," Gunnar commanded. Sam nodded and with that Gunnar and Zaharrah moved off.

190

"Come on doc, time to relieve your sister and her man," Sam muttered. Anna nodded and the pair moved out of the kitchen back into the parlor. They found Vince sitting near the window. His eyes watched the perimeter ever glancing to the sky. "See anything?"

"Not a thing. All is quiet," the other man answered.

"Good, I'm here to relieve you. Go get some rest," Sam stated.

"Gladly, come along Terra-Anne, let's to bed," he murmured as he took his wife by the hand to lead her away.

"Sounds like a plan," she answered as she stifled a yawn. Her eyes settled on the other agent for a moment. "You'll come get us if anything changes?" she questioned.

"Of course," he assured her and watched with satisfaction as they moved off down the hall.

"Now what?" Anna asked.

"We wait and pray," Sam replied as he settled into the seat Vince had abandoned. Anna sat down in the corner where her sister had been and it wasn't long until she drifted off. "Sleep well love," he whispered before turning his attention back to the street outside and the dark sky beyond.

191

Lance pulled up outside the flat with the address Sam had provided. After the jet landed in Tele-Viv he'd made short time of procuring a rental car. As he pulled in the lot he noted the clock read three a.m. and groaned. Sunday three hours until sunrise. He was running on little to no sleep and had been for almost a week. Not the best idea but he'd had little choice. Everything inside him had demanded haste. Each hour that passed brought them closer to disaster.

As he stepped out of the car he watched as Sam and Anna emerged from within the flat. Good. He was glad to see someone was keeping watch. Lance ignored the pair, they could wait. Rounding the hood of the car he opened the passenger door and unfastened Catharine's seat belt. She stirred briefly when he drew her into his arms but only for a moment. Long enough to snuggle closer to his chest. He kicked the door shut and made his way towards the house.

"Sorry for the late hour," he whispered.

"No, need, we're just glad you made it," Sam stated as he stepped aside to let Lance and his burden in.

Lance carried his sleeping beauty across the threshold and followed Anna down the hall to the living room. He deposited Catharine on the couch and brushed a kiss on her forehead before moving out of the room.

"So, what did you learn?" Anna asked as they came back to the parlor where Sam sat watching.

"We learned that this is our only chance at defeating Hades' beast," Lance said as he drew the sword from the scabbard at his hip. The moment the blade was exposed he felt a wash of power spill over him and the fatigue that had begun to dog him began to recede.

"Is that--" Anna began with disbelief, Lance watched as Sam shifted her behind his frame, keeping her away from the blade.

"You shouldn't have taken up that sword detective," Sam warned.

"Do you think I don't know that? There wasn't much choice," Lance snapped.

"Meaning?"

"It was either wield this thing and slay the beast or sit by and watch it destroy all of you," Lance muttered.

"Ares is lying to you to get control of your mind," Anna warned.

"He's not even in my head. He's not allowed to push me for control it's in our bargain."

"What bargain?"

"All he wanted was for me to stop the dragon."

"Why?"

"He wants Hades accent to power slowed down. I've got no problem with that," Lance said.

"Assuming you manage to kill this thing then what?" Sam asked his eyes gleamed with barely contained anger.

"It's over. This sword will go back in the damn rock it was pulled from," Lance said agitated at Sam's apparent lack of faith in his judgment.

"Do you really think Ares will just let you walk away?" Anna asked stunned.

"I don't see why not, he's changed his host three time now, if he doesn't it won't matter because I will," Lance stated as he shoved the blade back in its sheath. "Now, if you'll excuse me it's been a long week. I'd like to get a little sleep before Hades arrives," Lance added before he headed back in the direction of the living room where he'd left Catharine, as he closed the door he heard Anna ask.

"What do we do now?"

"Wait, and prepare. This is not good." Sam muttered.

"I know. Why would he do this? I mean even if what he said is true I can't see him biting on Ares line, he smarter than that," Anna stated.

Lance was aware of Sam replying to her question but ignored them as he sank down in the chair beside Catharine. "It's almost over Serenity," he whispered in assurance as he closed his eyes.

"YES, IT IS BEFORE THE SUNSET'S TOMORROW YOU'LL HAVE DEFEATED THE DRAGON," Ares stated as Lance's mind fell into unconsciousness .

192 <small>SUNDAY DAWN</small>

As the first light of dawn began to rise over the horizon Sam saw the form in the heavens they'd all been dreading. In the distance small but still clear was a reptilian form with leathery wings.

"Anna, go get your sister, her man and Gunnar as well, he's coming."

"What about Lance?"

"No, I want to try to take this thing without that sword first. We don't know what it will do to him; besides we've got some weapons out there that the knights of old didn't. I'll take my chances," Sam muttered.

Anna nodded and moved off to gather the others. Sam got to his feet and whispered a prayer. It was going to be a rough morning. He hoped that everyone survived it.

193

Anna moved down the hall past the living room as quietly as she could manage and prayed that her passage would not disturb Lance or Catharine's sleep. She worried they were taking too great a risk, as this gamble was not just with their lives but those of the citizens as well. If she'd learned anything about Hades during her captivity it was that the god of the underworld had no interest or regard for human life. He'd not hesitate to let his beast hurt others around them to get to them and the bloodshed would not end with them either. Despite all this she was in agreement with Sam's choice. They didn't know what Lance's wielding the sword to slay the dragon would do to him.

While the detective appeared in control of his actions at the moment she had no desire to watch her friend become the same hollow shell she'd seen Ian become. If they could hold back his hand it would be better. Ares actions thus far confused her. The war god was taking his time with his return, had given up certain rights to win his new host, made deals and promises. Was even going out of his way to aid them. Why?

He was war. Shouldn't he be eager to see the battle that was brewing explode? The dragon attack would do that. It would lead to bloodshed, suffering, death and war so why try to prevent it? What was he playing at?

As she pondered the matter Anna reached her destination. She knocked on the door of her host's room and waited for a response. A moment later it opened to reveal Zaharrah and Gunnar side by side.

"We were just coming to relieve you," Gunnar whispered. "No, need. It's time. Sam sent me to get you and my sister."

"I'll get Terra," Zaharrah murmured.

"I'll go help Sam get ready," Gunnar stated before moving off in the direction of the parlor.

Anna followed the tomb raider back into the kitchen and through the other corridor to the room where Terra and Vince were left to rest. She watched as the other woman knocked and waited as the news was past. Turning she moved to return to the parlor.

"Hey, Annalynn, where da ya think you're goin," Terra's voice demanded in a low hiss.

"Back to Sam."

"The hell ya are lass, ya've done enough playin at bein a spy. Ya stay here where it's safe," Terra muttered.

"I don't want--"

"Aye, I know ya don't, but if ya want ta keep your love alive ya'll stay out this mess so he can focus on the beast," Terra reasoned.

"I'm not going to just sit and wait."

"Of course not, but your sister is right, the best chance Sam has is if you stay clear of the dragon and Hades. I want you to keep my boy safe," Zaharrah stated.

Anna blinked startled by the request but nodded her acceptance.

"Thank you, he's across the hall, just make sure he's out of harm's way."

"I will," Anna assured her and she watched as her sister and her husband moved on down the hall in the direction of the front of the flat alongside a woman she'd once thought of as an enemy. With care Anna opened the door to the boy's room and stepped inside taking a seat at the desk, she turned the chair to watch the sleeping child and whispered a prayer for his parents' safe return.

194

Zaharrah stepped into the parlor as Gunnar unlocked the front door. Her husband and Mr. Abrams were both dressed in full body armor and ready to collect weapons. She crossed the floor to the black duffel and began pulling out her protection as the woman Terra and her man did the same.

"Where's Anna?" Sam asked with concern.

"I asked her to keep an eye on Caleb," Zaharrah replied.

"I wish you'd do so as well," Gunnar grumbled.

"Don't start with me. I've been running and hiding from this bastard for too long. We both know I can handle this. I will be there when he falls," Zaharrah hissed as she pulled on her flak jacket.

Gunnar nodded, knowing her well enough to understand that arguing would only hurt them and waste time they didn't have. Instead he helped her to secure the rest of her gear. Once they were suited up the small team exited the flat and moved into the direction of the weapons shed as the dragon looming on the horizon began to get larger. It was close now as was its master she could feel his icy touch on her but ignored it she was done running. Hades had called her Persephone but he'd soon learn she was nothing like his docile maiden of old, manipulated and deceived. She had fangs and he was the one who was going to end up trapped in hell alone.

195

Artemis watched from the distance as the humans prepared to face her uncle and his prized pet head on. The dragon's maw parted and fire burst forth from the beast's throat. Scorching the land below and setting various buildings around them ablaze. The warriors answered with gun fire and rockets.

The great serpent roared in pain and rage as hot metal tore through wing and scale. Their weapons were more than adequate to bring down the beast but its master's power surrounded it mending torn muscles and tendons. Repairing charred flesh keeping the dragon in flight as he exacted his revenge.

A powerful hand drew back the string of Eros's bow as blue eyes lined up the shot. She'd only get one chance at this. If she missed the game would be up. The arrow's flight had to be perfect, unexpected. She'd have to make it count.

196

Sam cursed as the dragon's fire poured down around them. Their efforts to bring it down were proving fruitless. He could see they were doing damage but it wasn't lasting. The Fallen's power was undoing their work too quickly. They'd soon run out of ammo and have nothing to show for their efforts as the beast was still coming.

"Terra!"

"Yeah."

"Get your sister and the boy out of here!"

"Aye!"

He watched as the *Rogue* retreated from the field to see to Anna and the child. At least they would live through this he reasoned as he fired a rocket from his bazooka. Sam watched as the beasts side ripped open; a gaping hole that had the dragon falling abruptly. He closed his eyes and drew a breath, hands shaking.

Eye lids lifted hoping that this time he'd see the reptilian form on a collision course for the earth bellow. He cursed as the smoke cloud split and the dragon rose in the heavens once more. The damage he'd created mended before his eyes. How was Ares sword going to fare any better against such power he wondered as fire fell from the heavens yet again. The homes around them burst into flames. Half of Jerusalem was burning and there wasn't a damn thing they could do to stop it so long as Hades was there to undo the injury to his beast.

197

Lance's eyes shot open as Ares voice warned of danger. He rose from the chair where he'd sat resting; keeping guard over Serenity. Ares threw open the door with his power pressing the man for haste as the woman Terra walked past startling her.

"GET HER CLEAR OF THIS PLACE AS WELL," Ares commanded.

Terra nodded without a word, her green eyes held fear and shock. It seemed she'd witnessed first-hand the beast and was now aware that they warred not with mortal flesh as she'd believed but something greater. Good. The man Sam had tried to face the monster without him and saw now that the act was futile. Hades would use his power to keep his pet alive.

Lance lifted Catharine from the couch and followed Terra down the hall to collect Anna and the boy. He'd see that his charge got away then he would join the others he told himself even as Ares roared at him to not waste time. He moved down the hall behind Terra and watched as she disappeared into the small room only to emerge a moment later with her sister at her side and the sleeping child in her arms. The trio moved silently to the back door and the waiting vehicle.

"Get them as far from here as you can," Lance said.

"What about the others?" Anna asked in protest.

"We'll follow," he assured her.

"But--"

"GO!' he snapped in a voice not his own and drew a breath fighting for calm.

"Lance, you can't use that sword," Anna warned with alarm.

"IF HE DOESN'T YOU'LL ALL BE DEAD," Ares snapped. He slammed the door in her face before she could say anything more and watched with satisfaction as Terra sped away.

Lance's ice blue eyes moved to the heavens. He watched as a rocket flew at the dragon ripping muscle and flesh, burning it like overcooked hamburger meat only to be repaired. "What good will this thing be if a rocket can't phase that thing," Lance muttered to the war god with disbelief.

"TRUST ME, THIS WILL WORK," Ares whispered as the detective headed for the battlefield.

198

Sam cursed in frustration as the beast circled overhead, fire now surrounded them. Their attempts to stop it had done nothing. Hades magic undoing any damage they inflicted. So long as the god of the underworld remained in the shadows they were going to die there and the city would fall with them.

Something had to be done.

"Hades!" Zaharrah roared the name in rage as she laid down her weapon. "Is this how you'll end this then? A coward that swats at his enemies from the shadows. No more than a child throwing a tantrum because he lost his favorite toy!"

"Zaharrah no!" Gunnar shouted in objection to her actions.

"Come out and fight us like a man," Sam challenged. "Your host was a more worthy opponent," he taunted jabbing Zaharrah's knife deeper in the fallen one's sense of pride. Hoping her blade was well aimed.

A cloud of green smoke erupted between Sam and the others surrounding him. Cutting him off and blinding him to the world beyond.

"THAT MORTAL WAS A FOOL! I LED HIM ABOUT BY THE NOSE LIKE AN ASS. EVERY STEP TOWARD POWER HE TOOK WAS AT MY URGING. MAGNUS HALDEN WAS NOTHING WITHOUT ME!" Hades hissed in rage as his hands wrapped around Sam's neck.

"I PLAYED HIM LIKE THE PAWN HE WAS, JUST AS I'VE PLAYED YOU. I GAVE YOU A CHANCE TO GET OUT BEFORE IT WAS THROUGH BUT YOU REFUSED; NOW I'LL CRUSH YOU AND WHEN I'M DONE I'LL DESTROY EVERYTHING YOU CARE FOR, ANYTHING YOU LOVE STARTING WITH YOUR PRECIOUS ANNA," Hades mocked as he squeezed the life from Sam.

"No," Sam gasped as he tore at Hades hands and fought to survive. "

199

A fist entered the green smoke to strike the god of the underworld and his gaze moved from his enemy to his rival as the man Gunnar dared to challenge him. Sam could wait the other man's time however had come. Hades would no longer tolerate the direct challenge of another man for the hand of HIS PERSEPHONE.

"GUNNAR, AT LAST WE MEET. YOU JUST COULDN'T REMAIN IN YOUR PLACE OF ORDER IN THIS AFFAIR. SO BE IT. YOU SHALL BE THE FIRST TO FALL," Hades whispered as he came forth from the smoke. Sam fell to the dust, motionless but still breathing, having blacked out. Hades ignored him catching the second fist directed at him crushing it in his grasp.

Gunnar hissed in pain but gave no other response. With his good hand he drew a knife. "You'll pay for what you've done," he muttered.

"FOOLISH MORTAL, CAN AN INSECT SWAT AT MAN WHEN IT IS WRONGED? WHAT MAKES YOU THINK YOU CAN CHALLENGE A GOD?"

"That's enough Hades," Zaharrah snapped as she stepped forward to stop him.

"No Zaharrah," Gunnar snapped keeping his body between them like a shield.

"AH, MY SWEET ZAHARRAH, THE DESERT BLOOM, HOW YOU'VE DISAPPOINTED ME. I KNEW I'D FIND YOU HERE. YOU SHOULDN'T HAVE LEFT. IF YOU'D STAYED BY MY SIDE WHERE YOU BELONGED MY DARLING, THEN NONE OF THIS WOULD HAVE BEEN NECESSARY," Hades murmured as he reached past the man to brush a finger down her cheek.

"Get your hands off MY WIFE," Gunnar snapped as he took a

swipe at the god of the dead with his blade.

Hades grabbed hold of the other man's wrist twisting the arm until he heard the bones snap and the knife fell from powerless fingers.

"Stop this," Zaharrah commanded.

"YOU WISH THIS TO END?" Hades asked as his fingers slid into her hair.

"Yes," she answered instantly. His hand fisted in her dark locks and pulled drawing her past her protector so that they were face to face.

"THEN COME WITH ME NOW AND PROMISE NEVER TO RUN AGAIN."

"Zaharrah No! Don't listen," Gunnar shouted.

"If I do this ends?"

"IF YOU DO I'LL CALL OFF MY BEAST BEFORE IT CAN KILL YOUR SON."

"And them?"

"THEIR FATE IS SEALED," Hades hissed.

"I want it unsealed," Zaharrah challenged.

"I CAN'T LET HIM LIVE AND YOU KNOW IT," Hades snarled as his other hand wrapped around Gunnar's throat to crush his wind pipe.

"Spare him or I'll die here as well," Zaharrah hissed.

Hades roared in fury at her price for their bargain. His pride demanded the man before him die. She'd left him once and run back to her lover, the only way to ensure it didn't happen again was to crush his rival but if he did she'd deny his offer, choosing to perish here instead, a death that once done could not be taken back.

In the sky above his pet screamed in agony. Green eyes wheeled to the heavens to see a lone arrow buried deep in the left breast of the dragon. "ARTEMIS!" Hades snarled as his beast fell from the heavens it's wound one he could not mend.

"There will be no bargains today fallen one," Zaharrah whispered as the tide of battle shifted and his spell failed.

"YOU'VE LOST," Ares voice mocked as the man Lance walked through the flames, sword drawn ready to fight.

"DETECTIVE ROMAN, I SEE ARES MANAGED TO GET HIS CLAWS IN YOU AFTER ALL. CONSIDER CAREFULLY YOUR NEXT STEP FOR IT WILL HAVE A PRICE. YOU KNOW WHO I AM, DO YOU REALLY WANT TO MAKE ME YOUR ENEMY? ALL YOU KNOW, ANYTHNG YOU CARE FOR, WHATEVER YOU LOVE I'LL TEAR IT APART. NOT

EVEN YOUR BELOVED DANA IS NOT BEYOND MY REACH," Hades hissed.

"HE'S BLUFFING DETECTIVE, SO LONG AS ZEUS'S CROWN IS BEYOND HIS REACH, HIS POWER IS SEALED. HE CAN'T TAKE ANYONE BEFORE THEIR ORDAINED TIME," Ares answered.

"I CAN IF THEY'VE HEEDED MY CALL. YOUR SERENITY IS WITHIN MY REACH. WE BOTH KNOW SHE'S NOT MUCH FURTHER FROM THE EDGE THAN THE LOVELY DANA WAS," Hades warned.

"SHE CAN BE PROTECTED. I'LL SHOW YOU HOW," Ares vowed.

"WHY DO YOU INTERFERE WAR GOD? WE HAVE ALWAYS BEEN ALLIES," Hades snarled.

"I'M THROUGH BEING YOUR PUPPET HADES," Ares answered, as the man Lance swung his sword cutting threw scaly hide, muscle, sinew, flesh and bone; separating the reptilian head from the long serpentine neck.

Hades roared in fury, as his beast passed from existence to the underworld, and vanished in a cloud of smoke aware that Ares would not hesitate to turn that sword on him as well.

200

Zaharrah looked on with horror as the war god's blade was lowered into the fire. The blaze of the flames sealing the dragon's blood within the swords edge. Half the jewels on the hilt gleamed from within as its true power began to wake.

"Lance, put the sword in the scabbard," she commanded as she began to understand what was happening.

"What is it?" Gunnar asked besides her trying to understand her sudden mood shift from relief to fear.

"When he killed the dragon he broke the first seal holding back Ares power. The fire broke the second, if the detective doesn't sheath that blade Ares hold on him will grow stronger. The war god will use him to break the final seal." Zaharrah whispered.

201

The detective trembled where he stood as sweat dripped from his brow. He drew a deep breath and blew it out as the sword in his grip flashed with power and the flames around him died out. He looked down at the blade he held tight in his hands and the carcass of the fallen beast.

He'd just killed a dragon.

"WITH MY HELP," Ares reminded.

"Okay, fair enough," Lance muttered. He felt the press of the war god's power around him now in a way he'd not before and wondered why. "You vowed not to press me," he grumbled reminding Ares of their deal feeling uneasy.

"I'M NOT. I'M STILL OUT HERE," Ares assured him.

"But, you're more pronounced," Lance muttered.

"A SIDE EFFECT FROM THE DRAGON'S BLOOD, IT INCREASES OUR STRENGTH," Ares explained.

Lance looked up at the sound of Zaharrah's voice. "Why did you have me put the blade in the fire?"

"TO CLEAN IT," Ares answered.

"Lance, put the sword in the scabbard!" he heard his comrade shout but the cry was muffled as if from far away.

"Why?" he shouted back but she gave no reply as if she'd not heard him.

"WE HAVE TO MOVE NOW," Ares commanded.

"Why?"

"YOU HEARD HADES. HIS THREAT WAS NOT AN IDLE ONE. HE WILL STRIKE BACK AT YOU THROUGH CATHARINE AND HE'LL DO IT SWIFTLY."

"You told me she could be protected."

"SHE CAN. IF YOU WANT TO KEEP HER SAFE YOU'LL NEED TO HOLD ONTO MY SWORD A BIT LONGER. I MUST

OBTAIN MY TRUE POWER."

"If you're not going to go back on our deal how can you do that?"

"I'LL TEACH YOU," Ares vowed.

Lance drew a breath to quiet his mind, feeling Ares power wrap around him tighter. He put the blade in its scabbard as Zaharrah had instructed and felt the power dissipate. He blew out his breath with relief. He needed time to think, plan and most of all rest. He'd made too many hasty choices of late and it didn't sit well with him.

Crossing the field he moved to Sam's side and helped his friend to his feet.

"What happened?" Sam asked groggy.

"The beast fell. Hades fled," Lance stated.

"How?"

"I cut off its head."

"That worked?" Sam asked with disbelief.

"Yeah."

"How are you?"

"Fine," Lance assured him though he wasn't sure if that was true. Even now he could hear Ares voice whispering to him. It buzzed around him now constantly on the edge of his consciousness. "Not sure how we're getting out of here though" he muttered seeing the fire around them in the distance begin to spread closer.

The sky overhead grew dark with storm clouds. Thunder rumbled and lightening cut through the smoke. Rain fell dousing the fire as Artemis moved into their midst.

"Thank you," Zaharrah murmured as her dark eyes met with the goddess's blue ones.

"No, thank you. Your little battle of wills was enough to give me a clean shot," Artemis replied.

"COME WITH US," Ares voice requested.

"I cannot. I have vows to uphold."

"WHERE DOES YOUR ALLEGIANCE LIE HUNTRESS?" Ares voice asked demanding a reply,

"MY HAND WILL STRIKE OUT AT ANY GOD WHO REACHES FOR MY FATHER'S CROWN," she answered before departing.

"We should get moving as well," Lance suggested.

"Why?"

"Ares thinks Hades will seek retaliation for his defeat. If he's right the god of the dead will strike out at the others to hurt us. The sooner we get back to our loved ones the better," he explained.

"Ares thinks?" Sam asked with disbelief. "Well, I think--"

"Sam, now's not the time. He's right."

"Then let's get going," Gunnar said as he moved in the direction of the SUV.

Lance followed after him aware the others were moving in that direction as well. He stretched out in the back seat and closed his eyes. The adrenaline in his veins fading, his muscles ached as exhaustion began to settle in. The first battle was over they'd won but the war was just beginning, he'd need to be ready.

2O2

Ares spirit slid out of the confines within the sword for the first time since he'd woken after Kurt Dryden drew his blade from the stone in which it had been sealed. The dragon's blood had done its work the scabbard that had confined his power had begun to decay. After centuries of imprisonment he was nearly free.

The war god turned his gaze upon the man Lance whom he'd tricked into wielding his mantel and pressed his power lightly against his mental guarding, testing their strength. Ares laughed as the wall began to crumble; small fissures opening. The war god peeked through the cracks to the mind beyond and found the detective lost in a dream with the wine gods taint.

He smiled it seemed the detective was lost now to his carnal desire for the lovely Serenity. Perfect that was just the distraction he needed now to make his move, besides it would make for an enjoyable distraction once he made it inside. Ares licked his lips as he pictured the pretty writer before him naked, bleeding, body shaking with fear but defiant. The only lady he'd encountered in his wandering worthy to be his.

Ares pressed both palms against the stone barrier blocking his way and let his power flow over it. "LET ME IN DETECTIVE, WITHOUT ME YOU'LL NEVER BE ABLE TO PROTECT YOUR WOMAN FROM MY BRETHREN," Ares whispered. He watched as the wall rather than part further became a heavy door locked tight and cursed.

The detective's ability to resist him was stronger than he'd anticipated. It didn't matter, with time and coaxing Lance Roman's mind would surrender to him. It was unavoidable. After all it was a door now before him and not a stronger wall. All doors could be opened, with enough time he only needed to find the right lock to open it. He already knew what his key was: SERENITY was the way past the gate, he just had to determine the best way to turn that key.

203

Anna paced the floor of the hotel suite a bundle of nervous energy. She hadn't been able to sit still since they arrived and knew she was driving her sister crazy, but she didn't care. She was worried for Sam but more so for Lance.

Ares was playing an angle. He had to be, but what it was she couldn't see. The only thing she was sure of was if Lance used that sword to kill the dragon it would have some unknown consequence. If Ares wanted the beast dead it was a good bet it meant trouble for Lance but after what she'd seen as they fled it didn't seem like there was any other option.

All of Sam's efforts to bring down the beast were undone by Hades power, only the power of another fallen could stop it now. Anna prayed as she walked, aware that unless a miracle happened Sam and the others would die. As soon as they fell Hades would come for them as well. The god of the underworld would not be satisfied until all of them were dead at his feet or worse enslaved to his will.

When the door opened she froze midstride fearing the worst. Hazel eyes wheeled to the door to fall upon a face she'd thought to never see again. "Sam," she called his name and was across the room in his arms within moments. "Thank God," she breathed as the others moved past them. She felt his arms enfold her and buried her face in his neck as she blinked back tears.

She felt his fingers sink into her golden hair and felt the terror that had been driving her melt away. "Anna," he breathed her name and she lifted her head to look at him with wonder. "How?" she whispered. Sam opened his mouth to answer but her eyes darted away from him relief becoming dread as Lance walked past her. Ares presence surrounded him and brushed against her awareness. "What happened?" she asked with concern.

"Nothing happened, I'm fine," Lance assured her as he moved to Catharine's side.

"Sam?"

"He cut off the dragons head. He claims he's okay though."

"Something has changed," Anna muttered.

"Meaning?" Sam questioned ill at ease.

"I can feel the war god about him now, his presence is more apparent."

"He sheathed the sword, Anna, he's still in control," Sam assured her.

"Maybe--"

"Don't borrow trouble doc," Sam whispered.

Anna nodded and rested her forehead against his before closing her eyes. She lost herself for a moment in the feel of his hand against her face as it sank once more into her hair, but her peace was disrupted by the sense of being watched. Opening her eyes she looked about and found that Lance was watching them, his ice blue eyes were lit with an orange glow for a split second then reverted back to their natural state.

Anna swallowed nervously.

"What's wrong doc?"

"Ares is getting stronger. We've got to get Lance to get rid of that sword," she whispered.

"We will," Sam assured her as he let her go.

"Where are you going?" Anna questioned with alarm.

"I just need a minute," Sam muttered before he headed for the bathroom.

Anna sat down at the table as she looked around her. Her sister and Vince stood off in one corner holding each other close whispering back and forth. In another part of the room Zaharrah, Gunnar and Caleb were gathered a family once more. Her eyes shifted back to where Lance stood. Hazel locked with ice blue and for a moment they gleamed orange as a smirk curved his lips. Anna flinched as those lips parted and the war god spoke.

"RELAX DOC, I WON'T HURT YOU," he whispered before the glow faded and Lance turned his focus to his sleeping charge. Lance knelt beside Catharine and murmured something to her before lowering his head to brush a kiss on her brow. His eyes lifted meeting Anna's again and glowed orange as they touched her flesh. Anna's skin crawled at the image Ares message coming across loud and clear only for her to hear. The sleeping beauty before him was his.

"Leave her alone," Anna breathed and felt relief wash through her as those eyes became blue once more and peace settled over her. She wished it would last but her spirit warned it would shatter all too quickly.

Hazel eyes settled on the door Sam had disappeared behind and she wondered how long he'd be gone. She hoped it wouldn't be too long, she didn't want to be alone with Ares spirit for too long, it seemed he found taunting her amusing and took pleasure in tormenting her.

Her thoughts wandered back to just what game the war god might be playing and reasoned that whatever it was the prize he sought at the end was the woman resting on the bed blissfully unaware of the things going on around her and the detective's soul. Anna sighed as she steered her thoughts from her own musings as they were depressing.

204

Sam moved into the bathroom needing to get away from the others. His mind and spirit troubled. He turned on the sink and threw cold water in his face. When he lifted his head his eyes settled on his reflection, at his side his hand coiled into a fist as he cursed. In his mind he counted their losses and felt frustration become despair.

"We failed," he muttered with regret. His head fell in shame with defeat.

"Why is it you humans look at any set back as a failure?" An all too familiar voice questioned with exasperation. The words came from nowhere and everywhere.

"Three of the fallen are walking the earth another is riding my friend in there, waiting to take him over. How is that not failure?" Sam questioned with annoyance as he looked up at the mirror. Upon it he found the reflection of the angelic figure that seemed to be watching him and the others at every turn.

"Lance's fate is not yet sealed, another may yet become war."

"Then that will be four of them in all."

"True, but have you considered the possibility that you were never meant to stop them all," the angel asked.

Sam turned to face the messenger with disbelief. "But you said--"

"I told you that you were to prevent the mantels from falling into human hands and those that were not already found you did. The whip, the gauntlets, the bow and even the crown will never get the chance to corrupt a mortal."

"But the others--."

"Were not within your power to contain, I never said you had to hold back all the fallen. Just to keep the mantels out of mortal hands."

"If we couldn't hold them all back then why did we bother to try?"

"Four is more easily managed than nine."

"Why put us through all this?"

"Consider what has changed Sam Abrams, since you began your journey. Anna who once sought knowledge at every turn now looks for truth and she will find more of it than she ever dared to dream of. Detective Lance Roman who once hunted monsters until the day one nearly consumed him is now reinvested in his life's call. Serenity, Catharine, Jade Collins who had hidden herself behind lies fearing she was a monster has taken back her name and seen herself through the Creator's eyes as a writer, her work will now fill the world with light and hope rather than darkness and despair. Zaharrah Lynch who abandoned her life and the call upon it due to Hades torment has embraced her existence and returned to the life she left with Gunnar. His fear that he was unlovable has been silenced and the anger and despair washed away. The Ancient huntress's loyalty has turned from the fallen she served to that of men. In time she will be given a choice as you were and will take her place in the war to come."

"And me?" Sam asked afraid to hear what the angel would say and yet unable to hold back the question.

"Sam, you who were a great warrior have taken up your fight once more. The love you thought was yours in your youth that was lost has been given to you anew," the angel answered with a smile.

Sam shook his head as the winged messenger's word sank in. "Okay, maybe my measuring stick for success is a little off," he muttered.

"Each of your lives has been brought full circle and set on the path the Father chose for you before you were born."

"So you're saying that Hermes, Ares, Dionysus and Hades were meant to be unleashed. Why? What sense does it make to turn these monsters with their power over humans loose in this world?"

"It was prophesied long before you were born that four would one day walk the earth. What the Father says will come to pass, for his word is true."

"Then times up?" Sam asked with disbelief.

"No, no man will know the appointed day or hour of His coming. But that doesn't stop the enemy from trying to set it in motion early, in a vain attempt to change the outcome."

"Okay, so if this is one such attempt then what comes next?"

"Now the four will battle for the crown of Zeus. In the process the last mantle the scroll of Chaos will be brought to light. Only one can rule; it is the way of them. Artemis has slowed their accent to power but not for long."

"Where do we fit in?"

"Your steps will be dogged by these fallen as you possess something they seek. Guard well the keys you hold and seek answers in the pages of the Black Hand. Hold true to each other as you begin this new leg of your journey."

Sam cursed as the angelic messenger vanished with his final words. He really wished the guy would stop doing that. Despite his irritation at the abrupt end to the conversation he found his spirit renewed and his mind eased. So maybe they hadn't failed as he'd believed moments ago. Whatever lay ahead of them; he intended to be ready for it?

THE END

MANTLE OF THE GODS

BOOK 4

NIGHT RISING

BY TRICIA SPARKS

A major victory has been won, but one battle does not make a war.

Haunted by the spirit of an ancient god, Detective Lance Roman returns to Los Angeles with the sword of war in hand, and Catherine Nichols at his side. Yet they have not left their struggles behind them. Still in danger of becoming a pawn in evil's elaborate game, Catherine must rely on Lance. As a wielder of god's mantle, Lance must make a .choice in order to protect the woman he loves – a choice with far-reaching consequences.

One man's need...

Arthurian enthusiast Fox Elwood has made the discovery of his dreams in Zeboim: evidence leading to the legendary city of Camelot. Hoping to make another awesome find, he races to the modern site of the city only to be frustrated once more in his search – until he meets a man carrying an eldritch artifact. The artifact is incomplete and it will require a true expert in Arthurian lore to locate the missing piece.

...and another man's ambition...

Sam Abrams and Annalynn Gallagher now stand at the edge of failure. With opposing forces converging on Zeus's crown, and the efforts of the only deity who seems to share Sam and Anna's goal foiled, one shadowy figure prepares to make her move. When she does, even the unleashed power of a god may not be enough to stop her.

...may speed the world into the hands of Chaos.

READ ON FOR A SAMPLE

1

Sam stepped out of the bathroom and back into the main room of their hotel. His mind free of turmoil it was time to discuss their next move.

"You okay?" Anna asked as he reemerged.

"Yeah, I just needed a minute to clear my head," he assured her.

"What's our next move?" She asked as he reached her side. Rather than answer her he drew her into his arms and held her close for a moment brushing her forehead with a light kiss. When he drew back his eyes locked with hazel ones that had turned gray.

"Are you okay?" he asked seeing her fear.

"Yeah, I just went a round with Ares," she muttered.

At the words Sam let her go and looked her over for injury. "What happened?"

"It wasn't like that. He's just taunting me. Making it pretty clear that despite whatever deal he made with Lance he has designs for Catharine still." Anna explained.

"Yeah, I'm not surprised there; I figured that a deal made with a fallen wouldn't end well," Sam grumbled.

"What are we going to do?" Anna asked.

"We'll deal with Lance in a minute first we need to get people on their way and figure out what we can do to stop these four wanna be gods from jump starting the apocalypse," Sam whispered.

Anna nodded her understanding as Sam drew her back to his side. He watched as the others in the room moved away from each other and in his direction all but Lance he stayed at Catharine's side. That was just fine by Sam he didn't want Ares privy to whatever plans they set in motion. "All right yank quiet times over what are we gonna do?" Terra demanded her green eyes sharp and cold.

"You and your Mr. Fenton are going to get back to the states and monitor the movements of these fallen. The second any of them pops up on your radar I want to know about it."

"But--" Terra began in protest.

"Will do," Vince answered stalling his wife's protests.

"Thanks. Zaharrah you and Gunnar take your kid and run; after what Lance did earlier today I have a feeling

Hades undivided attention will be on him and Miss Nichols--"

"I can't do that there are artifacts, still at those digs, I can't let them find. As a member of the order it's my duty--" Zaharrah began with objection.

"You said it yourself the order is done." Gunnar stated.

"Anna and I know what to look for we'll see to it Hermes doesn't locate any more," Sam assured her.

"But--"

"You gave up five years for this it's time to walk away. Your family needs you," Anna reasoned.

Zaharrah nodded. "I'm going to go back to the library see if anything useful survived the fire," She muttered.

"We will. If we come up with anything I'll let you know," Gunnar corrected.

"Fine," Sam answered.

"Not fine, do ya expect me to sit by and watch while ya go gallivantin about with me sister, with those fallen chasing ya," Terra snapped in objection.

"Do you think I'd risk taking her if I didn't have to? Believe me, I'd like, nothing better than, to put her on a plane with you; but whether we like it or not she's a part of this. Has been from the start and nothing we say or do can take her out of the middle of it," Sam stated.

"So we do nothing Mr. Abrams?'

"No, you keep your eyes on their movements let us know when they're closing in on us and trust me to protect my fiancé by doing my job," Sam corrected.

"I don't like this," Terra muttered.

"Well, I do not like your trying to step in and run my life. Sam is right if I go back with you I'm in more danger than out here with him," Anna stated.

"I liked ya better when ya were obedient," Terra muttered.

"Tough, miss prim, proper and responsible grew up," Anna snapped.

"I think ya best let this go Terra-Ann, my love," Vince said amused.

"Laugh it up Mr. Fenton when we get home ya'll be paying for it later," Terra grumbled. "What about him?" she questioned pointing over at Lance.

"I'll be going to LA with Catharine. I've no intention of leaving her unwatched with Mr. Hardagen or unprotected from Hades reach," Lance declared in answer to the question.

"Well, then, it would seem we're splitting up again," Sam stated.

"Right, good luck Sam," Lance offered.

"Thanks, be careful detective," Sam replied. "I suggest we get moving it won't take long for Hades to find us here."

Gunnar nodded and Zaharrah lifted her son into her arms and moved for the door.

"Stay safe," Anna urged.

"You too." Zaharrah answered before the family of three walked out.

Sam looked back to where his friend sat and watched as the detective leaned over and brushed a kiss on CJ Nichols forehead. The pretty writer's lashes fluttered and she looked up at him with question in her blues eyes.

"Sorry, Catharine, time to go home," he murmured.

"Home?" she asked groggy.

"Back to LA," he elaborated, before gathering her into his arms. Catharine snuggled close to him and closed her eyes.

"Be careful and stay in touch," Anna entreated.

"We will," Lance assured her before he walked out.

"Well, if we're gonna be watching your gods for ya we'll be needing a list of names," Terra muttered.

"Magnus Halden, Ian Broody, and James Hardagen…"

"The actor," Vince asked with disbelief interrupting him.

"Right," Anna replied.

"Do I even want to know?" Terra asked.

"You got a glimpse of him when we rescued her," Sam stated.

"Do ya want us to keep an eye on your cop friend as well?" Vince asked.

Sam hesitated unsure of how to answer the question. He wanted to believe he could trust his friend's word that he was fine but his gut told him not to. Before he could respond Anna spoke.

"He'll be in the same area as James only if he leaves abruptly do you need to worry about monitoring him," she stated.

Vince nodded. "Come along Terra, my love, it's time we were off as well. Say good-bye to your sister."

Terra drew Anna into her arms and gave her a hug before brushing a kiss on her cheek. "So long Annalynn, ya keep your head down as best ya can," she requested before letting her go.

The Rogue then took Sam's hand in hers and shook it. "Good-bye Mr. Abrams ya take care of me baby sister. If anything happens to her I'll be holding ya responsible," Terra stated.

"I will," Sam assured her as he shook her hand. He watched as Vince took Anna's hand in his and kissed her knuckles.

"Farewell Annalynn, it was an honor to finally meet ya."

"It was nice to meet you also. I want to hear how you two met next time I see you."

"It's a deal," he assured her before turning his attention to Sam.

"Sam, it's been interesting," Vince muttered.

"Yep. Hopefully next time we meet it won't be to fight a dragon," Sam stated with a grin.

"Or if we do it won't have a god mending it back together," Vince chuckled.

"After this little adventure I imagine getting back to normal operations will seem dull by comparison," Sam said amused.

"I'm looking forward to the everyday run of the mill terrorist threat and a normal night's sleep," Vince stated.

"I'll bet."

"We'll be in touch, hopefully the next time we meet will be under less dire straits. Perhaps even for a celebration," Vince speculated.

"That would be nice," Sam answered thinking about his recent proposal to Anna and their future ahead if they lived long enough to get there.

"Good luck," Vince offered before he took Terra by the shoulder and guided her toward the door.

The door opened and a moment later it closed a third time leaving him alone in the room with Anna.

"Where are we going to go?" Anna asked curious.

LOOK FOR MORE; SUMMER 2014

WANT TO SEE WHERE IT ALL BEGAN?

THEN CHECK OUT

AVAILABLE AT WWW.AMAZON.COM

www.ingramcontent.com/pod-product-compliance
Lightning Source LLC
Chambersburg PA
CBHW071148250626
47159CB00001B/24